Please return/renew this item by the last date
shown. Books may be renewed by
telephoning, writing to or calling in at any
library or on the Internet.

Northamptonshire Libraries and Information Service

**Northamptonshire
County Council**

www.northamptonshire.gov.uk/leisure/libraries/

Read about Arlo and Usha's first adventure in

ESCAPE FROM GENOPOLIS

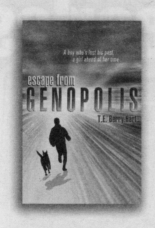

T.E. BERRY HART

fearless

■ SCHOLASTIC

First published in the UK in 2009 by Scholastic Children's Books
An imprint of Scholastic Ltd
Euston House, 24 Eversholt Street
London, NW1 1DB, UK
Registered office: Westfield Road, Southam, Warwickshire, CV47 0RA
SCHOLASTIC and associated logos are trademarks and or registered
trademarks of Scholastic Inc.

Cover illustration © 2009

ISBN 978 1 407 10289 4

Printed in the UK by CPI Bookmarque, Croydon, CR0 4TD
Papers used by Scholastic Children's Books are
made from wood grown in sustainable forests.

3 5 7 9 10 8 6 4 2

www.scholastic.co.uk/zone

For Ron
who loved the first book,
but couldn't be around for the second

And David
For every reason

PROLOGUE: BEYOND YOUR IMAGINATION

"Today is the day of uprising! We march on Genopolis!"
The voices of the revolution in Region Three reached Angus as he lay imprisoned in the dark and suffocating hut, feeling the turf shake under him with the stamp of the marching rebels. The Natural tribe had torched the woods to provide cover for the rebellion, and he could hear the greedy crackle of the flames already licking at the roof of the hut. Desperately, Angus twisted and turned, feeling the rope tighten on his wrists and ankles.

"Help!" he cried weakly. "Help!"

From outside the hut, he could hear Naturals arguing.

"What about the traitor?" cried one.

"Leave him!" shouted another. "Let him burn!"

"No!" Angus cried, but his voice was lost in the hubbub,

and seconds later the procession had marched out of the forest, leaving him to his fate.

Smoke filled his eyes and mouth, and he choked and coughed as he struggled. He must get out! He could not be left to die a cowardly death while his people marched on Genopolis! Nor could he leave his child in the clutches of the Doctor who had undoubtedly betrayed them! With the last of his strength, he rolled over on to his back and struggled uselessly against the cords that bound him. But as he did so, a wicked whoosh and roar erupted from the ceiling. The wooden roof of the hut had caught fire. The first of the rafters fell blazing, collapsing the lower end of the roof, centimetres from where he lay.

But through the gap he saw for the first time in hours a square of smoky light. The sight gave him hope. Gritting his teeth, he rolled over to the rafter, and pressed his bound hands against the glowing wood. The pain was terrible, but he hung on, willing the fire to burn through the knotted rope. Above him the second rafter trembled and swayed. . .

At last! The last fibres of the cords smoked into ash, and Angus rolled away, pulling the ropes from his wrists and ankles. One side of the hut was now blazing. Covering his face with his arms, he kicked at the burning reeds and, taking his courage in both hands, burst through the flames into the smoky dell. He rolled on the floor, beating and kicking at his smouldering clothes, as the last of the roof hut collapsed with a fiery crash where he had just been lying.

Dragging himself to his feet he started to run. But the flames and smoke were gaining on him, almost faster than he could go. Blundering through a thicket of trees, he forced himself to stagger down to the dried-up river bed where the smoke hung thinner, ignoring the pain and fatigue, with one thought only in his mind. He must reach the City of Genopolis, and rescue the son that he had so foolishly given away into the hands of its Citizens.

But his strength failed him. Even as he reached the river, his legs gave way and he collapsed in a heap.

How long he was unconscious, he did not know. When he finally awoke, his body was racked with pain and stiffness. An eerie calm hung over the ashy woods, and a voice that he dimly recognized was calling him.

"Uncle! Uncle!"

He struggled to rise but his weakness was too great.

"Where are you? Where are you?"

"I'm here!" Angus tried to cry back, but he could make no sound. He strained eagerly to listen, but there was no longer any sound save the whispering of the wind through the burned branches of the Regions.

Where was Kira? Hadn't she marched on the City with the others?

He heard nothing more. After a while he dozed, too far-gone now to feel any suffering. Above him the smoke cleared and at the edges of his mind he could hear the drone of a Citizen airship, and the sound of Citizen voices calling.

This is it, he told himself. This is where it all ends.

The crunch of footsteps grew steadily nearer, and the shadow of a uniformed Citizen soldier fell over him. A babble of voices broke out, and Angus felt himself raised up in the merciless grip of many gloved hands.

"We've found him, Captain!" cried a soldier. "We've found the Natural!"

A ghastly face seemed to float towards him through the mists, charred and ruined, attached to a body in shreds of blackened uniform that seemed more dead than alive. Angus stared back, hardly recognizing his proud captor, Captain Hacker, her body now devastated by the flames. Only one eye remained, glaring triumphantly out of her wasted face as she took in the appearance of the exhausted Natural.

"So," she ground out through her melted lips. "When will you Natural devils realize that you cannot escape us?"

Angus struggled to speak. "What have you done to them, Hacker?" he stammered miserably. "What have you done to my clan?"

Hacker smiled maliciously, as well as she was able. "The traitors in Region Three are all dead," she replied. "Wiped out as they attacked Genopolis."

"And my son?" stammered Angus, feeling the world reeling around him.

Hacker made a tiny motion with one charred finger, and the soldiers stepped forward and trained their guns on him.

"We will find him soon," she rapped out. "But now we will take you back to Genopolis, Natural, and before your own death, we have something waiting for you, something beyond your imagination."

4

ONE

It was the Dead Season in the wilderness outside Genopolis.

A blinding sun rose over a barren desert, its rays scourging the earth with fire. The heat had dried the earth to its core, transforming the shallow sea that once separated Genopolis from the outer Regions into a dusty plain that stretched as far as the eye could see. Heat-winds shimmered on the horizon, sometimes forming the illusion of pools of water spilling through the dust, but fresh water, or even the memory of water, was a long-gone dream. The rains were late in coming, and such springs as there were had retreated to their deep caves below the earth, leaving the topsoil drying into powder, to scatter here and there as the winds carried it. Underneath that fierce sun, nothing and no one moved.

Except one. A small form, almost invisible against the parched soil, was padding wearily across the desert, like a tiny ant crossing a sun-baked pebble.

The dog snuffled with a dry nose through the stony fissure. His feathery tail drooped down despondently as he loped along. Dust and mud clung to his shaggy pelt, and months of living and feeding off insects in the wasteland had shrivelled the flesh along his back so much, it seemed a miracle he could move at all. As he reached the shadow of an overhanging boulder, perched perilously in the jumbled incline of a dried-up waterfall, he slunk into what tiny shade there was, and lay down.

A human would have despaired in that terrible wilderness, but with the practical sense of animals, the dog paid little attention to his prospects, preferring to concentrate on the slight respite from the toil and heat. He sighed, yawned, rested his head on his paws and dozed.

The image of a red-haired boy who had fed and patted him was still uppermost in his mind, serving as an invisible and instinctive compass through the terrible land. Other memories the dog had also, tangled skeins of pictures and sensations, of sausages, of the scent of wet earth, of trees and kindly words and the feeling of hands stroking his ears in shady gardens. There were bitter memories too, of the events that had led him here; the feeling of a lash on his back, the sound of crowds roaring, a race through dark tunnels, the smell of salty, fishy air and the sensation of a rocking floor underneath his paws, and the crowd of yelling, savage men who had surrounded them and taken the red-haired boy away from him.

Instinct told the dog that water was not far away, and after a brief rest, he shook himself and prepared for the next gruelling trek.

Through the desert ran the remnants of a dusty road. Where it had come from, and which city it used to lead to, had vanished into the earth. No trace remained of the people who had first built the road, or travelled on it. Only from time to time, ruins rose out of the clay, the lost civilizations of the old Naturals, the ancient people who had built up a world of civilization and high buildings, but who since the floods and earthquakes of the Apocalypse had all but disappeared into the dust.

As the dog limped up and over the dusty bank, he came to a sudden halt, teeth bared, growling. Before him, towering out of the desert, rose the skeleton of a huge ship; the carcass of an old Citizen food-boat, attacked by Natural pirates on its way from the pharms, scuppered and left to die. Listing badly to the right as if it would sink beneath the engulfing sands, its tattered rigging was encrusted with dust and the scarred planks protruded like broken ribs from its flaking hull.

But it was not the ship that made the dog's hackles rise. On the deck of the stranded boat stood two Naturals dressed for the desert, scarves wound around their face to protect them from the searing dust-winds, and armed with sharp spears and a quiver of arrows. The larger of the two figures saw him immediately and pointed.

"Look, Liana! A wild-hound!"

The speaker vaulted over the side of the ship and approached the dog, carefully keeping out of reach of the sharp teeth. Slowly, he unwound his scarf. Underneath it, he was probably no more than thirty years old, though Naturals aged fast in this forsaken land. The blistering sun had tanned his skin dark, and his green eyes shone sharply from underneath his hood. It was a good-looking, though wild, face, with heavy arched brows, a wide mouth that seemed equally capable of both smiling and snarling, and shoulder-length hair that was a deep reddish chestnut, touched with threads of gold.

He caught his breath as he looked at the dog with a keen eye. "Why, I do not believe it! I am sure this is the litter-pup! Remember, the smallest of them all, whom we did not expect to live! See the ridge along his back and the black markings on his legs!"

The woman appeared beside him, peering closely at the dog. "It looks to be the same hound, I agree. But how. . . How did he come *here*, of all places?"

With a calm deliberation of movement, the man reached for his water-skin and poured a few precious drops on to his outstretched palm.

Recognition stirred in the dog's brain at the sound of the man's voice, of his first-milk and tumbling with his brothers in the shadows of the forest, of the order to hunt and the hand who gave him his share of pig-meat. Slowly his hackles subsided and he took a step forward, then another, to bury his nose in the fresh water.

The next moment a noose was slipped around his neck

and drawn tight. He tried to lunge away, but he was too late. The Natural stood up, pulling on the rope to subdue him. He barked and snapped his jaws at them. The man aimed a sharp kick at the dog's ribs.

"We will have a great task with him now, Liana, for he seems to have changed much. Truly, it is a mystery how he came here at all. But I am sure we will discover this, sooner or later."

A few moments later, all three had disappeared into the dust, and the wind swirled and blew, eradicating with a layer of grey dust the slight trail of prints that they had left behind.

Corin ran and ran, unable to breathe. His legs felt as if they were moving through water, and his outstretched arms grasped at nothingness as the ground slipped away from him. He felt himself falling, falling, plunging into an icy darkness.

A voice was calling him desperately, a voice that he knew, of someone that he recognized, but he could see nothing. He tried to move, to make his way towards the voice, but something heavy was on him, pressing him down. Frantically he struggled, but he could not move.

"Master! Master! Wake up!"

Corin blinked awake, scrabbling at the heavy damask blankets which seemed to be almost suffocating him. "Ivar? What is it? Is there a fire?"

"No, sir," returned his impassive Gemini bodyguard, bending over him. "You are only dreaming. But now your afternoon nap is over, and it is time for you to get dressed for the New Year Ball."

"I had such a nightmare," said Corin vaguely, as he was assisted from his bed and stood waiting for Ivar to dress him. "I'm almost glad you woke me up."

"Too much pudding at lunch time, perhaps?" reproved the servant mildly, as he sponged his master's face, and started to help him into the heavily embroidered and padded robe of purple and green silk that he was to wear.

Corin sighed impatiently. Wearing the ceremonial costume of a Higher Citizen was like putting on a suit of armour. Slim sensors that measured and regulated his body temperature ran invisibly through the seams of the jacket, while the material itself had been custom-made to the highest Genopolis security regulations; bullet-, blade- and even explosive-proof. Carefully, Ivar checked that the hydration and nutrient delivery systems were functioning correctly, buttoned the jacket fastidiously and brushed away a few invisible specks of dust.

All this trouble, thought Corin carelessly, for a silly dance! All the same, he could not help looking forward to the Ball. He had heard talk of chocolate fountains and honeycombs, and even rumours of real frozen ice cream, which was something so wonderful and rare that Corin would not be able to believe it until he tasted it.

"All *right*, Ivar!" he said curtly, pushing the servant aside. "I want to go down to the party now!"

"But, sir, your father has not yet sent for you," replied

the Gemini, folding his hands and staring at the floor as was expected of servants when they addressed their masters. "Your entrance should be at eight o'clock precisely. Your father was very insistent on that point."

"Who is your master, me or my father?" retorted Corin, pulling back the velvet curtain that hung over the chamber door. "The first purpose of every Gemini is to serve a Citizen, so you must do whatever I want!"

Yet despite his bold words, the mention of his father made Corin rather less confident as he made his way out on to the mezzanine and leaned over the banister to catch a glimpse of the bustle beneath. A Palace Ball was always a grand affair, and this one was of special importance. The New Year Rains were late in coming this year, and the summer had been long and hot. The huge entrance hall had been decked with ruby-red hangings that fell like great silken flags to the marble floor. Golden swags had been entwined around the huge staircase and from the ceiling hung great chandeliers, sparkling with light and diamonds.

"Who is coming tonight, Ivar?" he asked the Gemini, who as demanded, was never more than three steps behind him. "I hope the Maian girls have been invited. They are so easy to tease! Do you remember the time that I shot one of them with a sausage from my catapult?"

Ivar shook his head. "Since the Maian Inn was disbanded for treason last year, sir, the Maian scholars have been kept in prison, awaiting sentence."

"Well, at least I hope Priscilla di Angelo is not

coming," returned Corin, idly shredding a strip of the golden decorations between his fingers. "Father is always ordering me to dance with her, and all she talks of is the new dresses she wears and the parties she has been to. She bores me silly."

"But her father is an important Governor," said Ivar softly, picking up the shreds that Corin had dropped on to the thick carpet. "I am sure that your father is keen to give you a promise that befits your status when you grow up."

Corin considered this. Ruling Citizens of Genopolis were often promised early and always to other Higher or Ruling Citizens, even though marriage might take place many years later. Corin had never really thought about the meaning of this before, and the idea made him turn to Ivar in sudden surprise. "But I'm not even twelve yet, and I know final-year students who don't have to dance with anybody!"

"It is your father who will have the final word," replied Ivar.

"I don't want to grow up," said Corin, obstinately, starting down the staircase. "Too many City meetings and talking to Governors and silly dances like this one. People talking about you and never leaving you alone. And to think about living my whole life with Priscilla chattering in my ear is a terrible idea!"

The Gemini raised an eyebrow and coughed discreetly. "You may wish to talk lower, sir. Governor Angelo has just arrived."

Downstairs the great doors had opened and a litter borne by twelve Gemini had drawn up to the steps, even though it was a light ceremonial litter and really required no more than six bearers. In Higher-Citizen society, the size and appearance of one's entourage determined one's status, and many Senators brought with them their entire Gemini staff, from bodyguards to foot-servants, to wait on their every need during important events. As a result, social occasions were crowded with Gemini, all wearing the differing regalia of their Citizen masters and mistresses, and who if there was no room, waited outside with the carriages.

Governor Angelo emerged first from the litter, dressed all in black, with a high collar and soft shoes that made no sound on the floor. His daughter, Priscilla, was wearing an exquisitely-patterned robe of white and silver, and her black hair was braided up around her pale face in a style that made her look much older than her eleven Citizen-years. Corin waited for the Governor to bow and for Priscilla to curtsey, as was to be expected, while their Gemini servants prostrated themselves on the floor around them.

Corin restrained a grin at the absurdity of it all. Since the Anti-Outbreak Law, one was forbidden to show any expression on one's face, as even the ancient customs of *smiling* or *frowning* had become punishable, a rule that he in particular found extremely difficult to keep. But he knew he must set a good example. "Welcome, Governor Angelo," he said with his best Citizen manners. "Welcome,

Priscilla. You may go through to the Reception Room, where my father is expecting you."

Governor Angelo inclined his head politely. "I am most honoured, Your Lordship, to be received by you," he said smoothly. "I look forward to the pleasure of your company during the Ball, and no doubt my daughter would be privileged to dance with you if Your Lordship pleases."

Corin nodded back resignedly as the Angelos disappeared through the main door to the Palace, and suddenly, despite the great space of the entrance, he felt as if the walls were closing in around him, and the richness of the decorations seemed heavier than the chains on the feet of the lowest Gemini yoked to the waterwheels or the furnace in the Palace kitchens. Was this all his life was meant to be, narrow, planned out, pushed and guided by his father and the Citizenry around him?

The clock chimed eight Citizen night-hours. Slowly, with the attentive Ivar always at his heel, Corin walked towards the Palace hall as his father had ordered.

Arlo lay back on the crumbling ruin of the stone tower, dangled his bare feet over the gritty edge into the cool water of the lake, gazed up at the full moon sailing overhead and sighed with contentment.

A year living in the tribal wilds of the Regions had seen great changes in both Arlo and the small band of Citizens that he had led out of Genopolis. Now nearly thirteen years old, he was almost unrecognizable from the awkward skinny boy who had escaped from the City. He had grown taller and his uncut reddish hair hung down around his ears; he wore it pushed back by a piece of rag bound round his brows, Natural-style. He was still thin but his new height had given him confidence, and he had long since reduced his Citizen-clothes to tattered rags by scrambling through the scrubland and desert. Instead, he dressed in the roughly-woven cloth tunic and skins of the tribes, and his proudest possession – a tightly-strung bow that old Onofre had showed him how to make – was always slung over one shoulder, though his aim was still poor. But yesterday he had shot his first squirrel! He reached down, and touched the fluffy tail that he wore dangling from his belt as a trophy.

"Did my father catch many squirrels, Kira?" he asked his cousin, who was sitting next to him, her face upturned to the moon.

"Hundreds," returned Kira, smiling. "Uncle Angus caught wolves and bears and many other things besides. You are becoming more like him every day."

Arlo smiled happily. Over the past year, he had fitted effortlessly into the life of the Orphans – the remnants of his Natural family – led by his cousin, Kira. He felt so happy to be surrounded by people who felt, thought and understood exactly as he did. People who laughed when he laughed, who gave comfort in the touch of their hands or who felt the same joy in the taste of food that he did, and who had words for Emotions that Arlo had always struggled to express to Citizens, like . . . *anticipation*, and . . . *contentment*, and . . . *suspicion*. . .

The only sorrow that still sometimes visited him was the regret that he had been unable to find Rem. For months he and Ozzie had searched the surrounding Regions but without finding so much as a paw-print. Kira had tried to comfort him, telling him of the remarkable ability of dogs to find their way back to their masters, but as time passed slowly by, Arlo's hopes had slipped further and further away.

A splash and a cheer echoed across the lake, rousing him from his thoughts. On the rocks across from them, outlined against the clear night sky, Arlo could see the forms of his Citizen friends Talia, Ozzie and Toby plunging their harpoons into the water in the hope of catching fish.

Toby was jumping up and down excitedly. "Well caught, Talia! We're going to have a feast tonight!"

"Better be careful you don't skewer anybody out swimming!" called Kira, looking in some awe at the dark point of Talia's bloodstained spear.

"No chance of that, boss." Ozzie grinned back. "They're all down on the east bank with Onofre around the bonfire."

During the last year, Arlo had grown closer than he had ever imagined to Ozzie. The surly Citizen had appeared to resign himself to life outside the City and the gang of Kids they had left behind far quicker than anyone had expected, and set himself to establishing the Orphan camp with gusto. Before losing his eye and becoming part of the underworld of Genopolis, Ozzie had come from a family of masons, and put his skills to good use in draining the caves that they lived in and using the water to irrigate the surrounding soil. Like Arlo, his skin had been tanned perceptibly by the sun until he was almost indistinguishable from a tribal Natural, while the younger Toby's freckles had grown and expanded until he looked like one huge freckle, as he always liked to complain. He still wore his glasses, even though one lens was cracked, as he was almost blind without them. Finally, the least changed of them all in appearance was Talia, though she now wore a bandanna around her black braids and bore a fishing harpoon and a clutch of dangerous-looking knives at her belt.

Yet, despite Arlo's new-found happiness, there was one thing that was still niggling at him. Nervously, he turned to his Citizen friends.

"Isn't Usha with you?" he asked.

"No, she went over the other side of the lake about half a Citizen . . . I mean half an hour ago," said Talia distractedly over her shoulder, as she knelt on the edge of the rock, scanning the dark water beneath.

Arlo left Kira and the Citizens gutting their catch, and wandered off into the moonlight. Now that the heat had reached its height, the Orphan tribe – or *clan*, as they preferred to call themselves – spent most of its time outside during the cooler night hours. They would have breakfast in the glow of the evening sunset, a picnic under the cooling moonlight rays, and supper (if there was any) watching the dawn come up. Then they slept away the heat of the day in cool, dark catacombs.

On the shores of the lake, he could see a huddle of people sitting attentively around a taller white-haired figure, standing, finger outstretched, pointing at the moon. He quickened his pace, temporarily forgetting Usha. Only one thing could keep a large group of Naturals sitting still for so long, he reasoned, and that was a story.

The New Year Ball was in full swing. The Highest of all Genopolian Citizenry were present, and the Palace was crowded with silks and satins and polite chatter. Through it all wandered Corin, distractedly, unheeding of the bows and curtseys that greeted him, feeling only the ever-present Ivar like a shadow at his elbow. If he wished to eat a delicacy borne on the silver salvers, Ivar would taste it before him, if he wished to drink anything then Ivar would first put the cup to his lips.

It had not always been like this, Corin thought to himself. When he was younger, Ivar had seemed like a constant companion, someone to talk to, carry his staff and sword, clean up the mess he made or take the blame for the constant tricks that Corin played on everyone. But lately his servant seemed to have become a weight around his neck, never leaving him alone from bedtime to bath time, during lessons or free time, either sleeping or waking. Though Corin knew the Gemini's purpose was to guard him to the death – and as a Higher Citizen these days you could not be too careful – he often longed to be alone, with nobody but his own thoughts. But the only order that Ivar would not obey, *could* not obey, was to let his master out of his sight for one single minute.

Ivar was already murmuring in his ear. "Over there, sir. His Lordship is summoning you."

Up on the raised dais at the head of the Palace stateroom, Corin saw his father reclining on the richly-covered couch, surrounded by attentive servants, his arm upraised and beckoning to him. As Corin neared the couch, he bowed his knee low to the ground and waited for his father to speak first.

"So," said the Regis, and paused, taking in the sight of the boy kneeling before him. "How do you find the festivities, my son?"

Corin lowered his eyes respectfully. "Most interesting, sir."

"I trust it will become even more interesting, once you see the entertainment that I have planned for this evening." His father patted the couch beside him, a signal for Corin to stand up and take his place at his side. Instantly a footstool was pushed beneath his feet by the attending Ivar and a tray of sweetmeats was waved under his nose. As he selected one – *no ice cream then*, he thought glumly – his father stood up imperiously, clapping his hands, and instantly silence fell.

"My dear fellow Citizens," the Regis began, speaking in the deep, soft tone that he used for ceremonial occasions. "I bid you welcome. As you know, the Rains are late this year, but our scientists are telling us that they will start within days, and then the first food-ships will come to the City from the pharms.

"To celebrate this occasion, we have a special amusement planned for you. As you know, in the Bestiary of Pharmopolis, our talented scientists have created many Chimaeras, beings previously known only in myth and legend. Our airships have braved the heat-winds to bring one of the fruits of their labours to grace our festivities. Guards, bring out the Medusa!"

A fanfare of trumpets greeted the Regis's command, and the doors were flung back. For the first time, Corin sat forward in interest. Last time there had been dancing slaves, jugglers and beautiful acrobats that had swooped from the ceiling on silken ropes, performing dizzying stunts as they flew from one rope to another.

But what was *this*? Corin's sweetmeat fell untasted from his fingers. Around the Hall there was an intake of breath, as they stood transfixed at the sight of the creature which shambled in, before each of them immediately covered their noses at the terrible inhuman stench which issued from the doorway.

Tall, naked and covered with green scales, she was in appearance female, though taller and stronger than many a man there. Yet as she raised her head a simultaneous gasp ran around the room. Fanged teeth protruded from her bluish lips, and her long ears tapered into points. But worst of all, instead of hair, long writhing snakes curled and hissed from her skull, and from her hideous face two horror-filled, blue-green eyes stared back at them.

"Gentle Citizens, I give you – a Gorgon!"

Corin could hardly believe his eyes. Though he had seen a Minotaur last year at the Circus, he had never seen anything like *this* – and so close to him too!

Bound and prodded with lances and whips by the attending guards, the creature lunged and shrieked into the middle of the Hall. Applause broke out as her chains were released, and two uniformed soldiers – one male, one female – strode forward to duel with the monster.

Slowly they circled her, carefully keeping their distance as the snakes darted and spat poison at them. The Gorgon lashed out with one clawed hand, and they leapt aside, dodging the forked tongues of the serpents by a whisker.

"Come on!" cried Corin in excitement, almost forgetting himself, and the Regis shot a sharp, reproving look at him.

One soldier leapt forward and aimed a stroke at the Gorgon, but her long nails shot out first, raking him across the face, and he fell with a crash. But the female soldier sidestepped her neatly, and as the monster hurtled howling past, the bright blade of the soldier's sword flashed through the air, and with one stroke, severed the Gorgon's head from her body.

Instantly, cheers broke out from the audience. It had

been a short fight, though a good one. But with the momentum of the stroke, the head fell to the floor, in a frenzy of lashing snakes, and rolled towards the foot of the dais where Corin sat.

All rose to their feet. The guards sprang forward, swords drawn, but to Corin's amazement, it was the Regis who, moving as if in a dream, suddenly stepped down from his chair, bent, and picked up the head by its serpent-hair.

"Careful, Father!" cried Corin, but there was no need. The snakes now hung lifeless from the skull, and the eyes were shut. But as the Regis stood and held out the head at arm's length, the terrible eyes suddenly opened again, and in the stunned silence the Gorgon began to speak.

The language was sibilant and hissing, but for all that, still recognizable. A forked tongue darted from her lips as she fixed the Regis with her horrifying gaze.

"So, Citizen, do you breed us only to kill us? You use your knowledge to distort Nature and destroy it? Be warned, Regis. Your time is near. The days of Genopolis are ending, and your pride will be its downfall."

Corin sat as if turned to stone. With an effort, he turned his gaze away from her dreadful eyes, and even as her stare faltered and her eyelids drooped at last, he looked up at the high ceiling, which seemed to be getting lower and lower until the air itself got thick and heavy and he could not breathe.

*

Sound travels quickly across water, and from where she wandered on the far side of the lake, Usha could clearly hear snatches of talk, laughter and singing from the clan's picnic. Quietly, the Gemini girl pulled her cloak around her and retreated into the shadow of the ruined watchtower on the north-east shore. Nobody would find her here.

The lake was in reality no more than a stagnant pond, lying in a flooded valley in a cleft of the mountains above the catacombs. On a clear night such as this, you could just about make out the buildings of the old Natural City that had stood in the valley before the floods of the Apocalypse, dark shadows of spires and archways which flickered and swayed underneath the ripples of water. Sometimes, it was rumoured, and heard with a delicious shiver, you could hear the bells of the old steeples ringing. Though why the bells might have rung, and what the steeples were for, no one could tell. No one remembered the name of the place, nor of the valley, and in the tongue of the Orphans it was simply the Drowned City.

Naturals would not venture on to the north-east shore because of their fear of what they called *ghosts*, the spirits of people long-dead who would rise out of the lake if they were disturbed. If you heard the bells ringing, then it meant the ghosts were abroad. The ruined stairway where Usha now stood, with its graceful steps descending into the slimy water, held a particular dread significance for them. Some said it was the way between this world and the next, and any who walked down the stairs into the water would disappear and never return.

Usha had heard this ridiculous theory with astonishment. How could people possibly walk about if they were dead? And what on earth was "the next world"? Moreover, the idea of Natural death had to be explained to her, because back at home in Genopolis, dying Citizens were recycled to provide blood or body parts for others. But even so, thought Usha, the idea that there was another world to go to when you died seemed foolish in the extreme, as foolish as the stories about the Apocalypse that old Onofre loved to tell to the clan during the long nights. Didn't these people know that these were only dreams and fantasies? But, when she said as much to the Naturals, her opinions were met with an equally incredulous response, and from that moment, the rift between the Gemini and the Natural clan had begun to widen.

Suddenly, from behind her, came a tiny cough, closely followed by a strange, wailing cry. Despite herself, Usha jumped in surprise, before mastering her thoughts firmly. Honestly, she was getting as touchy as a Natural! Curiously she took a few steps towards the bushes, and saw a small wailing bundle, wrapped in dirty skins, lying in a cleft between two shattered tree-trunks.

A baby! Usha stared around amazedly, but no one was in sight. What on earth was it *doing* here? Usha knew that Gemini could not have children, since their purpose was to be created, not to create; but the sight of a baby still fascinated her. Slowly she bent forward and pulled back the wrappings to see a scrunched-up, squalling face, and a tangle of dark hair.

As her fingers touched the tiny cheek, a sensation like a clap of thunder broke upon her, and suddenly the air around her was thick with the noise of voices calling. Usha threw up her hands as shadows suddenly filled her mind, of blood, and terror, and a ghastly orange sun that flooded her vision. Instinctively, she groped for the baby and raised it in her arms to shield it from the horror around them.

"Get away from her!" came a shout, and instantly Usha was back beside the lake, and all around her was suddenly quiet, apart from the screaming baby in her arms. Confused, Usha turned to see Annis, one of the younger women of the clan, not much older than seventeen summers, emerging from the forest with a sack of harvested roots. The Natural girl lunged towards Usha and pulled the baby roughly from her arms.

"What are you doing to her!"

"Nothing!" gasped back Usha. "I wasn't—"

"Don't you touch her!" shouted Annis. "Ever! Do you hear me, you witch?"

Stunned, Usha watched as the girl ran off with the baby in her arms, to disappear towards the distant firelights and laughter of the picnic.

Although she had been rebuffed, it was not the first time. Visions such as these and her remarkable facility for foreseeing things that had not yet happened, had earned her no friends. Rumours had slowly circulated, born of old wives' tales and Natural superstition, and murmurs of "witch" often followed her as she walked alone through the clan, and even the kindly words of Onofre or the care of Kira could not make them accept her.

For her part, there were so many things about Naturals that Usha would never understand. For example, they had an unspoken language consisting of the tone of voice they used and the expressions on their faces, which might change the meaning of a sentence completely. A wink or a smile might change a *Yes* to a *No*, or even a *Maybe*. A different tone of voice might change a simple statement to a thing of ridicule or merriment. At such times, especially when the Naturals told what they called *jokes*, Usha and the Citizens were left bewildered, wondering at the outbreak of laughter that would rise around them. They had to understand scientifically what the clan already knew intuitively, and apply reason to even the most unreasonable situations.

So it was that Usha the Gemini, with no fear of Natural ghosts, moved lonely and phantom-like through the dark trees, as out of place in the Regions as Arlo had ever been in the City of Genopolis. Yet even as the peace of the forest again descended around her, something kept niggling at her, refusing to let her rest. Another vision had visited her, and she did not know what it portended. She could only wait to see what would happen. As she wandered, Usha could feel that something was out there, unseen in the darkness, awaiting its moment.

In the cold silence that followed the Gorgon's words, Corin felt his heart beat suddenly faster with a sensation that he could not name.

Be warned, Regis. The days of Genopolis are ending...

But, with a contemptuous stare as if nothing amiss had happened, the Regis stepped forward and handed the head to a servant, who instantly bore it away on a silver platter. Slaves ran in to carry out the body of the monster and strew fresh silver sand over the dark stain where she had lain. Then the Regis nodded to the conductor, who raised his baton. Swirls of music again livened the air, and the awkwardness caused by the Gorgon's prophecy was swept away from all present.

All but Corin. While the other Citizens began to circulate and chatter, he sat brooding next to the Regis.

I've had enough of this Ball, he thought. *I've had enough of my father and the things he calls entertainment. Actually, I've had enough of pretty much everything here. Ever since he became Regis he's got worse and worse!*

It was not the first time that Corin had had these thoughts. Over the last few years, his father had grown in power, from being a Senator to becoming Regis of the Inn of Court, and most recently to being Regis of the whole Consulate of Genopolis. Now Corin hardly ever saw his father, apart from state occasions like these, and when he did, he saw him with new eyes.

"Well, my son?" Corin realized that the Regis had turned towards him, smiling expectantly. "Priscilla di Angelo is your guest here tonight. Are you not going to ask her to dance?"

Corin suddenly found that he could move again, but when he spoke his voice was low and halting. "If that is what you wish, sir, I will dance with her."

"That is what I wish." His father sat down regally and surveyed the proceedings, while Corin turned reluctantly to Priscilla, who had stood watching the spectacle, her face impassive.

Corin took a deep breath and made the first step. Priscilla kept pace with him; she was a far better dancer than he, and even managed to add some extra twists and turns to make the dance look more professional. One after the other, watching Citizen-couples started to join in, until the whole hall was alive with dancing and movement, the incident of the entertainment already forgotten.

But Corin's quick brain was already working out a plan to escape the festivities. Over Priscilla's shoulder he could see Ivar waiting patiently by the dais next to his father, further away from his master than he had ever been before. *Good*, he thought to himself. Another turn, another step and Corin was further away still. Dancing couples encircled them, moving between him and Ivar as he and Priscilla progressed slowly across the floor. One more turn, and a few more paces, and they were almost at the outermost reaches of the stateroom.

Any time now, thought Corin quickly, awaiting his chance. It soon came. A tall Senator momentarily blocked the line of sight between him and Ivar. Instantly Corin knew it was time to act. He dropped Priscilla's hand, dodged behind a crinolined Citizeness and bolted.

Through the servants' door, where Corin had often visited the kitchens, there was a small twisting staircase that led up to the back-quarters of the Palace. In a second Corin had wrenched the door open and pelted up the stairs three at a time. Though there had been no public outcry at his escape, he had no doubt that Ivar had seen him make a break for it and was at that very moment pushing unobtrusively through the crowd in order not to cause a scene. There was not a moment to lose. As he gained the upper corridors that ran past the servants' quarters, he could hear the heavily-built Gemini's feet already echoing on the wooden steps after him. Corin threw himself round a corner and took the first door that led off to his left.

In a second he realized he had made a mistake. He was heading up the staircase of the upper Tower of the Palace, a place where the Regis often kept prisoners for his own private amusement. How fitting that he should be cornered here, thought Corin, as he blundered along the dimly-lit stairwell, trying first one locked door and then another with no luck. His father would not be so careless as to leave an open door in the Palace.

As he hurtled up the steps, he felt all hope leave him. From the top of the staircase he could hear booted feet descending. No doubt it was a guard from the tower who had been alerted to his dash from the ballroom. Rebelliously he sat down, folded his arms and waited for Ivar to make his way up. At all costs, he would not go back to that awful Ball! He grinned to himself wickedly as he imagined the insult that it would be to the di Angelos to be denied his company for the evening.

Above him he heard the footsteps suddenly stop. Then there was a rumbling, as if something heavy had been pushed aside, and then silence.

From below Corin could hear the voices of Ivar and another servant discussing whether to ascend the staircase. But from above there was no sound. He pricked up his ears in sudden hope. Who had been at the top of the stairs, and where had they gone?

Quietly, he got to his feet and tiptoed along in the deepening darkness, one hand trailing against the wall. Before he reached the second turn of the stairs, his hand suddenly disappeared into darkness and he realized that one of the panels that lined the stairs had been pushed aside to reveal a concealed passageway. At the end of the passageway a door stood ajar and from the room beyond a dim lamp was shining. Silhouetted against the light, her back to him, was Brigadier Hacker, his father's chief adviser, Commander of the Army and the most powerful – and dangerous – Citizen in Genopolis.

"In the beginning," said Onofre, having waited impatiently for Arlo to clamber into the circle and be seated, "there was Nothing on the face of the earth. Darkness had not yet been created, nor yet light. No living person has ever seen Nothing so great as that which existed before the beginning of time.

"Into this empty, featureless place, came the Great Mother. Where she came from, and what she looked like, we cannot tell. But what we do know is that when she clapped her hands, the thunder was created. And when she laughed, the sun was born, and brightened the skies with its radiance. And when she sang aloud, the music became the earth, which unfurled and lay beneath the sun like a great Road, whose journey continues for ever.

"Yet all the earth remained empty, and the Great Mother was saddened because there was no voice to answer hers, no laughter, no music, and no singing. So the Great Mother wept from the heavens, and her tears fell like rain, and from those tears, the trees grew, and the flowers blossomed, and the birds chipped their way out of their eggs and sweetened the air with their song. But still she had no children, and no word yet existed to describe her loneliness.

"So then the Great Mother sent forth Love on to the earth that night, and the next day, when the sun rose again, there were footprints on the Road, and there were voices chattering, and there was the smell of food cooking; there was the sound of flutes playing and babies crying. And she smiled down on them because she saw all her children, and it made her glad."

There was a brief interruption as Annis, carrying her baby, pushed her way into the circle next to Arlo. Her eyes were reddened with tears but she shrugged away all offers of help and turned her back to nurse her child. From the back of the crowd, a voice called out, "And then, Onofre? Don't stop there!"

"But then," continued Onofre, "the laughter and the chatter of the Great Mother's children turned to quarrelling and hatred. And the arguments became so loud and so fierce that they woke the Great Mother from her slumbers, and she sent forth a flood on to the earth, called the Apocalypse, to punish her children. And the floodwaters remained on the face of the earth for twenty years. And when the waters receded, and the sun came up, there was only one child who still dared to challenge her, the man that the Citizens call Leuwenkind, who had studied the evil art of Science (which we call Knowledge) and who had it in his mind to defeat his Mother.

"So Leuwenkind gathered around him all that was remaining of his tribe, and built a city on the highest mountain, a city with towers so high that he had it in mind to cross the bridge from earth to invade heaven and to become more powerful than the Great Mother herself. Yet even while the tower was still being built, the Great Mother saw what he was planning, and sent forth all her power to the earth. And she took from Leuwenkind and his descendants the gift of Love, with which she had created all her children. So then in that City, which they called Genopolis, there was no more emotion, no more feeling. The Citizens could not love, they could not hate, they were strangers in their own family.

"And those people also did not have compassion, they did not have mercy, they did not have pity. So they stole from the other tribes everything that they had and killed them; and the survivors ran to bury themselves in the cracks of the earth, to hide in the caves, to the water's edge, and called to the Great Mother for help.

"Yet the Great Mother did not answer, because she knew the price that had to be paid for taking away her love. And, as the sun went down, she withdrew into a deep cave in the sky, weary of her labours, and slumbered. And there she still lies, and all that now passes on the earth is but a dream in the mind of the Great Mother."

Applause broke out as Onofre finished his story, and voices babbled questions to the storyteller. Arlo shifted uncomfortably. Back in Genopolis they had told quite a different version of history, one that laid the blame for the Apocalypse squarely at the ancient Naturals' feet for their misuse and poisoning of the earth. But such a story would never be told here. How different the world seemed, he thought, depending on where you lived. The Citizens would never be understood by the Naturals, nor the Naturals by the Citizens. Not for the first time he felt himself unsure, uncertain which side his loyalties lay on, and for a moment not even the lively chatter of his own people could prevent him from feeling lonely and afraid.

*

From where Corin crouched in the shadows, he could see that the Brigadier stood in a dimly-lit turret room hung with maps and muskets. All her attention was concentrated on her desk, on which were placed a number of small glass vials. As the lamplight caught them they flickered with many different colours as if a living flame was inside them; violet, azure, golden, emerald. As they sparkled, a small rainbow seemed to be playing around the walls.

What on earth could make lights so beautiful? Fascinated, Corin moved slowly forward down the dark passageway in order to see closer.

A voice echoed faintly up from the stairwell behind him, Ivar calling softly but respectfully. "Is Your Lordship there? Will you please come down?"

Corin ignored him. *Let the servant shout*, he thought contemptuously. But unfortunately, the Brigadier also heard the Gemini's voice and marched up the corridor, in her haste sweeping by Corin, who stood unobserved in the black shadows behind the door. She peered out into the stairwell.

"Who is that? What are you doing in these quarters?"

There was a startled pause, and then, "I beg your pardon, Brigadier," as Ivar turned away and clattered down the steps, evidently assuming that Corin must have taken another turning. As he departed, the Brigadier slid the panel shut with an impatient sigh, before she stalked unseeingly back past him and into the dimly-lit room beyond.

Quickly, Corin took stock of the situation. He had succeeded in escaping from Ivar, only to be trapped in the company of the most dangerous Citizen that he knew!

The Brigadier had been one of his father's advisers from Corin's earliest Citizen-hood, and he avoided her whenever possible. It was not only her appearance that made her so forbidding. Ancient scars sustained in a battle against rebellious Naturals had melted her features like wax down one side of her face, from which one naked eyeball protruded. It was also her manner, a cold hostility that seemed to regard everyone in Genopolis – even the Regis! – as under suspicion. And if she realized that Corin was in her study, then he would be in more trouble than he had ever been in before; more than the time he had strung a trip-wire between two statues in the Palace Museum; more than the time he had put a bucket of water at the top of the banquet door; more than the time. . .

But the Brigadier had already walked back into her study and disappeared around a curve in the turret room. Corin peered around the door after her. The Brigadier was nowhere to be seen. Where had she gone? Corin scanned the room uncertainly, before realizing that the curve of the turret meant that the room was circular, leading around to his right, where he could not see.

Something made him take a step into the study. He had never been into this secret place, nor ever wished to, but something about the strange flickering vials of colour drew him irresistibly on, until he could see the inscriptions on the bottles.

Felix hilarius

Tristem melancholia

Phobia aggressa

Colours played over his face as he read the names to himself, light that changed into all hues of the rainbow, each with their own deep lustre, transforming from the darker shade to the lighter. Transfixed, he stretched out his hand and closed it over the most beautiful vial, of streaks of swirling gold, and flecks of silver shimmering inside the glass.

Whatever was in that bottle must be very precious, thought Corin. Could it be a perfume, a poison, or something to drink?

As if in a trance, he picked up the vial, reached for the stopper and began to draw it out.

A clink of metal on stone made him jump back to consciousness and he realized that the Brigadier's metalled boots were coming around the corner towards him. There was only one place to hide, and quickly he ducked underneath the table, concealing himself with the fringes of the military flag. Too late he remembered that the golden vial was still clasped in his hand.

Corin fingered the bottle in indecision. He would be in great trouble if they found him there, but actually handling the possessions of the Brigadier would be worse still! Rapidly sizing up his situation, he was on the point of giving himself up and risking whatever punishment would be given to him, when he heard the sound of other, shuffling steps and the creak of an iron chain.

Cautiously, Corin peered underneath the folds of the flag. The Brigadier strode back into the study, with two hunched prisoners stumbling after her, one young and fair-haired, around twenty-five Citizen-years, the other older, white-haired and bearded, perhaps more than fifty. Their feet were manacled and their clothes in rags. Dirt and cobwebs stained their hair and their skin was grey and brittle from a year spent locked away from the sunlight and the open air.

Corin had seen many such captives, but there was something about the elder prisoner that locked Corin's attention.

Hadn't he seen him somewhere before?

The Brigadier seated herself comfortably in a chair, and gazed at them.

"So, Doctor. What will you say to save yourself from Regeneration?"

The old man, his voice dulled by imprisonment and lack of nourishment but still spirited, answered her. "You seek the child that has escaped from your clutches, Brigadier. You have searched for many years without success."

There was something about the voice that made the hairs prickle on Corin's neck with a strange uneasiness. Now he remembered. The Doctor had sat on his father's

High Table for the Anointment Ceremony almost one year ago. Though he had only seen the elderly Citizen once before, a sense of mistrust touched him.

The Brigadier coughed, a deep rattling cough that echoed around the stone chamber. "I know this already, old man. My question is, what bargain will you make in exchange for your life?"

There was a brief silence, before the younger prisoner spoke up.

"I will make the bargain. I alone k-know where he is to be found."

"Do you?" sneered the Brigadier. "How am I to know that this is not an idle trick of yours, of a stuttering librarian to save his own skin?"

"Give me one week, until the seas begin to rise," returned the younger prisoner. "I can l-lead you to the place where the Naturals hide during summer."

The Brigadier considered this for a moment, nodding her ghastly head as if deep in thought. "If you are lying, then it will be the worse for you. The pharms hold many secrets, and we have punishments of our own there which would drive even a Citizen mad, before he dies."

"Then take me there, and you shall see for yourself," returned the younger prisoner calmly, and as he spoke, the eyes of the older prisoner fell upon Corin, crouching beneath the table, and widened in sudden surprise. He opened his mouth as if to say something but Corin shook his head mutely in appeal, his finger on his lips.

No . . . no . . . please . . .

After an agonizing second, the older prisoner turned his gaze away as if he had not seen the boy, and spoke. "You must trust us, Brigadier. When the seas rise, you will know whether we speak the truth."

The Brigadier stood up in decision. "First, I will take you back to your cells and we will spend a short time in the company of these pretty bottles, to give you a taste of what may be, if you will betray me."

Corin shrank away as she turned towards the desk and picked up the tray of vials, but the Brigadier did not seem to mark the missing one. Moments later, the sound of the shuffling footsteps had faded and Corin was left alone in the study. His heart pounding, he scrambled out from under the desk and ran for the door, remembering too late that the panel to the outside staircase was closed.

There had to be a way out! The Brigadier would surely never have shut it if it could not be opened from the inside, reasoned Corin. He must get out first, and give the vial to Ivar to arrange its return later. In terrible haste he pushed at the wood, jabbing here and there in the darkness. Finally, as he was almost about to give up hope, his fingers finally hit a lever. He pulled at it. The panel slid open and Corin stumbled out on to the staircase, right into the arms of Ivar, who was blundering confusedly up and down the steps in search of his master for the umpteenth time.

"Your Lordship!" began Ivar, but Corin pushed past him, finger on his lips, beckoning him down the steps.

Suddenly he realized he had never been so thankful to see his servant in his life before.

"Quickly, Ivar, let's go. I'll explain everything later."

Once Onofre's story was finished, Arlo remembered Usha. Cursing himself for his forgetfulness, he pushed his way out through the circle and made his way around to the lake. Repressing a momentary shudder that ran through him at the thought of the bells, he turned his mind to the problem of his Gemini friend.

Though all of the Citizens had struggled to fit into clan life, it was Usha who had most difficulties. With her extraordinary pale eyes and fair hair, she stood out from the Naturals – and even from her fellow-Citizens – like a birch tree in a family of dark oaks. Mistrust had started slowly, with the realization that though Usha endured the same amount of wind and sun as the others, her skin had not browned, nor even reddened slightly. Instead she remained the same milky shade she had always been. And when the Naturals had heard that Usha had no biological parents but instead had been Created in the laboratories of the pharms, their disbelief knew no bounds.

Born in a bottle, they murmured amongst themselves. *No soul was ever made by human hands. She's not one of us.*

While Arlo occupied a protected position as the cousin of their leader, his influence to change other's minds was limited. Often he had heard whispers about him as he passed.

"Natural-born, he is, but Citizen-bred. And breeding will always come out in the end."

"Aye, but blood is thicker than water, they say. And whose side will he be on if he had to choose?"

For some time Arlo could not see Usha, and thought she had made her own way back to the catacombs. Finally he saw the glint of her hair as she passed through the trees and called to her. Though he was certain Usha had heard him, she did not pause to wait. Eventually Arlo caught her up, panting, and pulled her sleeve so that she had to turn and face him.

"Why are you out here all on your own?" asked Arlo, more for something to say than because he did not know her answer.

"Because your clan don't want me with them," answered Usha.

Arlo shook his head, but he could not think of a way to deny this convincingly enough. "It's not that, Usha, they're just not . . . *used* to you, that's all."

"Your clan will never be used to me," replied Usha unconcernedly, making her way towards the lake and seating herself on the ruins of the haunted staircase.

After a momentary qualm, Arlo joined her, though her words stung him. Usha did herself no favours sometimes by distancing herself from everybody. But he could feel that something else was up, apart from the usual problems.

"What's wrong, Usha?"

Usha folded her arms and turned away from him. For

some reason she had no desire to tell him of what had happened with Annis or her baby. "I had another vision," she said, shortly, staring into the slimy pool.

"What. . ." started Arlo and then stopped. Usha had told him that her visions came in pictures or images, not in any coherent pattern. "What exactly did you see, Usha?"

"I don't know," answered Usha, staring stubbornly into the water. "I saw smoke, and burning and blood. There were many cries of pain, so it must have been Naturals who were being hurt. And I saw people who carried bows and arrows, and the sun was in the east."

She paused, but Arlo caught her drift. "Do you think . . . something bad is going to happen at the New Year Hunt?"

"I don't *know*!" flashed Usha. "I'm just telling you what I saw!"

"You need to tell everybody," said Arlo uncomfortably.

"How can I?" snapped Usha. "Remember what happened the time of the waterfall?"

Arlo did remember. A few months ago Usha had a similar vision about the dried-up rocky waterfall where the Naturals often went climbing to search for roots or berries. The images had been a confused mixture of rocks, screaming and falling. Though Usha had tried to warn the clan that the waterfall was not safe, she had been ignored. When a child had fallen from the rocky outcrop two days later, he had broken his neck and died. Since that incident, people had drawn their cloaks away from Usha as they passed, almost as if they thought that she had caused the accident herself. Despite himself, he could not stop a shiver, and it was not all to do with the cool night air.

"Listen, Usha. We'll talk to Kira and get all this straightened out. Perhaps we can do the Hunt another day, or something. . ."

Usha shook her head. "They will blame me," she said hopelessly. "They do not understand me, and you Naturals always fear what you do not understand."

"I don't understand it either, but I'm not afraid," said Arlo, rather too resolutely to be convincing. Though he had been raised as a Citizen, only a few months in the Regions had strengthened instincts that he could not fully explain. Darkness and mist now brought out a fear in him that he had never had before, even during the most terrible times in Genopolis.

But Usha was his friend and had stuck by him, so he would stick by her, even if it meant going against a few superstitious Naturals. In sudden resolution, Arlo put out his hand and took hers. She resisted but he was not to be put off that easily.

"Don't worry, Usha. I'll help you convince Kira. Nobody will blame you again. Trust me."

The success of his escape from the Brigadier's study had put Corin in quite a different frame of mind, and he returned to the Ballroom with a new spring in his step, blithely brushing aside the reproaches of his bodyguard.

For the first time in ages, a gleam of excitement had touched his humdrum existence. The Gorgon's prophecy, the mystery of the prisoners and his theft of the golden vial had suddenly opened up new doors of adventure in what had become a stifling existence, and he felt quite brave and resolved as he checked to see that the vial was secure in the pocket of his sleeve.

Downstairs, the orchestra had broken into a fast dance, and the floor was bright with swirling dresses. Few of the guests had seemed to notice Corin's absence, and Ivar had been quick to cover it, knowing full well that he would be sent for Regeneration if it were ever known that his master had been out of his sight for ten whole minutes. But as they entered, Priscilla stood before him, her hands on her hips.

"What's happening? Where did you go? Don't you want to dance with me?"

Corin exchanged a glance with Ivar, daring him to say something. Was he not the Regis Apparent of Genopolis, and Ivar just a common servant? But the Citizen could see in his servant's eyes that the Gemini had lost. Ivar could say nothing of this little escapade to the Regis or the Brigadier. It was more than his life was worth. Nobody would doubt Corin's word against a slave, and Ivar knew it too, though he stood closely behind his lord with one hand lightly brushing his elbow, ready to seize his master if he should bolt again.

"I had something important to do. Sorry," lied Corin, and though suspicion still lingered in Priscilla's eyes, she held out her hand again, resignedly. But as Corin raised his arm to take it, a passing dancer jogged his elbow. The golden vial slipped from the pocket in his sleeve and fell to the floor. Instantly he stooped to retrieve it, but too late. Kicked out of his reach by a passing dancer, the tiny bottle shot skittering across the floor.

With a cry, Corin plunged after it, but the vial had already been knocked towards another crush of dancers even as he reached out to seize it. On his hands and knees, he chased the bottle across the polished dance floor as it was flicked from toe to toe, from heel to heel, from unseeing dancer to unseeing dancer. Finally it fetched up against the bottom step of the winding staircase, miraculously unbroken.

With a sigh of relief, Corin wriggled forward, and stretched out his hand to pick up the vial. But the next second, the dainty slippers of a beautiful Pharmopolis merchantess descended from the stairs above, stepped on the bottle and crushed it to powder. Like a golden mist, its delicate contents evaporated into the air.

"No!" cried Corin, grasping wildly at the shattered glass. But at that moment the strangest sensation caught him and he doubled over.

For a moment it felt as if someone had punched him in the stomach, but with it came a feeling of such dizzying and complete happiness that he could not breathe. In confusion he fell forward on to his face, unable to stop himself.

What on earth was happening? What was going on?

But he was not alone. The same thing was happening to the merchantess, and all the other guests around them; everyone was tripping or falling to the ground, a stunned expression on their faces. And from the pit of his stomach Corin felt himself begin to laugh, a great deep bellow of pure joy, gasping for air, laughing as if he could not stop. He tried to restrain it, but he could not help himself. There was no holding it back. The more Corin tried to stop, the more he laughed.

And with that Outbreak, merriment suddenly erupted within the Palace. Every person there, master or servant, Higher Citizen or lowest Gemini, fell to the floor, holding their sides and each other, screaming with laughter as if they were in the grip of an invisible hysteria. Like a wave, the sensation was sweeping over the dance floor, rendering the entire court helpless with mirth, shaking faces and bodies like puppets, held in the grip of something far stronger than they.

What was going on? What was this feeling?

The next moment the door was flung open with a crash, and the Brigadier towered in the entrance, her military cloak flying behind her.

"My Lord Regis! Emergency! Spies are loose in the Palace, and there is an Outbreak of Emotion in the City!"

TWO

Arlo and Toby sat in the mouth of their cave as the sun came up, flushing the sky pink in the early dawn. It was an hour before bedtime, and from the depths of the cave, the smell of Talia's fish frying for supper was already emerging.

Arlo was teaching Toby how to read using the book and map that had been written about Arlo and his parents many years ago. In truth, he had started off trying to teach everyone to read, but the task had very soon proved futile. Although the Naturals loved stories, they preferred telling them around a cooking fire or at bedtime to send the younger ones to sleep. Most of their old tales had been handed on from mothers to their children, then remembered and embroidered until the story itself had almost totally changed from its original. When Arlo tried to write them down so that they would not be changed or lost, the Naturals had been bewildered. What good, they said, was a story that could not breathe, a story that could not grow? Who on earth would plant a seed and not expect to see a fruit?

Even trying to teach them practical uses of writing had no effect. Every Natural counted on its fingers up to ten and then used its ten toes. Hunters had a complicated arrangement of pebbles and sticks to indicate the presence of animals, or to show the way back through unfamiliar territory. What use had they for books or writing? Or indeed what time, when you thought how many mouths there were to feed, and every child to every grandparent was out from dawn to dusk searching for scraps of food or performing the tasks allotted to them. Every moment out in the Regions was a struggle to survive.

Only the hour before bedtime was free to study, and though at first Arlo had been surrounded by interested observers who giggled at the strange marks scraped on to the cave mouth or into the dirt floor, now only Arlo and Toby still sat at their task every evening. Amongst their current personal projects were trying to update the map of the Regions that Arlo had brought from Genopolis; and also (rather ambitiously) attempting to finish the book of Arlo's history by writing a chronicle of their own adventures since escaping from Genopolis.

Arlo scratched a sentence into the dust at their feet, smiling a little sadly to himself as he remembered the schoolroom back at the Inn of Court. How often he had not appreciated Doctor Ignatius's efforts to interest and amuse him, and how hard the job of a tutor really was! For a moment, he missed the kindly old Doctor bitterly.

"That's very good, Toby. Try to read this one."

"Horse ... Shoe ... Gorge!" spelled out Toby, curiously. "Arlo, what's a gorge? And what's a horse?"

Arlo pushed his hair out of his eyes. Though he knew what the words meant well enough, he could no longer remember the images from the books of the Inn of Court, nor most of the lessons that he had once learned.

What on earth is happening to me? he thought confusedly. The task seemed too great for him, and he shut the book with a snap.

"I'm sorry, Toby, I can't remember. I've ... I've been here too long."

The clock in the State Room chimed six morning hours. The hush of the assembled courtiers was absolute. It was unusual for so many people to be standing in absolute stillness, thought Corin. The Brigadier's face was grim as she made her way to the pedestal at the front of the State Room. For a moment her eye caught Corin's, and the boy forced his face to remain smooth and impassive.

He had slept little that night. Whenever he closed his eyes, he saw a medley of visions – the eyes of the headless Gorgon opening, the shimmering of the rainbow-bottles on the Brigadier's desk, rows of courtiers collapsing like dominoes – and heard again the shrieks of laughter, so foreign and strange-sounding, not to mention treasonous!

What on earth had been in that vial?

The whole incident reminded him of what had happened at his father's Anointment Ceremony as Regis of the Inn of Court last year. Corin had two distinct memories of that event; firstly, the smile on the face of an ugly, red-haired boy, slightly older than him, who had lived as a novice in the Inn and who had upset the luncheon party by letting out a pet dog that he had kept secretly. The second was the confusion that had suddenly swept the assembly when the animal had run riot. Ivar had swept Corin up and carried him to safety before the creature had even come near, but the sight of the Dean tripping over the tent-ropes and bringing half the canopy down on top of them was one of the best things that he had ever seen. In a way, Corin had envied the red-haired boy. For a brief moment, he had been the sole centre of attention, in a way that Corin, though continually fussed over and guarded, had never been.

There had also been a rumour that the red-haired boy had been a Natural, but Corin had doubted this. First of all everybody knew that Naturals had tails and Corin was quite sure that the red-haired boy had been tail-less. And secondly it was common knowledge that the Brigadier had an obsession with Naturals and saw them lurking behind every wall, often accusing perfectly harmless Citizens or anyone who disagreed with her in the Senate of being Naturals in disguise. The test was to tie them down and pull their arms and legs from their bodies in order to discover whether they would scream.

Of course, nobody ever screamed, but they often died from their appalling injuries, so even being innocent would not help anybody once they had come under suspicion from the Brigadier.

So, despite his external calm, Corin's quick mind had already leapt to some conclusions. Whatever was in the Brigadier's vials must be something incredibly powerful, so powerful that the Brigadier must keep it secretly locked away. And also it must be highly contagious, because even one tiny breath of it had been enough to reduce more than a hundred good Higher Citizens to worse than silly children!

For the first time Corin realized the enormity of what he had done, and secretly inside him was a deep longing to once again experience that overwhelming, sweeping sensation of. . .

Whatever the sensation was, Corin had no words for it. All he knew was that he would give anything – *anything* – to feel like that again.

The Brigadier coughed. "The Enquiry into last night's Outbreak of Emotions is now under way. As you all know, last night's attack was the most serious yet. Though there have been a few isolated incidents of Laughter or Tears over the last year, never before has a whole group of Citizens been affected like this. But now the reason is clear."

She opened a small metal case and placed it on the pedestal. From its depths, she produced a number of the small vials that Corin had seen in her study. They caught fire with the rays of early sun coming through the window and sparkled with vibrant colour.

"Inside these vials," said the Brigadier, "are some of the most dangerous essences known to our City. Though they seem beautiful to the eye, do not be misled. They are part of the evidence seized from the Inns of Court and the Maia. You recall the Cleansing of the Inns last year for treason. Upon inspection of the studies of these Inns, it appears that certain Doctors had been abusing their powers of experiment, and had actually dared to produce artificial *Emotions*."

There was a murmur around the Palace, quickly stifled as the Brigadier fixed them with her baleful eye. "With these they prepared a secret Rebellion within the City whereby they planned to engineer Outbreaks of Emotions to break down public order. Though the vials were impounded and kept under guard in my study, it seems that a sympathizer broke in and stole one, precisely to cause chaos and a breakdown of civilized Citizenry. And what is worse, one of *you* has done this."

No murmur this time, as the courtiers kept silent. Corin kept the same impassive expression of any Higher Citizen on his face, though inside him a number of things were falling into place.

Well, *let them investigate*, he thought disdainfully. One of the other fools would surely take the blame! Was he not the son of the Regis? Who would ever think to investigate *him*?

The Regis coughed. "By your leave, Brigadier, I have

one thing to say. Let my son, Corin, come forward for a moment."

Corin shot a look like a dagger at Ivar, but in his servant's eyes he saw the same stunned surprise as most of those present. With a shrug, he decided to brazen it out. After all, nobody could prove anything! All the same, he felt very unsure as slowly he made his way down through the packed courtiers to stand alone in front of the desk, while the light from the vials played across his face.

"My son," said the Regis pleasantly. "You were, as we all know, one of the *innocent* victims of the Outbreak yesterday."

Corin nodded. "Um . . . yes, sir."

"Can you describe to the Palace what it was *like*, Corin?"

Corin was lost for words. Nobody ever discussed Emotions under the threat of Regeneration.

"I'm sorry, sir, I . . . don't know what you mean."

"You need not fear," said the Regis carelessly. "You were an unwitting victim, were you not? You had nothing to do with the theft of the vial from Brigadier Hacker's quarters."

Corin could not meet his father's eyes, but he realized that his father knew rather more than his words let on.

"Er . . . yes, sir."

"Therefore it is no crime to describe how you *felt*. Please proceed."

Corin took a deep breath. "It was . . . it felt good. . ."

"*Good?*" The Brigadier rose to her feet, but the Regis

idly waved her aside. "Let him speak please, Brigadier."
To Corin he turned. "It was a good sensation, it was
pleasant, and it was something that you would want
more of, yes?"

Corin was confused. How could he admit that he
wanted more of something that was strictly Outlawed?

"I . . . er . . . I don't know, sir."

"I think you do," said the Regis smoothly, taking the
boy by the shoulder. "For this you cannot be blamed, for
the effect of some Emotions is pleasurable, some might
even say *addictive*. But you should know that not all
Emotions are so joyous."

From the row of bottles he selected another vial, this
time coloured with whirling grey streaks that entwined
themselves around a core of inner darkness. Even as he
gazed at it, Corin felt a dark sensation come over him, as
if his heart had suddenly turned to stone and sunk deep
into the pit of his stomach.

"What . . . what is *that*, sir?"

The Regis uncorked the bottle and held it under
Corin's nose. "Breathe in, my son, and you will soon
learn what it is."

Down in the depths of the caves, flickering firelight
danced on the faces of the assembled Naturals
clustered in the supper circle. Talia's catch had been
delightedly received, and every clan member sat
contentedly around the embers, devouring great hunks
of the enormous pike that had been roasted over the fire.

Finally there was a stir from the far end, and Kira stood up, clapping her hands for silence. "My friends, I am glad to see everyone together tonight. As you know, for months we have endured the great Heat, the curse of our land, and the Rains have been long delayed. But the skies show that the Rains will soon arrive. And with the Rains will come the New Year Hunt. When the wild beasts come out of their long sleep, we must be ready for them."

Sitting next to Arlo in the shadowy light, Usha listened as Kira handed out instructions to the clan; the men were to form themselves into hunting parties, the women were to be in charge of priming the weapons for hunting, salting and drying the meat and collecting the precious rainwater.

Talia snorted impatiently and Arlo felt a prick of apprehension. "Catch me jugging sky tears and sharpening somebody else's sword? I don't think so! I'm off at the head of the Hunt, and I wager a boar's head that I'm the first one bringing home the bacon!"

There were murmurs of disapproval from the men, and Kira waved them down. "Talia is as able as any man to fish and spear. Is it not her catch of pike that you are feasting on this evening?"

The oldest man in the clan, Gunthar, knocked his eating knife loudly on a rock to make himself heard. "But she is a woman. Everyone knows that women disturb the Luck during a New Year Hunt! She will bring us evil fortune!"

"A woman's place is in the caves!" cried another. "Let the men do men's work!"

Talia rose to her feet, her black eyes glinting dangerously in the firelight, and all were reminded that she stood a full head taller than most of the men, and her stature in limb and muscle gave her greater strength than any they possessed. Though they knew that she had already proved her ability in fishing and tracking, a New Year Hunt was a different matter, and one where it would be perilous to trifle with Luck.

"If it is a matter of strength alone," said Talia dangerously, shooting a look at Gunthar, "then you can be assured that I will not let the clan down. Yet if any man doubts my worth, then let him come now and try his spear against mine."

A sullen ripple rose from the ranks of the clan, but no Natural got up to meet Talia's challenge. After a triumphant moment, Talia sat down again, rolling her eyes, and dug Usha with her elbow. "That's the way to manage 'em, Blondie. All talk and no trousers. Like I'd sit back and let them get all the glory? No chance!"

Quickly Arlo knelt up, waving to attract Kira's attention. "Kira! Before you go on, I've got something to say about the New Year Hunt. Or rather . . . Usha has something to tell you. Something she saw in a vision. Go on, Usha."

Usha stood up unwillingly. There were disapproving mutters from the crowd, and some shaking of heads and tutting, but she was used to this by now.

"I had a vision," she explained breathlessly, not daring to look towards Annis, who glowered darkly at her. "I think it is telling me that danger is coming. I don't think that we should go to the New Year Hunt."

An outcry followed, and a Natural woman leaned forward. "But the Hunt is important! We are in need of fresh meat. Our children are starving. We need furs and skins to clothe ourselves, we need bones and teeth for spears and needles, we need guts for cords."

"Every Hunt is a danger," proclaimed Gunthar, contemptuously glancing at Usha, "and every Hunt has its risks. We cannot put your daydreams in front of our needs!"

In vain Usha tried to explain the meaning of her vision, but the Naturals remained unconvinced. Whatever the hazards, the chance of fresh food was too great to miss after their long starvation through the Dead Season. Eventually Kira broke up the heated discussion by banging a plate with a spoon until she could be heard above the din.

"Enough, all of you! I have made my decision. The Hunt will go on. But whatever our traditions of the New Year Hunt, they will be swept into the past. This is the beginning of a new beginning. Any woman who wishes to go to the Hunt is permitted, and any man who wishes to stay behind may do so."

There was a shout of laughter from most of the men at the very idea of being left behind, with the exception of Arlo and Toby, who exchanged relieved glances. But the moment was ruined by Talia, who sprang forward gloatingly and rapped them both on the heads with the butt of her spear.

"Thought you could get out of it that easily, hey, boys? No, I bet you'll be on the front line with me, won't you?"

"Don't worry, Toby," said Arlo comfortingly, seeing the look on the younger boy's face. "If we take extra special care then everything will be all right. We'll all look out for each other, I promise."

"I miss Genopolis," said Toby unexpectedly. "I miss being in the Kids' den, with Nanda and Mindie and everybody. It was hard enough, but at least we understood things. It's all so strange here. Do you think Nanda and Mindie remember me, Arlo? Do you think they're thinking of me?"

Arlo pushed at his shoulder, teasingly. Though he had never met the Kids, Toby, Usha and Ozzie had spoken frequently of Nanda, the blind girl who had looked after them in the underworld of Genopolis, and Mindie, the girl who had lost her legs in a wagon accident. The only way of dealing with their memories was to keep them happy ones. Though some Emotions were valuable for a Citizen to learn, he thought, Grief should not be one of them.

"Of course they are, Toby. I bet they're saying to each other, 'If only Toby were here, to keep us all awake with his silly chatter. . .'"

Toby giggled, and soon they were making their way to bed in the clammy dark of the catacombs, while in the world above them the sun wheeled across the harsh sky, and the rocks burned like a furnace.

Corin closed his eyes and breathed in the vial held under his nose. For a second nothing happened. Then it felt as if the world went dark around him. His legs became weak and his stomach heaved. For no reason that he could think of, the face of the red-haired boy flashed in front of him, clearer than he could ever remember, but with it came the most terrible reaction, as if he wanted to burst into tears, cry, scream, throw himself out of the window. It was so intense that he could not move for a second, and then his knees buckled under him and he sank to the floor. His eyes burned, and he clutched at the forbidden, telltale tears to try to hide them from his father, but it was too late. From a great distance, he could hear a voice moaning unintelligibly, before he realized it was his own, as he lay slumped against the dais, weeping as though his heart would break.

A metalled claw pulled at his shoulder, and he found himself forced upright to his knees. He was conscious that a hundred eyes were fixed on him but the faces blurred and swam before him until all became grey. He was barely conscious of Ivar crouched next to him, dabbing quickly at his eyes and nose with a handkerchief.

"Grief!" pronounced the Brigadier loudly above him. "Grief is one of the most powerful Emotions known to us. See this child, reduced to an inhuman state, powerless in its grip. Tell me, Corin, does this seem *good* to you?"

Corin shook his head frantically. *Make it stop, make it stop!* As if obeying his unspoken command, the terrible pressure eased, and he came to himself again, soaked in tears and coughing. He snatched at the handkerchief and blew his nose. Shakily, he got to his feet and turned away from the incredulous stare of the other courtiers.

"Emotions are destructive!" declaimed the Regis grandly. "For all the beauty that Joy can bring, Grief can sweep it all away. For every shout of Laughter, there are a thousand Tears. The scales are weighed against us. Who in their right mind would live one minute of Joy knowing that they must pay the price of years of Sorrow?"

His eyes swollen and red, Corin tried to slip away, but the Brigadier blocked his path. Corin struggled, but the metal arm held him tightly. From behind him, the Regis advanced to the dais and picked up another ebony vial.

"Not so fast, Corin. For while Joy is temporary and Grief is powerful, there is one other Emotion that you shall learn, and it is the strongest of all."

Corin cast a bewildered look at the black bottle that his father held in his palm. At the very sight of it, suddenly a sensation came over him that made his heart race and his body tremble. He shook his head frantically. "No, sir. Please! Please!"

But the Brigadier held him fast as the Regis advanced

towards him. "I confess, Father!" cried Corin. "It was me! I am sorry! I didn't know. . ."

As if he had not heard his son's cry, the Regis uncorked the vial and held it underneath his nose. Corin tried to pull away but he was helpless in the iron grasp of the Brigadier. *I mustn't breathe*, he thought quickly. *I mustn't breathe*. Around him the room went black and the blood beat in his ears like a drum. He was scarcely aware when he opened his mouth and took a deep gulp of the dark vapour, and then another. There was a petrified silence that seemed to last for ever between one racing heartbeat and another. Then Corin stiffened, threw his head back and began to scream.

He was not at first conscious that he was screaming. It was as if he was held down, tied down, under the glare of a bright light, and he was crying out with a voice that he did not know he had for someone to help. Gazing down on him were strange faces, white-masked, impassive, and in the same second, he had the sensation as if a thousand needles were being pushed into his skin, all at once—

Abruptly the vision faded, and now he saw his father before him, still serenely impassive at his son's distress. But in place of the familiar features of thin cheekbones and dark eyes, instead his father appeared as something dreadful and ghastly to Corin's bewildered gaze. An evil and savage light burned in his face, transfiguring what was once recognizable into something terrible and strange. With a scream, Corin pulled himself out of the

Brigadier's grasp. All around him seemed a confusion of hideous faces and outstretched fingers, and he stumbled down the aisle towards the doors, holding his arms over his head to protect himself.

As he neared the doors, he pulled desperately at the great handles to open them but they were locked. Ivar approached his master to aid him but Corin shrieked and flung himself under an adjoining table. There he cowered, pulling at the ceremonial cloth to try to hide, while Ivar tried in vain to coax him out and the Regis strode to the centre stage and held up the vial to the crowd.

"Gentle Citizens, before you is the greatest and most terrible Emotion of all, and the one that has been the heaviest burden over thousands of years of human history. When our Founder destroyed Pain, he destroyed Fear also; for what can we fear if we do not fear pain? We have triumphed over our greatest weakness, we are held back by nothing, we are afraid of nothing; we have rid ourselves of centuries of Natural instinct and become true supermen! Who amongst you would wish to become like this foolish child here? Who amongst you would dare to sympathize with those terrorists who plot to overthrow our stable City with such terrible Outbreaks as this? Who amongst you would ever wish to feel what he is feeling?"

With his final warning delivered, the Regis descended the dais and strode swiftly towards the table where his son crouched. From beneath the tablecloth, Corin could see the long gown and the gleaming boots stop opposite him. There was an icy pause. His teeth chattered uncontrollably and his muscles shook in spasm. Finally his father bent down and peered under the table, where his eyes met his terrified son's.

"The next time you plan to go exploring, Corin, I counsel you to keep to the places where you are allowed, and to keep your hands to yourself regarding things which are not yours!" With his stare never leaving Corin's stricken face, he reached into his pocket and pulled out a shred of purple fibre, torn from the bottom of the ceremonial robes that Corin had worn the night before.

"I found this piece of material in the hinge of the door of her chambers which exactly matches the rip on the hem of your robe. You are very lucky that you are the Regis Apparent, otherwise it would go badly with you, my son. Be careful with your curiosity now, for next time I shall not be so merciful."

When Arlo woke that evening, he could sense that something had happened. The coolness of the catacombs had changed to a muggy, wet heat. It was stuffy and hard to breathe. Shaking Toby awake, he scrambled out of the cave and made his way to where Onofre and Kira were standing looking up into the sky.

"What is it, Onofre?" he panted as he caught them up.

"Look," said Kira, pointing above her. "It is starting."

Arlo looked up and caught his breath. Where before

the sky had stretched from horizon to horizon in an unbearable blaze of blue, now the evening steams hung above the Regions in a huge, sullen cloud of dirty yellow, towering above them like a mountain about to fall. There was no wind, but a strange tension in the air, as if the whole earth was waiting for something. One by one, the other clan members emerged from the camp to stand staring up into the clouds.

"What's happening?" shouted Usha and Ozzie as they ran up, but at that second the question was answered. From the swollen sky, there came a deep rumble and the first splashes of rain started to fall on their upturned faces.

Parched from the long months of drinking chalky cave-water, or fish blood, the clan tilted their heads back and let the cool droplets run down their faces and into their mouths, welcoming it with cries of laughter and gratitude. Children ran around playing and shouting, splashing through the shallow puddles in excitement, while the grown-ups hugged each other, sang songs of joy and laid themselves down to soak their dried leathery skins as if they were flowers unfurling to drink in the water. It seemed to Arlo as if the whole earth itself was a living being, sighing, breathing and slumping in relief as the Rains poured down.

After half an hour, the heavens suddenly darkened as a clap of thunder split the air. Great rods of water streamed from the sky, and the Naturals with one accord, turned and ran to their duties.

Kira had laid her preparations well. Pots and troughs had been set out to receive the precious rainwater, while a fresh reservoir had been dug out in front of the catacombs to channel the flash floods that would sweep down from the overshadowing hills and divert them away from their caves. This would be the first of many night storms that would flood the lower Regions and the wasteland around the City, turning it into a shallow sea over which the first food ships from the pharms would presently sail.

Arlo and Ozzie were in charge of the sandbank patrol to make sure that the new reservoir did not overflow and flood the catacombs. Running up the slope towards the dugout, the soil beneath their feet was already becoming slippery with mud. With vicious rain stinging their eyes and drenching their ragged cloaks, they slipped and slithered over the banked walls of the dugout to where Gunthar was waving them in frantically.

"Come on, boys! Get a move on! We need some help over here!"

Already the first waters were starting to stream down from the mountains above, the baked earth unable to absorb rain so quickly after months of heat. Arlo and Ozzie threw themselves into line beside the other Naturals and started to shovel the loosened earth up on to the sandbanks to make sure that the reservoir channel did not overflow. The slow trickle of water was swiftly turning into a running torrent. Though it was hard work, and uncomfortable, there was a new mood of cheeriness within the clan. The arguments of the night before had been swept away. Even Gunthar laughed and sang as he swung his shovel. In his excitement, Arlo did not even feel the pain as he grazed his knuckles on the gritty soil.

Behind the catacombs, Usha and Toby had been detailed to run up and down fetching and carrying troughs and pots of water. At first they had both stared in surprise at the sight of the pouring rain, and had to be cajoled by Kira into venturing out. Though they had seen gentle rain on occasions in the streets of Genopolis every New Year, never had they been caught inside a Regional storm's vicious fury.

"They are the tears of the Goddess, children," shouted Kira over the tumult of the storm. "Do not be afraid. She has not forgotten us."

Inside the catacombs sheltered the very young and the very old, for whom it would be dangerous to venture outside in the treacherous water and the icy rain. Their job was to sharpen spears, weave rope for the coming Hunt, and store the rainwater that they were brought. As Usha brought down yet another pot of water, struggling underneath its weight, Annis came to fetch it, the baby strapped to her back. As she reached for the jar, their hands touched. Annis flinched away as if she had been struck, and made the sign of the Evil Eye. Usha said nothing, climbing back out of the catacombs and back to her task.

As the night progressed, the storm worsened. The sky lowered and another loud rumble of thunder cut across the quivering air. Arlo had never been so wet in his life, and the icy wind that pierced him and his sodden clothes made him shake to his bones. The elation of the Naturals gave way to fatigued desperation as the rain poured down. From the direction of the Drowned City sprang an arc of lightning that threw a sheet of fire across the mountain tops, temporarily blinding those who watched. From where he gazed, Arlo felt a shuddering coming from deep within the mountain, a tremulous vibration that he could feel in the soles of his feet. The other men felt it too, and turned in confusion to one another.

"What is that, Gunthar?" Arlo shouted. "What is that noise?"

Gunthar pushed his dripping hood back and gazed up the mountain. The next moment he was flinging his shovel down and waving his arms frantically. "The Drowned City has burst its banks!" he cried. "Run! Run! We will all be drowned!"

Corin watched the rain of the night storm splashing on his window. Many hours had passed since his ignominious flight from the Enquiry, and he had taken refuge in his bedroom and spoken to no one as night fell. Through the walls came the sound of chatter and the clang of pots as the kitchens prepared to receive the food from the pharm-ships that would soon be launched. It was now officially the start of the New Year and arrangements had begun. Yet despite the delicious smells seeping through the Palace corridors and the new flurry of anticipation, Corin stayed on his own silently in the bedroom, with only the grey shadow of Ivar hovering in the background for company.

Opening his desk, he searched for his canvas, his oil paints and brushes. He assembled a canvas, mixed his paints and without particularly thinking of a subject, started to paint, a little awkwardly. In the long hours of solitude, he had discovered a remarkable facility for painting – how to mix the colours and blend in the shadows – and he had taught himself about perspective and proportion and how everything could be a subject for a picture if you framed it well enough.

Without thinking, he painted a face. Not a familiar face, not of Ivar or his father or anyone else that he had been accustomed to draw, and certainly not the face of any Citizen that he had ever met. Instead he drew from a sense other than memory, the face of a young man, in his early twenties, with brown hair, a pale face, and dark eyes. He was not smiling, and his eyes seemed to be looking through Corin at something else.

"Who are you?" whispered Corin.

Without thinking, his hands moved across the canvas, adding a touch of blue here, a glint of white there. So lost was he in his work, that he did not hear the door softly open behind him, and only a sudden gust of cold rainy air made him realize that his father was standing in the doorway.

"My son," said the Regis, and on him again was the black look that Corin had seen during the Enquiry. Corin automatically took a step away from him. "Why do you waste your time on idle painting when your sparring practice is so behind? The Brigadier tells me that you will make a fool out of yourself on Sports Day!"

Corin shook his head. "But, Father, I'm no good at fighting!"

With a lunge, the Regis reached around his son and pulled the canvas from the easel, scattering paints and brushes on to the floor. As he looked at the picture, his face darkened.

"What is this? Who are you painting, boy?"

Corin clutched at it wildly but the Regis held it above his head and out of his reach. "You are not worthy to be the son of a Regis! Not only do you insult Priscilla di Angelo, but you sneak into the Brigadier's study and meddle with forbidden Emotions! You will not challenge me again, boy! You will paint and draw no longer! I will make a proper Regis of you yet!"

The Regis swept out of the bedroom and down the corridor, Corin running after him. "I'm sorry, Father, I'll spar more, I promise!"

But the heavy iron-barred gate that protected his father's apartments slammed in his face, and in vain he clutched through it at his father's robe as he ascended the steps to his chambers.

"Please, Father! Please!"

From above came the sound of voices talking, and

Corin strained to hear what his father was saying, but his father was already out of sight. Presently he was cut short by the impatient tone of the Brigadier.

"The seas are rising, Regis! From tomorrow the ships can be launched, and the search unit should start straight away!"

"But almost a year has passed!" responded the Regis, and Corin noted in surprise his father's sulky tone, as if being reproved by a parent. "The child could be anywhere by now, and most likely dead!"

"Nevertheless," retorted the Brigadier, "in questioning the prisoners I have reason to think that he can be discovered. The younger prisoner will be sent with the ships so that we can identify the Naturals' whereabouts."

"Can the librarian be trusted?" asked the Regis sullenly.

"Whether trustworthy or not, he will not return from the journey," replied the Brigadier calmly. "I wish only to be led to the place where the Naturals hide during summer, and my soldiers will do the rest."

The door closed and Corin could hear nothing more. He had not understood most of the conversation, save that it seemed to have nothing to do with the upcoming Sports Day or his painting. He walked back to his bedroom, under the mute gaze of Ivar, knelt on the bed and stared out of the window, to where he could see the dark clouds raining down fury on to the distant Regions.

He had never been so alone in his life.

*

The terrified Naturals stared up at the mountain. From between the cleft of the hills sprang a torrent of water as the valley of the Drowned City, engorged and swollen by the sudden savage rain, overflowed and cascaded down the slopes. Though they were not to know it, the arc of lightning had struck and weakened the body of an ancient tree that had dammed the lake, and as it blazed, the pressure of the swollen water had built up behind it until finally it burst with a roar. An enormous wave of mud, larger than anything Arlo had ever seen before, was surging down the mountain towards them, bringing down an avalanche of trees and boulders with it.

Instantly all was confusion. Some Naturals who were in the flood path were swept away in the fierce onslaught; others scrambled to higher ground in the nick of time. Kira's party had a few precious seconds of warning and fled aside from its destructive passage, while the channel and sandbank defences that they had dug were swamped. Gunthar gripped Arlo and Ozzie in each hand and together they sprinted for cover, but not quickly enough. As the side of the wave hit them with its dying fury, Arlo felt his legs go from underneath him as the ground turned to mush, and the next thing he knew they were caught up in a tangle of briars and flood-water and whirled around and around. Mud and grit filled his nostrils and he scrabbled frantically to keep afloat. Screams filled the air as the Naturals desperately dragged themselves clear of the debris and stumbled to find their families.

Coughing and spluttering, Arlo pulled himself out on to a lip of stony ground, and looked around desperately. The main wave of mud had tossed them aside and roared downhill, leaving a trail of devastation as it passed. To his left Ozzie was crouched, dazed, with Gunthar standing over him, tending to blood flowing from his head. But from down the slopes came the sound of hysterical wailing. His heart in his mouth, Arlo slid down the slimy banks towards the catacombs.

Instantly his worst fears were realized. The landscape had entirely changed. Where before had stood the two rocks that signalled the entry to the Naturals' caves, now only a huge grey mound of sludge stretched in every direction as far as the eye could see. The great landslide had coursed down the slopes to where Usha and Toby were working, and engulfed the catacombs where the young baby and children had sheltered, burying them under an impenetrable weight of mud.

"Usha!" screamed Arlo against the roar of the wind. "Toby!"

But there was no answer. Around him, cries of pain from the wounded filled the air, mingling with screams as mothers and fathers flung themselves into the mud and dug desperately to try to reach their loved ones. But it was all in vain. No one could even see where the standing stones had been, much less find the entrance to the catacombs.

Staring around desperately, Arlo could see only the blaze of the burning tree where the lightning had hit it, and the thick smoke as it met the heavy rain pouring from above. Through the lessening rain, a pale streak of light appeared to the east. The next second, Talia and Onofre splashed their way towards him.

"What happened?" shouted Talia frantically. "Are you all right?"

Arlo could not answer her. "Usha! Toby! Where are you!" he yelled frantically into the wind. "Where are you!"

Talia pulled his shoulder and forced him round into the driving rain. "There! See! There!"

Against the storm-wrecked clouds, swiftly clearing with the first light of morning, tottered a thin, drenched figure, almost unrecognizable underneath the thick grey mud that coated her, and in her arms a small, squalling bundle. Hanging on to her cloak was a smaller boy, helpless in a pair of smashed glasses, clutching blindly in front of him. Behind them crawled a group of wet and muddied forms, crying and holding out their arms for help. With screams of joy, their parents ran towards them and clasped them tightly, none quicker than Annis, who tore her baby from Usha's arms and howled in relief.

"Usha! Toby!" Arlo grabbed at her frantically. "Are you all right?"

But there was a strange light in Usha's eyes as she stared at him, as if she was not quite taking him in, as if she was looking straight through him—

"Smoke," whispered Usha, so softly that Arlo could barely hear her. "Smoke, and burning and blood. The sun is in the east, and there are cries of pain. This is what I saw in my dream, Arlo. Before the mud came down, I knew I had to get them out of the caves. I just knew it."

THREE

ANew Year mist hung heavy over the valley and a light drizzle coated the early sky as the sun struggled to break through the lowering clouds. It had been a long night since the catacombs had been destroyed, and the starving tribe, with no dry firewood available, had resorted to searching out and eating raw reptiles and rats that had been drowned in the flood.

Arlo pulled his sodden sack closer over his neck and shivered in the cool wind. After months of heat, the sudden change in temperature had brought on a light fever, making him sneeze and cough. Most of the Natural tribe were similarly suffering, but the Citizens, though as susceptible to illness as the Naturals, felt nothing of the effects of sickness, nor the weakness that came with it.

The dazed Orphans had collected themselves together on a patch of higher ground that had escaped the worst excesses of the floods. Through the goodness of the

Goddess, many said, no one had been killed or seriously hurt, though many shook with ague or limped on a twisted foot. The children and old people who had narrowly escaped being buried in the caves were lying down in a huddle, dazed at their ordeal, and the fine rain was gently washing the thick mud away. However, the greatest damage had been to their home. With the destruction of the catacombs they had lost most of what they possessed. Pots, tools, swords, spears, knives, blankets, cloaks – most had been swept away or buried. Only a few paltry belongings remained, and one by one the Citizens and stronger Naturals returned from their searches and flung what they had gathered on to the pile: a broken cooking pot, a couple of notched spears, and a few spades and trowels with which they had been digging before the floods came down.

Defeated, Arlo watched them, feeling no strength or hope in his body to rise and search alongside them. Everything he had fought for . . . his spear, his squirrel-skin, the book collection and map that he had started with Toby . . . everything had been swept away and destroyed as if it had never been.

"While there's life, there's hope!" called Kira comfortingly. "Our little ones are still with us, and for that we must give thanks to the Goddess."

Arlo pulled Kira out of earshot of the others. "Listen, Kira, it wasn't the Goddess who saved the children. It was Usha. She got them out of the caves before the wave came down."

But Kira just smiled and kissed his brow carelessly. "The Goddess works in magical and invisible ways, cousin. Her power was shown through Usha."

Exasperatedly Arlo watched her go. Though Kira did not think badly of Usha or subscribe to the same superstitions as many of the other Naturals, she never exactly stuck up for the Gemini either.

As Arlo trudged sulkily away, he became aware of Toby calling him excitedly. "Arlo! Look! Look!"

Bursting with excitement, the Citizen tore up to him, waving a muddy object in front of him. "It's your book, Arlo! The one about your family that we've been writing in! We found it down the hill! Isn't that lucky!"

A wave of sudden warmth welled up in Arlo's heart as he met Toby's eager eyes and put his hand out to take his book. One of his possessions had survived, and the fact that he had borne it out of Genopolis and through many hardships since, made it all the more special. Even crushed, stained and muddied, it seemed something infinitely precious, a part of his history and himself.

Hardly able to speak, he managed only a brief, "Thanks, Toby. I don't know how I can ever repay you for this."

Meanwhile, Usha sat at a little distance to the others, as had become her habit, staring out into the whitish fogs that were drifting across the valley. She had not joined in the salvage mission to find their missing possessions. Instead she had greater problems to ponder.

A hand touched her shoulder, and she turned in surprise. Naturals usually avoided physical contact with her, so she was expecting it to be a fellow-Citizen or Arlo. Instead, old Onofre stood over her, his blue eyes kind and smiling.

"I came to thank you, Usha. On behalf of our people. You have saved them from a fate worse than death."

Usha blinked. Thanks from a Natural was one of the last things she had expected. "I didn't really do anything. I suddenly knew the mud was going to come down, and so I asked them all to come out and picked up the ones who couldn't walk."

Onofre sat down next to her and took from around his neck an amulet on a thick cord.

Darkened and dulled by dirt, nevertheless the stone shone with a dull silver radiance as he held it in front of her eyes.

"What is this?" asked Usha, mesmerized. Many of the Naturals had special polished bones, jewellery or precious talismans that they used to bring them luck or to guard against evil, but to give one away was unheard of.

Onofre sighed. "I have something to say to you, Usha. You have a great gift, and I do not think you realize it, nor do you know how to use it. We Naturals have the five senses of touch, smell, taste, sight and hearing, but you have the sixth sense, the *knowing*.

This is something that is very precious and given only to a few."

Usha looked at him in puzzlement. "You mean my visions? But they're all mixed up! I *see* things, but I don't know what they *mean*! It's terrible to know something but not to know when it's going to happen!"

Onofre smiled and took her hand, turned it face-up and laid the amulet in Usha's palm. "My grandmother was a seeing-woman, and I know there are things in this world that are invisible to the eye. When she died, she passed me on this moonstone, to guard against the future, but I have never seen anything in it."

"But how should I use it?" asked Usha, puzzled.

Onofre shook his head. "For me it is a pretty stone, and nothing more. For those who cannot see, it will remain just a thing of beauty. I cannot tell you how to use it. But you, Usha, should take it and see if it helps you. With practice, you could make the most of the gift and help many."

Usha turned the moonstone round and round in her fingers. It shone with a darker lustre as if it were spinning rapidly, and beneath its surface she was almost sure that she could see something moving.

A pair of arms were thrown around her shoulder from behind, and the moment was lost. Arlo had flopped down next to her, his face flushed and his eyes bright with excitement.

"Well done, Usha! You saved them! That was what

your vision meant! Now nothing will happen at the Hunt!"

"I hope so," answered Usha, quickly slipping the amulet into her pocket. Arlo's sharp eyes noted her movement, but he did not remark on it. Instead, he held out the muddy book, its pages stuck together.

"Toby found the book, and it's the only thing I have left now. You're on lookout, aren't you? Will you take care of it for me during the Hunt?"

The next moment Kira passed by, clapping her hands and crying out.

"To the waterhole! Bring anything you can find! The wild beasts will be awakening from their long sleep, and we must be ready for them!"

The dog shivered in the windy caverns that overlooked the west range of the mountains. Since the Rains had come, coursing down the rocky walls and flooding the floor into a shallow puddle, he had been secured by a stout cord so that he did not stray into the wilderness. He stood forlornly and patiently as the tumult of the wind and rain roared into the mouth of the cave and lapped around him.

A few weeks under the care of his new master had brought about surprising improvements in him. He had more flesh on his bones and his joints no longer ached when he moved. But now, with his shaggy pelt drenched and loose with rain, he looked more like a skeleton than ever.

Footsteps echoed around the cave walls, and he began to bark, an excited, happy sound. Footsteps meant food and pats and pulling on his ears; footsteps meant love and attention and the dark-tasting insides of bones. He pranced around, pulling at his bonds, until his new master, accompanied by the woman, came into view, both buffeted by the force of the water, their sand-coloured cloaks now dirtied and browned with rain.

"Forget her, Tambar!" snapped the woman, pulling off her dripping cloak and hurling it into the driest corner of the cave. "She is a disgrace! No background, no breeding, the daughter of black-legs!"

"Take that back!" cried the man, wheeling to face her. "You do not know what you are saying! You may be my elder sister but you cannot control me!"

The dog watched as they glared at each other, then with a shrug the woman stepped away, reached up above a rocky shelf and pulled down a knife. With curling golden-brown hair, she was in voice and appearance similar to her brother, though her nose was longer and her jaw thinner. Her greeny-gold eyes were gimlet-sharp as calmly she began to whet the knife against a stone.

"When our father died," she snapped scornfully, "I thought that you would continue the Cause, not hide in the wilderness with a bunch of thieving pirates!"

"Liana, you are being ridiculous!" returned the man.

With a glare, his sister had caught up her knife and ropes. "The Meet will start tomorrow, but it seems you prefer to bring only dreams and fantasies to barter. Myself, I will go to find fresh meat, for minds cannot be fed while the body is starving."

"Wait!" cried the man, but the woman disappeared into the night with a parting shot over her shoulder. "Do you want to lose everything that we have fought for, Tambar?"

"You know I will never abandon the Cause, Liana!" shouted the man after her retreating figure, but no answer came back. Left alone in the cave, he sighed deeply for a moment, and then turned to the dog, squatting down and running his hand gently over the brindled back.

"Well, sometimes lost things return, don't they, wild-hound? We never thought to see you or your brothers once we led you into the tunnels of the City to spread confusion and disease. Yet here you are, back safe and sound, with not a scratch on you! Ah, what stories you could tell of Genopolis if only you could!"

The dog thumped his tail but the man's eyes were dreamy and elsewhere.

"And minds change as well, don't they, wild-hound? I know that mine has. If you come with me to the Meet then I shall show you the most beautiful creature that ever lived, one that appears only once a year when the Rains come. She has escaped me these last few years, but perhaps this time I will be able to snare her, and make her mine for ever. Are you with me?"

The dog heard the words, and even understood the tone in which they were uttered, but still they meant nothing to him. Instead, he was more interested in the smell of dried mouse coming from the man's pockets, and nosed inside, his tail wagging excitedly. The man chuckled, his wild, weather-beaten face softening as the dog nudged against him and nearly pushed him over.

"Hold on now, greedy! There's plenty more where that came from!"

Arlo blinked away the thin trickle of sweat that ran down his forehead and into his eyes, and his aching fingers shook with fever as he gripped his spear. They had been crouched in the bushes surrounding the waterhole for almost two hours, but though his legs were cramped he dared not move for fear of disturbing the fragile shelter of branches under which they waited for the wild beasts to come and drink.

Onofre had told him much about the ways of animals in the wild. Hundreds of years ago, before the Apocalypse, when the earth was still cold, creatures had slept through the chill months, waking when the earth was warmer. Now most of them retreated to the depths of the earth in caves to sleep through the long Heat, until they were awakened by the Rains. When they emerged from their hibernation, they could be unpredictable and dangerous. Arlo had been warned to stay as far away as possible and to leave the slaying to the experienced hunters of the tribe.

Next to him Talia, Toby and Ozzie crouched, impervious to the discomfort that Arlo suffered. To his left Onofre lay, his eyes trained on the hills above for any sign of movement. The drinking hole itself was some hours from the destroyed catacombs, on the wilder, east side of the neighbouring mountain range, and was actually a concealed stream that bubbled up once the subterranean water-courses had been filled by the Rains. Surrounding the drinking hole were many other concealed contingents of Naturals, and around the pool were strung many hidden nets and deep troughs. Arlo's forehead burned and ached, and he gritted his teeth with the pain.

"Sssh," murmured Onofre suddenly. "Look, here they come."

Down the muddy tracks left by the storms of the night before, two bulky four-legged forms were cautiously nosing their way. Arlo had never seen anything like them in his life before. Covered in grey hair with short jointed legs and low-lying round bellies, they grunted as their short hooves slipped on the wet soil and their squinting eyes blinked nervously as they looked around for predators. The smell of man hung in the air, confusing and frightening their senses, but with their instincts dulled through long months of sleep, the thirst for water proved more powerful still. Slowly they trundled towards the hole, narrowly avoiding the hidden traps, and buried their snouts in the cool stream. Talia's spear twitched.

"Wild hogs," whispered Onofre. "Good meat, but not enough. Keep waiting. There will be more coming."

And there were. With the advent of morning and the lessening of the rain, one by one, more animals were emerging into the valley and making for the drinking-hole. Next came a pack of loping wild dogs – like Rem but without his feathery tail, thought Arlo with a sudden pang – and after them a couple of lithe, long-bodied creatures with speckled short fur and pointed ears; *wildcats*, murmured Onofre quietly. Strangely, though Arlo had been told that feral creatures hunted and ate each other, these beasts took little or no notice of the others, instead moving around the drinking hole so that each animal had its own space. It was as if the need for water had overridden any urge for killing for the moment. Arlo could see that they moved as if dazed or exhausted, for months without food had dulled their aggressive instincts. Even when three shaggy-looking wolves, such as Arlo remembered from the savage tribe of the Wolf-men, padded into the valley, their only thoughts were for the cool stream and not for the wild pigs clustered in the shallows.

A low bird call cut across the waiting valley, Kira's signal to be on the alert. Quietly, Arlo took a deep breath. He could not stop shivering and his feet were suddenly icy cold. From the corner of his eye he could see Onofre slowly raising his hand towards the cord of the net. . .

Then something happened that made even Kira abruptly halt and refrain from giving the attack signal. From the top of the trail came a clear, brittle sound as if someone were banging two stones together, or tapping on glass, though what it could be Arlo could not tell. He peeked over his nest of branches and his jaw dropped. Down the stony trail that led from the forest and directly towards the concealed troughs dug into the west bank of the drinking hole, came a creature, taller and more proud than the rest, with its long legs lifted delicately as it navigated the boulders, its silver hide gleaming in the early sun and with a full mane of creamy hair that blew in the breeze.

"A *horse*!" murmured Onofre in wonder to himself, and Arlo gazed in amazement. Suddenly, the learning from his old history lessons came back in a rush. In Genopolis they had taught him that *real* horses, like cows, had been extinct for many years, perhaps even before the Apocalypse once most of their grazing grounds had been submerged or otherwise taken over. The scientists of the pharms could still Recreate horses and cows, but they would not be *real*. As with the first time he had seen Rem in the long-distant gardens of the Inn of Court, he found himself trembling again, and this time it was not from fever.

Slowly and gracefully, the horse skirted the pool,

keeping its distance from the other animals, and bent its long neck to drink.

Unable to contain himself, Toby squeaked in excitement. "Oh! So that's a *horse*, Arlo, is it?"

"Sssh!" hissed Onofre, but Toby's voice had been too loud. The horse suddenly jerked itself upright, and turned to run. But as it sprang away, the ground gave way underneath it, and it plunged into the concealed trough with a neighing scream. Immediately the animals, with one instinct, turned to flee but it was too late. From the top of the ridge came a flurry of movement. Gunthar had pulled the first net that sealed off the gorge from the pool, and the first animals had entangled themselves in it, snarling. Instantly Onofre's hand shot out and pulled the cord of the lower net, and with a slithering thump the net shot up and blocked the trail next to them. The two wild hogs charged into it and entangled themselves in its ropes, goring the ground frantically as they struggled to free themselves. The wolves and the wild dogs tore around the enclosed arena, snarling and baying, as one by one the Naturals peppered them with arrows and rocks. With his head whirling, Arlo flinched as Onofre drew his hunting-knife and plunged it deep into the chest of one of the wolves. Tears suddenly prickled his face as he thought of Rem. He must have already been killed in a similar fashion, by wild tribesmen or perhaps by other animals. . .

Throwing himself to the ground, he covered his ears

with his hands, but nothing could keep out the terrible sounds of slaughter from his ears.

From where she lay on the boulder on the highest point of the mountain that rose above the watering pool, Usha looked down on the carnage happening below her and wrinkled her nose. Though she could never feel or even imagine pain, she was strangely affected by the noise, smell and appearance of death, and seeing it inflicted on others, even wild beasts, made her uneasy. As a compromise for Usha's warning over the Hunt, Kira had given her the job of lookout, as the Gemini's far-sighted eyes could see over many miles and perhaps, as Onofre had added, could see further than anyone could even imagine.

Turning away from the screams and snarls that drifted up from the killing fields, Usha stood up on the boulder and scanned the horizon, feeling the heavy weight of Arlo's book where she had slipped it beneath her tunic. Something was not right. She had no Natural instincts, and a Citizen would not have picked up that anything was wrong, yet Usha knew that she was being watched. Carefully she climbed down from the boulder, pushed her way through the dripping forest of bracken to the west side of the mountain – and stood rooted to the spot.

Before her fell a steep drop down to the plains, but where once there had stretched a barren desert all the way to Genopolis, now there lay a shallow muddy sea, perhaps no more than a few feet deep, but still deep enough for the sleek military catamarans of Genopolis, which had silently encircled the mountains and lay anchored in the flooded bay behind them.

Instantly Usha turned to run, but through the screen of bracken in front of her, appeared a group of Citizen-soldiers, dressed in camouflage green and brown. From the leader issued a curt command, and two of them raced towards her. With no way in front, Usha scrambled down the steep incline towards the sea, clinging with her fingers and toes on the slippery ledge. The red warning flag was torn from her fingers and flapped away on the wind. From above she could hear the crashing of the soldiers as they beat through the bushes to where she had vanished, but no shouts or bullets followed her, and in fact the whole ambush had been oddly silent. Puzzling on this, Usha decided that the soldiers were unwilling to alert the Naturals to their presence by any sound or shot until they had completely surrounded them. The thought gave her hope. If the soldiers were not yet in a strong attacking position, then the clan could still escape if they were given sufficient warning. But there was only one way that she could avoid the soldiers and reach the lookout point, and that was by inching around the side of the mountain with the steep drop down to the shallow sea and the ships.

Bit by bit she crawled around the slippery crag, gripping hard with her toes, knees and fingers, knowing that any false move could start a landslide or see her plummet hundreds of feet to the stony shallows below. Finally her fingers hit the harder pebbles of a rocky shelf and with an effort she pulled herself back up on to the other side of the mountain-top. She froze. In front of her lay a short open area leading to the lookout point, and to the left, a Citizen-soldier with his back to her, scrutinizing the Naturals at the watering hole with a telescope.

There was no time to think. With a blind dash, Usha pelted over the open ground behind the soldier before he had time to turn and draw his gun, and threw herself into the shadow of the great boulder that overhung the plain. Below her she could see the Orphan clan intent on capturing the last of the Hunt. Leaning perilously forward, Usha waved her arms wildly.

"Run!" she screamed. "Run! The soldiers are here!"

But her small cry was swept away by the wind, and without the red flag to command attention, nobody noticed the small figure desperately signalling from above.

With only seconds to go to warn the tribe, she had to resist capture as long as she could. Usha pushed herself further into the shadow between the two rocks. Her heel slid through the loosened soil as she braced herself, and as she did so, the smaller boulder to the left moved slightly. In sudden hope, she scrambled so that the boulder was between her and the soldier, turned and pushed at it desperately. If she could only manage to move it, if she could just manage to. . .

But her idea had come too late. The next second, a

shadow darkened the sky. The soldier had leapt up on top of the boulder and trained the barrel of his rifle on to the trapped Gemini. Usha saw herself reflected alone and isolated in the dark visor of his helmet and, with no escape, slowly put her hands up.

The soldier adjusted his sights and leaned forward to guarantee a better shot at his target. But the move was his undoing. With the extra weight of the Citizen pressing down on the unstable boulder, the weakened soil groaned, shifted, and the great stone moved. Almost in slow motion, it rocked on the precipice, tipped forward, and plunged down the mountain. The soldier twisted round and fell with it, and as he did so, his fingers tightened on the trigger, spraying the sky with bullets. The crack of the shots ricocheted and echoed around the valley, and the Naturals down on the plain turned and looked up at the falling boulder and the small figure of the Gemini now outlined against the sky, frantically waving the lookout signal.

"Run!" screamed Usha. "The soldiers are here!"

But the next second a uniformed arm seized her from behind and she was dragged from the ledge. The rest of the Citizen-patrol had arrived.

Down on the plain, Kira took in the situation in an instant. A lifetime spent on the run in the wilderness had well prepared her for the job of tribal leader, and she knew the necessity of taking control before panic could sweep her people.

"Citizen attack! Quick! Follow me!" she shouted, sprinting towards the narrow gorge that led towards the wilder mountain range. The tribe, scattered and confused as they were, torn between their fear of the Citizen soldiers and their need for fresh food, stumbled after her, dragging whatever kill they could with them.

"Leave it behind!" ordered Kira. "It will slow you down. We can catch more meat, but we cannot do anything if they catch us!"

In panic and confusion they plunged after her. From the plain of the waterhole, the winding Horse Shoe Gorge ran between two mountains and out into the wilder scrubland of the Regions from where the wild animals had come. Panting at her heels, Arlo realized what Kira meant to do. If they could gain the safety of the gorge before the Citizen soldiers made their way around the headland, they could pass into the wilderness, where any Citizen would find it hard to track them, as long as they could keep their head start. But as the tribe scrambled down the rocks and through the narrow pass, Arlo hung back through the press of running Naturals. Talia and Ozzie stumbled close behind him, and Toby, his glasses almost completely smashed, was hanging on Kira's sleeve, but of Usha there was no sign since the frantic wave of her lookout signal.

"Wait!" called Arlo. "Usha's still back there!"

Kira shook her head, tugging at him. "Arlo, we must

go! We cannot endanger everybody here for the sake of one person!"

"But they'll take her back to Genopolis!" cried Arlo.

Gunthar, one of the remaining Naturals who waited impatiently for his leader's direction at the mouth of the gorge, spat angrily. "Leave the witch! She's brought nothing but bad luck to us, ever since she joined us!"

Arlo wheeled to face Gunthar. "You stupid old man! She saved your children from the flood!"

"We cannot stay here—" began Kira, but Onofre came to Arlo's rescue. "And what if they interrogate her in Genopolis, Kira? If Usha tells them all she knows, then your hideouts will be in danger!"

Talia forced her way through the Naturals, pushing aside Gunthar impatiently. "You're going to leave Usha after she was trying to warn us? Then I'm going back for her, if you won't!"

"Then we're coming too!" cried Ozzie and Toby from where they had been listening. "We can't leave her behind to die!"

Onofre stepped forward and raised his spear. "Better a Natural to attack on Natural home ground. Talia may be the best at fighting, but I am skilled in tracking and hiding and I know these woods. This is a job for a small group only, otherwise we will attract too much attention."

"Let me come with you, then!" returned Arlo hotly. But Onofre was immune to his begging. "Blood is thicker than water in times like these, Arlo. You did not come all this way to leave Kira at the first misfortune. Believe me, Talia and I will find Usha better on our own."

Unwillingly, with his feet feeling like lead, Arlo followed Kira, Ozzie, Toby and the last of the Naturals into the gorge. Talia picked up her spear and the next second both she and Onofre had melted into the bush and disappeared.

Kicking and struggling, Usha was carried down the winding track towards the catamarans by a burly soldier, her wrists and ankles clasped in iron shackles. Disoriented as she was, the only thing that comforted her was that the Citizen attack was in chaos. With the falling boulder forewarning the Naturals, most of the attacking patrol had been left in disarray and had raced off after the escaping tribe with little plan or organization.

The sky wheeled beneath her feet as she was tipped head over heels and dumped unceremoniously on to the sand. Half-stunned, she lay quietly as the soldier quickly loaded another rifle and scudded off up the path in the direction of the rifle fire. A couple of younger soldiers remained on guard by the moored catamarans, plainly confused and uncertain what to do.

Rolling dazedly on to her front, Usha raised her head and looked about her. She was lying on a stony beach surrounded by military catamarans, so to escape up the mountains without attracting the attention of the guards was impossible. But as she turned her head, her eyes widened. Beside her lay a huddled form, its hands tied behind its back and its head and shoulders covered in a ragged cloak.

Who on earth could that be? Perhaps another captured Natural? Usha could not see his face but his appearance seemed male. He was dressed in tattered remnants of formerly fine clothes, such as a merchant of Pharmopolis might wear, and a glint of fair hair protruded from underneath the hood.

"Hey!" hissed Usha, but there was no response. She pushed at him with her foot, and the body rolled limply. Usha gasped as she saw a trickle of blood snaking from underneath the head and disappearing into the sand.

"Oi there, Natural!" shouted one of the soldiers roughly at her, catching her movement. "You move, and you'll get the same as that traitor! Won't be pulling any more stunts now, he won't!"

Usha turned her head away, and surreptitiously strained at her wrists, but they had been bound with thin cord that, struggle as she might, would not budge. Time was running out! Soon the soldiers would be back and all chance of escape would be lost. Usha struggled to think, but her mind was blank. Then she felt the cool surface of the moonstone amulet against her cheek, and despite her situation its touch comforted her. She lay still.

Suddenly there came a whistling thud and one of the soldiers fell forward on to his face, an arrow protruding from his shoulder blades. The other one jumped up and swung his rifle around, but too late. Two more arrows pierced his chest and the gun slipped from his hands. In sudden hope, Usha twisted around in time to see two familiar figures leaping down the rocks towards the catamarans.

"Talia!" she hissed excitedly. "Over here! Quick!"

Talia knelt down beside her, pulling her knife from its sheath and cutting at her bonds. "You don't half get yourself into some trouble, Blondie. We asked you to keep a lookout for wild beasts, and you go and find yourself some wild Citizens!"

Usha dragged herself to her feet. As she did so, the figure lying next to her groaned and stirred. "He's not dead!" she cried.

"Who on earth is that?" called Onofre, but Talia shot the figure a wary glance. "He's not one of ours, so I say leave him here. Probably had a fight amongst themselves and he came off worst. That's soldiers for you."

"But they shot him and left him here to die!" protested Usha. "They said he was a traitor to Genopolis, so he must be on our side!"

Wearily, Onofre stooped and pulled the cloak back from the figure's face. Bloodied and dirtied though he was, Talia and Usha could recognize the features of a Higher Citizen, fair-skinned and blue eyed, though it was no one that they knew. They were about to withdraw when suddenly the man moaned, coughed away the blood in his mouth and struggled to speak.

"Arlo. Where is he?"

"He's asking for Arlo!" cried Usha. Instantly Talia was kneeling over the Citizen, her hands around his throat.

"Who are you? What do you want with Arlo?"

"I am a friend," gasped the man. "Take me to him."

"Not on your life!" argued Talia. "How many more of you are there? How did you know we were here?"

The man's breath gurgled with the blood in his throat. "Please," he whispered, so quietly that only Usha could hear him. "I need to warn him."

Talia and Onofre exchanged glances. "I believe him," muttered Onofre. "He speaks the truth. Untie him."

Unwillingly, Talia cut the cords from the man's wrists. "Any funny business, and I'll finish you off, understand?"

Together they helped him to his feet, but the man was clearly in no condition to either resist or double-cross his helpers. Though as a Citizen he felt no pain from his wounds, he was extremely stunned and confused. With Talia and Onofre assisting him on either side he was just able to stumble along. As fast as they could, they made their halting way around the other side of the mountain and into thick brush, Usha scouting in front. Only a few more feet remained until they could reach the forest path which led to the gorge. Already the evening steams were starting to descend and the air was thick and dark underneath the dripping forest. If they could gain the shelter of the gorge after the rest of their tribe before the Citizen-patrol returned. . .

But even as their hopes revived, a volley of shots broke out in front of them. Talia sprang instantly for cover, fitting an arrow to her bow as she did so. Unsupported, the man staggered and fell aside into the deep bushes. Usha turned around and ran for her life but in front of her leapt a Citizen-soldier, his finger already tightening on the trigger. Usha gasped, closed her eyes, and waited for the sound of the shot.

But instead, with a cry, Onofre flung himself in front of her. Usha's eyes flew open only to see the old man throw up his arms and take one, two, three bullets in his chest. Spinning around with the force of the shot he fell to his knees, but still his fingers went to his spear and he threw it with all his diminishing strength at the soldier as the Citizen turned to reload. Dazed, Usha ran to his aid, but even as she reached out to touch him a final bullet took Onofre in the throat and he fell like a stone. Talia shouted a warning, but Usha could not hear her. A thick, burning sensation was choking her throat, and the air seemed thick and watery. As if drowning in a dark mist, she stumbled blindly forward and into the arms of the masked Citizen-patrol, who, armed with gas-guns and protective breathing-equipment, had emerged from the depths of the forest.

"Stop the shooting!" called one, his voice distorted and muffled through his protective mask. "Naturals are no good dead, and we want these two to talk!"

"The Citizen-prisoner!" called another from the shores where the catamarans were moored. "He's disappeared!"

"Forget him!" snapped back his leader. "With the wounds he's got he won't last a day in the wilderness. There's no sense in us staying here any longer now that mangy tribe has escaped. No, we're to get these Naturals back to the Palace as soon as we can. Special Orders from *Her*, and we must not delay."

Night was falling in the dark of the wood, and a pale moon slid through the dark silhouettes of the trees, illuminating the clearing with faint light. For the first time in forty-eight hours there was no rain, for which the Naturals were grateful. Exhausted from two days of disaster, the tribe had come to a halt near a jumble of rocks covered with withered creepers and ivy. Here the floods and the Rains had been less unkind, and they could still find a dry space to crouch and some scraps of firewood that they collected, though Kira would not let them burn it. Some, fatigued with hunger, gnawed at the raw, bloodied kill that they had brought from the Hunt, but Arlo sank gratefully on to his stomach as if dead.

Suddenly a sickening thought struck him. He no longer had his book! Usha had been looking after it when the Citizens had arrived. If she had been caught with it on her person, they would have no mercy on her when they discovered what it was.

As he lay, tormented with worry, hoping against hope that Usha could have escaped the soldiers in the confusion, the Naturals quarrelled amongst themselves.

"There is the stink of wolf here," hissed Gunthar. "I do not think we should stop in this place."

"Wolves will not attack a group as large as ours," argued Kira, "And we cannot keep running for ever. The weakest of us need rest for a few hours. We shall press on again before morning."

"Press on? Where?" argued Gunthar. "We have nowhere to go!"

"We must go to the New Year Meet," responded Kira calmly. "That is the only place where we might be safe."

"The Meet? But that's miles away!" returned the Natural. "And the Hunt was a disaster! We have nothing to trade and no one will welcome us! It is foolishness!"

"Then find yourselves a food-ship to attack, and good luck to you!" flashed Kira, turning her back on them and throwing herself down on to a bed of dry leaves next to where Arlo, hot and feverish, was drowsing.

"Arlo?" she whispered gently.

"Go away," snarled Arlo, a sudden hatred leaping up in his chest. How dare she talk to him after abandoning Usha to her fate? He rolled away and covered himself with his cloak.

With tears prickling her eyes, Kira reached out to touch his shoulder, but Arlo recoiled. "Don't you dare touch me! You left my friends behind, and now they're probably dead, or worse!"

"You stupid child!" spat Kira furiously. "Being a leader is no game! Believe me, Arlo, I am sorry about Usha. But it was a choice between her and us. I could not endanger the clan!"

At the sight of her tears, Arlo felt his own eyes burning, and a wave of regret seized him. "I'm sorry, too, Kira. I know you had no choice. But she was my friend! I want to go back there and see if she's still alive."

"She won't be," called Gunthar from the shadows. "For the love of a witch-girl born in a bottle, will you abandon your own people?"

"Be quiet, you old fool," snapped Kira, wearily getting to her feet. "Arlo and I are going back to see what has become of our friends."

"What?" mocked Gunthar. "Do you prefer to die at the hands of the Citizens?"

"If we are not back in four hours, then you have my permission to leave before sunrise," answered Kira, gathering her cloak and spear around her. "Gunthar, as you are so certain you know what is right, then you must be leader of the tribe in my stead. I command you to go to the gathering of the Meet and trade what little we have. If the Goddess is willing, then we will join you there."

Despite his fatigue and fever, Arlo felt a small prick of pride at his cousin's haughty words, and followed her down the rocky crags on the path back towards the waterhole while Gunthar and the tribe gazed, stunned, after them.

"Wait!" shouted Ozzie. "You're not going alone?"

Arlo turned wearily to face his friend. "Ozzie, please, stay here. Look after Toby – he's never going to make it otherwise. You can't leave him!"

"I can do it," protested Toby. "I wunna come, Arlo, I wunna help!"

"But you can't see well, Toby!" insisted Arlo. "You've smashed your glasses! And you can't stay alone here. You need another Citizen to look after you."

Ozzie, grumbling, capitulated, but Kira bent close to them for a last warning before she left.

"When you go to the Meet, Ozzie, at all costs, no one must know you are a Citizen. Wear cloaks and keep your heads bowed. Talk to nobody. The Meet can be a dangerous place, even if one is a Natural."

As he lay with his face in the dust, Onofre was to remember, quite distinctly and clearly, the last time he had ever seen his father.

On the beach in front of him, his father's back was turned, dragging the thick, barnacled fishing nets towards the boat bobbing in the shallows. The smell of the sea rose up around them, the tangy, brutal and elemental odour of salt and fish.

His father was already knee-deep into the water, pushing the boat out. Onofre shouted to him in his high-pitched, childish voice, but the wind tore his words away. His father sprang nimbly into the boat and took the oars. Suddenly a sense of foreboding seized Onofre and he stumbled down the last sand dunes towards the disappearing figure. But it was all in vain, and as he waded the first few steps into the water, still shrieking his father's name, the shadow of the boat faded into the dusk.

The icy waves lapped around Onofre's ankles. He took one step, and then another into the water. He felt the coldness rising up his body. The night fogs were descending and it was impossible to see where sea met sky. He took another step and the chill reached his chest. His heart laboured in his body. He would have to swim. He did not know how. Already he felt the waves pulling at him, slapping against him, surging over his head as he fell forward into the water.

And then, quite incredibly, Kira was by his side, turning him over, putting her arm underneath his head, and rocking him as if Onofre himself was a child. In confusion and terror the old man stared around him, hearing comforting words but not understanding what they meant.

But it was no good. The coldness still drenched his body, paralysed his limbs. He tried to focus on the faces above him, but his own body seemed to have lost its sense of balance, of up or down, left or right. His head lolled uselessly as Arlo helped Kira settle him. At one glance it was clear his wounds were fatal.

"The Citizens have captured Usha," Onofre managed to murmur, with his final strength. "I tried to stop them, but I was shot. They have taken her back to Genopolis."

"And Talia? What happened to Talia?" urged Arlo.

But Onofre never spoke again. As his eyes dimmed, he felt once more the rocking sensation as if he was adrift on the seas of his boyhood, floating gently on the waves in his father's ship. But even as his sight faded, the smell of salt rose about him again, and now he heard the creak of oars, felt the rough warmth of boards supporting his back, and the gentle rise and fall of a boat beneath him.

FOUR

Onofre was buried at dawn on the southernmost peak of the mountain, on the flat shelf of the lookout point. At morning, the first rays of the rising sun would warm the crag, and in the evening, the last rays of the dying sun would touch it. On the mound of his grave, Arlo and Kira raised a cairn of grey stones to mark the spot. Though they could leave no inscription on the grave, privately Arlo named it Onofre's Point, and resolved to put a small X on the site on the map that he and Toby were compiling, if he should ever find it again.

When it was finished, they stood for a while in silence. Kira murmured a prayer to the Goddess, but Arlo stood silent with the noise of the wind and the waves in his ears, his face streaked with mud and stained with tears.

During the year that they had spent together in the wilderness, Onofre had become like a father to him, almost (though not quite) like a second Ignatius. It was through Onofre that they had escaped the savage Wolf-men, and it was by his skill that they had crossed the stormy shipping channel into the path of Kira and her Orphans. So too it had been Onofre who had interceded for them, been a tower of strength by explaining the ways of the clan to the Citizens, and those of the Citizens to the Naturals. It was he who had taught Arlo to handle a spear, weave a net and tie a knot that would not come undone. And he had been the only other Natural who had looked after Usha, tried to help her. . .

And with the thought of Usha an overwhelming hopelessness entered Arlo. Usha was gone, taken back to Genopolis, to Regeneration or worse. He turned and stared over the flat sea towards the horizon. How far away she was now, and he could see no chance of bringing her back. With the sea risen, it was too wide for him to cross, and he had no boat, no weapon, nor knew the direction in which to sail.

"Come," said Kira, taking his hand. "Grieve no longer. There is a time for living and a time for dying. Onofre has left at his own time, and we must not hold him back. Our time is for living now. We must hurry."

Arlo felt as if a burning hand had clenched his chest. Kira was right. A Natural's place was with his family. Now that Usha was taken, they could linger no more. With the last effort of will, he buried the memory of his friend deep inside his heart, together with Ignatius, and Doctor Benedict, Kristo, the Abbess, Rem, and all those whom he knew he would not see again.

For the last time, he turned his face to the east so that he could breathe the fresh air and feel the wind on his face. Slowly his gaze travelled over the horizon, and on to the brush-lined waterhole and the forest that led to the gorge. Suddenly he stopped and stared, pointing with a trembling finger.

"Kira! Look! There's something down there, and it's moving!"

Corin ducked, not a moment too soon, as the stout staff of his attacker whistled perilously close to his ear and smashed into the wall above his head. Throwing himself aside he rolled away from the descending blow and brought up his own staff to hit at the knees of his assailant. But his own strike was ably dodged and the next moment his staff was pinned down beneath the boots of his aggressor while the laughter of the Brigadier echoed around the small courtyard from the balcony where she had been watching.

"The son of the Regis caught out again? You will have to do much better if you are not to come last in Sports Day this year!"

Corin got to his feet and dusted himself down. He disliked sparring practice with his Gemini trainer intensely. Though he was quick-witted and sharp, his body never acted as fast as his mind did. To act rather than think – that was the mantra drummed into him by his trainers. All Citizens relied on logical thought and planning rather than instinct, and a soldier's training was designed to unlock that quick, intuitive power that only Naturals possessed. But Corin, though skilled in drawing and painting, had little ability in physical exercise or combat, and often found himself face down underneath his trainer's staff with his nose rubbed in the dust. He looked over his hands and saw that one of his thumbs had been injured in the struggle; it was dark red and already beginning to swell.

The Brigadier examined Corin's thumb brusquely, pronounced the injury superficial, and summoned the Gemini trainer to fetch an ice pack. Ice was almost unheard of in the City but for the Regis Apparent no expense would be spared. With the pack wrapped bulkily around his hand to reduce the swelling, Corin practised with his trainer for a few more moves, but his aim was poor and, as he expected, he soon found himself flat on his back with his trainer's staff poised above his nose. Thankfully the sparring was to be short-lived. Seconds later the tolling of the great gong above Traitor's Gate sounded through the air.

As the great gates were rolled back, from behind came a sound of shouting and jeering.

"See the wild Naturals! Show us your tails, Natural scum!"

Prisoners! And better still, *real Naturals*! This was a chance not to be missed! With his face almost betraying his excitement, Corin threw down his staff and ran after the Brigadier as she stalked down the causeway. But Ivar, as always, was immediately behind him, pulling at his sleeve, and urging him up to the small balcony that overlooked the courtyard.

"Stay here, master, and watch from a distance. Natural devils cannot be trusted. You never know what they will do when cornered."

Arlo's heartbeat thundered in his ears from his rapid sprint down the mountain as he fell to his knees beside the fallen figure. Who could the survivor be? A Gemini foot-soldier, a traitor-Natural, a Citizen-spy? Though the man's head had been covered in blood from some brutal injury and his clothes were rent and torn, he had summoned the strength enough to crawl some way out of the forest, as if seeking water from the shores of the muddied waterhole, but now lay, hand outflung, on his front. Struggle as he might to rise to his feet, the effort was too much for him. As Arlo reached out his hand to touch the man's shoulder, Kira ran up behind him, her spear pointed at the ready.

"Careful, Arlo! Perhaps it is a trick! An ambush!"

But at that moment, as the man's arms gave way beneath him and he rolled over on to his back with a groan. Arlo gasped in shock and delight as he took in the well-remembered features of someone that he knew of old.

Incredibly, beneath the grime and bloodstains, the face of the librarian Kristo from the Inn of Court of Genopolis stared up at him, his lips faintly curving into a smile.

"Hullo, Arlo," murmured Kristo vaguely. "It's been a b-bit of a journey to get to you. I'm sorry I'm so late."

The splash of gritty, salty water in Usha's face woke her, and she became aware that she was lying face down on one of the catamarans, strapped to the outside wing with both her ankles and her legs bound tightly together. She coughed and choked as the wave broke over her again and tried to hold her head clear of the sea but with no success. Suddenly a long-buried memory floated back to her; it was as if she was lying immobile on the operating table, while the faces of Auntie and the scissor-man stared down at her, laughing, pointing. ...

A black-clad soldier stood on the opposite wing, a rifle trained on her. "Don't move, Natural. You're lucky you're alive, though not for much longer! Oh yes! *She* will have some fun with you!"

Usha turned her head away. What the soldier meant by *She* was unclear, but she could guess that whoever *She* was there would be little mercy shown them once they arrived. From her horizontal position, she saw the enormous gates of Genopolis open before them, and the great bulk of the Lighthouse threw its shadow over her.

Genopolis had two means of entrance once the sea had risen. The first was the commercial docks to the south, where pharm-ships arrived, encircled by a wide protective harbour that spread like a crescent-shape into the sea; the same docks where the Kids had plundered the warehouses almost a year before. But this time they were landing at the military marina at the north-west of Genopolis.

Here, the entry to the Port had been designed in the form of a lock, with three different levels of gates to bring the returning soldiers as far inland as possible. Teams of huge, sweating Gemini heaved on levers to pull the sluice gates together. A great rumbling and splashing thundered around them as the pumps began to pour water down the slimy, moss-ridden sides of the lock, and the water level began to rise. As the fleet entered the third lock, there was a shout and clatter as the guards ran down to receive them. Like a Pharmopolis food parcel, Usha felt herself hoisted up and carried by two soldiers along the huge stone platforms that ran alongside the marina and thrown down roughly into a corner.

Then, for the first time, she saw the figure of Talia being dragged from another catamaran and pulled on to the dock. Bloodied and bruised though the gladiator was, her appearance flooded Usha with new hope. If the two of them were together, then the situation might not be so desperate. Talia's unerring confidence, her swordsmanship and her ability to seize opportunities were the best qualities to have in a situation like this. But Talia's head was strangely bowed in a way that Usha had never seen before, and her hands hung loosely at her side. She did not meet Usha's eyes or hear her encouraging whisper.

Usha could not understand it. She had never seen Talia like this before. "Talia!" she hissed under her breath. "Look at me! Talia!"

But the gladiator merely stared at the ground, and at the vicious tug at the chain around her neck, she moved forward like a trained Gemini. The sight threw Usha into utter confusion. If Talia was giving up, then they would all be lost!

A chain tightened around her neck, and in a daze she hobbled after Talia as the guards led them down a flight of steps and through a high iron gate. Inside a wide courtyard there stood a tall fair soldier-woman in a crimson uniform and black cap. She slowly turned to face them.

Usha stared in astonishment, feeling as if she was trapped in a bad dream. One side of the soldier's face was horrifically maimed and injured, and instead of a right hand a metal claw shone wickedly from her decorated sleeve, though the soldier bore the mutilation with as much pride as the row of medals across her chest that sparkled in the sunshine.

And then, at last, Talia raised her head for the first time since she had entered Genopolis, and on her face was the smile that Usha knew of old, a caustic raising of one eyebrow, and her voice was proud and clear.

"It has been a long time, Hacker, since we last saw each other? I trust that you have not forgotten me?"

*

"**B**ut how are we going to get him *out* of here?" wailed Kira in despair. "It's going to be hard enough with two of us, and we can't carry him!"

Arlo looked down at Kristo, now dazed and rambling in a fever, and sighed. "I don't know, Kira, but we can't go without him. He's come too far. I'm not leaving any of my friends again."

As they stared at each other, locked in a stalemate, a faint neigh from the pit startled them. Together they sprang up and ran to the side of it. Beneath them, still struggling wearily in the mud, was the horse, its creamy sides now stained with mud and sweat, blood bubbling from its nose as it beat with its hooves on the pit's crumbling sides. But the pit was too deep, and its strength was failing. Once it was exhausted, it would slip beneath the surface of the water and drown. Arlo gazed at the suffering animal in pity and fear.

"The horse!" cried Kira in excitement. "We can take the horse!"

Arlo blinked in perplexity. "What for? We can't carry it, and we can't eat it all."

Kira snorted with sudden laughter. "You numbskull Citizen! Horses are used for *carrying* or pulling things, not for eating! See its long back? You can put things on there and it'll carry them for you. It can even carry us!"

But the idea of putting anything on a wild creature's back, especially the desperate animal before them, seemed a little far-fetched to Arlo. "Are you sure it will let us?"

His cousin smiled, unwinding a long rope from her pack and fashioning a rough lasso from it. "No wild creature will *let* us. No, first we must capture its heart, and then it will do anything for us."

Under Kira's direction, the cousins gathered as much driftwood and as many rocks and stones as they could and started to roll them down into the pit, where the horse continued to struggle feebly in the muddy water. Hour after hour they worked underneath a light drizzle of rain. Sweat streamed into Arlo's eyes and his stomach ached with hunger, but Kira worked as a woman possessed, not allowing him a single minute to rest. Slowly Arlo began to see what she was planning. The pit was so full of mud and water, it was impossible for the horse to climb out, but as the rubble piled up inside, it started to create a slope up one side. Feeling the debris forming a slippery pile beneath its hooves, the horse started to try to pull itself up and out, but its weight still made it sink. Finally Arlo, frustrated by tiredness and hunger, turned away with a cry of anger.

"We'll never do it, Kira! It's impossible!"

In desperation, Arlo sank to his knees next to Kristo. The librarian had fallen into a slumber, and his face was flushed and sweating. He did not respond to Arlo's urgent pleading.

"He's unconscious, Kira! What should I do?"

Kira snorted. "A Citizen does not suffer. He will last a few hours more. Save your breath and your pity for us! Work!"

Searching around, Arlo came across the trunk of a tree about ten feet long, smashed from its height during the storm and lying up the slope from where the pit had been dug. "Kira! Can we use this?"

Kira turned round and her face lit up. "Yes! Come on! Pull!"

Arlo, his teeth clenched with the effort and his muscles cracking, strained to roll the huge tree down to the pit, but the ground was soft and yielding and instead his feet slid from underneath him. Kira ran to help him, but still the trunk remained immobile. Angrily, Arlo beat at it with his fists. "Come on! *Move!*"

With tears of anger more than sorrow pricking his eyes, he fell down beside the tree-trunk, exhausted by fatigue and emotion. This could not be happening! How could Kristo have come all the way out into the wilderness to die in front of him? With his head in his hands, he fought against the fear that was consuming him. Black clouds were already starting to darken the valley. If another downpour started then it would all be useless. They would have to leave Kristo to die alone and the horse to drown; they would have to save themselves, but at a terrible cost. . .

But the joy that had been awoken in him at his first sight of Kristo refused to let him surrender. He could not give into despair while life and hope still surrounded him. There had to be a way! There just had to be! Springing up he gazed around and his heart leapt in sudden hope. By the crumpled body of the soldier who had fallen from the crag while trying to shoot Usha, lay his rifle and a crossbow. They were almost too heavy to lift, but somehow he managed to drag them over to the pit, an idea already forming in his brain.

Kira looked up in surprise as he approached. "Arlo, you're not thinking of shooting them both, are you?"

This time it was Arlo's turn to laugh. "No, Kira, look. If we push the rifle underneath the other side of the tree-trunk, we can make . . . I think they call it a *lever* in Genopolis . . . and perhaps we can make it move and roll it downhill. And if you make a lever out of the crossbow, then it might just work," he cajoled, seeing her doubtful expression. "Let's try!"

The first few attempts were unsuccessful, and Arlo almost shot himself in the foot by accident before they worked out how to unload the rifle, but then somehow it all came together, and by pushing down hard on the levers, the great tree came loose from the mud and rolled a few feet downhill. With their fatigue forgotten, they ran after it and repeated the procedure. Finally, after another hour of levering and pushing, the tree was poised on the brink of the pit, and then, slowly but surely, slid down into the bottom and on to the rubble-slope, forming a rough but sturdy bridge on to solid ground. The horse, weary though it was of its struggles, immediately forged its way towards it, found a foothold and started to pull itself out of the mire.

Quickly, Kira coiled her rope around her arm and

threw it over the head of the horse, pulling the lasso tight. "Come on, Arlo! Be ready for him!"

At first the horse slipped as it tried to gain its balance, but, wild as it was, it was naturally sure-footed and managed a few steps on the slimy trunk. Then it gathered itself together for a great leap. For the first time Arlo saw how big and powerful it was, the great muscles moving under its haunches.

"Watch out!" cried Kira. "It's coming!"

Corin leaned over the balcony for a glimpse of the new arrivals. The press of soldiers at the gate entered and fell back while two dirty and bedraggled figures, draped in chains and with their hair long and unkempt, emerged from the shadows. Disappointingly, despite their appearance, the Naturals were not as he had expected – no horns, no tails – and even more surprisingly, they were both female. The first was a tall, black-skinned young woman dressed in greeny-brown trousers and tunic, her hair tangled into long ropes. Her face was twisted into a glare that was half-smile, half-scowl, and she spat at the soldiers, who despite themselves, moved away as she passed.

Yet it was the second prisoner who made Corin crane amazedly over the railings, shock and surprise sweeping across his face in equal measure. Smaller and thinner than her companion, she was a few years younger, not much older than Corin. Underneath the mud and grime, her skin was as pale as stone and her hair was as fine and fair as any Citizen. Her eyes were grey and blank as she stumbled under the soldiers' prods and pokes. But it was not her appearance that rooted Corin to the spot.

It was the face of the fair-haired girl-gladiator from last year's Circus, the girl who had escaped from the Labyrinth with the red-haired boy who Corin remembered so well.

And in that moment he felt again the sensation that had swept him when he had breathed in the fumes of the stolen vial, the same strange, dizzying feeling of joy, which he thought he would never feel again.

"Guards!" shrieked the Brigadier, and Corin was startled to hear such an Outbreak echo around the courtyard walls. "To the prison turret! Now!"

Quickly, Corin ducked under Ivar's restraining arm and headed excitedly after the soldiers as they bundled the prisoners up the stairs of the Tower and towards the Brigadier's quarters.

As the horse gathered itself together for a great leap out of the pit, Kira was ready. Her rope whirled through the air and coiled itself around its neck. In the same second that its hooves met solid ground, she passed the other end of the rope around the tree trunk and pulled it tight. As the horse tried to gallop away, the rope fastened and pulled it back. With a terrible scream, the horse reared up, its hooves beating the air.

"Stay away," shouted Kira. "Do not get in its way. Wait until it tires itself out."

It did not take long. Exhausted by the battle to get out of the pit, the horse pulled and strained, but the rope held fast. Finally it stopped, its legs buckled and it dropped to the ground. Its head drooped and its eyes closed.

This was the moment that Kira had been waiting for. Immediately she sprang forward and leapt on its back, holding tightly to the rope around its neck. But the horse, unused to a rider, was suddenly spurred into panic. It bounded to its feet and bucked frantically, trying with its last strength to throw off the human that clung immovably, gripping with fingers and toes on its back. Arlo watched in stricken admiration as the horse plunged and reared, yet his cousin stayed on, until with a mighty heave, it bucked and sent Kira flying over its head. Panting and trembling, she got to her feet, tired, but apparently otherwise unharmed.

"How on earth did you do that?" asked Arlo, in open wonder.

Kira sighed, running her hand along the sweat-soaked neck, and patting the heaving sides of the horse gently. "Once I knew a man who could tame any wild creature. Horse, hound, even wild bears. He taught me all he knew, and I have never forgotten it."

Though Arlo's curiosity was awakened – his cousin had never mentioned this man to him before – there were other things to attend to. Fat droplets of rain were beginning to fall from the sky, heralding the advent of another storm. Quickly, he and Kira carried Kristo in to a shallow cave underneath the mountain's feet where the ground was relatively dry. In the contents of the soldier's pack, Arlo had found dry Citizen-biscuits and a bottle of water and some sachets of nutrient powder. Together they shared the biscuits between them, and Kira tipped a few droplets of water and nutrients into Kristo's mouth, though he was still unable to talk. As night fell, Kira gathered rainwater in her pannier for the horse to drink. Though refreshed, the mare still refused any approach from her and bucked and reared every time she attempted to caress it.

"It is going to be long until she consents to bear me," said Kira tiredly, at last abandoning her task and crawling into the cave next to Arlo. "I cannot tell how long such a beast will take to tame. But in the meantime we can do nothing. Another storm is setting in, and we must ride it out. Go to sleep, cousin, for we will need all our strength for the day in front of us."

Slowly, Arlo fell into an uneasy sleep, buffeted by the howling of the wind, the sound of the horse neighing from a distance, and the occasional spatter of raindrops from the storm. But, before his eyes closed, he saw that his cousin now knelt over Kristo, gently sponging his face with a piece of rag. On her face was an expression that Arlo had not seen before, and her hands were unusually gentle as she rolled back the librarian's head and examined the wound on his temple. And every time

Arlo woke up, he saw that his cousin was still awake, sitting close by Kristo, checking his fever and giving him water, drop by drop, all through the night.

The Brigadier hurled her cup against the wall of the Palace, where it smashed in a flurry of glittering fragments, showering the cowering soldiers with red wine.

"I said find me the *Naturals*! And you bring me a renegade Citizen gladiator and a runaway *Gemini* of all things? What on earth is the use of *those*?"

"I'm sorry, Brigadier," stuttered the captain. "It seems that our reconnaissance party ran into one of their lookout posts, and . . . well, the Naturals that we were following managed to. . ."

"Managed to *what*?" bellowed the Brigadier.

"Managed to . . . er, escape, Brigadier."

From her place in the corner, Usha turned her head away as she realized what was to come. Moments later the sound of the gunshot echoed around the Brigadier's turret room, closely followed by the crash of the captain's falling body. As Usha looked away, her eyes met those of the small, curly-haired boy who had followed them up from the courtyard and stood gawping at the door. He put his finger to his lips and shook his head in warning, before his lips widened into a faint smile.

Usha blinked. A smile on the face of a Citizen was the last thing that she had expected to see, especially towards a prisoner. Who he was she had no idea, but evidently he meant to ask her not to draw attention to his presence, and to show her that he was on her side. Perhaps he was a servant, or a courtier of some sort, or someone who sympathized with her plight.

But what was the good of one friendly face? They were back, imprisoned in Genopolis, under the cruel guardianship of the very Citizen that Talia had tried to kill some years previously, and from her first sight of the Brigadier, Usha had no doubt that something particularly nasty was waiting in store for them.

Arlo hung the last of the strips of meat out over the smoking fire and washed the dried blood from his hands with a shudder. Three days had passed since they had rescued Kristo and the horse from the pit, but they were still marooned at the killing fields and the watering hole, and every day he expected to see the long brown Citizen canoes nosing their way back over the horizon. With Kristo still ill and incapable of walking, Kira had set herself to tame the mare, whom she named Ash on account of her grey colour, and in the meantime set Arlo to skin and dry what meat could be salvaged from the remains of the Hunt. Arlo hated preparing meat from the dead animals – Gunthar's sneer of *women's work* still rang in his ears – but there was nothing else for it.

He gathered a little of the dried meat and took it to where Kristo lay. The Citizen had been fed on nutrient-soup for the last few days, and little by little his fever had left him, though he had still been unable to talk clearly. But this time the librarian's eyes were clear and undimmed and he even struggled up on one elbow as Arlo entered the cave with the meat and a cup of water. With a cry of joy, Arlo embraced his friend and hugged him tightly, but surprisingly the Citizen pushed him away.

"I'm s-sorry, Arlo," said Kristo faintly. "I have failed you."

Arlo shook his head, gently raising the cup to the Citizen's lips and coaxing him to drink a small amount of water. "No, Kristo, don't talk like that. You're safe now. As soon as you're a little better, we're leaving."

"It is all m . . . my fault," said Kristo weakly.

"But how?" asked Arlo anxiously. "How can any of this be your fault?"

"Because it was too late," replied the Citizen flatly. "After you escaped from the Circus, freedom in Genopolis became an impossibility. Ignatius was imprisoned and other known members of the Circle were rounded up and thrown into jail – Sir Herbert, Sasha, Tariq, Sofia. . ." Kristo sighed. "We should have acted sooner."

Arlo hugged him. "You couldn't help it, Kristo. But how in Genopolis did you escape yourself?"

"I arranged my capture with sympathizers of our cause who remain in the service of the City Guardians," stammered the librarian. "Even in the highest ranks of the Guardians there are members of the Circle, although they guard their identity secretly. I masqueraded as a misguided but repentant member of the Inn of Court, and, while pretending to recant, I formed a plan with Ignatius and my captors for my own escape from the City. We decided that I would pretend to have secret information about your whereabouts, and that I had struck a deal to lead them to the Regions when the Rains fell in order to ambush you. Upon arrival, we had arranged that they would cut my bonds and we would escape into the wilderness to make it look as if I had escaped and killed them both. It was a wild plan, but we knew that if we could be free in the Regions, then sooner or later we would encounter a group of Naturals, and perhaps gain some news of you.

"But I was betrayed. On the day that the Rains started, other Guardians suddenly replaced my agents, and I knew our plan had been foiled. The Brigadier knows our ways too well. As the fleet was launched, I knew that I would not be coming back. I tried to lead them to another place, but they must have had information that I did not know, for they ignored me and sailed directly to the watering hole where your tribe were. I tried to escape, but I could do nothing, and they shot me and left me on the beach. But some of your tribe helped me to escape, and brought me away, but the Citizen-patrol was returning, and captured them."

Arlo's heart skipped a beat. "Who? Who helped you to escape, Kristo?"

Breathlessly, Arlo listened as Kristo related the final moments of Onofre's end and the capture of Usha and Talia. When the Citizen had finished, he sat a while in silence, fighting against despair. There seemed no way out. He could not possibly go after Usha to Genopolis under the iron fist of the Brigadier, and yet if they stayed in the Regions, it seemed that Citizen-spies were already watching their every move. What was he to do?

"And what is happening to Ignatius and the Abbess, Kristo?"

Kristo sighed. "Ignatius was imprisoned with me, and now that our attempt has failed, he will be on trial for his life, while the Brigadier roots out every single member of the resistance in Genopolis. The Abbess Binah left Genopolis to petition the Senate's stronghold in the North, but on arrival she was arrested and jailed also while the Senators debate what is to be done."

There was a jingle from outside the cave, and the next second Kira rode into view, urging the recalcitrant mare up the path towards them. Ash had been tamed enough to allow Kira on her back, but she was still skittish and awkward. At the sight of Kristo, Kira's face suddenly lit up and she reined in quickly.

"He's . . . you're awake!"

"Kristo, this is my cousin, Kira," said Arlo uncomfortably, wondering what on earth was the matter with her. Her face was flushed and her eyes were shining as she gazed at the Citizen, who looked steadily back at her, politely and impassively. "Kira, this is Kristo. . ."

"I've heard so much about you!" returned Kira, slipping off the horse and holding her hand out. But, as Kristo took it, she reddened slightly, pulled her hand back and stammered. "Well, it looks as if we'll be able to move off tomorrow. Ash is almost completely broken-in now. She'll bear you, as long as I am with her. Come on, Ash," and she hastily busied herself with tethering and feeding the mare.

Kristo looked questioningly at Arlo, who shrugged. "I don't know. She's not usually like that. Perhaps she's tired."

The light that was shone in Usha's eyes traced itself in a mesmerizing pattern, up, down, to the left, around in a circle and back again. It reminded her of the flights of some of the insects that she had seen in the Regions, an outline traced by a wild bee or a butterfly. The effect was curiously hypnotic and soothing, and she found herself almost lulled to sleep, despite the fact that both her hands were manacled high above her head from a hook suspended from the roof of the Brigadier's study.

Behind the light, the Brigadier's voice came out of the shadows. Usha was glad that she could not see the bulging blind eye, the ruined face, for the tone itself was so gentle, so calm. "And then? After you left your auntie's house?"

Usha tried to remember. It seemed a reasonable enough question, and she felt it terribly important to tell the kind Brigadier everything, but her memory was jumbled and slow-moving. "I met . . . I met a boy called Ozzie. He was a bit older than me, but he lived in the sewers, with a group of kids who lived by stealing food. I tried to tell him it was unCitizenly, I tried. . ."

The Brigadier murmured approvingly. "It does not matter. And then?"

"Well," Usha bit her lip in concentration, "I was kidnapped by some smugglers, and they put me in the Circus, where I met Talia."

"Ah." The Brigadier nodded. "And Talia tried to recruit you as an enemy of Genopolis in order to help the Natural boy escape?"

Usha shook her head. "No! I had no idea who either of them were! Ozzie and the Kids were trying to help me get out before the Minotaur came to kill us, but this boy . . . he just fell out of nowhere in the middle of the Labyrinth. He had a dog with him, or at least I think the dog belonged to him. . ."

"Anyway," pressed the Brigadier. "You escaped, and what then?"

"We got on a boat," replied Usha dreamily. "We sailed, and sailed, and we ended up in the Regions. There was a fierce tribe who tried to eat us alive, but we escaped and met an orphan called Kira, who let us join her clan. Arlo was her cousin, you see."

The Brigadier drew in her breath in interest. "So Arlo is out there now, with the remnants of Region Three?"

"What's Region Three?" asked Usha, puzzled.

"Never mind. And then?"

"They didn't like me," admitted Usha frankly. "They thought I was a witch, because—"

"Because?"

"Because . . . I don't know." Suddenly Usha began to feel uneasy. Something was warning her that she should hold her tongue. But how could she not tell the Brigadier everything? It was her purpose, it was. . .

The Brigadier held out a small object, hardly recognizable as a muddied and stained book, its pages crusted over with earth. "And what do you think this is?"

"I think it's a book," replied Usha. "Arlo said that people use it to remember the past."

"And if I destroy the book?" mocked the Brigadier softly. "Does the past vanish also?"

Usha stood silent, confused, as the iron claw of the Brigadier scored open the dried pages and surveyed the writing within.

"It's a book about Arlo," said Usha truthfully. "It's got his history in it."

The claw pointed to the pages written in Arlo's sloping hand. "And what is this?"

"I think Arlo was showing Toby how to write. They were writing down everything that happened since they escaped. I think they. . ."

Then, unbelievably, the mist before Usha's eyes cleared with a flash, and she saw Arlo standing before her. For a moment she could not recognize him. Dressed in strange, almost military clothes of camouflaged grey and brown, his face was daubed with black, and a green rope was threaded around his waist. Usha's mouth dropped open at the suddenness of his appearance, but she found herself unable to speak. For a moment he stood, looking around, searching for something. Usha shook her head to clear it, but Arlo had already disappeared. She blinked again, but they were once more alone in the chamber.

Yet the Brigadier had evidently seen nothing. "And where has Region Three . . . I mean Arlo, gone now?"

"I'm not sure," answered Usha vaguely. "They ran away when the soldiers came, but only Talia and Onofre came back to get me, and they shot Onofre and killed him dead."

"So you are friends with Talia, then? Do you admit that Talia recruited you as an enemy of Genopolis? Do you admit that she has a grudge against me and would do anything that she can to betray me?"

"No," said Usha simply. "I just don't think she likes you very much. And neither do I, as a matter of fact."

Even Arlo could not have recognized Kristo after Kira had finished his disguise. His fair hair had been darkened with the juice of roots and berries, and his skin stained a deep brown by a paste of pounded wood-bark and dirt. Wrapped in the ragged weave of Kira's tribe, even his bright blue eyes would not give him away – plenty of Naturals had blue eyes – and as long as he kept his head down and acted like a wounded Natural, Kira had every confidence that his disguise would pass muster, despite his lack of a beard and his Citizen-fine skin.

"For if they see a Citizen at the Meet, Kristo," she said, "they will kill you without a moment's thought, and there are some that would feast upon you too, and not only from hunger."

"I don't think I'd make much of a meal," returned Kristo mildly, trying in vain to pinch a centimetre of flesh from his starving ribs. "There's hardly enough of me here to keep myself alive."

Arlo tried to laugh, but a knot of fear started to coil inside his stomach at the thought of the danger that Ozzie and Toby were already facing.

With Kristo slumped over the neck of the mare, and rough panniers of the smoked meat hanging from either side of Ash's flanks, Arlo and Kira made their halting way down the tussocked slopes towards the wood where the Meet happened every year. The entrance was so concealed by briars and scrub that they could not see it until they had almost passed. Seeking entry into the forest, Kira cupped her hand to her mouth and sent a bird's call floating upwards, three times, then rested her hand on Ash's neck and listened. After a moment, two spears suddenly swung down from the branches above them, coming to a stop centimetres from their faces.

"Who are you? Declare yourselves!"

Arlo stiffened but Kira remained calm and did not

flinch. "We come in peace with a wounded member of our tribe to barter at the Meet. We are the Orphans, of the South Regions."

"Orphans? Scavengers more likely!" spat back an unfamiliar voice, and an olive-skinned, hazel-eyed Natural woman, dressed in the same shade of green as the forest, swung herself down from the overhanging boughs, her spear poised at the ready. Two heavily-armed men followed her, carrying spears, their faces unfriendly. "What do you want, pirate-girl?"

Kira's face registered shock and embarrassment. "Greetings, Liana," she stammered, and for the first time Arlo noticed that her eyes were unwilling to meet the other Natural's, and she seemed strangely unsure as she held out a pannier of the dried meat and skins for the other's inspection. "I . . . I come to exchange and trade, and do not seek a quarrel over times past."

Liana took a piece of the dried meat and chewed on it cautiously, before wrinkling her nose at the taste. "Bitter food you bring, scavenger-girl. Is this what the children of black-legs live on?"

"Enough of this, Liana," broke in her companion impatiently. "Leave your weapons with us, Orphan, and be quick. Entry fee is half of the meat you are carrying."

"But. . ." began Arlo but Kira nudged him quiet and handed over one entire pannier of meat to the man with no resistance. Their spears and hunting knives were taken from them by the other Naturals, a move that made Arlo deeply uneasy. Ash stood champing and stamping impatiently, and the man's eyes flickered in wonder and envy as they passed over her strong back, haunches, and well-muscled shoulders.

"That is a fine horse you have there. How did you come by her?"

Kira's fingers tightened involuntarily on the rough hemp that served Ash as a bridle. "Many things are brought down from the hills with the New Year Rains, friend, and I was trained well how to capture a wild heart."

Liana stiffened as if Kira had slapped her. "Capture them and break them, you mean, pirate-girl. If you speak of my brother, then he is here recruiting for the Cause, but I counsel you to leave him alone today, if you wish to leave the Meet in one piece!"

"What on earth was all that about?" asked Arlo curiously as the guards pulled back a curtain of brambles to let them pass, but Kira shook her head and urged Ash quickly through the narrow opening. "It's better you don't know, Arlo. Keep near to me, and don't speak to anyone unfamiliar, understand?"

Arlo soon recognized the truth of Kira's advice. As they passed through the wood, they came across groups of other tribal Naturals, more akin to the Wolf-men than any of Kira's clan, who turned to study Ash covetously as they passed. Some had evidently come from miles away, for their dress and accent was harsh and difficult to understand, some costumed outlandishly in animal skins that Arlo had never seen before.

"Kira, Goren's tribe aren't here, are they?" he ventured nervously.

Kira shrugged. "They may be. But no one can harm you. It is against the Rules of the Meet, for within these woods all tribal differences must be set aside and we are on protected ground."

"I really hope they're not!" began Arlo, his heart beating fast at the thought of seeing the Wolf-men again, but at that moment they pushed their way out of the woods and into an enormous, crowded clearing, where the Meet was taking place.

Arlo had never seen so many Naturals from different tribes together in one place before. At first sight it seemed a chaotic and random affair, with campfires and rickety stalls set up heaped with animal skins, crudely-woven cloth, carved wooden utensils and bundles of kindling. Lengths of dried meat and berries hung from the trees, and piled on the ground were wild roots and tubers still crusted with earth. Occasionally one might see a pile of captured Citizen army rifles, uniforms or pairs of mismatched boots. The air was thick with smoke and coarse laughter, as each tribe sought to trade the best bargain they could with each other.

While Kira disappeared to search for the rest of the clan, Arlo helped Kristo down from Ash's back and found a quiet place beside a tree where he could lie down and rest. Once they had found the Orphans, they would have safety in numbers, but here they were alone and exposed, easy prey for the wilder tribes that surged and chattered around them. Tethering Ash to a trunk, Arlo made sure that she had food and water, certain that if he so much as disappeared for a second, the precious horse would be stolen.

Through the hordes of jostling Naturals, he could hear a voice, declaiming as if on a stage, pitched high above the rumble of the crowd. Something about it pricked his curiosity, and over the heads of the crowd he could see the figure of a man, standing on a boulder above the rest of the throng, well-built and broad-chested, though not particularly tall. Arlo could not see his face properly but he could hear him well enough; the man had a powerful, thrilling voice that moved Arlo deeply in a way he could not name. Fascinated, he stared at the man, who was dressed unusually in a tattered Citizen-uniform over a tunic made of skins, so that he seemed half-Citizen, half- Natural. His waist was bound by a rope of thick hemp and dyed a deep green in colour, and around him were a small group of similarly-attired Naturals who attempted to hand out green ropes to the passers-by.

"How much longer, brothers and sisters, will you let the Citizens rule over us! Join us, the Rebels! We need to rise up against them!"

His words soared above the chattering, argumentative mob as they quarrelled over bargains, too intent on their day-to-day life to consider changing the world that they lived in. But occasionally a solitary or wandering Natural, who seemed to be attached to no particular tribe, would come forward to listen and nod, and be given a place in the ranks of the others, with a green rope bound around his or her waist.

So these must be the Rebels, thought Arlo, those Naturals who attacked the convoys of soldiers and staged their own resistance in the wilderness. How different seemed these people, he told himself wistfully, to the Orphans with their fear of confrontation and change. Not for the last time he felt a stirring of guilt and shame over the cowardice of his tribe. *Pirate-girl*, the woman Liana had insulted Kira. *Orphans? Scavengers more likely!* And perhaps scavengers and pirates were all his family were, destined to steal and hide in the wilderness for ever.

But as he turned away from the sight, his cheeks burning, there was a flurry of hot breath and barking, and the next second he was lying on his back with the weight of two delighted paws on his stomach. In disbelief he stared up at the brown eyes, the laughing mouth and the feathery tail that wagged excitedly from side to side. Though terribly scrawny, covered in burrs and brambles and a year older, Arlo would have recognized him anywhere.

"Oh, Rem!" he gasped, screwing his face up from the hot dog-breath that panted in his ear. "How on earth did you get here? *Rem!*"

Usha lay slumped on the clammy stone floor in her prison tunic. How long she had been imprisoned in the tiny cell, she could not properly calculate. It felt like weeks but in reality it could not have been more than a few days since her interview with the Brigadier, marked solely by the occasional scrap of food and mug of water that was banged down through the small flap in the door. But no matter how she tried, Usha could uncover no memory of what they had talked about that evening. She thought that there had been a light, and she had been asked questions, but for the life of her she could not remember what had been said. All that she knew for certain was that Arlo's book had been taken from her, though she had promised to keep it safe. The only thing that they had overlooked was the moonstone that Onofre had given to her, being obviously unaware of its significance. Its lustre had now dulled and it resembled nothing so much as a pale pebble.

More than the conditions, it was the lack of companionship that bothered Usha in a way that she had never known previously. Since their arrival some days earlier, she had been separated from Talia, and had no news of her. Usha tried not to think of what might be happening to the proud gladiator in the meantime, and to distract herself, brought out the moonstone and concentrated on it.

"For those who cannot see, it will remain just a thing of beauty. I cannot tell you how to use it. But you, Usha, should take it and see if it helps you. With practice, you could make the most of the gift and help many."

Onofre's words echoed in her head as Usha stared

down at the amulet, the way she had many times over the past few days. How on earth could you *see* anything in it? At times, such as in the early dawn or the late evening, the creamy swirls on the face of the moonstone seemed to float and coil, like mist over the lake of the Drowned City, but actually *seeing* something in it seemed like the wildest kind of Natural superstition to Usha. Her visions came in flashes, uncontrollably, when they wanted to – it was not a talent which could be called up at will.

But this time was different. Summoning all her energies, she willed herself to concentrate, to enter into the space between waking and sleeping, between understanding and forgetting, between knowledge and confusion. As she let her mind go blank, as empty as a silver bowl, she breathed gently on the surface of the stone. As the mist evaporated, Usha's eyes widened. She was seeing something – not seeing in the amulet or even inside the cell, but as if looking into another entirely different place – and saw herself on the deck of a ship, chained in a long line with a host of other prisoners. The vision changed and suddenly she felt grit underneath her feet and saw before her an iron cage containing—

Abruptly the image melted away as a voice hissed through the darkness, "You're in a lot of trouble, you are!"

Usha jumped. For a moment she thought it was Arlo – hadn't he been in the Brigadier's study with them? – even though she knew that she was totally alone in the cell. Puzzled, she knelt up and looked around her.

"Talking to the Brigadier like that! She could have shot you, like she did that captain!"

There was a quiet chuckle from the other side of the door, and immediately Usha realized who it must be. It was the curly-haired boy who had watched her being brought into Genopolis and smiled at her. He appeared too well-bred to be a servant, but he seemed to want to be Citizenly, and somehow he must have found out where she was being kept. Despite herself, she could not help being comforted by another Citizen's voice, though she turned her face away and quickly stowed her amulet beneath her tunic. The voice sighed impatiently.

"I could get into terrible trouble if they knew I was here. Don't you want to hear what's going on?"

Usha fought against her curiosity for some moments, but in the end her need for companionship overwhelmed her and she crawled over to the flap set in the door, where she could hear better.

"They're charging you with murder of a Middle Citizen and a scissor-man! Listen, Gemini, did you really *kill* someone?"

Usha remained quiet. If they thought they could get a confession out of her by trickery, then they could think again. But the boy was undeterred by her silence. "Are you really a Gemini? You don't look like most of them. My servant's a Gemini and he's really ugly. And stupid too. Most of you made-to-measures look like someone else, but you're different for some reason."

Usha snorted and turned her back on the door. So he

was not a servant himself, then, but one of the inhabitants of the Palace come to gawp.

"What was it like out in the Regions?" persisted the boy, but finally Usha had had enough of his questions. She had plenty of her own. "What's happening to Talia? What are they doing to my friend?"

"Friend?" asked the boy, confused, and Usha hastened to explain. "A friend . . . I mean, the other person I came here with. What's happening to her?"

"If I find out for you, will you tell me about the Regions?" asked the voice cleverly, and Usha sighed impatiently.

"Yes I will, but you have to tell me where she's been taken first."

"Then I'll have to put some more sleeping powder in Ivar's tea," returned the boy mystifyingly, wriggled out of earshot and disappeared.

Two muddy and weather-stained boots approached Arlo and stood in front of him. Gazing up and over Rem's shoulder, Arlo could see two green eyes gazing down at him from a tanned face that somehow seemed much younger than the creases that had been etched into it by the sun and the winds. The leader of the Rebels stood opposite him, hands on hips, his reddish, shoulder-length hair held back by a tattered bandanna, one eyebrow raised in sarcastic surprise.

"I see that my dog has taken a liking to you, boy."

When Arlo looked around him, his worst fear had

come true. Almost the entirety of the Rebels had formed an interested circle around him. Other Naturals were slowly edging into the circle to see what it was all about. More attention Arlo could not have commanded if he had suddenly fired shots into the air. Slowly, he rose to his feet, trying vainly to push Rem down as the dog lurched and jumped up at him, whimpering with excitement.

"Don't, Rem! *Stop it!"*

"Sit!" commanded the Rebel fiercely, and at his stentorian tone, Rem squeaked and crept sideways, bunching his haunches so that he cringed before Arlo, his head bowed. Instinctively the boy's hand went to Rem's ear and patted him reassuringly.

"No, actually, he's *my* dog, sir."

A ripple of amused laughter came from the watching Rebels. Their leader, however, did not laugh. He had furrowed his brows and seemed to be scrutinizing Arlo closely. Under his intense stare, Arlo became uneasy. "You see, I lost him for a bit . . . I was travelling and. . ." His voice trailed away under the other's haughty gaze. "Well, it wasn't exactly my fault," he resumed shakily. "We were kidnapped by the Wolf – I mean another tribe, and in the confusion, he ran off, and I've never stopped thinking about him, or looking for him, and. . ."

The man took a step forward and folded his arms. "If he is indeed your dog, then tell me, who was his sire? When was he weaned? What place did he have in the litter?"

"I can't tell you that," said Arlo anxiously.

"Yet I can. I can tell you how three of his fellow-whelps died, yet he, the youngest and weakest, survived. I can tell you how I fed him on warm gravy and scraps when his dam could no longer produce milk. I can tell you the cave where he hunted his first rat, about the small scar underneath his foreleg, and about the holes he tore in my best breeches. I can tell you—" The man broke off, biting his lip.

Through the confusion of his mind, Arlo struggled to think. Surely this rough-looking man could not really have brought up Rem as a cub? Yet Rem had fawned and grovelled before him as he had never done for Arlo, and obeyed him at one simple command when sometimes it could take all Arlo's begging to get Rem to do *anything*.

Suddenly a sharp indignation flared within him. "Well, you must have lost him yourself, sir, because . . . I found him, running around somewhere . . . about a year ago, and he's been mine ever since."

The Rebel's eyes narrowed. "*Where* exactly did you find him, boy?"

Arlo bit his tongue, and hardly needed Kristo's swift warning poke in the back of his leg. *Dangerous*, he thought to himself. A question that had always puzzled him was exactly how Rem had found his way into Genopolis. Though he had been well-received amongst the Orphans, he was smart enough to realize that being the Natural-born child whose kidnapping had precipitated the disastrous Rebellion could easily cause many complications amongst other tribes. He forced himself to think quickly. From the man's expression, he judged that discovery was not far away.

"I think that dogs will always know their true master," he said, his voice ridiculously high and shaky. "You may have raised him as a cub, but as a dog he chose me, and I gave him his name. I suggest that we leave it to him to decide."

The assembled Rebels burst into laughter. "Leave the dog to decide? What foolishness is this!"

Yet their leader did not smile and his eyes rested on Arlo with a sad thoughtfulness. "You speak well, boy. Both of us have a claim on the animal, but no one may serve two masters, be he man or beast. I accept the challenge."

His heart pounding, Arlo backed away so that Rem was left sitting in the open circle, with the man standing at the other end. For a second his mind went back to the study at the Inn of Court and the deadly bargain that he had struck with the Regis for Rem's life. That bargain had ultimately been betrayed. Would this man also betray them both?

The man knelt down, so that he was on Rem's level, and made a soft, odd, clicking sound in his throat. Instantly Rem began to caper on the spot with excitement.

With a peculiar pain in his heart, Arlo watched as his dog sat, begged, rolled, fetched and played dead, caught pieces of dried meat as they were thrown at him, balanced pebbles on the bridge of his nose and offered his paw to be shaken. Deep within him, he knew that he had never trained Rem as rigorously, and it hurt him to see Rem's affection freely given to someone else. Often it had been all that he could do to make Rem walk to heel, though Rem never wilfully misbehaved, and in fact, Rem had taught him many of the games and tricks that he had played with him in the gardens of the Inn. Sighing, he knew that he had no authority to match that of the man. Yet even so he could not help but admire the Rebel, as far from using strength or intimidation to inspire Rem's obedience, he seemed to understand Rem completely, and his quiet commands were uttered in a voice so compelling, so fascinating, that even Arlo himself could not see how Rem could refuse. As he watched, Arlo realized that the Rebel wielded a power more than any that he possessed, for only something stronger than mere force could compel his troops to follow him for what was surely a fruitless cause. But even in his despair, a thought strengthened him.

I gave Rem his name. Surely he will remember that.

Arlo held his hands out, palms uppermost, and called Rem.

Rem's tail thumped on the ground, and he panted and grinned at the boy, but he made no move.

The man got to his feet and again made his gentle clicking noise. Rem's ears twitched, but again, he did not stir.

Arlo became aware that he was trembling all over.

Sweat ran down his back and pooled beneath his rough shirt. He was barely aware of the faces turned towards him. One thought rose above everything and drowned all else.

Please, Rem, please...

"Rem," he whispered softly. "Here, boy. Rem. Rem!"

Rem got to his feet, slightly stiffly, and stood uncertainly, looking from one to the other. The man's soft click echoed in the silence. Arlo's breath escaped from him in a quiet sob.

"Rem . . . here . . . *Rem. . .*"

And suddenly, in a flash, it was over. Rem wheeled around and pranced over to Arlo and reached up his forepaws as high as he could, his tail lashing. Arlo dropped to his knees, pulled Rem down and kissed the shaggy head in a blaze of happiness. As if from far away he could hear the Naturals exclaiming, and the soft click-click as the man sought to make Rem turn around, come back to him, but to no avail. Despite the tumult, Arlo's heart was perfectly at peace as he knelt, his arms around Rem's neck, and took deep breaths of relief.

I named him. He knows me. He chose me.

At that moment, Kira forced her way into the circle and stood protectively next to Arlo, putting her arm around his shoulders. The Rebel drew in his breath, and momentarily something like a flicker of pain passed across his confident features. To Arlo, watching, he suddenly seemed years younger, and equally unsure as Kira had been in front of the guardswoman at the edge of the forest. Again, there was a murmur of wonder as the Naturals took in the similarity of face and feature of the cousins, though changed in age and colouring. Across the man's face flashed dawning realization.

"Yes, Tambar," said Kira, as if answering the man's unspoken question. "This is my uncle Angus's child, Arlo."

Corin edged quietly through the ventilation shaft that opened out into the prison cells, and tuned his quick ears in to the voices within. It had not been easy to procure enough sleeping powder to put a full-sized Gemini to sleep, and all of the next day after his talk with the fair-haired girl he had needed to sit calmly in his room, hiding his excitement, as little by little Ivar's eyes had closed and his head had drooped on to his chest. Finally a deep rumbling snore had emerged from his servant's throat, and Corin had wasted no time in putting his plan into action. Deftly unhooking the key from the ring that hung around Ivar's belt, he had unlocked his bedroom door, slipped through, and locked it again from the outside.

That'll keep him quiet for a bit, he thought to himself with satisfaction. If Ivar awoke, then he would not kick up a fuss for some time, under threat of what would happen if anyone discovered that his master had tricked him.

Why exactly he had chosen to help the fair-haired girl he would, if questioned, have had no clear idea. But it was yet another way to strike back, to rebel against his father, against the Brigadier. Something had been unlocked within him once he had first tasted Emotions; the need for joy, excitement, happiness. He felt as if he had been living in a black-and-white world all his life, but with one breath, life had suddenly opened up a universe of colour. And also, though he did not even admit it to himself, the fear and anger forced upon him by his father were stronger reasons still.

Quietly, he peered through the grid at the scene within.

In the middle of the cell floor, the Brigadier towered over the other captive who had been brought in with the Gemini, strapped to a chair. The prisoner's face was bloodied and battered, and her arms were lashed behind her, but she still stared proudly at the ceiling as if her captor was of little importance.

"Do you confess, at last? That you, Talia, have been part of a secret plot against Genopolis for the last few years, that in the guise of a Circus gladiator you aided and abetted the Natural to escape from the City after your murder attempt against me?"

The gladiator laughed, and the forbidden sound echoed around the turret walls.

"Nice try, Hacker. You will get nothing out of me, *Captain*."

"Then if not," said the Brigadier silkily, drawing close

to her prisoner and breathing in her ear, "I will have no choice but to send you for Regeneration."

The other's expression did not change. "I am not a Natural, and the idea of death or Regeneration does not frighten me."

The Brigadier scowled, turning away and picking up a small vial from the table. Corin saw the deadly shimmer of its contents, and a sudden surge of the fear that he had felt during the Enquiry suddenly froze his stomach. "But what if I told you that you could *be* as a Natural, *feel* as a Natural, suffer emotions like them? How courageous would you be then?"

Talia sniffed. "I know that fear and grief are temporary. Citizens are made of stronger stuff."

"Citizen-born indeed, but your blood and bones still belong to us. You have lived amongst Naturals this past year. How would you like to become one yourself?"

Talia looked back at her, uncomprehending, as the Brigadier curled back her lip, showing her shattered, pointed teeth. "In the laboratories of the pharms we could send you for Regeneration. But then you would still tell us nothing, and we would be no better off. But if you were to undergo a procedure, say, if you were to be able to feel pain ... suffering ... grief ... loneliness ... *permanently* ... then perhaps you would feel differently?"

Talia's face paled, but she did not move as the Brigadier leaned closer, triumph glinting in her remaining eye. "Do you remember the injection that you took when you were still under my patronage during the Games? Do you remember what it was like?"

Talia closed her eyes and sighed. "The injection did not kill me the first time, Hacker, and it will not kill me now."

"But there is a lot of time to talk before dying," said the Brigadier maliciously, "and a lot of time to tell me where *they* are. And tell me you will, once I have made a Natural out of you."

Kira seized Arlo's wrist in an astonishingly painful grip and drew him away from the group of Rebels and towards the small grove of trees where he had left Kristo lying. Arlo could see that the Orphans had returned, and were now clustering around Ash, patting her admiringly and feeding her handfuls of bitter leaves, while a small campfire had already been lit.

"What on earth are you *doing*, Arlo? Whose is that dog?"

At that moment there was a sudden flurry of movement as Ozzie and Toby, their faces shadowed by hoods, pushed their way through the other Orphans, and threw themselves upon him.

"Arlo! Arlo, you're all right!"

"I'm fine," muttered Arlo, suffering Ozzie's rough hug, but it took all his strength to look into Toby's piteous pleading eyes, through his fractured glasses, as the younger boy tugged at his sleeve. He knew only too well what Toby was going to ask.

"And Usha, Arlo? Did you find Usha?"

Arlo shook his head, barely able to speak. "They – they took them, Toby. They took them back to Genopolis."

Ozzie drew in his breath with a hiss. "Took *them*? You mean—"

Arlo forced himself to speak with an effort. "They captured Talia also, and they . . . they killed Onofre."

His friends gazed at him, dumbstruck. But it was Toby's reaction that surprised Arlo the most. The child's eyes gleamed with sudden water, brimmed over, and a single tear trickled down his freckled cheek.

"They're – they're not takin' 'em back to the *Circus*, are they, Arlo?"

Arlo had never ever seen a Citizen cry before. "No, Toby," put in Kira comfortingly, quickly pulling the boy to her. "Don't think about it. They're gone now. We can't help them any more."

Ozzie blazed with a sudden Outbreak and wheeled upon her. "Don't *think* about her? Usha saved all our lives, and Talia and Onofre went back to save her, and you say don't *think* about 'em?"

Kira faced him down with a bitter expression. "You must learn to live with loss, Ozzie, when you are a Natural. You must get used to your friends disappearing. One day you wake up and your father is gone, the next day your mother, the next your own baby. If you tried to think about it, you would go mad. If I thought about everyone I had lost, I could not bear it. It is the only way."

Ozzie stood silent, dark and mutinous, as Arlo told

them of the search, of Onofre's last minutes, and of finding Kristo at the landing strip. The only time he roused himself was when Arlo spoke of meeting Rem and his tussle for mastery of the dog. Then he shook his head, sighing, with the ghost of a smile flickering around his sneering lip.

"Can't get rid of that mangy mongrel, can we? My old man used ter say that bad things happened in threes. Can't wait ter see what's comin' up next!"

There was a sudden stir, and Kira looked up sharply. At the edge of their circle, the rebel girl Liana had silently appeared, and stood calmly, waiting for them to finish their discussions.

Arlo felt a sudden shudder of warning. How long had she been there, and how much had she heard? Not for the first time he felt terribly aware of the responsibility of having so many Citizens amongst them. One false move, one careless word, and even the peace of the Meet would not serve to protect them. He bit his lip. There were too many enemies on either side, both known and unknown, and he felt his own clan, scattered and scavenging as they were, as an island adrift in a sea of warring tribes.

Liana bowed with mock ceremony as Kira rose to her feet. "I beg your pardon for my unseemly interruption, miss," she said before the other could speak. "My brother bids you to join him for tea in his tent in one hour. He wishes you bring to him the red-haired boy and the hound. That is the end of my message."

"Liana—" began Kira, but the haughty Rebel had

already departed. In the evening dusk, Arlo could see that his cousin's face was strangely flushed and her lips trembled with anger.

"Bids me join him for tea, indeed! Who does he think he is?"

Arlo bent over so that he could whisper unobtrusively in her ear. "Kira, listen. I think we should go. We can't afford to turn away friends. There are too few people here that are on our side."

Kira turned to face him and he was shocked to see the fierceness of her gaze.

"We will go, because we have little choice. But, be careful with this man, Arlo. There are many who have fallen under his spell, and many are the lives that have been lost in the following of him and his big ideas. For it is not just for gain that they follow him, it is because he possesses the ability to control hearts as well as minds. They follow him because they love him, Arlo." She blinked and Arlo could barely see the glint of tears in her eyes before she continued.

"They love him, and that is the tragedy of it. Be careful who you love, Arlo. For when you love, it will pass a chain around you that cannot be seen and cannot be broken, and you will find yourself doing things that you never believed that you were capable of, both good and evil." She paused and drew her cloak tighter around them both. "There are times that I think it might be no bad thing to be a Citizen."

*

Usha listened wordlessly as the boy finished relating his story. He was incoherent and confused, and several times she had to ask him to go back to iron out some detail that remained vague, but fairly soon the substance of it all became clear. Talia had been broken at last. Whatever the Brigadier had in the vials, it was a great power that could persuade even the strongest Citizen to confess whatever she wished to know. The thought of it made Usha rack her brains in consternation. Again she realized how much she relied on Talia's strength, both physical and mental. But to think of Talia, weak and sobbing in front of her enemy, struck her like a thunderbolt.

"You've no idea what it's like, Usha," the boy was gabbling nervously. "One day they found out I'd stolen one of the bottles, you see . . . I didn't know what it was, and when they found out, they. . ."

"And what else?" broke in Usha impatiently. If she didn't keep him on track he would come out with all sorts of irrelevant chatter. "What else did Talia say?"

"She told them all about Arlo. He's the Natural, isn't he? The red-haired boy, the one that had the dog?"

"That's right," said Usha calmly, though already she could see where this was leading. How much had Talia been made to tell them, and might the Brigadier already be on her way to attack Arlo and his clan?

"I saw him a couple of times," confessed the boy. "His dog got out at the Ceremony, and they took him away to the Circus. I would've liked to talk to him a bit. What's he like, Usha?"

"Arlo?" answered Usha in surprise. "He's. . ." For a moment, words failed her. "He's . . . he was my friend. The other Naturals didn't like me, but he did. . ."

Almost without realizing it, she found herself telling him everything. He hung on every word, asking questions, totally fascinated. Usha told him all about the Hunt, about Auntie, about Annis, and even about the bad dreams that haunted her, though she did not explain about her waking visions.

"I have nightmares too," said the boy softly. "I feel sometimes as if they are trying to tell me something."

"Perhaps they are," said Usha. "You just have to find out what they mean."

Finally the faint echoes of the Palace dinner gong put an end to the conversation, and immediately the boy said that he must go. He would try to come again the next day, and bring her some better food.

"Listen," he said as he was about to depart. "You mustn't blame your friend, Usha. Once Emotions get you, then there's nothing you can do."

"One day," said Usha grimly, "I'll make sure that the Brigadier gets a full dose of Emotions so that she knows exactly what it's like. She can't go round doing that to everybody."

"Oh, it wasn't the Brigadier that did that to me," replied the boy, as he got up and prepared to leave. "It was my father."

"Your *father*. . ." began Usha. Suddenly a terrible thought struck her. "What . . . what's your name?"

"My name's Corin, and my father's the Regis of Genopolis," answered the boy carelessly, and Usha heard the sound of his footsteps retreating down the corridor.

Left alone in the cell, Usha covered her face with her hands. What on earth had she *done*? Why on earth had she not asked him his name straight away? But she had confided in the son of the Regis, of all people! It must have been a trick, a subterfuge to get her to tell all she knew!

But then again, she reasoned desperately, the boy hadn't *seemed* as if he was part of a plot. In fact, he had appeared as if he were totally on her side. But why? Was it because of Emotions? What must Emotions be like, to cause you to turn against your own father?

At a loss to know what to do, she drew out the moonstone for comfort and stroked it. Whether it was because she was so bewildered, or else because of the fatigue or lack of food, the surface of the stone seemed to shimmer and disappear beneath her fingertips almost at once. At first she could not believe what she was looking at. Her eyes grew bigger and bigger, and her face paled.

Icy wind roared around Usha's ears and a thick blue mist swirled before her so that she could hardly see. Dimly, she could make out the flickering shapes of flames, but flames of a fire that burned like no other, as cold and blue as in the heart of a candle. She tried to struggle but she could not move. Her breath hung before her in a silver cloud.

Where was she?

She put her hands to her head, but her fingers touched only a prickly scalp.

Where had her hair gone?

In that moment, the mist parted. She gazed at the horrifying vision before her, wide-eyed, and was unable to scream.

FIVE

Night had fallen, and with it a new peace within the Meet. Within the encircling scrub of trees, a cluster of acrid-smelling but cheery campfires had sprung up, well-shaded against any roaming Citizen air-patrols. Here and there different tribal groups sprawled quietly, toasting small strips of meat or seed-potatoes over the glowing embers. Some of the wilder tribesmen had taken to drinking their strange fermented bark-juice (smelling something like chorley, thought Arlo) that caused hallucinations and torpor, and occasional outbreaks of either singing or fighting. But at that moment, most of the Meet lay bathed in calm, cheered by the spoils of barter, some with full bellies for the first time in a year.

Away from the main fires, a small tent had been rigged up against the low-lying branches of a tree, a green rope tying the front flaps together. Within this dark and scanty structure, illuminated by a single smoky candle, sat the Rebel leader, Tambar, with his sister, Liana, crouching suspiciously at his side, and in front of him, Kira, Kristo, Ozzie, Toby and Arlo.

Arlo had given an account of his life and escape from Genopolis with occasional additions from Kristo. In return, Tambar had told the story of how the Rebels had arranged to send animals into Genopolis by secret tunnels to spread confusion and disease amongst the Citizens. Rem lay with his head on Arlo's foot, not taking his eyes off his master for a second.

A bowl of acorn tea, drizzled with wild honey, was being passed around from hand to hand. Liana took the barest of possible sips before passing it to Kira, without looking at her. Tambar drank deeply before offering it to Kristo.

"It is strange that I share tea in my house with Citizens," he said slowly. "I have killed many of you before, and you in your turn have shown no mercy towards my people. I accept you because you come here under the protection of Kira and her family, but otherwise I would not tolerate it."

"Not all Citizens are like the soldiers," said Kristo calmly. "There are many people in Genopolis who are against the Rulers and were actively seeking to overthrow them."

Tambar leaned forward, interest flickering in his green eyes. "Others, you say? Within Genopolis?"

"There were," replied Kristo. "But they are all dead now, or in prison, or sentenced to Regeneration. We few are the only ones who escaped, in one way or another."

Arlo, who had been listening in wonder to the guerrilla captain, suddenly burst out. "But what are *you* doing, sir, at the Meet?"

The man smiled grimly. "We are the Rebels, boy, born in the Cause and dedicated to fighting for a better world. Here at the Meet, instead of food, we barter ideas, hopes, desires and wishes that the world can be changed. We recruit men and women who have lost their tribes and will lose nothing but their lives in our service. We attack Citizen convoys and lay explosives underneath their feet. We ambush their soldiers and steal their arms. We are captured, tortured and executed, and every day our comrades disappear, but still there come more to take their place. Every day we wake to hopelessness and despair, every day we keep making plans, and every day the City is no closer to falling."

But despite the man's grim words, his tone seemed almost merry and the candlelight flickered in his smiling eyes. His powerful hands rested, palms up and open on his crossed legs, and Arlo found himself marvelling both at the man's physique, his broad shoulders and deep chest, and his indomitable spirit, the way he could talk of death, suffering and despair with lightness and hope. For the first time in many days, he found himself thinking about his father, and secretly wondering – *wishing* – whether he had been anything like the man before him.

"The trouble with Naturals is this," said Tambar. "We spring from a thousand different mothers, we worship different gods, we speak many dialects. Each of us has our little patch of land to defend, our own babies to feed, our own enemies to escape from. But within the Cause, all things are equal. The Cause is greater than the individual. Any enemy of Genopolis is our friend, even if he killed our own father yesterday."

"And even though he be a Citizen himself?" asked Kristo quietly.

Tambar smiled. "I see that you understand me. To join the Cause means to put aside all differences against the greater enemy. No man may bring his history to this fight. He must leave everything that he was behind, the moment he binds himself with the green rope.

"I am offering you a chance to join us. Together we could form such an alliance as Genopolis would never expect! You have skills that we do not have, and we both share the same wish."

Arlo's heart leapt in hope. At last! After all this time, he had finally come across one man who thought as he did. And Tambar was a real leader, he thought, confident and brave, full of conviction and passion. But why had Kira never told him of Tambar before? Why had she left him in the belief that there was no hope? He shot a sneaky glance towards his cousin and was momentarily confounded by the look on his cousin's face. Instead of regarding the speaking Tambar, she was gazing at Kristo, where he sat poised opposite the Rebel.

The difference between the two men, so similar in age, one rugged and scarred, the other fine-featured and clear-boned, was remarkable. Her lips moved slightly and only Arlo, sitting next to her, half-caught what she was saying.

"As the ghost in the night, with the tripwire, the poison, the silent arrow, with these things you may fight them."

Arlo nudged his cousin sharply. Since they had entered the tent, she had seemed dreamy and faraway, taking little part in the discussions.

"Yet I counsel you," said Kristo, speaking in the same calm tone that he had used throughout, "to attack against the City of Genopolis in the way that you have been doing, will prove fruitless. You have many, but they have more. You may shoot, and snipe, and lay explosives, but they are expendable; you are not. Since Arlo escaped the City last year they have been searching. They have eyes that you do not know, they have more information on your movements than you would think. They knew where the settlement was to be found. Only you will waste more blood, more lives, and as you say, the City is no closer to falling."

"Then what would you advise?" asked Tambar, and Arlo noticed with admiration that there was no arrogance or ridicule in his tone. He leaned forward as if almost to touch the Citizen, his eyes intent.

"You would turn your troops to greater advantage if you attack the pharms," said Kristo thoughtfully. "Pharmopolis is an island once the Rains come, and it is the weak spot in the design of Genopolis. Capture their food supplies, and you will soon have the City at your mercy."

"But Pharmopolis is a thousand miles around!" snapped Liana. "It is a fortress, surrounded by open sea and vicious rocks! And within its walls the scientists have created monsters and beasts more hideous than we can imagine! Do you think we have not thought of that? How could we ever take it?"

"I don't know," replied Kristo mildly, "but there must be a way. We should not act in haste. We should turn our brains, not our bodies to account."

"I agree," said Kira unexpectedly, speaking up for the first time. "Genopolis is too strong a fortress, and since my grandmother Ira died in the rebellion, I have known the waste of human life in acting without thinking."

"Your grandmother was an inspiration," said Tambar humbly. "Even now, the mark of Ira is given to those who attain great honour in the service of the Cause. Though your clan is despised by some, the Rebels know her worth."

Kira smiled, and quietly, so that no one could see it but Arlo, she moved her hand slightly, so that her fingers were resting on the back of Kristo's neck, touching the small streak of fair hair at the nape where the bitter dye had not darkened it.

But Tambar had seen it too. Instantly, black jealousy leapt from the green eyes, and he recoiled as if he had been slapped. Quickly, Kira pulled her hand back but it was too late. The others, sensing the change of atmosphere but not its cause, looked round in confusion. Gathering herself together, Kira rose abruptly, and with her, the Citizens and Arlo. Rem staggered to his feet, sneezing.

"I thank you for your hospitality," said Kira quickly. "We will think over your offer and meet again."

Tambar did not reply. Instead his eyes, narrowed almost to slits, followed Kristo as the Citizen left the tent after Kira. Arlo dithered, torn between wanting to follow his cousin and the realization that the spell had been broken. Exactly what had happened he was not quite sure, but he felt strongly that the fellowship that they had begun to forge with the Rebels now lay in pieces at their feet, and that the one man who might provide an answer to his questions was already turning away from him.

As the canvas of the tent shut behind him, he could hear Liana's voice raised in outrage.

"Are you happy now? Not content until she humiliates you once again? I swear, I don't know what ails you! There are a thousand prettier women than her, a thousand truer hearts than hers. You will be an old man soon, Tambar – you are almost thirty! You should have a woman and children of your own, not still be running after a filthy traitor, a pirate, a. . ."

Arlo could listen no more. Dumbly, he set off after the others, feeling as if he had been on the brink of something new and exciting, which after the first bright blaze of hope had suddenly dulled into the bitter ashes of the dying campfire.

Usha sat dazed, lost in time and space. How many hours had passed, how much had been revealed before her eyes, she did not know.

Before her rose a towering mountain, cloven in two as if cracked through the middle by a mighty fist, and lashed on each side with spray from a pounding sea. And from the midst of the mountain marched a great army, but an army strange and terrible, formed of creatures that Usha had never seen before. Hideous and grotesque, formed of monsters with the heads of beasts; of men and women distorted by misshapen limbs, or with copious arms and legs that sprouted unnaturally from their bodies, followed by other things that seemed neither human nor animal, nameless, faceless. . .

"No!" screamed Usha. "Don't make me go back there! Please!"

An urgent tapping broke through into her consciousness, and the vision snapped and fizzled into darkness as if it had never been. For a moment, bewildered, she fancied she was back in the Regions with the fire-speckled shadows leaping on the walls of the catacombs. The next second she was fully awake and realizing that it was the deep of night in her cell, the flickering light of a waxen candle was streaming through the bars, and a familiar voice was hissing her name.

"Corin!" gasped Usha, struggling to her feet. "What are you doing? What time is it?"

The boy pressed his face against the bars, and for the first time, Usha saw the marks of Emotion etched deep into his face.

"Nearly midnight. Usha, listen. I'm afraid I've got bad news."

Usha gave a start and Onofre's amulet clattered abruptly to the ground, as instantly the dream became clear to her with an awful meaning.

"They're sending me back to the pharms, aren't they?"

"How do you know?" gasped Corin, and Usha shook her head. "I just – I just *know* these things, Corin. They'll send me for Regeneration."

"But that's not the worst, Usha," muttered the boy. "I've seen Minotaurs and Gorgons and awful monsters from there. There's terrible punishments that they can do to you there if you have Emotions. And there's awful Experiments to turn you into a Natural, or . . . worse. . ."

Another, deeper voice came from behind the door.

"Master, we have to go! If we're caught here—"

Immediately, Usha threw herself against the shadow of the wall so that she could not be seen. "Who's *that*?" she hissed sharply.

"Oh, shut up, Ivar," returned Corin's voice irritably. "Hold your tongue if you don't want me to tell my father about you falling asleep the other day. . ."

"What's going on, Corin?" pressed Usha. "Who *is* that?"

Corin sighed. "It's all right, Usha, it's only my manservant. He's a Gemini too. Listen. We have to decide what to do. . ."

Usha warily eyed what little she could see of him through the bars. Could she trust him? Now the realization that he was the son of the Regis came back to haunt her. What did he have to gain, risking all to visit a condemned prisoner in jail? And to bring his servant with him, at a time like this!

"Master," came the voice again. "Master, I can hear footsteps. . ."

Corin pressed his face against the bars. "Usha, listen. There's a key. I don't know how to get it, but Ivar knows, don't you, Ivar?" There was a brief pause. "Yes you *do*, and you're going to get it for me, aren't you?"

"Master, please. I can't. . ."

"Yes you are. Otherwise. . ."

The boy's tone was threatening. Usha grasped the bars with both hands. "But, Corin. . ."

Now the footsteps were so loud that all of them could hear. A door clanged. The next instant, both Corin and the Gemini had disappeared. Usha stood transfixed, waiting as the footsteps rounded the corner, clean and crisp, as of iron-heeled boots on stone. She could hear another, staggering tread accompanying it, as of feet manacled together. The bolt of the door slammed back, and outlined in the lantern light Usha could see the hideous face of the Brigadier, and next to her, a crumpled shadowy figure in chains. For a moment, in a sudden surge of hope, she thought it must be Talia, and started forward. The next minute she stood transfixed, staring at the face of a man she had not seen since her imprisonment in the Circus. . .

At the prompt of the Brigadier's truncheon, the man moved forward into the light, his feet bound. One sleeve was hanging loose and empty, and his remaining arm was bound to his side. His top hat had long gone, and his lank hair was streaked with grime. The bright clothes of the Circus hung around him in tatters, but the mood of arrogance was unchanged, and the sneer as he looked down at her was unmistakable.

"Long time no see, eh, Blondie?" said Ringmaster Mephisto Merco.

Arlo lay in a dark dream without light. Somewhere in the Inn of Court they were throwing books on the bonfire that surrounded him, and one of those was his own. Crying out, he rolled over and woke with a start in a patch of thorny plants, Toby wriggling out from underneath him.

"You're squashing me! Listen, Arlo, I can't sleep. I keep thinking about Usha, I keep imagining—"

"Me too," cut in Ozzie impatiently from where he lay curled up underneath a bramble-bush. "There's her and Talia locked up in Genopolis, and old Onofre in the ground, and we're on the bleedin' run surrounded by a bunch of crazies who'd kill us the next second if they only knew who we were."

"Look," muttered Arlo, with an uneasy glance at the sleeping forms huddled around them. "We can't talk here. Let's find somewhere private."

Together they crawled out of the clump of bushes where they had spent the night and picked their way towards the centre of the wood, where a rise of higher ground gave way to scrubland. Morning was filtering through the trees, grey and cheerless, with a white mist that caught at their lungs and made them cough. Wet smudges of cloud above the treetops spoke of more rain to come, and Arlo felt an ache that he was not accustomed to in his bones. Rem panted and sneezed at his heels, and he worried that the dog might have caught the ague too.

A clear trickling sound alerted them to a small running brook that, swollen by the previous rains, made the surrounding grass marshy and chill. Without discussion they splashed cold water on their faces and hands and drank deeply.

"Right," said Ozzie in his matter-of-fact way as soon as they were clear of the camp. "I don't like things one bit. You know I never wanted to come 'ere, and I wouldn't have if I'd had my way, because we left Nanda and Mindie and everyone back home without anyone to look after 'em. And now it's all gone from bad to worse. That cousin of yours is all right, but there's a lot of others who don't wish us well and just want shot of us. That Rebel bloke last night, though, he seemed to have the right idea, and I'm going crazy just sitting here doin' nothin'."

"I don't understand why they hate Usha so much," added Toby soberly. "I just want her and Talia back."

Arlo bit his lip in indecision. "But you heard what they said. Genopolis is a fortress. There's no getting out or in. And Tambar doesn't want to team up with Kristo any more, that's for sure. Things are all just so complicated."

"*Things* ain't complicated, it's you Naturals who're complicated!" began Ozzie roundly, then broke off short. "Eh – what's that? There, in the water?"

Arlo turned around. The stream had broadened out next to where they were sitting, and past them floated a series of great, flat white flowers, some almost as big as a soup-plate, with waxy petals and pale stamens. Since the Heat, Arlo had not seen one single flower in the Regions, and their sudden appearance, like glossy pearls on a rippling necklace, surprised him. Leaning forward, he reached for one.

"Do not touch them," said a voice. "They are the souls of the departed. Let them be."

Annis, the young Natural girl from the Orphan tribe, sat opposite them on a stone, nursing her child.

"What do you want?" snarled Arlo angrily. "Why are you spying on us?"

"I heard you talking about Usha," said Annis evenly, patting her child on the back. "She saved my baby."

Ozzie shifted nastily at Arlo's side. "Well, it's a pity no one feels the same about her, ain't it? Reckon she could do with some gratitude around here."

But Annis seemed unmoved. "I am sorry about Usha," she said. "Come with me. I want to show you something."

Arlo looked at Ozzie, who shrugged. "Let's have a look then. Seeing as how nobody can have a chat in private around here any more."

Annis led the way around to where the stream ran out from a rocky pile of stones. As they neared the top, Arlo realized that they were not the only ones awake at this early hour. Through the pale mist he could see a ghostlike procession of white-draped figures. Rem bridled at the sight, his hackles rising, and Arlo patted him nervously, not only to soothe his pet but also to seek reassurance for himself. Something about the appearance of the figures chilled him, and it was not only the cold. "What is this?" he asked sharply. "Where are you taking us?"

"It is the dance of the departed," answered Annis, watching the forms as they threaded their way back and forth in an eerie, wraith-like fashion. "They mourn those that have disappeared, those they have loved, and for each lost soul they send a flower down the river."

As she spoke, one of the figures came forward. Arlo saw that her face – for the dancers were all Natural women – was covered so that he could not see if she was young or old. Turning towards them, she held out a basket that was covered with the pale blooms and offered it to them.

"Take some," said Annis. "Take one for the old man, one for the warrior-girl, and another for the Gemini. It will bring you peace."

Arlo picked up three flowers. Their touch was icy, for they had been plucked from the pool around the brook's mouth only moments before. He looked at Ozzie, who shrugged, nonplussed.

"Go on," encouraged Toby.

Leaning over the brook, Arlo cast the first blossom on to the water. It floated downstream before it joined the procession of flowers snaking their way down the river and through the mist.

That's for Onofre, thought Arlo, and glancing at the faces of his friends, he could read the same thought on all of them. How many more flowers would they send down the river? There was Usha, there was Talia, Ignatius, Benedict, there was ... his mother, his father. . . How long would it go on? His eyes prickled, and his hand trembled as he held out the second flower over the stream, *Usha's flower*.

"Arlo?" said Toby, his face puzzled. "What's wrong?"

But something inside Arlo would not let him cast the blossom into the water. His arm wavered and fell back. Instead, he turned and pressed the remaining flowers back into the arms of the woman beside him.

"No. Keep them. I don't need them yet."

The Brigadier's eyes met Usha's expressionlessly. "On your feet."

Usha shook her head. "What? Where are you taking me?"

"No questions," spat the Brigadier, and Usha noticed how she pushed the Ringmaster forward roughly so that he stumbled with his bound feet and fell against the rocky wall of the passageway. Usha watched soberly. Though Merco had treated her cruelly enough when she had been under his power in the Circus, she took no satisfaction in his punishment.

The Brigadier smirked. "Come here, Gemini."

With no other choice, Usha moved forward and stood in a daze as the Brigadier manacled her ankles in front of Merco. All she could think of was Corin's face as he said his last goodbye and darted off into the blackness. Where was she being taken, and would the Brigadier bring her back? If Corin risked everything to bring her the key, and she was not there. . .

"Move!" snarled the Brigadier, and Usha moved off, feeling the drag of the chains on her ankles and the stench of Merco's breath enveloping her from behind. Twisting into the depths of the turret, the passageway was dark and dripping, and proved a perilous path to follow. Usha found it hard to move without tripping, as her feet moved at different times to Merco's, and as they clumsily started to descend a staircase, she frequently had to clutch at the wall for support.

"This is all your fault, Blondie," muttered Merco evilly in her ear, as they made their uncomfortable way along. "You wait till I get you alone, and then you'll be sorry."

Despite the impotence of Merco's Outbreak under the heavy chains that bound him, Usha realized with a shudder that nothing would prevent him from carrying out his threat, if he had the chance. If only the Brigadier would not put her in a cell alone with her old tormentor!

Summoning up all her wits, Usha turned her head so she could murmur to Merco undetected by the Brigadier, who strode behind them both, evidently taking no chances with her prisoners. Her only hope was to calm him down, gain some information. . .

"But why is it my fault?" she whispered. "What have you got to do with all this?"

Merco snorted. "'Cos you were in the Circus, weren't you, and then you run off with that Natural boy that they were looking for."

"But why have they imprisoned you, though?"

"Because *She*'s after him, isn't she? *She* thinks it's all a plot that we're all in together. Everyone who's ever come within twenty metres of that boy has been rounded up and charged with treason. I'd never seen that little rat before, but the minute he comes rolling down into my Circus, the whole show gets cancelled. I tried to tell her that, but she even had my left arm pulled off to see if I was a Natural or not! She said I was a traitor! Infecting the masses with Emotions by letting them watch a Circus! My whole life, my business, my whole reputation! Destroyed because of that dirty little Natural!"

Usha remained silent, unmoved by Merco's speech. A

business such as the Circus, which had thrived on the blood of others, whether Natural or Citizen, was in her view well deserving of destruction. Yet it was more important that she try to get Merco on her side. With an unfamiliar cunning, she realized that she could only succeed if she offered him something to his advantage. But what?

"Listen, Merco," she hissed back cautiously. "I didn't know the . . . dirty little Natural either. He's to blame for getting us both into this. I promise you, if we ever get out of this, I'll hand him over to you, and you can do what you like with him."

Merco grunted scornfully. "We ain't ever getting out of this, Blondie. Do you know where they're taking us now?"

But at that moment, they reached the bottom of the staircase, and two armoured guards threw wide a pair of metal gates. From within came a terrible stench of unwashed Citizens and a babble of many voices yelling. Over the noise rose a harsh, rhythmic thud, as of heavy stone crashing down against stone. *Boom*.

Usha almost forgot the presence of her sullen enemy at her back as they hobbled forward into a huge vaulted chamber, windowless and airless, hung with the scarlet flags and tapestries of Genopolis and flanked with courtiers holding scented handkerchiefs to their noses. The Brigadier stationed herself at the back, arms folded.

Boom. At the far end of the chamber stood a huge iron gate, wickedly spiked, and on each point were impaled shapeless, dripping things that Usha could not recognize. Along the centre of the chamber wound a long file of people from which the smell was rising, in such a state as no respectable Citizen would ever have been seen in. Dirty and unkempt, pale as if they had not seen the sun for many months, some with their hands or wrists bound, others with arms missing, but each with their feet shackled like Usha's; men and women alike. Though all present seemed to be Citizens, the air was alive with shouting, weeping, entreaties, as if the long-forbidden Outbreaks had finally come to the surface now that the Citizens had nothing else to lose. Pressed with Merco into the end of the line of prisoners, Usha's feet were bound to those of the thin, curly-haired girl in front of her. She could see no one whose face she knew, and though she scanned the room desperately, she could see no trace of Talia.

Boom. The heavy thud rang out again, but Usha could not see what was causing it. At the far end of the room rose an enormous stone pillar, draped in a flag, behind which a thin, hawk-eyed man was standing. A heavy padded ceremonial robe, deep crimson in colour, fell heavily over his shoulders and rose to a peaked hood behind his head. His black hair was sparse and framed his narrow face and pinched eyes. Though his expression was impassive and his demeanour deathly still, his long white hands were in a state of continual, almost nervous movement, the bony fingers plucking unceasingly at the embroidered flag in front of him, and shredding the delicate needlework viciously to pieces.

For a sudden blinding second, Usha thought that the scissor-man had returned from the dead and come to pass judgement over her, for the man was like him in colouring and bearing. Then as the mist cleared, she realized that it was not him, and decided that it must be the Regis, though she clearly remembered Arlo telling her that the Regis had no hair. On closer examination, she knew that it could not be, as the man bore no trace of Corin in his features or manner. By the style of his dress, he seemed to be of high importance, and the neighbouring courtiers cowered before him, but she could still find no clue as to his identity. As the queue of prisoners edged slowly forward, jumbled and indistinct, Usha could hear the man proclaiming over the hubbub.

"Tariq Atir and Sasha Abramovitch, merchants of Pharmopolis. Guilty of treason in the first degree. Sentenced to Regeneration."

Boom. The heavy thud echoed around the chamber again, and this time Usha could see that it came from a huge stone hammer, suspended from the rafters by means of a great pulley, and wielded by two sweating Gemini. After every pronouncement by the man, the Gemini heaved the hammer up and let it fall with a resounding thump, and after every stroke there was a groan as the prisoners were ushered away by the waiting guards through the great gate that towered evilly above them.

"Tutu Abadwe and Tarissa El-Samir. Professors of the Academy. Guilty of treason in the first degree. Sentence: Regeneration."

Boom. After every sentence, the queue shuffled forward, and yet another prisoner was hauled before the judge. The heat thickened from the press of bodies around her, and the red flags swayed before Usha's eyes until the entire scene seemed to pulse like a beating heart. Behind her, she could hear Merco muttering incoherently.

"This is it, Blondie. Traitor's Gate. Nobody who passes beneath it ever comes back."

Boom. "Yoshi and Yuma Ikinowa. Scientists. Guilty of grand treason, and sentenced to Regeneration for their crimes."

Usha became aware that the curly-haired woman in front of her was weeping bitterly, her thin shoulders heaving. Still unused to seeing tears on the face of a Citizen, Usha shuffled uncomfortably.

"Are you all right?" she whispered, but the woman seemed inconsolable. "Do you need help?"

The woman shook her head, almost fiercely, and her words were so distorted by frantic sobs that Usha could hardly hear her. "It is all lost," she stammered, between bouts of weeping. "It is all over."

Boom. "Sir Herbert Brasenose, former Lawlord of the City of Genopolis. On charges of treason: guilty. On charges of aiding and abetting a Natural: guilty. On charges of Love and Emotion. . ."

But a great bellow arose from the front of the prison-band, and craning forward, Usha could see the figure of an elderly yet burly man, struggling powerlessly against the guards who had come to lead him away.

"My children!" the man was crying. "Let me say farewell to my children! They have nothing to do with this!"

But the face of the judge was inexorable, watching as the soldiers dragged him away. The woman in front of her wept hopelessly. Even Merco cursed at the sight.

Usha gazed around helplessly. Most of the Citizens present appeared to be losing their minds. For a second she doubted the wisdom of bringing Natural feelings back into the lives of Citizens. How powerful could Emotions be, that they caused one to behave like this? How could they ever hope to triumph over a race whose minds and bodies were so much stronger than they?

But her concern was nothing to what happened next. With an armed guard each side of him, a gaunt figure dressed in the filthy remnants of a gown of the Inn of Court, his face deeply lined and his hair touched with white, was marched up to the dais. His beard had grown ragged and clods of matted blood hung about his face. He stood, crumpled and drooping, in front of the Lawlord as he was announced.

"Professor Ignatius Bonaventura, Doctor of the Inn of Court."

*

Tambar was shaving inside his tent when Arlo arrived at a run with Ozzie and Toby in tow. Unusually for a Natural, who out of necessity and warmth usually wore beards, he had covered his cheeks with hog-fat and was scraping it off with a wickedly-sharp knife. Although he had not been expecting them, he did not look particularly surprised as a reluctant Liana, after first sharply attempting to turn them away, finally opened the tent flap and showed them in.

"We've come to join the Rebels," said Arlo breathlessly.

Liana let out a snort of laughter. "Rebels indeed! Three boys and not a decent set of eyes or limbs between you!" Her eyes rested contemptuously on Toby's withered hand and cracked spectacles, and Ozzie's missing eye.

But Tambar did not laugh. He merely laid down the knife, and reached for his shirt, for he was stripped to the waist, and again Arlo noted the sheer physical strength of the rounded muscles of his arms and back as he moved. As he dressed, he eyed them a little sadly.

"I do not train children to die," he said softly. "My offer was to your cousin and the other Citizen. But our paths do not lie in the same direction. I see that now."

"Hang on! I'm nearly nineteen!" protested Ozzie.

"Nevertheless," answered Tambar shortly, opening the tent for them to leave, "recruitment is over for this season."

Arlo pulled the flap shut again. "Listen," he said

urgently. "We have a plan. Kristo was right about one thing. We can't storm Genopolis. But we could get inside with a small group. We know – or at least Ozzie knows – the way out of the City, and he knows all about the underground paths there. We escaped on a boat, and we could return on one too. And if we could get in there, get inside the Palace. . ."

Tambar looked at him, and for a second Arlo saw the bright blaze of excitement leap up in his eyes as it had last night, although his face remained stern and guarded.

"I'm listening," he said.

An unexpected Outbreak of Hope coursed through Usha as, heedless of the effect she was causing, she waved and shouted over the crying crowd towards the bedraggled Doctor as he stood before the judgement chair. Here was the man who had brought Arlo up at the Inn of Court! Here was the leader of the Resistance! If only she could reach him!

"Ignatius! Ignatius!"

But the noise was so great that Ignatius did not, or would not hear her. Instead he raised his head with a calm that Usha could not help but admire in his pitiful, degraded state. Around the chamber the tumult grew to such an extent that the guards were forced into action, and set about the prisoners with their sharp pikes. Blood flowed and presently it was quiet enough for Ignatius's voice to be heard. Yet despite his demeanour, Usha could see that the marks of strain were set deeply into

Ignatius's face, and he trembled as he spoke, though his voice did not waver.

"So it has come about, Lawlord Kane. You have been set in judgement over me. I do not expect mercy from you, but even less do I wish it."

Kane's twitching fingers paused momentarily and the tiny eyes glittered coldly. "Professor Ignatius. How have you been finding your experience of Emotions? I hear that you cried like a Natural baby when the Brigadier showed you what Fear was. And how you begged to be spared when you first experienced Grief? Do you still persist in your belief that such Emotions are vital and necessary for the health of Genopolis?"

Ignatius paused, and Usha could see the struggle that was going on inside him. His jaw quivered and his fingers clenched momentarily as if reliving some old agony. Yet he still faced Kane with as much dignity as he could muster.

"There are many Emotions other than those which you choose to torture us with," he said at length. "And it is to your shame that you deny your Citizens the ones most beautiful, in order to spare them of those which can destroy."

Kane sneered in what seemed like triumph. "It is my duty to sentence you in my position of Lawlord and defender of Genopolis. You have been the leader of the Resistance Circle within the City, and you have harboured a Natural within its walls. Therefore, for the good of all Genopolis, I sentence you to Naturalization."

A shocked murmur spread through the crowd. Kane took a step forward, his beady eyes glinting delightedly. "As someone who has long wished to bring Pain back to the Citizens, now you will be given that desired gift yourself. Our scientists have perfected a procedure to create Naturals out of Citizens, so that they can now experience Pain, Suffering and Despair, all those beautiful feelings that you crave so much. . ."

The woman in front of Usha wailed loudly, stretching out her hand as if to touch Ignatius, who, however, seemed unmoved by the Lawlord's threats.

". . .And once the procedure is complete, a sentence of execution shall be passed upon you, in such a manner as befits your crimes. You shall be hung, drawn and quartered. Firstly, you shall be hanged by the neck until you are almost dead—"

Involuntarily, Usha put her hand out to try to calm the woman down, but she was inconsolable. "Ssssh," murmured Usha, stroking her arm as she had often seen Natural mothers do to their children. "Ssssh. Please. Don't lose hope."

But Kane's next words seemed indeed to suck all belief from the assembled prisoners. "Then you shall be taken down, your stomach shall be sliced open, centimetre by centimetre, and your entrails pulled out in front of your eyes. When you are dead, you shall be cut into pieces, your body burned into ashes, and scattered to the four winds so that your heresy and treason shall never contaminate the pure Citizens of Genopolis."

Throughout Kane's speech, Ignatius had not flinched, and as the heavy hammer fell down with a crash, he stood unbending, and seemed to pull himself together with a great effort.

"You may torture my body, Kane, you may destroy my bones so that all trace of me is struck from this earth, but the truth you will never be able to erase. Others will come after me, Kane, who hold the same ideas as I do, that can pursue the same ideals that I have started. Yet though you grind us into dust and mix us into the sands of the Regions, you cannot alter one indisputable fact. The Circle has still succeeded in the most important thing, that Arlo the Natural boy is safe and beyond your reach."

Kane's eyebrows shot up so that his tiny eyes bulged white like marbles against the sallowness of his skin. "Indeed?" he hissed. "Then mark this."

From the pocket of his gown he produced a muddy object, almost unidentifiable under its crust of dirt and sand. "Do you recognize it?"

Ignatius gazed at it without comment, but it was instantly familiar to Usha, who pushed forward with a horrified gasp, her breath almost taken away.

"It is the book of your Circle, Ignatius, that the Maian Abbess Binah Solomon gave to the Natural before you arranged for his escape from the Inn of the Maia. Our soldiers captured it when they ambushed and eradicated a group of Naturals scavenging near to the Western Regions. They called themselves the Orphans, I believe. Formerly known as Region Three."

Despite himself Ignatius moved with a cry as if to seize it, but it was swept from his reach by the Lawlord, who raised it triumphantly above his head.

"The boy is dead, Ignatius! The Circle has failed! Face your own death – for it will be a long time in coming, though in the end you will beg for it!"

Usha saw the look of despair as it swept across Ignatius's face, more hopeless than she had ever seen on the face of a Citizen before. In the sudden uproar that followed Kane's disclosure, Ignatius, moving as one already dead, was marched away; not under the Gate, but back towards the Palace, as the wails of the Citizens echoed around the chamber.

"No!" screamed Usha. "He's not dead! Ignatius! He's not dead!"

A vicious club from behind her brought her back to reality. "Shut up, Blondie! One more yell out of you, and they'll stick your head up there on the Gate with the other Gemini! You want to die right now, or give yourself a few days more?"

Usha looked up and saw to her horror the objects that studded the spikes of the Gate were heads of lower-caste Gemini, perhaps the servants of the condemned traitors, cruelly hacked off at the neck and impaled upon the wickedly sharp ironwork. Blind eyes, white and rolling, or dimmed and crusted with blood, gazed down at her. A sense of revulsion grew upon Usha such as she had never felt, even helpless on the Operating table beneath the scissor-man, or in the wild savagery of the Regional

Hunt. She stood transfixed, unable to move. Merco coughed and spat.

"Better hope that they sentence you to Regeneration, Blondie, otherwise you won't even be getting through the Gate alive."

Many hours later Arlo, Ozzie and Toby left Tambar's tent, each with the green rope of the Rebels tied around his waist. The morning had been spent in performing oaths, in learning the codes of the Cause, and in forming a plan of campaign. Even Liana, as soon as she had resigned herself to her brother's decision, had thrown herself into their training with enthusiasm. Already they had learned the Rebels' system of bird-calls and hand-signals, signifying warning, attack, retreat or silence. Though his head was buzzing after many hours of whistling and memorizing gestures, as Arlo stepped out into bright sunlight he felt as if he was at last on the right path, and when his eyes met Ozzie's, he knew that at last he had conquered his fear.

They were going to rescue Usha.

But the next second his new-found ardour abruptly disintegrated as he felt a furious box on his ears. Stars wheeled around his eyes and he staggered. Kira stormed up behind him and wrenched him away from the tent.

"What are you doing! Take that rope off! Get away from him!" (This to Tambar, who had emerged from the tent and stood looking sullenly at her.) "Arlo! I had no idea what had *happened* to you this morning! I thought you had been kidnapped, or killed, or . . . *worse*!"

"Kira, stop it!" Arlo shouted back. "I'm sick of this! I'm sick of running, of hiding! I have to do something for a change! Can't you understand?"

"But you're not yet thirteen!" blazed Kira. "You're still just a boy! You're the last member of my family and I'm not letting you go anywhere!"

It was all too much for Arlo. "You're a coward, Kira!" he screamed. "A coward, a scavenger, a pirate! You're scared, you're weak, but I'm not going to be like you!" For a moment, as he searched for words, one of the oaths of the Rebels suddenly came back to him. "I'm a Rebel now! My past life is over! I'm not scared of losing anything! Not even my life!"

Pulling himself away, he ran blindly from her, away from all of them, down along the riverbank towards the other camps of Naturals. Rem bounded at his heels, and he heard Ozzie and Toby calling for him. Through the hubbub he could hear Kira screeching wildly at Tambar.

"Your words in his mouth! He never spoke like that before! What have you *done* to him?"

But as Arlo pushed his way through a small thicket of trees, his foot slipped on a tussock of grass, and he tripped into the clearing beyond, and on to something grey and stinking. Crawling up on his knees, he could see that he had fallen on a pile of skins, spread out on the grass as if to make a great carpet, and from each pelt, a shaggy, long-toothed wolf-head grinned sightlessly back at him.

His heart pounding, Arlo struggled to his feet, but it was too late. A group of surly, straggle-haired men sat cross-legged in front of him, grey skins draped over their shoulders, and before them, a large man, heavy boned and dull-eyed, bald and swathed in a dark robe. Even though almost a year had passed since they had seen each other, during which the man had become fatter and the boy taller, recognition was instantaneous.

For a moment they stared at each other, too amazed to speak. Then Goren got slowly to his feet. One of his tribe, a thickset, surly-looking man, pointed excitedly.

"I told you he was here! He came in with the Orphan girl!"

Goren's eyes bulged. "You?" he hissed, in a voice that was all the more terrifying for its quietness. "*You?*"

Rem yipped and planted himself snarling before the Wolf-men. Arlo staggered backwards through the trees, and collided with Ozzie, who had been running after him. Ozzie stumbled, and instantly they were sprawling again at the Wolf-men's feet. Goren roared in fury, and sprang forward, his drinking horn upraised like a club.

"The dead-flesh will not escape me again!"

Arlo threw himself against Ozzie and buried his head in his friend's shoulder. But the expected blow never fell. Suddenly a shout broke out behind Arlo, and the next moment the small clearing was full of people. Goren's horn quivered, poised above his head. There was a flash of green as Tambar and Liana burst through the trees, leapt over the boys and positioned themselves protectively by the growling dog.

"Let them alone, Wolf-man! Remember the peace of the Meet!"

"Rebel, I have no quarrel with you," ground out Goren in his thick accent. "This is an old score that I have to settle. It is none of your business."

"If you quarrel with Arlo, then you quarrel with a fellow-Rebel," answered Tambar dryly. "Look around you, Goren. You are outnumbered. Do you really want to trouble us?"

Goren's bleary eyes took in the stern faces of the Rebels as they pressed into the clearing and formed four well-drilled lines. Against such a sight, Goren's tribe looked ragged and undisciplined. For a moment, his brutal expression appeared to soften, and after a moment's pause, he stepped backwards, motioning the ranks of his men away. But as soon as he was safely out of reach of the Rebels, his hoarse voice rang through the woods.

"Spies! Citizen-spies! Attack! Attack!"

The rest of his tribe took up the chant, shouting and blowing horns, scattering here and there through the trees. "Citizens! Citizens amongst us! Attack! Attack!"

"Stop!" cried Tambar, running after them. "Naturals! Stop this! Calm down! Enough!"

But the camp had been roused. From all sides came

the clamour of voices shouting for their weapons. The accusation that they had *Citizen-spies* in their midst was like setting a light to dry tinder. Shouts of fury echoed around the woods, along with the crunch of a hundred running footsteps. Imprisoned in the small clearing, Arlo gazed round, terrified. Even the Rebels, trained and confident as they were, would be no match if every Natural in the Meet came down to slaughter the Citizens. And stern though the Rebel oath was, surely it could not force them to fight against their own people? Would they not just be handed over to Goren to keep the peace, to do as he wished?

A sudden gust of wet wood-smoke suddenly furled across the clearing, making them cough. "The fools!" shouted Tambar. "They are torching the forest! They will kill all of us!"

But a kind of madness seemed to have swept over the Meet. Inflamed by fury and the bitter bark-chorley, men from all tribes were piling into the fray, eager for a fight. Shouts and screams broke out around them as Natural turned upon Natural, and others took advantage of the confusion to try to steal another's goods or women, and were savagely set upon in their turn. All was chaos and ferocity.

"Keep close!" shouted Tambar. "Take your positions! Quickly!"

Even in the midst of his panic, Arlo could not help but marvel as the Rebels quickly assembled around them, forming a wedge-shaped formation, and, bending low, took off at speed through the forest. He had barely time to lunge at Rem's collar and draw the dog against his side before his arm was gripped by Liana and dragged forward. But despite their order, their path was beset by obstacles. Branches snapped back painfully into their faces, their feet slipped and slid on the stony ground, and all around them came the sound of screaming and cursing. Icy water soaked Arlo's legs to the knee as they splashed through the stony shallows of the stream, and overhanging brambles swung down to scratch at his face. A few stones flew whistling around their heads, but because of the smoke and the cover of the branches, their hunters evidently chose to save their strength until their prey reached clearer land. Arlo tripped and nearly fell again, but was dragged up in the same instant by Liana and set on his feet.

The camp was descending into pandemonium. Nightmarish visions rose before him, as tribesmen appeared through the thickening smoke wielding eating knives and great branches, and were beaten back. Through the choking fumes, Arlo could dimly see the outline of the great trees that marked the entrance to the Meet, and around them the Wolf-men and a great many other tribes, rearming themselves with the weapons that all the Naturals had left at the barrier thicket.

"There they are!" bellowed Goren, flinging his battleaxe towards the Rebels. "Seize them!"

Arlo dodged as the vicious stone blade whistled past his ear and buried itself in Liana's shield. Jeers and catcalls followed the vicious stroke. They were surrounded. More and more tribes were emerging from the smoke behind them, enraged with hatred and the love of battle.

"Dead-flesh! Dead-flesh!"

And another chant went up. "Kill the Orphans! Kill them! Kill them!"

"Stop!" cried Tambar again, and Arlo could see him now, breaking out of the front of the formation, his hands upraised. "What are you doing, Naturals! Let us pass!"

A movement above him caught his eye, and Arlo looked up. Poised in the branches above the barrier, a smirking Wolf-man was fitting an arrow to his bow and pointing its jagged head directly towards Tambar.

Arlo opened his mouth to shout, but it was too late. The bowstring curved, tightened. . .

But suddenly there was a neighing scream, and a thudding sound of hooves shook the ground. Tambar jumped and looked back, and that small movement saved his life. The tautened bowstring slackened as the arrow flew, but it went wide, whistling harmlessly into the ground behind the Rebel. Immediately the huge form of Ash thundered into the clearing, sending the Wolf-men scattering. On her back clung Kira, desperately reining the mare in before wheeling around to charge them again. Ash's great hooves beat at the air as she reared up, and those Naturals manning the barrier scattered.

"Come on!" cried Tambar, ducking back underneath the safety of his shield. "Charge!"

With a cheer, the Rebels surged forward into the path cleared by Ash and broke upon the barrier. Branches and brambles were thrown aside as they forged a path into the open air by sheer strength. There was no time to retrieve their weapons in such chaos. Scratched and bruised, Arlo was pulled along by Ozzie through a splintering thicket and into the fresher air beyond. Glancing wildly over his shoulder, his eyes met Kira's for a split second before she turned the horse around and disappeared into the trees. He coughed, retched and nearly collapsed as he stumbled down the rocky path, one hand clutching vainly at Tambar.

"Kira – Kira – she's back there—"

"We cannot stop!" shouted Liana from behind him. "We must get away from the Meet with all speed. Look!"

Arlo looked, and behind them, the smouldering woods sent up a thick column of smoke into the evening air, a sure sign of Natural presence to any Citizen-patrol within fifty miles.

Boom. The heavy stone hammer crashed to the ground. Shuffling under the weight of their chains, the prisoners moved forward one by one, to be sentenced and marched to oblivion underneath the hideous Gate, until only the weeping curly-haired young woman remained between Usha and the Lawlord, awaiting her fate.

Kane looked down at her coldly. "Sofia Hagia, of the Inn of the Maia. For your association with the Natural and your involvement in his escape last year. . ."

Usha's ears pricked up at the name. The Maia! She had heard about Sofia from Arlo as he related his many adventures, and here she was, right in front of her!

". . .by assuming the guise of a Citizen soldier in order to do so. . ."

A sharp hiss of excitement escaped Usha's lips. Her confidence was steadily growing as she realized that she was surrounded by friends. She knew well the story of Arlo's escape from the Cleansing of the Inn of Court by Maia comrades disguised as soldiers, for Arlo had told it many times. She hoped that beneath the riot of the girl's Emotions still lay a spirit as stern and reliable as Talia's, if only it could be roused again. But could anybody come back unscathed from such a turmoil?

"Sofia," she murmured in the ear of the woman in front of her as loudly as she dared. "Sofia. Can you hear me? I have a message from Arlo."

Sofia suddenly started, and Usha was momentarily concerned that she might have overplayed her hand while only feet away from their enemy. But the Maia managed to control herself and only nodded curtly, still facing the other way, to signal that she had understood. Usha paused as Kane raised his hand to pass sentence.

"For your crimes, I condemn you to Regeneration. Leave Genopolis by the Traitor's Gate."

Boom. The stone hammer fell, but before the Maia could be ushered away, Usha leaned forward urgently.

"Arlo is alive. Do not lose hope. We still have everything to fight for."

As she was pulled beneath the Gate by the guards, Sofia glanced back over her shoulder, where her eyes met Usha's for the first time, and flashed her thanks.

Now only Usha and Merco stood before the Lawlord. Usha's mind was in a whirl. Though she shrank from the sentence of Regeneration being passed upon her, she wished to be allowed to pass the Gate, for while she was in the company of comrades of Arlo, she was not alone. *While there's life, there's hope*, Kira had said after the flood, and Usha knew the truth of it. She dared not peer up at the ghastly heads that bristled on the Gate, nor meet the eyes of the Lawlord. Instead, she stared meekly at the ground as Kane leaned forward, his beady eyes boring into her forehead.

"Gemini 740323, mark G, created 3001, given the name of Usha by her Citizen-owner, now deceased. Your crimes are manifold and treacherous towards our City. Firstly, for the murder of your Citizen-mistress, Cybella Aquina of the West Quarter, and Citizen Xerves Castor, scissor-man of the Academy. Secondly, of the escape from the scene of your crime, and failing to give yourself up for Regeneration. Thirdly, for your association, aiding and abetting of the Natural both inside Genopolis and outside in the Regions. Though all these crimes are abhorrent, one stands out supreme. For a Gemini to reject their purpose is the supreme transgression against Genopolis. Therefore. . ."

Kane's eyes swept over Usha contemptuously and his fingers twitched. "As a warning to all other Gemini who might have been tainted by your felony, I sentence you to Death by beheading forthwith, and for your head to be displayed for all to see upon the Traitor's Gate."

SIX

After hours of relentless running, Tambar led his small band, their feet lame and sore, down the track of a plunging ravine that had been turned into a raging torrent by the waters coursing down from higher land. The gorge was precarious and slippery, and one by one they crept in single file until they reached the jumble of huge boulders that formed a water-break while the river poured over the top, creating a shallow cave behind. Arlo closed his eyes and covered his mouth. Pounding spray filled the air with a vicious hammering as the water surged overhead, and it was difficult to breathe. The only way into the cave was through the sheer curtain of water, whose force threatened to sweep them over and dash them on to the rocks below if they missed their footing.

"Go, Arlo!" Tambar was behind him, his hand steady on the boy's shoulder. "On the count of three! One, two—"

Arlo braced himself and, as he had been told, lunged into the cataract and scrabbled to find the rocky shelf behind. For a brief agonizing second he was pierced to the bone by the icy flood and feared that he would lose his grip and fall, but mercifully the next moment he was through and staggering, dazed, to the back of the cave to seek respite from the pounding water and the despair. One side of the cave was composed of mud and rocks from the landslide, while the other formed a perfect screen of water, shot through with the last rays of the golden afternoon sun, almost too blinding to gaze at.

One by one the small group of Rebels emerged through the curtain of water and threw themselves down to rest. For the first time since their desperate flight began, Arlo realized that Toby was not amongst them.

Ozzie fell to his knees beside him, coughing and spluttering the water out of his nose and mouth. "I can't believe it, Arlo. I can't believe it! We lost Toby! We left 'im behind! I told 'im I'd look after 'im—"

Arlo beat his knuckles fiercely against the slimy wall, remembering his cousin urging Ash back towards the barrier and the tribe of Goren running before her. "Do you think they're all right? Do you think the Wolf-men got Kristo or Kira?"

"But Toby lost his bleedin' glasses!" snarled Ozzie, and at a loss to know what to do, he picked up a stray stone and hurled it savagely across the cave, at the precise moment that Tambar ducked through the curtain of water, carrying Rem under one arm. The rock caught him on the cheek, painfully, but he did not flinch.

"You cannot go back, Arlo," he said gently. "The Wolf-men are raising the tribes to rioting, and the camp is ablaze. It was all we could do to get out of there alive."

"But Kira!" burst out Arlo. "She's still there! And Toby! And Kristo!"

A momentary flicker, almost imperceptible, crossed Tambar's face, before he set the sodden Rem down in Arlo's lap. "There was no choice to be made," he said flatly. "It was them or us. I had no choice."

I had no choice. Kira's words echoed painfully in Arlo's head, as he covered his head with his arms. Even the hot licking of Rem at his ear could not rouse him, and he did not touch the dried provisions that the Rebels distributed amongst themselves. He sat as if turned to stone with the silent Ozzie beside him, a weariness that was not merely physical consuming him. At first his heart beat fast with hope every time another weary figure ducked into the cave, but he soon realized that these were the last of Tambar's group returning to the hideout, and that no Orphans were with them. Nevertheless, some of the Rebels had been left behind at the battle, and had later made their way, in much danger, back to the meeting point by other paths. It was from these last stragglers that Arlo could piece together what had happened after their escape from the Meet.

Goren's tribe had been thrown into confusion by the

appearance of Ash, and as well as aiding their escape, the pursuit of the Rebels had been effectively delayed. Within the forest, the wetness of the trees had prevented a serious fire taking place, but the smoke itself had been cause enough for concern for the Meet to be abruptly disbanded. In the commotion, some said, many of the tribes had abandoned the fight, and only Goren had remained, trying to urge them on, until finally common sense had overcome him and he had ordered his tribe away. Others told of groups of weeping Orphans, running scattered and witless through the forest, and others of Wolf-men waiting outside the barrier to hunt down screaming women and children as they tried to escape the smoke. Arlo shuddered at the thought. But one, the last to arrive, remembered a mounted Kira charging back into the woods, even after the Wolf-men had left, back towards the smoking thickets where the Orphans had made their camp.

"Why would she return to such danger?" asked another. "We had already escaped!"

Arlo made no answer. He knew why, and Tambar knew it too. He could not look at the Rebel leader, and stared hopelessly at the ground, not trusting himself to think about what could have happened once Kira rode into the forest.

"But, many hours later as I came up the lower path to the waterfall," said the last man to arrive, "I saw a trail of hoof-prints leading away from the Meet. Fresh they were too, and heading north."

Tambar's breath escaped from him in a sharp hiss of relief, and Arlo turned and looked at him hopefully.

But nobody had seen Toby, and no one, even when they compared notes as to what had happened in those first few crucial moments of the stand-off with the Wolf-men, could remember exactly where he had been standing, nor why he had not been seized and protected along with Ozzie and Arlo. It was generally hoped that the boy had been overlooked in the confusion, and been able to escape the smoke unseen by the Wolf-men.

With a heavy heart, Arlo watched as Tambar organized his troops and ordered, from a concealed place at the back of the cave, boxes of replacement weapons and a barrel of an evil-smelling black substance to be rolled out.

"We have until sundown today to rest," he said curtly. "At nightfall the first food-ships will set sail, and we must be ready for them."

Arlo looked at him in disbelief. "The *plan*. . .? You mean, we're still going to continue after all that's happened?"

Tambar glanced at him grimly, plunging his hands into the dark barrel, and smearing the black viscous mixture over his hands and face until he was totally transformed before them.

"That's exactly what I do mean," he snapped. "If we wait any longer, there'll be none of us left. Like it or not, Arlo, our paths have been brought together. This is the way that you were meant to take. You cannot leave it now. And in the meantime, I suggest that you get some sleep. We will have a hard night ahead of us."

With a slithering sound of steel upon stone, the guard nearest to Usha unsheathed her sword and held it over her head. Usha stiffened as she saw that the anvil of the suspended hammer was also darkened with streaks of blood, where doubtless the previous Gemini whose heads adorned the Gate had knelt after sentence. She stood dumbstruck, her ears ringing with the Lawlord's last words. Her mouth was so dry with the unexpected shock that she could not speak. It was a few moments before she became aware that a voice was shouting from behind her.

"Here now! Hold on! What's all this about?"

At the sudden interruption, the assembled courtiers fell silent. As the sound of the voice filtered into her consciousness, Usha raised her head and looked up. Incredibly, the voice belonged to Merco. The Circus-leader, loaded and shackled with chains though he was, lurched forward until he stood before the crowd.

"Why should the Gemini be spared Regeneration when she too is a traitor? Why should she not be taken to the pharms along with all of us? One reason only! This trial is a miscarriage of justice! The Lawlord himself is acting under Emotions!"

At this piece of news, the chamber suddenly buzzed with surprise, and Kane seemed to whiten underneath his pallor, pointing a shaking finger towards Merco. "Silence!" he hissed. "Guards! Seize him!"

But Merco was unstoppable and his voice rang out above the clatter of arms. For a second, despite her confusion, Usha saw a glimpse of the compelling Ringmaster that he had once been, holding his arms aloft, declaiming above the noise so that all eyes were drawn to him.

"The Lawlord is not impartial! He has *not* told the Court that the scissor-man that the Gemini murdered is his Citizen-brother, from the same family-unit! He is judging the murdering Gemini with Revenge!"

Uproar from every corner of the chamber broke out. Stunned, Usha stared at Merco, who continued his diatribe, but the noise was so great that she could no longer hear what he was saying. Through the clamour, the Brigadier strode from the back of the chamber where she had been watching, and approached the Judgement Chair.

"Is this true, Lawlord? Was Scissor-man Xerves your Citizen-brother?"

Kane shot a look so vicious towards Merco that even Usha could feel his guilt radiating off him, like the powerful smell of sweat. "Yes," he spat out finally, "but I do not judge through Emotions. I have always sworn for pure justice in my station as Lawlord. I would never—"

"Then why did you not declare this connection?" said the Brigadier.

"I . . . I . . ." stammered Kane.

"You have been Contaminated!" returned the Brigadier. "Contaminated with Hatred by the Natural! I can see Emotions in your eyes! This case is rendered void by your actions, and it is my duty to overturn it!"

Her steel-tipped boots ringing against the stone steps, the Brigadier mounted the dais so that she stood next to the Judgement Chair. Kane edged away and his eyes flickered towards the Gate. But the Brigadier stood, her hand upraised.

"Gemini, important though your purpose may be, the crime of Treason remains the supreme crime in the laws of Genopolis. Accordingly, you are sentenced, along with your fellow-conspirators, to Regeneration."

A dread sentence indeed, but ironically, the only one that Usha wished to hear. A guard unchained her ankles, and almost thankfully she stumbled forward and underneath the dark shadow of the Gate. As she did so, she could hear the Brigadier shouting behind her.

"Lawlord Kane! You are arrested immediately! I will have no Emotions in these courts!"

As a guard led her down a slippery path, Usha could smell the air of the docks again, and saw the file of prisoners ahead of them, being herded up a ramp into an iron cage. The next second, she could hear another shuffling tread echoing under the Gate towards her, and she knew that the Circus-master too had been sentenced.

"Why did you do it, Merco?" gasped Usha. "Why did you speak up for me?"

An evil chuckle sounded through the darkness. "Because Kane ain't the only one who's acting through an Outbreak of Revenge, Blondie. Citizens like to pretend they're immune, but we're all prey to it really. The Brigadier's acting through it, because of nearly being burned alive in the Regions. And I'm acting through it because I'm going to get my remaining hand on your filthy little neck before we get to Pharmopolis, Blondie. And they can do whatever they want to me afterwards, so long as I get my Revenge first!"

Night had long since fallen before the first lights of the food-ships appeared across the glimmering stretch of shallow sea that ran past the rocky foothills of the Regions. There was no moon, and only the bright points of the stars wheeled above the small wooden raft that bobbed unobtrusively next to the outlying rocks.

Arlo lay flattened on the raft next to Rem, his hands and face blackened like Tambar so that nothing would betray him in the darkness. Around him he could feel rather than see the other Rebels, up to their necks in the sea, treading water as they awaited the sign from their leader. No word was spoken, but the soft warning bird-call had put all on the alert. He could not see Ozzie hanging on to the side of the raft, but he knew he was there, and the knowledge was a bitter comfort for him. Fear of the deep water and the creatures that swam in it overwhelmed him, and despite Tambar's reassurances that the great fish would only gradually make their way down from the outer seas after the Rains had finished, still every second he expected to hear splashing and agonizing screams.

With an effort he forced his mind on to the task at hand.

When the last boat passes, Tambar had said.

Food convoys travelled as well-disguised as they could; firstly the main ship, with teams of rowers and navigators aboard, and then after them, great flat-bottomed barges about twenty feet across, heaped with produce, strapped down with tarpaulins and each with an armed guard riding pillion on top of it.

"But no Citizen ever wishes to ride the last barge," Tambar had said, back in the waterfall-cave as he explained what Arlo was to do. "They know that this is the weak point in the convoy. Often they leave the last one unattended, so if they are attacked, they can sacrifice the final load rather than themselves. You must latch our raft on to the end of this final barge."

"But what if there is a guard there?" worried Arlo.

Tambar tossed a slender, evil-looking harpoon across to him. Its point gleamed wickedly in the candlelight.

"Then you know what you must do. But it must be instant, do you hear? He or she must not be allowed to raise the alarm."

Arlo's trembling fingers clutched the slippery harpoon. *Please, please*, he thought, *don't let there be a guard there. Please.*

Another warbling bird-call, the ready-signal, cut

across the night. Instantly, the raft started to move as the Rebels took their positions and started to manoeuvre out of the shallows and into the shipping lanes; some swimming ahead and dragging the raft with them, others kicking from behind.

Arlo strained to see into the blackness. The huge mass of the rowing ship was almost on them, eerie in the silence save for the splash and dip of the oars. As long as they kept their heads down, they would pass for a floating piece of debris, swept down during the floods. The Rebels crouched low and immobile in the water. Arlo felt exposed on the raft, as if all eyes could see him. But finally after an agonizing wait the first ship was past them, and the raft began to rock and plunge wildly in the wash. Instantly the Rebels paddled frantically to keep in position and avoid being swept aside by the surging waves. Next came the barges, usually three or four at a time, Tambar had said, and Arlo craned forward, trying to make out where the convoy ended. A move too soon, and they would be entangled in the barge-chains, overturned, drowned, or cut to pieces. Too late, and they would be left helplessly far behind in the huge sea. *Usha would have been better at this than me*, he thought miserably, squinting into the darkness.

That was it! Suddenly the paler black of the sky sprinkled with stars shone around him once more and he realized that the last barge was passing him. Low in the water and, with great good fortune, no guard atop it! Scrambling to his feet, he lunged forward and thrust with his harpoon at the shadowy bulk, using it as a grappling hook. The curved blade slid over the side and lodged on the wood with a dull thud. He staggered and fell to his knees, but out of great luck the sharp point held and though the harpoon was wrenched from his fingers, the rope fixed to the end of it and tied to the raft's corner, tautened. The next moment the raft swung around wildly and suddenly they were being towed at the end of the convoy at a rate of knots through the rolling sea.

But it was not yet over. They could not simply ride on the back of the convoy all the way to Genopolis. Firstly the raft was pitching and bucking in the wash left by the barges so that it was all that the Rebels could do to hang on, and secondly to leave a raft attached to the barge would leave a sure sign of their presence once the fleet arrived at the port, especially if they arrived after the sun had risen. So it was that the most difficult part was still to come.

With his heart in his mouth, Arlo wriggled forward and hauled himself on to the straining harpoon-line. Being smaller and lighter than any of the other Rebels, this task had been allocated to him. He had indulged his passion for climbing many times in the Regions, shinning up trees much taller than the one he had climbed in the Inn of Court – how many years ago that seemed! – or up the long creepers that trailed beside the barren waterfalls. But here in the pitch-black, dripping wet and pelted by spray, bounced and jolted every time the raft hit a wave, his nose and mouth so full of gritty water that he could hardly breathe, the task seemed impossible. The weight of his body and his sodden clothes meant that he hung upside down over the lurching sea, his arms and knees hooked over the slender line, trying with all his failing strength to haul himself up like a spider, bracing and pushing with his feet, and reaching vainly over his head to search for the hull of the boat.

At last! His scrabbling fingers found the rough wood of the stern. Twisting around, Arlo grasped frantically at the lip of the barge, hooked his arm over and tried to pull himself aboard. But in the lurching motion of the barge, he slipped and almost fell, lying splayed over the edge, his feet dragged away from him by the force of the water and threatening to pull him off altogether.

No! he thought grimly. *Not now!* With another mighty effort he let go of the harpoon-line and swung his other arm over the side. His hand found the tarpaulin edge, gripped it firmly, and pulled. At that moment the barge gave a great roll and he half-wrenched, half-tipped himself over and on to the last boat in the convoy.

He was aboard! With the blood rushing excitedly through his numbed fingers, he took hold of the line and began to reel in the raft until a soft bump told him that it had fetched against the side of the barge. Instantly the night was alive with other figures clambering over the edge of the boat to huddle next to him. There were about twenty of them, and last of all, Tambar, with Rem under his arm.

But as the Rebel started forward, Rem yipped suddenly and piercingly. His feathery tail had snagged on the rough end of one of the cabers that had been used to make the raft. Everyone froze. But the sound of the dog's yelp had been drowned in the rushing of the water. No alarm was given, and no light was shone upon them. Tambar lifted Rem bodily and threw him into the boat, leaping in after the dog. Taking a knife from its sheath around his ankle, he slashed at the harpoon-line until it frayed and broke. Then, without the line to secure it, the raft bobbed and lurched and disappeared out of sight in the darkness.

Arlo found himself aching and shivering all over, not so much from exhaustion as from emotion. But Tambar was next to him, pulling up the tarpaulin and ushering him underneath to where the other Rebels crouched.

"Well done, Arlo," he muttered. "Lie low now, for we still have some hours to go. Save your strength and eat whatever you can find. I will call the watch."

Gratefully, Arlo wriggled underneath into the warm darkness, from where the smell of biscuits was rising.

Usha sat in the cage on the docks alongside the other prisoners as the night deepened. Though communication was difficult, she had whispered fragments of her story to Sofia every time the guard's back was turned, and it had been relayed around the small group of convicts.

Through a guarded system of winks and waves, she had been introduced to the other members of the Circle; amongst them Arlo's old allies Tariq, Sasha, Tarissa, Tutu, Yoshi, Yuma and Sir Herbert. With new hope, the wild Outbreaks exhibited by the condemned seemed to have calmed down, and there was a mood of optimism in the air. She felt as if they were watching her intently for some clue, a signal, but she knew she must wait until they could speak freely. If it had not been for Merco sitting threateningly behind her, Usha would have felt as positive as she could.

Yet even so, she tried to remind herself, the slave-driver had still spared her life, for whatever reasons.

But suddenly the sullen orange lighting that flickered along the dockside was suddenly extinguished into pitch-darkness, and there was a loud clang as the cage doors were thrown open. A wild scream echoed through the darkness, and she was struck with a thud by something unseen and knocked to the side. From all around broke out the sound of cheering as the prisoners, no doubt assuming that this was the start of a rescue attempt, poured out and turned on the soldiers in the darkness. In the midst of the confusion, two merciless hands picked her up and dragged her out of the cage. For a terrible second, Usha thought it might be Merco seeking his revenge already, and hit back at the shadow. Her fist connected with a sickening thud on the side of her assailant's face. But the next moment, a familiar voice was hissing frantically at her.

"Stop it, Usha! It's us! It's Corin and Ivar!"

Usha stopped struggling immediately and the same second the meaty hands of Ivar released her. "What are you doing, Corin! What's going on?"

"Ivar's shut the lights off. We've only got a few minutes. Come with me, Usha. I'll make sure you're safe."

A rifle blazed frantically through the darkness, shedding a stream of sparks as it went. From the sound of it, prisoners appeared to be escaping through the darkness while the guards pursued them. A better opportunity to flee had never presented itself, and she had only seconds in which to take it!

Yet still Usha hesitated. The memory of what she had seen in the moonstone had been strong and vivid. If what she saw was true, then her path led to the pharms. Should she throw all her decisions aside, now that luck had sent her an ally?

"Usha, please – the door's just here—"

For one moment, Usha was tempted to run with him. What if she was wrong? What if the vision in the moonstone had not been what she interpreted it to be? Yet could she willingly return to a life of hiding and running in the darkness, inside an ever-closing net? What good would that do?

The moment was passing. Usha stretched her fingers out, found Corin's hand and held it briefly, Natural-style. "Corin, I can't. I have to go to the pharms."

"What? But, Usha! You'll never come back!"

But Usha was unmoved. "I need to go to Pharmopolis, Corin, for reasons that I do not yet know myself. But you must stay here. You need to bear an important message for me. If – and only if – you pass this message on, then you will help me most."

A light glimmered somewhere above them. Emergency supplies of lighting were being fetched to the uprising, and soon they would be seen.

"Master—" begged the Gemini servant. "Quickly. They are coming!"

"You shut up, Ivar!" snapped Corin. "Or your head'll be up there on Traitor's Gate quicker than you can run!"

Usha knew she had only a few seconds left. She clasped Corin's hand closer.

"Corin. Tell him. *Tell him*: Midsummer's Night. Don't forget. *Midsummer's Night*."

Corin gazed back at her in the slowly-lifting shadows, uncomprehending. "Tell who? What? Midsummer. . . What do you *mean*, Usha?"

"You'll know," returned Usha, and felt surprise at the calmness of her voice. She could not tell Corin everything, for if he was ever questioned, then he could not be made to give too many details. "You'll know who he is, and you'll know when to say it. Don't forget, Corin. *Midsummer's Night*."

Before she had finished speaking, the lights suddenly blazed on, and Usha found herself standing alone outside the empty cage, with a ring of Citizen rifles trained on her. Around the docks, she could see the file of prisoners being rounded up and chained even more tightly together.

From somewhere in the shadows she heard the soft click of a door closing.

Slowly, she put her hands up.

Arlo felt himself being shaken awake. With a start he realized that the first pale lights of dawn were already snaking under the heavy dark tarpaulin. All around him the Rebels were rousing themselves and crawling out of the boat, slipping noiselessly over the side and into the sea, where they formed a chain and trod water, waiting for their leader's signal. Meanwhile, the convoy passed silently on, heading for the port, unaware of the arrival, and the departure, of their unexpected passengers.

"Are you sure you can find the smugglers' cave again?" Tambar had asked Ozzie as they planned the attack in the tent at the Meet.

"Sure," Ozzie had said. "If the port's here, then the cave's about *here*," and he had traced a diagram with his finger in the earth.

"But what if the Regis has discovered the cave and is waiting for us?" Arlo had stammered nervously.

Ozzie rolled his remaining eye in disbelief. "Once you went to all the trouble to escape from Genopolis, he won't be expecting you just to walk back in of your own accord, will he? The worst that'll happen is that they'll have blocked it up or something, and there's other tunnels around that I can try to take us through."

But all the same, the swim that the Rebels were proposing was terrifying. Although the great bulk of Genopolis was clearly visible on the horizon, rising like a stone leviathan from the sickly greenish water that surrounded it, they still had almost a mile to swim through shallow, tidal waters, navigating debris that had been swept out by the floods, all the time with the possibility of discovery and Citizen-alarms ringing in their ears.

Arlo gritted his teeth as he swung himself over the side. Icy water surged around his neck and chilled him to the bone. He had been assigned a stocky Rebel to swim with, a surly, suspicious-looking man called Uther, who looked distinctly unimpressed at needing to carry a skinny boy with him. Tambar himself was to swim with Rem atop his shoulders, and although Arlo had begged to be allowed to go with his pet, he secretly knew that without the Rebels' strength, neither of them would make the journey.

Uther was already waiting for him, and without a word, signalled for Arlo to put his hands on his shoulders and kick with his legs. Screwing his face up against the freezing sea, Arlo did so, and felt Uther's powerful arms begin to cleave the water. Glancing round, he saw Ozzie swimming next to him, two Rebels either side, ready to catch him if he should come into trouble. Ozzie had learned to swim in the Regions, and he splashed awkwardly, head held high from the beating waves, his only advantage over the Naturals being that he did not know pain or exhaustion.

It was a calm morning, and the pale grey of the sea faded into misty blue as the sun began to edge over the horizon. Arlo's teeth chattered violently in the cold, the gritty waves rubbed unrelentingly against his face, and his stomach cramped with a combination of fear and the dusty biscuits that he had eaten the night before. All he could do was grip on to Uther's broad shoulders, and kick feebly with his legs. *Keep going*, he urged himself. *Keep going. It's your only choice.*

Nearer and nearer rose the great, moss-stained wall that surrounded Genopolis, its blind stones seeming to gaze at them coldly as if contemptuously watching the approach of the tiny ant-sized humans floundering in the great sea.

Perhaps half a mile into their journey, Tambar, at the front, suddenly waved the warning signal. Instantly all the Rebels froze, put their heads in the water and floated. Despite his panic, Arlo hated to put his face willingly underwater, and instead, held on to Uther's floating body and peered over his shoulder. Then, through the fog of the early morning, he could see the huge bulk of a Citizen-ship gliding not a hundred metres from them.

Almost indistinguishable from the shadowy sea on which it moved, it carried with it an eerie calm, as if it was formed only of dark mist itself, and not a sound broke the air save that of the soft slap of the waves. So suddenly and silently had it appeared that the sight was deeply unnerving. Arlo shuddered as thoughts of phantoms crossed his mind. Tales of ghost ships, unmanned by human crew, were often spoken of by Naturals around their campfires, ships which, when they were attacked, melted away into the air. Despite the widely-held Natural belief that Citizens had no souls, some said that such vessels were inhabited by the spectres of murdered Citizens, condemned to eternity in their lonely wanderings across the waters, no longer part of the living, yet also refused passage to the world of the dead.

One by one the Rebels surfaced, but continued floating, while only their eyes followed the ship as it made its way along and over the horizon.

"It has passed," whispered Tambar over his shoulder. "But be careful, and keep alert! There may be many more!"

Keeping a wary eye on the rapidly-rising mist which could soon leave them exposed in the lonely sea, the Rebels swam on, shivering from their unexpected stop. They were almost upon the shores of Genopolis when one of the scouting swimmers at the front suddenly shrieked, put up his arms and thrashed about for a few seconds, before he sank like a stone beneath the water.

Sharks! thought Arlo in blind panic, and the same fear evidently crossed the others' minds, as confusion swept through the following Rebels, and they hung back. "What is it?" hissed Uther. "Tambar, what is it?"

Tambar, with Rem sprawled across his shoulders, floated cautiously up to the spot where the Rebel had sunk, and immediately swam back again. "Nets!" he called. "There are electric nets surrounding the City! Do not touch them, or you will be stunned and drown!"

Arlo's mind raced. There had not been nets outside Genopolis when he had escaped on the smugglers' barge only a year ago. Evidently the Regis had lost no time in setting up defences, and probably other obstacles too. How were they to get through the nets, and what would be the chances of the smugglers' cave being bricked up, or guarded, as he had feared earlier? Now they would be sentenced to a slow death, floating in the seas outside Genopolis, with no way in or out!

"What are we going to do?" gurgled Arlo miserably, his eyes watering.

He was in such panic that he did not notice for some seconds that Tambar had also disappeared and a sodden, wild-eyed Rem was now draped over the shoulders of Liana. Only when the Rebel suddenly resurfaced next to him, puffing and blowing, did he understand that their leader had dived down to investigate and already formed a plan.

"Good news," muttered Tambar softly to him. "The water is but twenty feet deep at this point, as the nets can only be fixed in shallower water, and they end a few feet from the bottom of the sea. We must swim underneath them."

"But I can't dive!" Arlo trembled. "I hate putting my head underwater!"

"You don't have to dive," returned Tambar exasperatedly, "Just hang on to Uther and keep your legs tucked in."

Arlo had barely time enough to close his eyes tight and clutch Uther around the waist, before Uther gave a great kick, heaved and duck-dived straight down beneath the waves.

Instantly all went dark. The crush of the icy water around him filled his ears and forced its way into his nostrils. Hold as he might on to Uther, the pressure was so great that Arlo felt his grip slackening. In fear lest he should be torn from the Rebel and swept into the electric nets, he tucked his legs in and hung on to the struggling man for dear life. But as they neared the end of the descent, even Uther's great strength seemed to be failing. The water seemed to be forcing them upwards to where the nets swayed wickedly in the current only a few centimetres above them. Suddenly a cloud of muddy grit surrounded them as Uther met the seabed, and burrowed as long and low as he could. Arlo felt a scrape on the back of his hands and his fingers numbing. He fought the temptation to take a breath, but the air inside his chest escaped from his mouth in a great burst, and his lungs seemed as if filled with fire. The scuffling in the cloudy mud seemed to go on for ever. *I can't*, he thought confusedly to himself. *I can't hold on any longer*.

But miraculously, after a fury of kicking and struggling, they were suddenly shooting upwards in a roaring cloud of bubbles. Arlo's head broke through the waves on the other side and took great gasping breaths of air, over and over again. He thought he would never stop. One by one the Rebels surfaced next to him, coughing and spluttering, heedless of the dangerous position that they found themselves in at the very foot of Genopolis. Only when sky and sea had arranged themselves again and he could breathe easily, did Arlo realize that Tambar and Rem were still on the other side of the net.

"I cannot dive with the dog," shouted Tambar. "I am sorry."

"No!" screamed Arlo. "You have to! You can't leave him here!"

Tambar's face darkened in frustration. "I cannot dive with an animal, Arlo! He will fight me every centimetre of the way, and endanger both of us. I must leave him, or we lose everything!"

No, thought Arlo desperately, *not again*. One by one they were all being left behind; one by one they were all failing. He could not bear Rem to be lost. "Wait," he begged frantically. "There must be a way. Let me look."

"We have no time, Arlo!" retorted Tambar. "The sun is already rising! We will be seen!"

"Then you'll have to leave me here as well!" shot back Arlo. In a blaze of fury, he realized what a predicament he was in. Who *was* this man, who could leave all things behind as and when it suited him? What a fool he had been to throw himself so blindly into his service after he had known him only a few hours! His cousin had surely had a point when she tried to warn him of what Tambar was capable of. And now, here he was, trapped in the middle of the shifting sea, with the last of his remaining companions, and he was going to leave Rem *behind*?

"Don't be a fool!" snapped Uther, and gripping the boy around the wrist with one muscular arm, began to tow him away from the nets. Without properly thinking what he was doing, Arlo shrieked and hit out blindly at Uther with his fist. Instantly, Uther twisted him around and clapped his hand over Arlo's mouth, and forced him down into the waves. Arlo struggled frantically, but Uther's huge hand was on the back of his neck, holding him underneath the water. Just as he thought he could bear it no longer, the pressure eased, and Uther dragged him upright, coughing and gurgling.

"Try something like that again, boy, and it will be the end of you!"

Arlo stared at him aghast as he gasped for breath. What in Genopolis had he got himself *in* for with the Rebels? What on earth would they do in the name of their Cause? Not knowing what else to do, he turned to Tambar with an appeal, but the Rebel's eyes were dark and shuttered. He merely said, "Enough, Uther," before unwinding Rem gently from his shoulders and setting him by himself. Rem began to paddle frantically, dog-fashion, as a wave almost submerged him. White-eyed and teeth bared, he tried to clamber back on to the Rebel, but was pushed gently away. Tambar dashed away the salt water – or was it something else? – from his red-rimmed eyes, swam a few feet away from the hysterical dog, prepared to dive. . .

"Hang on!" called Ozzie, from a short distance away where he had been examining the barrier. "Look! There's a gap in one of the nets!"

In a sudden surge of hope, Arlo broke away from Uther and swam towards his friend. "Where, Ozzie? Where?"

A gap it was indeed, but such a small one that none of the swimmers could have passed through it. One of the nets had come loose from its anchorage, and swayed loosely in the current, leaving a break no more than a couple of feet wide. Was it enough to admit Rem?

But there was no choice to be made. Arlo swam as near as he dared to the net and called Rem. The dog turned at the sound of his master's voice, and struggled through the waves towards him, his ears back. At that moment a sudden surge of water caught them and the nets rocked gently in the current, momentarily closing the gap. But Rem also had been pushed away by the force of the wave, and when the water receded, the gap swung tantalizingly open again.

"Rem!" whistled Arlo softly. "Rem!"

Rem paddled gamely towards him, though his eyes rolled in fear at the unknown expanse of water around him. Arlo held his breath. If the dog kept to a straight line then he might just squeeze through the breach, but if another wave came as he was passing, or if he swam even a fraction to either side. . .

He was through! The next second another surge of water came and lifted them all bodily towards the net. Arlo was ready for it, lunged forward, gripped Rem by the scruff of the neck and dragged him away. As the nets closed behind the dog, the streaming plume of his tail cleared the lines by a hair's breadth.

A fountain of bubbles exploded beside him as Tambar rocketed up to the surface and spat out a mouthful of water. Arlo did not trust himself to look at the Rebel, and ignoring the man's outstretched hand offering help, turned and with Rem's sodden weight over his own shoulders, stubbornly started to swim the remaining distance to where the rocky shores of Genopolis were now clearly visible in the morning light.

In the dim light of the early morning, the Citizen-ship moved silently away from Genopolis through the shadowy waves. No slaves powered these craft, for there was no need for anyone aboard ever to return. Instead, condemned prisoners would do their own rowing underneath an armed guard, and the silence under which they travelled marked the mood of hopelessness. *Death-ships*, they were called, for they bore the dead-flesh of Genopolis back to the pharms for Regeneration, and to be aboard such a boat meant to count oneself as dead.

Above them towered a storm-cloud, a hideous swollen purple, shot with sickening gold as the light poured through it, illuminating all present with a ghastly light. Yet the upturned faces took no hope from the morning, as it marked the last sunrise they would ever see.

Usha sat on the deck of the ship, her wrists and ankles manacled to the heavy oar that jutted through the side of the boat. The mists were rising. In front of her sat Sofia, her shoulders slumped, chained to the oars along with the other convicts that she had seen at Traitor's Gate. A dull creak of oars was the only sound that filtered through the sound of the waves, and for a second Usha had the curious sensation that they were part of the mist itself, and that she herself was not real, and she had to tap herself sharply to make sure. They were sailing on a ship of ghosts, she thought to herself, and from such a journey no Citizen ever returned.

For a moment Usha's mind swam, and the task she was about to perform seemed vague and nebulous. She regretted the way that she had chosen during Corin's failed rescue. Why had she not taken her chance to escape while she had it? From the faces of the other prisoners around her, she could see that they believed that they had missed their last opportunity of freedom.

But the cold touch of the moonstone at her neck calmed her, and with difficulty, she lifted one hand from the oar and held it. Now she knew that she must trust her visions. Only by entering the pharms and by passing through the place of fear and darkness, might they have any hope of overthrowing Genopolis.

As quietly as she dared, she leaned over, and whispered to Sofia.

"Listen, Sofia, we must first go to the pharms. We cannot try to escape before then."

The Maia nodded, her eyes downcast. "I will, but my heart shrinks from entering such an evil place. I do not think that many of us will come out alive. But I trust you, Usha. I cannot do otherwise."

With his legs feeling like lead, Arlo waded up on to the rocky shore and collapsed next to Rem. After all that they had been through, he had fully expected to find the caves bricked up and a platoon of soldiers standing guard, and only the total exhaustion of mind and body prevented him being surprised when their arrival on the shore met with no resistance. The crags of the smugglers' cave looked exactly as they had left it a year ago. But despite the plain sight that soldiers had been there in the meantime – large booted footprints, stray gun-cartridges and end cuts of pipe-tobacco – the cave bore no traces of current occupation. Ozzie, however, had not thought that the smugglers' cave would be the ideal means of entry in any case, and had lined up several other possibilities drawn from his extensive knowledge of the sewers.

"There's a waste pipe that comes out into the sea round about *here*," he had said, as they sat excited and confident that far-off morning around the map drawn in dirt on the floor of the Rebel's tent. "Or there's a flight of broken stairs – I don't know what they were used for – where they've collapsed a little and taken a bit of the wall down with it. We'll have ter see."

"Those stairs were once the gates of Genopolis, before this sea surrounded it," Tambar had answered. "It was on those stairs that the Naturals of Region Three were cut down as they tried to attack the City."

Arlo had said nothing, but the story of his grandmother's ill-fated rebellion had found a deep place in his heart. Privately he hoped that when they re-entered the City, he could somehow follow in her footsteps, and finish the work that she had started.

But now, shaking, exhausted, the taste of blood in his mouth and all hope at an end, he could barely summon up the energy to feel any pride at all as Ozzie cautiously led the way, snaking around the shore of Genopolis, shrinking into the shadow of the huge buttresses and darting quickly from hiding place to hiding place. Rem limped at Arlo's heels, and Liana and the rest of the Rebels were strung out in single file in front of him. Tambar brought up the rear, glancing sharply behind and above him for any sign of soldiers.

Ozzie turned round and held up a hand, making the sign. *This is it. In here.* Underneath the huge crumbling stone steps that led to a bricked-up archway, a tiny gap showed where one of the boulders had partially fallen away. Ozzie wriggled through the gap and there was a tense pause while the Rebels waited for any sound of ambush, but there was none. Presently Ozzie's hand emerged from the hole and beckoned them in. Arlo was so stiff and sore that even as the smallest and slenderest of them all, he had difficulty in crawling through the hole and fell with a splash into the flooded cavern beneath.

In the dim light, the water smelt filthy and bobbed with old rubbish. Tambar brought out tinder and flint from a waterproof pouch that was bound to his chest, and struck a light. In its dim radiance they made out that they were in a submerged chamber with crumbling arches of stone that supported the curving flight of steps above them. Stinking weeds hung from the ceiling and covered the walls in a green slime. Rem squeaked as he tried to scrabble up on to a rock and loosened a claw as he did so.

"There's part of a tunnel goes up here," muttered Ozzie, "perhaps an old chimney flue. When yer get up it, yer get into some tunnels, perhaps an old heating system or something."

"These must have been the old guard-chambers underneath the gates," mused Tambar, looking around. "When the plains began to be flooded, they must have lost their use. I wonder that they were not destroyed."

"They're pretty much destroyed anyway," answered Ozzie, pulling aside a pile of debris to reveal a sloping tunnel leading uphill in front of them. "Me and Toby," his face paled for a second, "broke through into the sewer system one day when we was looking for the storerooms. If we can get through there, then there's a short cut we can take into the sewers that go back to the Den, and try to find Nanda and Mindie and everyone."

"But do you think they will still be there, Ozzie?" whispered Arlo, as they made their way through the darkness. "Don't you think—"

He broke off abruptly, because it occurred to him that much of Ozzie's determination to return with him to Genopolis had been inspired by the hope that they would find the Kids where they had left them. It seemed a vain wish to Arlo, but was it any more vain than the hope that they would be able to rescue Usha, safe and sound? Perhaps even now she was sitting in front of the Regis, or in the hands of the Brigadier. Perhaps even now—

He turned his mind away from this thought, and busied himself with looking after Rem. The dog's paw was proving a problem and he was hobbling up the steep slope on three legs. Arlo walked protectively next to him, worrying all the time that Tambar would find another reason for leaving Rem behind. He was not sure whether he could control himself in such a situation.

They rested after half an hour of uphill journeying as the tunnel broadened out into a shelf of rock, where they lay, drinking what little water they had brought with them. Despite his worry, Arlo's eyes closed involuntarily as soon as they sat down, so that it seemed as if he had hardly rested before Tambar was shaking him awake again.

For all the Rebels it was a tiring journey, well-trained as they were, but for Arlo it was a nightmare. The roof of the tunnel had lowered significantly and the Rebels ahead of him were starting to crawl into the blackness. For a moment it reminded him of the catacombs in the Regions, the same heavy, suffocating weight of rock hanging above him in the blackness. "We must stop again," whispered Tambar. "Arlo is almost exhausted. We should wait here."

"But we're almost there," hissed back Ozzie triumphantly. "Just another few minutes! You can do it, can't you, Arlo?"

Arlo tried to answer, but at that moment everything dissolved in front of him, and he plunged forward into an unending darkness.

SEVEN

In the far north of the outflung arm of the Regions, Pharmopolis rears its monstrous walls. Where Genopolis is built on a huge outcrop of rock projecting upwards from a flooded plain, the approach to the pharms is gentler, but no less dreadful. At first, voyaging over the shallow seas around Genopolis, the horizon extends from east to west without a single landmark to break the awful monotony. After many hours, when the flooded plain meets the open seas, the water begins to boil and churn over wickedly sharp rocks until the ships can find only one of two routes to pass through without disembowelling themselves on the lethal crags beneath. Then presently – at either sundown or sunset for Pharmopolis is not entered or left at any other time of day – the dim outline of the pharms rises out of the sea.

No casual explorer passes within sight of the pharms, and for those Citizens whose task it is, the whiteness of the borders of the seafaring map seem to bear testament to the fact that they have come indeed to the very edge of the world; the undiscovered country from whose realm no prisoner returns. Those Naturals who have chanced the terrible waters outside the pharms and lived to tell the tale, return almost crazed with garbled tales that puzzle the listener, of creatures glimpsed that appear half-woman, half-animal; flying things like birds that circle the outlying rocks but call to each other in human language; and of monsters that lurk beneath the deeper channels, whose vast tentacles coil around unwary rafts but whose deep-set eyes seem human. But there is no sign of whatever science or magic has produced such creatures.

For those who pass beneath the archways of the pharms, the approach comes as a shock. Slowly, the out-lying rocks rise further and further above sea level until the ship appears to be navigating through a forest of whitened crags. Then a thunderous roaring fills the ears, as the current picks up and starts to propel the ship faster and faster towards what seems a sheer wall of rock which encircles and protects the pharms within. At the last moment, the vessel tilts and begins its headlong descent towards a narrow pass cut through the rock. The pharms themselves lie within the hollowed-out shell of an exploded mountain – a *volcano*, it used to be called in the language of the Old World – in a protective crater, walled off from the outside seas, inside which the rich fertile soil has been largely untouched by the ravages of the Apocalypse.

Buffeted by the wind and the waves, Usha held dizzily on to her oars, seeing in reality at last the awful vision that had appeared to her while she had been imprisoned in Genopolis. Slowly, she raised her hand to her head, but her hair was still there. Shaking her head, she concentrated hard. She must be patient. Surely the meaning of the visions that the moonstone had shown her would be revealed in due course.

Through the driving spray, Usha could hardly see Sofia or any of the other prisoners crouched in front of her. All that she could make out was a huge archway, poised between two crags, rising out of the fog. There was no longer any need to row, as the ship had picked up such a pace that the Gemini helmsman could all but keep the vessel on track.

Suddenly a shadow darkened the mist above her and she ducked as a huge flying thing suddenly dropped from the sky and grazed her cheek with a leathery wing. She glimpsed a woman's face, with long flowing hair, and sharp green eyes. Without thinking, Usha threw herself on to the deck, put her arms above her head to protect herself, and peered upwards in amazement.

Above the ship circled a number of creatures like birds, similar to the hawks that she had sometimes seen at a distance in the Regions, beating the mist with their huge outstretched wings. In the half-light their appearance was ghastly. Great feathered backs supported a huge wingspan, unlike any bird of the Regions, and their faces seemed of the human kind, though wild and obscured with flying hair. Through her bewildered daze, it seemed to Usha that their harsh crying could be understood, as they wheeled around the ship or hung upside down, wings folded, from the archway while they passed beneath.

"Flesh! Blood! We will feed well tonight, sisters!"

Toby wandered alone through the burned-out forest. With his spectacles now missing, he could see no more than a few feet in front of him, as the shadowy trunks and the early morning mists seemed to merge into one, and frequently he fell and stumbled over hidden roots and bushes until he was so scratched and blackened by the charred timber that he was almost indistinguishable from his surroundings.

"Arlo!" he called weakly into the silence, although he knew that there would be no answer. "Ozzie!"

But the dark breath of the forest came back at him in a silent hiss, as it had all the previous night and all the day before it. Toby knew that he was totally alone.

What had happened in the last desperate struggle during the Meet he was still not totally sure. He had been standing with the others outside Tambar's tent, when Kira had confronted Arlo after they had joined the Rebels. Then Arlo had run away, and Toby had tried his best to follow him, but had been left behind in the confusion. When he had heard the shouting and firing in the distance, he guessed that his friends had run into trouble, but in the wild stampede that followed the encounter, he had been knocked roughly aside into a shallow ditch by a rampaging tribesman and lost his glasses. With no way of seeing or meeting either the Orphans or the Rebels, he had judged it better to remain where he was until the tumult had died down. But when the first fumes of the burning forest had come wafting around him, he knew that he could not remain there for fear of being overcome. Remembering the Naturals' advice that water was the best place to get away from fire, he had made his way back to the river down which the flowers of the departed had been sent, and found himself cover underneath a scramble of briars that hung over the side of the bank. Lowering himself into the stream where the smoke did not lie so heavily, here he had sheltered while around him the Naturals fought and the Rebels (though unknown to him) had escaped from the smouldering woods. Even after the rioting had died down, he dared not leave his hiding place, and though once he fancied he had heard the sound of hoof-beats pounding the turf, by the time he emerged and shouted, the woods were deserted.

Now he had made his way back as best he could towards the Orphans' camp, only to find it abandoned, sacked and burned. In his search, he chanced upon the slashed and trampled tents of the Rebels. Slowly all hope left him, and he sank down, burying his head in his hands, and gave way to an Outbreak of crying.

"Shut up!" hissed a voice abruptly from behind him.

Toby spun round. Though he could not see the figure,

the voice was familiar. "Annis!" he cried in relief, forgetting all his earlier hatred towards her. "You're here!"

"Sssh!" warned Annis fiercely, pushing aside Toby's clumsy embrace. "The Wolf-men may still be around here somewhere. Quickly! We must be gone!"

Cautiously, with Annis guiding him, they stole through the remains of the forest until he felt the bare slopes of the hills beneath his feet.

Where they were going Toby was not quite sure. Tambar had told them about a cave underneath a waterfall, but although Toby's geography was better than most thanks to the map that he had spent long hours compiling with Arlo, he could see only a few feet in either direction, and had to rely mostly on the position of the early sun that burned his left cheek. Annis knew little of the paths through the wild but held on to Toby's hand and acted as his eyes as they navigated the treacherous flooded bogs and the slippery crags. Meanwhile the baby, strapped to Annis's back, first cried and then settled to sleep, as slowly they trudged over the plain. They stopped from time to time to listen, but there was nothing, save the empty sound of the wind sighing over the plain, and the distant screeches of a small group of vultures, who sensing their lonely predicament, circled ravenously above, waiting for weakness to overcome the tiny figures, so that they might feed.

*

Clinging on to Sofia's hand, Usha lay flat on the deck of the ship as the vessel thundered through a white-foamed pass cut through steep walls rising to a dizzying height on either side. Paralysed by shock and bewilderment, the Citizens lay rigid, as they floated adrift in a world that seemed to have gone quite mad. Even Usha, steeling herself by the warning of her visions, had not known the full horror of the situation.

Above and around them, strange creatures, like tiny humans covered in fur, scampered on the sheer face of the rocks, following the boat and chattering excitedly. Through cracks in the walls, Usha could glimpse other, more sinister, many-legged creatures, which scuttled swiftly and silently in a horrid, rippling fashion alongside the boat, keeping well into the shadows. The guards who manned the boat stood on guard at each side, cuffing off the various creatures that tried to attack the ship with spears and rifles. Suddenly Sofia let out a shriek. One of the tiny, human-like creatures had slipped between two guards and gripped a handful of her hair, screaming incoherently. Usha struck at it, and instantly it turned on her. Reddened eyes and huge yellow teeth filled her vision for a brief moment, before a guard hurled his spear with deadly accuracy and brought the creature down writhing on to the decks. At the sight, the others held their distance, though wailing and chattering their anger and defiance.

"What is it?" quavered Usha, staring at the upturned

face, the fierce eyes that were already glazing over, and the huge mouth convulsing in the rictus of death.

Sofia shuddered, touching her face where the animal's claws had ripped at her cheek. "I think they are *monkeys*, Usha. We heard about them in the halls of the Inn of the Maia when we studied the pharms. Some say that they were the ancestors of Naturals, and some say that they were used for experiments by the Naturals. Yet whatever they are, it seems clear that the scientists are breeding them here, though kept for what purpose I cannot say. But I think we will be fortunate if they are the only enemy that we encounter."

Cowering next to Sofia, Usha could only shake her head in desperation. The more she learned, the less her plan seemed to be possible. She might enter the pharms, but who knew what terrible creatures she might encounter, or whether she could really follow the purpose predestined for her?

A clanging of cages awoke her from her stupor. Ahead, an iron gate blocked the flow of the river, and she could see figures unlocking the gates and beckoning the ship through. As they passed through the gate, the walls of the rocks grew smoother, and well-chiselled like the canals that ran through Genopolis. Gazing up at the guards that surrounded the gated entrance, Usha's mouth fell open. The hairy faces that grinned down at her were broad and flat like the monkeys outside the gates, but now they belonged to huge, well-muscled simians, taller and stronger than the average

Citizen-man, though they stooped slightly and their limbs were longer so that they walked with a loping gait on overhanging passageways built into the rock. Dressed in ill-fitting black pharm-uniforms, their shambling forms seemed like something from a nightmare to the appalled Citizens, and their eyes glittered scarlet in the dim light as the Gemini guard saluted and addressed them.

"New traitors for Regeneration, sir. What should we do with them?"

The largest of them, a huge, white-furred, sloping simian guard with a crest of hair that fell over its shoulders like a mane, rolled back its lips over sharp, yellowing teeth. The voice that answered was roughened and hoarse so that Usha could hardly understand what it said.

"Traitors, you say? Then I think we should have a little fun with them before Regeneration! Take them to the Bestiary!"

Arlo woke to blackness. For a moment he thought that he was back in the catacombs of the Orphans, and automatically he felt to see if Toby was sleeping next to him, but he jumped as his hand fell instead on Rem's rough pelt. Slowly he began to remember. There had been a long journey. Something about a boat. . .

He felt as if he had been sleeping for hours and hours. Groggily, he sat up and felt about him. In the darkness of the sewer, he could hear someone breathing.

Something about the smell of the cave brought him fully back to consciousness and in that instant he remembered where he was.

"Ozzie?" he cried. "Tambar?"

But it was Liana's voice that answered. "Ssshhh. Quiet. They have gone on a reconnaissance through the tunnels."

"But where *are* we?" asked Arlo. "What is this place?"

At that moment he heard soft steps approaching, and the next moment the chamber was full of people. A dim light was ignited, and Arlo saw Ozzie's face. The sight of it struck him like a slap. His friend seemed suddenly years older; black shadows sprang from underneath his cheekbones and the hole of his missing eye formed a great crater underneath his dirty brows.

"Ozzie?" he gasped. "What's wrong?"

But Ozzie just stood, his hands hanging limply by his sides, staring around him. Following his gaze, Arlo looked and saw that they were in an underground chamber, with old blackened cables hanging from the roof. Around them the floor was strewn with debris and the tattered remains of clothes, boxes and smashed bottles. An old tin kettle lay on a pile of charred fabric that looked strangely like woollen socks of different sizes, and in the corner there was an overturned chair with wheels bolted to it. But three of the wheels had been wrenched off and scattered about, and the walls of the cavern were blackened with smoke.

"That was Mindie's chair," muttered Ozzie hoarsely. "I made it for her."

"What?" Arlo struggled to his feet. Dimly, he remembered the stories that Usha and Ozzie had told him about Nanda, Mindie and the other Kids. "Oh, Ozzie."

"Stupid," mumbled Ozzie. "Stupid. I was stupid. To think they'd still be 'ere. Stupid."

Arlo searched his brain frantically for words of comfort, but he could think of none. "You weren't stupid, Ozzie," he said finally. "You had hope. And that's all that we really have, isn't it?"

But Ozzie did not respond, and simply sat down and stared into space, even when Tambar called the Rebels to order, and sat them down in a circle, scratching a rough map into the floor.

"We're here under the site of the old Inn of Court," he said, pointing out directions with a stick. "The tunnels in each side lead off to the open air of what they call Central Square, but they seem to have been blocked from above. But the Palace, if what our friend here tells me is correct —" and he stole a glance at the unresponsive Ozzie — "lies somewhere up here, to the north. Now the sewer network leads up here towards the Palace. . ."

Arlo hardly heard him as the Rebel talked on, outlining plans, drawing diagrams, distributing tasks. It was too much, he thought dismally. It was too much for him, it was too much for Ozzie, too much for all of them. Why had he not stayed with his cousin, the last family he had, out in the freedom of the Regions? All that you could really ask for in life was a piece of meat when you were hungry, a mouthful of water when you were thirsty, a hug goodnight and the stars to sleep under. For a moment the memory of the hand-to-mouth existence of the Regions seemed almost compelling next to the danger that he knew they were in.

But then the face of Goren came towards him through the smoke, and he heard the sound of women and children screaming. Bitterly he realized that – in truth – Tambar was right. They had no choice.

Usha held tightly on to Sofia's hand as the boat bumped against a rocky docking-station and they were prodded at spearpoint on to the dark quay outside the inner mountain that housed the pharms. Night had now fallen completely, and only the dull glow of a distant fire illuminated the prisoners.

Ahead of them, the huge Simian whom Usha had privately named Whitemane, padded easily in front of them, his huge furred back almost bursting out of the pharm-uniform as he moved. Any thought of escape was impossible. In the darkness, nothing could be seen, and they would be brought down and savaged by the powerful limbs and jaws of the Simians within seconds. Though some Simians walked upright, others frequently dropped on all fours and bounded along, herding the small group of prisoners into a tight knot.

Stunned by the sights and sounds all around them, the

Citizens walked passively, but Usha kept a sharp eye out, noting each twist and turn and outcrop of rock for future reference. For hours they walked as the ground steepened underfoot. Usha could feel that they were climbing upwards on a stony path that wound from side to side as they scaled the outer wall of the volcano.

Presently, she noticed that despite their desperate predicament, Merco strolled along unruffled, his remaining hand in his pocket, as if he were merely out for an evening promenade. Before she could ponder on the significance of this, a chill wind whipped against their faces. They had finally arrived on the rim of the volcano, and all the ghastly majesty of the pharms was outspread before them.

Fashioned out of a vast natural crater, which seemed to stretch into nothingness from end to end, Pharmopolis was illuminated in an icy, bluish glow from the light of its distant furnaces. The walls of the encircling volcano were carved into a series of descending plateaux, and with her sharp eyes, Usha could count nine different levels, cut like huge steps disappearing down into the centre; each level thicker than the one before, some with shapes moving unfettered in the blackness, and in others forms were herded into pens or cages. And down on the ninth level, even at that huge distance, Usha could see the dark bulk of the Regeneration Factories, set in a dark forbidding mass, surrounded by rows of twisted barbed wire and guard-turrets and topped by enormous chimneys. In the north side of the volcano, vents were set in to the mountainside, belching out a bitter white smoke that made the Citizens retch and cough.

In front of her, the old Citizen that Usha knew as Sir Herbert tottered unsteadily. "No –" he moaned pitifully – "I repent it all! Let me see my children! Please—"

Whitemane turned, his eyes glinting unpleasantly in the light, his voice harsh and guttural. "Too late now, old man! Do you see those chimneys there? Inside their core there burns the icy fire that has no ending, in which all traitors end their lives. Too late, old man, too late!"

At his words, panic seized the Citizens and some of them turned to run, but the Simians surrounded them, on all fours, snarling. For a second, the life of the group hung in the balance. Many seemed to prefer being torn to pieces on the spot by the terrible guards than face the horrors beneath. Through her dry lips, Usha forced herself to shout above the din.

"Citizens! Remember Arlo! Remember Arlo!"

Then Sofia was behind her, adding her words of encouragement. "Do not despair, brothers and sisters of the Circle! Do not falter! Keep together!"

Another older man whom Usha remembered was called Sasha, part of his face slashed by a Simian claw, turned to face them. "They are right! Do not chase death faster than it chases you! We must keep our heads, if we are to remain together! We are not animals! Tame your fears!"

As a Natural would have done, Usha stretched her hand out and gripped Sofia's. The Maia herself put her hand out and took that of Sasha. One by one, the Citizens joined hands and the moment of desperation passed.

Grinning, Whitemane swung himself ahead of them and they started the grim trudge down into the depths beneath.

Along, low cloud lay sullenly across the horizon, blotting out the line where sky met sea. Evening had fallen, and it hung low over the Regions, darkening the morning with an ominous gloom.

Ash's hooves thudded down the softened sand of the water's edge and the small white crabs that appeared at this time of year scattered into the water and disappeared, leaving only a soft pop of bubbles behind. On her back, muddy and exhausted, clung Kira. With the last of her strength, she guided the mare to the mouth of a small cave, set into the rocky shelf of the mountains that faced the sea.

She dismounted and whistled twice, softly. From behind a curtain of creepers emerged Kristo. His hair was wet where he had washed and now his face and hair showed light and pale beneath the last of the berry-stains.

"Nothing?" he asked, seeing the expression on the other's face.

"Nothing." Kira turned aside and threw herself down wearily in a patch of shade. "No Rebels, no Wolf-men, no Citizens, nobody. Not a sausage."

Kristo looked confused, and Kira smiled tiredly at the

problem that the Citizen had in understanding. "I don't mean *really* a sausage, Kristo. It's an expression – well, never mind." But despite the lightness of her tone, her voice broke on the last word and she covered her face with her hands.

"I have failed. I have lost my tribe. I have lost my family. I have lost Arlo."

Kristo watched her uncomfortably, obviously unsure how to pacify a Natural in the throes of an Outbreak. He was even more confused when the woman turned to him, burying her head in his shoulder. As gently as he could, he drew away.

"What . . . what are you doing, Kira?" he asked feebly.

Kira opened her eyes and looked at him in surprise. "Don't you . . . don't you feel the same way as me?"

"Feel?" said Kristo, bemused. "Feel what?"

In a flash Kira was on her feet, her momentary weakness and the last of her tears burned away in a blaze of white-hot anger. "Feel *what*, you say? What a question!"

Kira stormed towards the horse, and started to untie the halter, her fingers shaking with emotion. "No, but the fault is mine! What a fool! To think that a Citizen could ever feel in the same way as a Natural!"

"Where are you going, Kira?" ventured the man, vainly trying to restrain her as she swung a leg over the horse's back.

"Anywhere but here!" snapped back the Natural girl.

"To find someone of my own kind, someone who is alive!"

"Someone like Tambar?" asked the man, mildly.

Kira shot him a fierce look that would have quelled any Natural, and wheeled Ash around and out of the dell only to come to an abrupt, quivering halt. Kristo ran up beside her, and followed her gaze to where four or five black shapes were circling over the plain beyond. "What is it?" he asked.

"Birds," answered Kira shortly. "Seekers of carrion. They follow any animals that are close to death, and wait until they fall."

"What animal could possibly be here?" asked Kristo in surprise.

Kira snorted, and slapped Ash on the flank. "That's the point. No animal would be in these parts, and that is why it must be human."

Toby was lying face down in a patch of weeds when they found him, and the first vultures had already landed on his back. A hundred metres away Annis knelt weakly, protecting her baby from the circling birds with her body. By the look of them, they had been wandering for almost two days, ever since the riot at the Meet, and they were covered in dirt and thistle-thorns. Kristo chased the hideous birds away, while Kira fell to her knees and raised Toby gently. His eyes were shut, and she could not hear him breathing.

"Toby!" she cried. "Toby! Can you hear me?"

*

Whitemane led the Citizens down the dizzying stair-path that wound around the nine levels of the pharms. Clearly, thought Usha, the layout of Pharmopolis had been designed specifically to prevent any prisoner uprising or mass getaway. Each level was bounded by high walls, and the pass between them was so narrow that only one might walk at a time. The Citizens ventured down in single file, but the Simians swung high above them upon the walls, gripping the rock with their prehensile toes, ever watchful for any sign of escape. At intervals they came across huge, studded doors that signalled the entrance to each level of the pharms, and from behind them came a cacophony of shrieks, hoarse laughter and speech that seemed both recognizable and yet unrecognisable, as if uttered by voices both human and barbaric. The Citizens shuddered at the thought of what might lie within.

As they descended deeper and deeper into the heart of Pharmopolis, Usha began to experience a serious unease. Was this what the moonstone meant for her? Could her visions have been wrong? And what on earth was the *Bestiary*?

Instinctively, she felt for the amulet at her throat. Its touch was cool and calmed her, though she dared not take it out and seek the answer in its creamy depths under the suspicious gaze of the Simians. Just as she was beginning to reconsider her plan, Whitemane stopped abruptly in front of a huge gate on the sixth level, produced a large ring of keys from his belt and unlocked it. From the darkness within came no sound, but a stench that Usha had never smelt before flooded out, and for a moment horror paralysed her.

"Welcome to the Bestiary, Citizens," Whitemane said mockingly. "I will see you tomorrow morning, for Regeneration – that is, if any of you are left alive by morning."

He drew back, doffing his cap in elaborate courtesy as the other Simians herded them inside and the huge gates swung shut behind them.

It was so dark that even Usha had trouble seeing where they were. Little by little, her eyes picked out the criss-cross grid of a great cage that covered the night sky, through which the blue fumes that hung in a vast cloud over Pharmopolis could dimly be seen. Along the right-hand side ran other shadowed cages, and above all a covered caged walkway, evidently a protected access tunnel for the use of the Simians. From underneath the walkway hung hooded shapes. As her eyes became more used to the dark, she saw with a start that they were similar to the great birds that had attacked them as the ship passed beneath the archways, roosting upside down with their huge leathery wings folded around them and their long hair hanging. Their faces, though narrow and pinched into beak-like noses and chins, were recognizably female, but all with eyes closed, sleeping.

"What are they, Sasha?" quavered Sofia in an undertone. "Where are we?"

But it was Tariq, Sasha's merchant companion, who whispered back, his voice shaking uncontrollably.

"The Bestiary is an experimental laboratory of the pharms, where scientists have devoted themselves to engineering mythical and miraculous beasts. I do not know the names of these creatures, but they are doubtless dangerous, for else they would not be kept in such a cage. Tread quietly, for we must not disturb them."

But as the Citizens strove to tiptoe forward, the hem of Usha's prison tunic caught on the roughened side of a drinking trough, and brought it over with a clatter. Instantly the night was alive with a flapping of wings and a screeching as the hideous inhabitants of the cage became awake. Usha flinched as the great shapes wheeled and hovered around them, spitting fearsomely.

"Awake! Awake! Strangers! Attack!"

"Toby!" gasped Kira. "Where is Arlo? Why isn't he with you?"

Toby struggled to a sitting position, coughing as the precious drops of water from Kira's flask trickled down his throat. "I don't know! He must have gone with Tambar and the Rebels!"

"Gone where?" pressed Kira urgently. "Which hiding place would they have gone to?"

Toby shook his head, his eyes huge in his smeared face. "They won't have gone to hide, Kira," he said haltingly. "They would have followed the Plan."

"What plan!" shouted Kira, and, as Kristo laid a

soothing hand on her, "Don't touch me, Citizen! Tell me, Toby! What plan!"

"They're. . ." Toby could hardly get the words out. "The plan was . . . to return to Genopolis."

Kira started to scream hysterically, and it was Kristo who took over, calmly reassuring Toby, and, little by little, extracting the story as Toby remembered it.

"Tambar said we could hide on the back of one of the food convoys," said Toby, avoiding Kira's gaze. "When they got to Genopolis, they were going to hide up in the den with Nanda and Mindie, and attack the Palace."

"With less than twenty Rebels?" yelled Kira. "Has Tambar gone absolutely insane?"

Toby blushed and stared at the ground. "Actually, Kira, it was Arlo who came up with the idea. Tambar organized the plan."

"Tambar prefers to die in a blaze of glory rather than succeed, it seems!" began Kira, but Kristo stood up slowly, his face grim.

"Listen," he said gently to the furious Natural. "Arlo has gone with the Rebels to follow the most foolhardy plan that I have ever heard. Of your tribe, there remain but three. What does this mean for you?"

Kira sat in silence for a while, then nodded. "I have a choice," she said flatly, getting to her feet and smoothing back her hair. "Either I stay in the wilderness with the last of my tribe, always running, always scared, or I go after the last remaining member of my family, and try to redeem my heritage, and my pride."

"But Annis and the little one cannot manage the journey," replied Kristo quietly. "They must stay here, in the cave, alone. The choice is yours to make, Kira."

Kira sat a long time lost in thought before responding, as Annis fidgeted next to her.

"Annis, forgive me, but I will follow Arlo," she said finally. "I do not know if we can reach him in time, or whether we can persuade him to leave Tambar and his fighting to others. But whatever it may be, I would prefer to die trying, than not try at all."

Annis nodded slowly. "I understand," she said softly. "We cannot go on doing as we have always done. You must leave us here."

Kira put her arms around the younger girl. "I do not expect to return," she said quietly, "but if I do, then I will come and find you. I promise."

"Then the question is, how do we get back into the City," replied Kristo thoughtfully. "We could try the same route as the Rebels, but I doubt our strength in making our way across the waters. There is only one way that I can think of, but first of all, you and Toby must agree to play a part. And somehow – I don't think either of you are exactly going to like it."

Kira and Toby exchanged glances. "Go on, then," muttered Kira. "Let's hear the worst."

Usha stared back at the winged monsters. Though their great wingspan made them appear far larger than they were, their bodies were around the same height as a Citizen, but clothed in feathers, and perched on sharp-taloned feet. Their beaked faces glared at her as they hissed and spat.

Behind her the Citizens clung together in a small group, shivering and moaning. "What are they?" moaned Tarissa. "What are these creatures?"

"They are known as the *Erinyes*, the Furies, or sometimes as Harpies," stammered Tariq. "The Naturals of Ancient Greece and Rome saw them as winged fiends of doom, who would punish the human race for its evils."

"As long as they don't punish us first," muttered Merco, but nobody laughed.

Yet Usha was strangely filled with a growing interest. For the first time she realized that she was face to face with some of the creatures she had glimpsed in the moonstone. Surely here was the first piece of the puzzle! These beasts would have their part to play. But what?

"Stop your chattering, old Furies!" came a commanding voice from the shadows behind them. "Some of us are trying to sleep!"

With the voice came a spring and a bound, and the bird-women scattered in confusion, squawking horribly as another form leapt into their midst, wheeled, and cut at them with its paws. Soaring into the air they clutched at the wire ceiling with their claws and screeched indignantly at the newcomer. But at the very sight of their rescuer, the Citizens fell back, gripped with even worse terror. For the beast — although human of face and voice — was also nightmarish to behold. From a bearded face that appeared male, the hair flowed back on to thickening shoulders covered with short bristling fur that reminded Usha of Arlo's dog Rem; then the pelt continued over a long back and four limbs that moved with a stealthy feline grace, like the tigers that Usha had seen in the Circus.

As the Furies perched clucking on the rafters, the creature paid both them and the Citizens no more attention, and turned its back as if to pad away to the quiet shadows at the other end of the cage. Despite her bewilderment, Usha thought quickly. So other beings were imprisoned here too, and luckily one of which the Furies seemed wary! Could they keep this new creature talking until the monsters lost interest and settled down for the night?

Immediately, she ran forward and stationed herself before the beast, brushing away Sofia's restraining hand.

"Thank you, sir!" gasped Usha. "They would have torn us to pieces if it wasn't for you!"

A tail switched behind the creature as it regarded Usha, while two glass-green eyes fixed her with an unwavering gaze. Usha experienced an unusual sensation; it was as if the creature looked through her rather than at her, with a stare that seemed to reach for a thousand miles.

"Ignore them," said the creature presently, after it had gazed through her and each of the Citizens in turn, apparently referring to the Furies, who twittered above

them, making ribald and obscene remarks, though none
dared approach again. "They enjoy welcoming visitors
in this way. But which creatures are you, who walk upon
two legs and have no fur or scales? Have our masters
created a new breed of beast, who must clothe
themselves as the Simians do?"

"We . . . we are Citizens," replied Sofia, coming up to
stand next to Usha. "They . . . we have been sent here for
Regeneration."

The creature considered them again, each in turn. "I
have heard of Citizens," he said presently. "But I never
imagined you would be so tiny, so helpless. Where are
your claws? Where are your tails?"

"We have no tails," replied Sofia, gaining confidence
from the creature's deep, unthreatening voice. "And for
claws we have only fingernails. Show them, Usha."

Usha obligingly held out her fingers for the creature
to inspect, and bared her teeth for good measure. But the
creature merely glanced with mild pity at her physical
shortcomings, before losing interest and beginning to
pad away. Above them, Usha could feel the Furies
preparing to swoop again, and darted after their rescuer,
seeking at all costs to detain him.

"Sir! Please, sir. . ."

The beast turned and looked at her as if he had
already forgotten who they were. Behind them, a Harpy
fluttered down to the ground and started to sidle
towards them with an inquisitive, pecking motion. Usha
thought quickly.

"Please . . . could you tell us *what* you are, sir?"

"*What* I am?" asked the creature, with mild distaste. "I am a Sphinx. Or rather, we are the Sphinx. Myself and my breed."

Sensing that the creature was about to leave again, Usha stepped in front of him. "But tell me, what is your name?"

"My *name*?" replied the creature, in what seemed like surprise. "What is a name?"

"A name is . . . well, it's *who* you are, rather than *what* you are," replied Usha quickly. "It's what would separate you from your, er . . . breed. Otherwise, how would anyone know the difference between you and another Sphinx?"

The Sphinx appeared to consider the issue for some time, frowning as if in deep thought. "It is an interesting question," he said finally, as if conceding a difficult point. "Come with me and we can discuss further."

Arlo and Ozzie sat slouched uncomfortably on a patch of rubble in the corner of the deserted Kids' chamber as the Rebels sat in conference, cross-legged on the floor. No one talked to them, and Arlo felt as if they were being totally ignored. Only Liana occasionally shot them a questioning glance, but Tambar appeared so preoccupied that he barely noticed them, much less picked up the expression on Arlo's face.

"Tomorrow, I'll lead one team into the Palace by this route *here*," Tambar was saying, pointing to the map sketched in the dirt of the floor. "Liana will lead the other around the back past the storerooms, *here*. . ."

"To tell you the truth," muttered Ozzie in Arlo's ear, "I'm not too sure about the plans this Tambar bloke's been making. He's got all sorts of mad plans in that head of his, and I keep telling him it's not a good idea. He won't listen to me, though, he wants to have it all his own way."

"I know what you mean," murmured back Arlo. "He doesn't care about Usha. I wouldn't be surprised if he didn't even have a plan of finding her at all."

Ozzie spat viciously on to the floor. "Well, lucky we're here then, ain't it? I tell you what, there's something that I know that I ain't been telling our friend and his snotty sister. There's a sewageway that me and the Kids tried once, goes up to the Palace dungeons. We didn't bother with it in the end, as there was no food there, but I was told that they keep the prisoners in there, the political prisoners, that is. Well, I thought you and me could do a little mission of our own in the meantime. . ."

Arlo choked so loudly that Ozzie was forced to shush him. "But why didn't you say this before?" he whispered back fiercely.

Ozzie grinned. "The problem with you, Natural, is that you trust your own kind too easily. First time I laid eyes on Tambar, I thought to myself, now there's someone who'll use people to get what he wants, and hang the rest of 'em. Quiet now, or they'll all be wondering what's going on. Follow me, and don't ask questions, or we'll be out of the firing pan and into the fryer, as Toby would have liked ter say."

Wonderingly, Usha and her companions followed the Sphinx as it padded noiselessly along the long stretch of cage that ran through the sixth level of the pharms. From the rafters, the Furies stole after them excitedly, upside down, twisting their heads this way and that, vigilant for any sign of weakness.

As their eyes became used to the dim light, the Citizens could see adjoining cages on all sides, filled with other nameless beings clustering behind the bars, eyeing them with wary curiosity as they passed. Even the hardiest Citizen could not restrain a shiver as they took in their silent, beastly spectators.

Out of the shadows appeared human faces, but each distorted with tusks, long teeth or slashed with gills; antlers branched from human heads and long tails curved behind them. Many creatures were formed like men and women, but with their bodies covered in rough hair or scales, their heads crowned with horns and their fingers tapering to sharp claws, or webbed fingers, or hooves. Some were hairless and smooth-faced and seemed neither male nor female, others were coarser and thicker with exaggerated limbs that had obviously been bred for singular purposes; turning wheels, shovelling, pulling, carrying, or working a treadmill. In some cages there lay creatures with their sides bristling with more than one pair of arms, or legs, using their limbs to drag themselves clumsily along. In others, there were hideously fleshly forms who had no recognizable features, but with their faces, backs and flanks studded with ears, or pairs of eyes that watched the Citizens' approach; some shrewd and calculating like humans, and others dull, instinctive and watchful like animals.

"These ones must have been bred for body parts," muttered Tariq. The Citizens turned their heads away in horror as they passed, but Usha walked in silence, memories long-buried slowly rising to the surface, of the early years before she had been brought, brainwashed and innocent, from the pharms to begin her life with Auntie in Genopolis.

Every moment she expected to encounter another Minotaur, as she had in the Circus, but finally – just as she thought they could take no more, the Sphinx stretched himself out languidly, like a cat, where the cage ended, flanked by other barred enclosures.

In the shadows of the pen, she could see a group of similar beings to the Sphinx, some sleeping, some raising their heads to take in the newcomers with scant interest. From all sides the other creatures clustered around the bars of their cages, gazing down at the new arrivals. The Citizens stood dumbly, their eyes passing over the hideous appearance of their audience in incredulous silence. Only Usha stood in thought.

With every creature in the Bestiary, and even more in the pharms, they would have the power to take on the City! For her vision of Arlo in the Brigadier's study could only mean one thing. He was going to Genopolis, and she would need to aid him.

"Sofia!" whispered Usha timidly to the Maia. "Maybe these creatures can help us!"

Sofia shot an understanding glance at her. "Leave it to me."

The Sphinx was looking at the new arrivals with mild boredom, and raised an eyebrow, as if to say, "Well?"

Instantly taking command of the situation, Sofia stepped forward, palm outstretched in greeting. "We have come," she said impressively, "to bring you freedom. We have come to take you out of your cages."

She paused, expecting some kind of response, but apart from a bemused stirring from her audience, there was little reaction, save only a jaded "What is a cage?" from a yellow-haired female Sphinx at her feet.

"This!" said Sofia, pointing upwards at the metal bars that surrounded them. "You are prisoners here! Don't you ever want to get out?"

"Out?" replied the first Sphinx, with a slight furrowing of his brow.

Usha could understand the creature's confusion. While she had been living in Genopolis, she never had any idea of a world that existed beyond the walls of the City. When Arlo, on the shores of the City during their first escape, had suggested the idea of a life beyond Genopolis, she had found it confusing and unimaginable. Yet still, the thought had inspired her, and now she had to inspire them too. But how?

"Where should we go?" asked the female Sphinx curiously. "Why should we leave? We are perfectly content here."

A Fury squawked. "Outside the pharms, nothing! Our sisters see only miles and miles of sea, or miles and miles of desert. Nothing there!"

"Yes there is!" insisted Sofia. "Further perhaps than you could fly, but there is a whole world out there. But you must break out to see it!"

Sofia paused, momentarily at a loss. "It is not working," she muttered in Usha's ear. "They do not understand. It is hopeless."

Usha shook her head. "I don't think that they're going to understand *freedom*, Sofia," she whispered back. "They don't know about the world outside! No, instead we have to make them understand that they are in danger here, and that we can help them escape it."

"But how?" hissed Sofia. "What should I say to them?"

"Let me try," said Usha gently, and moved forward to stand next to the Maia.

"Suppose we start with some introductions," she said falteringly, conscious that all eyes were upon her. "My name is Usha, and I am a Gemini. My companions are Citizens; their names are Sofia, Tariq, Sasha, Tutu, Tarissa, Yoshi, Yuma, Merco and Sir Herbert."

"We are the Chimaeras of the Bestiary," replied the Sphinx, calmly. "Half-beast, half human. Amongst us you can see satyrs, werewolves, fauns, lizard-people, centaurs, and other creatures that even they themselves do not know the breed. These —" indicating a cluster of the smooth-faced beings who stood curiously in an adjoining cage – "are the Androgynes, neither male nor female. You know that those wretched creatures there —" he indicated the bird-like women who spat at him furiously – "are the Furies. We, as I said before, are the Sphinx. But none of us, as far as I know, have what you call a *name*."

"Well, I didn't have a name, once, either," started Usha, falteringly, conscious that many eyes were upon her. "You see, I was Created here, then I was taken to Genopolis and given the name Usha. I didn't remember the pharms, I didn't remember anything that happened here. And what I didn't know was that I was actually bred to be killed, to be sacrificed for an old lady so that she might live. And the terrible thing is, I wasn't the first. . ."

Toby stood knee-deep in the dark sea, his wrists bound together with a strip of cord in front of him. With some difficulty, he held the sputtering candle fashioned from grease and a bit of rag, swinging it to and fro in the way Kristo had shown him. Without his glasses, he could see nothing on the black horizon.

They had left Annis and the child inside the shallow cave with the last of the scraps of food. Uneasiness tugged at Toby's mind. Perhaps after all they might be better off staying with them? Though Kristo's plan had seemed good enough during their first discussions, now Toby could see the drawbacks of it all too clearly. Sternly, he rallied himself. What alternative was there?

All his friends had left from the same shore to fight in Genopolis.

Behind him, Kira stood with her face pressed into Ash's side, as the horse snickered and jittered on the wet sand next to her. Her eyes were wet with tears, as slowly she undid the bridle, and patted the long back.

"Go, wild thing," she murmured. "Go back to where you came from."

But the horse only stamped doubtfully, and shook her mane and tail. "Go!" commanded Kira more fiercely this time. "You have your freedom! Leave us!"

The horse stood uncertainly beside her, confused. She did not understand her mistress's words, but the tone was clear enough to her. "Go!" cried Kira again, and this time struck Ash a sharp blow on the flank. Instantly, Ash neighed and plunged off into the darkness. Kira stood looking after her departing form as Kristo stepped forward, took her wrists and bound them together.

"She'll be all right," he said, in a tone intended to be comforting. "She'll go back to her own lands and be safe there."

Kira shook her head. "She cannot," she said. "She has been tamed now. I took something from her, and now she will be at the mercy of any wild animal, either beast or human. I just hope that the Wolf-men are no longer around these parts."

But resolutely she turned and faced back into the darkness. In front of them, Toby swung the lamp, up and down, up and down.

"Are you sure that this is the way the barges come?" murmured Kristo presently to break the tension.

"It is the nearest route," answered Kira. "But not every night. They feel safer to pass closer by the Regions with empty ships, because they know it is not worth our while to attack them."

Suddenly a distant shout came from the sea beyond them. "Ahoy there! Ahoy!"

Kristo instantly stepped forward and took the lantern from Toby, and shuttered it three times, on and off. From the sea came an answering flash, and then, unmistakably, the sound of oars splashing.

"What did you do?" whispered Toby, but Kira prodded him into silence. Kristo answered, "It is the Citizen seafaring signal. Quiet now. Let me do the talking."

A blinding light shone out of the darkness, flickered over Toby's face, and fastened on Kristo, standing dressed in the Citizen's military cap and uniform that they had taken from the dead soldier on the killing grounds.

"Who are you?" cried the voice. "Declare yourselves!"

Kristo removed his cap and held up his hands. "A soldier of Genopolis, with two Natural prisoners," he said clearly, in his best Citizen's accent. "I was part of a raiding party on the orders of Brigadier Hacker, but my catamaran was scuppered. I command you in the name of the Regis to turn over your barge to me and give me passage back to Genopolis."

"But we are not going to Genopolis," returned the voice, and for the first time the light swung out of their eyes and Toby could see behind it a long flat-bottomed barge, powered by eight or ten Citizen boatmen, two of whom held rifles trained on them. "We are on the way to the pharms for extra supplies for the Midsummer Ball. Surely your captains know of your situation? Can you not radio them?"

"My radio was broken in the raid, and I cannot wait longer on these shores," answered Kristo firmly. "My prisoners are two of the most dangerous rebels of these Regions, and even though the area is free of those devils for the time being, their tribe will soon return."

The light flashed again on Toby's face, and he did his best to look both menacing and Wolf-man-like. The man surveyed both him and Kira, ran his eyes over their dishevelled appearance and bound hands, but still hesitated.

"Am I to tell the Brigadier that you risked the success of a raid and two important prisoners, for the sake of a few sausage rolls and honey mead?" asked Kristo icily.

The man scratched his head in doubt. Toby could see that he was an elderly merchant boatman from the lower classes of Genopolis, obviously not given to making decisions on his own. The old sailor's eyes flickered over Kristo's ill-fitting uniform and the bent rifle uncertainly.

"What is the insignia which hangs above the door of the Guardian Headquarters?" he asked at length.

"Two rifles, crossed, with a black and silver inscription. 'Power Above All'," replied Kristo promptly. "There are two statues in the forecourt, one of our Founder, Leuwenkind, and another of Brigadier Hacker."

The boatman nodded slowly, as if partially reassured, and waded ashore. One man holding a rifle followed him warily. From his pocket the captain produced a small silver dirk that sparkled wickedly in the lamplight. "Hold out your hand," he said, and in an undertone, "Forgive me sir, but I must make certain."

He drew the blade of the knife deep across Kristo's palm, and a dark streak of blood appeared. Kira drew in her breath at the sight, but the Citizen did not flinch, and the boatman nodded and stepped back, saluting smartly.

"Yes, sir," he said respectfully. "Come on board." To his men he shouted, "Turn about! Set the compass! Make for Genopolis!"

In a breathless hush, Usha recounted the story of her life as she remembered it, of her early years with Auntie, and then the terrible revelation on the Operating table as she discovered the purpose for which she had been made. She told them of the scissor-man, and of her escape into the sewer-underworld of Genopolis, of Arlo and Ozzie and the Kids; and of the Circus, the Minotaur and the cruel sports that had been designed there for the amusement of the Citizens. As she had predicted, it was the last story that seemed to rouse the attention of her listeners at last, some of them sighing or groaning in sympathy.

It was clear that, whatever science had produced these creatures, they still possessed the capacity for pain, and the animal-like empathy that could make them feel when suffering was inflicted on one of their number. Perhaps this came from their half-beast nature? Minute by minute more and more creatures awoke and gathered around, listening intently until she paused for breath.

Amidst the sudden flurry of questions that greeted her at this point ("Why do they have a Circus? Where is it?"), Usha described the Circus, pointedly omitting Merco's part in the enterprise, and made much of the Minotaur's final moments at the sharp swords of Bjarn and Talia. Throughout the exchange, the Ringmaster kept silent, and Usha noticed a look of unease as he glanced at the creatures around him. For the first time she realized that if the beasts knew that he had been the leader of the Circus where many of them had been sent to fight and die, he would be torn to pieces. Yet still, he maintained a calm arrogance that seemed incongruous considering their circumstances, and she resolved to watch him closely.

"So this is where we are taken!" cried the golden-haired female Sphinx. "They tell us nothing of this!"

"They took the Gorgon a few weeks ago!" cried some of the Androgynes, from where they had been leaning against the bars, listening intently. "Our masters said she was being taken to a better place!"

"But your masters took her to kill her!" encouraged Usha earnestly. "Either for body parts, food, or their own entertainment! Will you wait here for that? Or do you want a world where you can run free, untroubled? Outside Genopolis there are miles and miles of land that you could roam in!!"

"But what can we do about it?" enquired another Sphinx. "If our purpose is to die, then it is to die. What good would this do?"

"No!" cried Usha passionately. "Your purpose is more than this! You are free to choose your own purpose! And the only way you can do this is to rise up against those people who are controlling you and overthrow them!"

"But how can we overthrow them?" objected the male Sphinx. "We are not fashioned like you. We do not have hands, we do not walk upright as you or the Simians do. We cannot fire guns or sail ships."

"But the Androgynes and the Gemini and some of the Chimaeras do, and altogether there are enough of you here to overcome the Simians!" said Usha urgently. "And others have teeth, claws, tusks and other weapons! You don't have to put up with this any longer!"

A tremor ran through her audience, and there was much chattering and muttering, and from the Furies, a squawking of "Blood! Blood!" which was quickly frowned down by the Sphinx.

"I do not think we should go against our masters," shouted another Androgyne, peering through the bars. "It will only lead to ruin."

"And what good will it do us afterwards?" croaked a fishy-looking Chimaera, her gills flapping. "Who will feed us? Who will look after us? We will be on our own!"

"But being free is about being on your own!" called back Usha. Forgetting herself, she climbed up on a drinking trough and waved her arms at the assembled crowd.

"You will not be *alone*. After we overthrow the pharms, our aim is to attack Genopolis! For every Citizen living there are many more creatures here! We need your help, and only by working together can we do this!"

Faces turned towards her, and finally she had their undivided attention. "For Genopolis controls the pharms, and only by attacking it can we finally be free. But you must choose, for time is running out! If we are to attack Genopolis, we must do so on Midsummer's Night!"

Arlo stared in horror at the slimy sewer-pipe, crusted with the filth of years of use, and shook his head.

"I'm sorry, Ozzie, but I can't go up there. It's . . . well, it's horrible!"

Ozzie snorted with impatience. "Well, what were you expecting? A velvet red carpet and scented candles? 'Course it's horrible! That's the bleedin' point! Now stop your Natural yapping and get going!"

Arlo gritted his teeth, as the Citizen swung himself up and easily into the pipe, and followed.

It was worse than he could ever have imagined. The stench was so powerful that it revolted him to his stomach, and he marvelled inwardly how Ozzie could have existed within the sewers for so long. Several times he nearly choked and was almost sick, and if it wasn't for holding on to Ozzie's ankle at times he might easily have been overpowered by the fumes and fainted. But finally he felt a breath of fresher air on his face, and the next moment Ozzie was grasping him by the scruff of his neck and they were grovelling on the floor of a dirty but disused latrine. Dank and unwholesome though the air was, it seemed sweet and refreshing to Arlo, as he heaved and retched in a corner.

When he had recovered himself, Ozzie motioned to him in Rebel sign language, being safer than ordinary whispers. *Up here, stay behind me, and quickly.*

A rusty door barred the exit to the latrine, but it was the work of a moment for Ozzie to use his knife to lever the hinges off it. Once through, they propped it back into position, and took stock of their surroundings. They were standing on the bottom level of a winding stairwell, unlit by any means, though a faint yellowish glow trickled down from above.

On all fours, they crawled cautiously up the stairs, pausing at every bend, but no footstep was heard. After they had ascended a couple of flights, they came upon a barred door set into the wall, but as Ozzie touched it, it swung open with a faint creak.

"It's empty!" whispered Arlo, momentarily forgetting their danger. "There's no one in there!"

Ssssh, signalled Ozzie. *There's other cells, upstairs.*

But as they crawled from level to level, the absence of light and of guards brought one fact home to them. Whichever prisoners the dungeons had once housed, either political or criminal, they now stood black and empty, and all that area was shuttered and quiet. On the final level, a group of empty cells bore traces of recent occupation: footprints in the dust, a bent plate with a rotting sausage still clinging to it, and a few scraps of threadbare garments.

If she's not here, gestured Arlo frantically to his friend, *then where would they have taken her?*

Ozzie shrugged. *Beats me. Fancy a look up above?*

Wearily, Arlo agreed, and followed the Citizen as they edged into a broader, faintly-lit corridor and looked about them. Here a smell of cooking drifted down from the higher levels, and distantly there came the faint buzz of feet and talk, though from how far away they could not tell. Arlo was seized by sudden panic. How reckless they had been, coming into the foot of the Palace! If they were caught, then the entire plot to overthrow Genopolis would be discovered, and all Tambar's plans would be in vain! He reached for Ozzie to pull him back into the darkness of the dungeons, but his friend was already hurrying along the passageway, uncaring of their danger. As Arlo ran after him, the corridor suddenly echoed with footsteps, and the next moment someone pulling a smoking food-trolley appeared around a bend in front of them.

Instantly Ozzie was upon him, and the figure crumpled with a muffled shout, the trolley flying with a clatter against the wall. In the quiet of the corridor, the noise seemed deafening. In an agony of fear, Arlo ran after him, and tugged frantically at his friend.

"Stop! Ozzie, let's go! Leave him!"

"We can't! He'll bring the soldiers down after us!" hissed Ozzie.

But Arlo hung on to Ozzie's arm, and the figure twisted easily out of Ozzie's grasp. But instead of shouting or raising the alarm, Arlo heard a muffled gasp. "Arlo! Arlo! It's you!"

Arlo gazed unbelieving at the face before him, the face of a tall, fair-haired boy that he had not seen since leaving Sir Herbert's house over a year before.

"Clarence!" he cried. "What are you doing here?"

The next second, Clarence had rushed at him, and Arlo cringed away, expecting a blow. Then Clarence's arms were round his neck and Arlo felt hot tears on his cheek.

"They arrested my father at the Circus when you ran away," sobbed Clarence. "They sent him for Regeneration, and then they cut off my hands, and they made me and Cecilia servants until we are fifteen, and then they will kill us too!"

"Arlo! What's going on! Who in Genopolis is this?" hissed Ozzie.

"This is Clarence, the son of Sir Herbert, one of the Circle, who let me hide in his house last year. . ." began Arlo, but Ozzie was no longer listening.

"*Clarence?* That bully?" cried Ozzie, remembering the story of Arlo's cruel treatment at the hands of the boy. "Let me at him! I'll show him!"

But for the first time Arlo realized that Clarence's arms ended in mutilated stumps where his fists had once been. "Stop, Ozzie," he said quietly, putting out a hand to restrain his friend. "Things were different then."

"Have you come to get us out?" begged Clarence. "I'll do anything, Arlo, anything! Just take us away from here!"

Arlo took a deep breath. The temptation to run with Clarence was strong, but he gritted his teeth and remained calm.

"Listen, Clarence. We need your help. . ."

With a feeling of disbelief, Usha watched as the discussions travelled from cage to cage around the Bestiary, with the inhabitants of each compartment being woken up and told the news. The babble rose to such a height that Usha could no longer hear her own voice, and was forced to murmur to the Sphinx, whom she correctly identified as possessing some kind of authority in the Bestiary, "Please, sir, can you get them to quieten down? We need to make a decision!"

"Silence!" bellowed the Sphinx, and sudden calm was

restored, save for a few Furies, who pecked excitedly at each other.

"But how are you proposing to *do* this?" asked the female Sphinx of Usha, voicing the questions of many present.

"We are members of the Circle, the secret society of the Resistance," broke in Sofia before Usha could speak. "We have been trained in fighting and attack as well as any soldier in Genopolis! Follow us, and we can lead you!"

"But lead us to where?" began the Sphinx. However Tariq quickly interrupted.

"I was formerly a merchant of Pharmopolis. I know the pharms well. On the north side there is a port, with many ships. If we can commandeer them, we make for the City."

"And with what weapons?" asked the Sphinx.

"There is an Armoury here which we could raid," answered Sasha excitedly, and Sir Herbert raised his hand in interjection.

"Wait," he said softly, "I have heard that weapons of great power are bred here in Pharmopolis. I do not know where they are, but if we could capture one of these, then nothing and no one could stand before us."

"What weapons are these?" asked Sofia curiously, turning to face him. "Why have you never spoken of this before?"

But Sir Herbert's eyes were veiled. "They are so secret

that they are kept hidden even within the pharms," he said slowly. "I believe that they are kept on the fifth level. They are things of terrible force, and to use one would be a mixed blessing. Though it might help us, it would be at a great cost to human life."

"And the Gemini!" called out Usha, not to be outdone. "There are hundreds of us bred every year in the pharms! If we can get them to follow us, then we can match the soldiers each for each!"

Finally the Sphinx raised himself on all four paws, suddenly imperious and commanding and turned to the Chimaeras.

"You have all heard the strangers, and the news they bring of the world outside. How many of you wish to stay here, knowing what we now know?"

A few hands were raised, or the appropriate limb.

"Or do you rather wish to seek a place of our own, in these . . . what do you call them . . . Regions?"

A cheer, along with much nodding of heads and flapping of wings greeted his announcement. Usha was secretly rather impressed at the way the Sphinx handled the creatures, and wished for a moment that she had as great a presence.

"Then we must send word around every cage in the Bestiary," decided the Sphinx. "Once the Bestiary has been roused, then we must break out and release the other levels. It will be up to you Citizens to lead us to where you wish, and take the weapons if you can. I do not know where the Gemini are bred, but there must be a way to find them. And if any Simian comes before me, let him watch out!"

"Indeed?" mocked a throaty voice from the walkway above. "Then I am sorry to say that you will have no such opportunity!"

So intent had everyone been on the plans that no one had noticed the stealthy approach of a contingent of Simians from above, the earlier noise surely having attracted them. Whitemane leaned over the top of the cage, his ugly face bristling from beneath his snowy fur. Next to him were two other Simians, with orange and black fur respectively, who swiped and snarled at the Furies as they snapped and screamed curses at them from the other side of the bars.

"Seize her!" commanded Whitemane, pointing at Usha. "Take the traitor for Regeneration immediately!"

With a roar, the Sphinx crouched like a lion and then sprang at the Simian guards who issued through the main gates behind them, but a huge net thrown by the Simians above entangled him in its folds, and he rolled over, spitting, howling, but powerless. The Furies soared screeching to the other side of the cage, leaving the Citizens alone in the centre of the floor. From the row of cages behind came a great roar as the assembled creatures threw themselves at the bars, trying to break through. The front of the cages buckled under their weight, and Whitemane and the other Simians leapt for safety as the walkway bent precariously under the pressure of many yowling bodies.

But there was no time to see more. Guards seized Usha and pulled her to the door, sending Tariq and Sofia flying as they tried to intercede. The next moment, Whitemane roared furiously from above.

"Two by two, we will feed you all into the furnaces tonight! Choose your death-partner, Gemini! Choose which of your friends will die with you!"

Usha gazed around the terrified faces of her friends, seeing the new-found hope paralysed and swiftly disappearing. "Choose!" commanded Whitemane. "Otherwise I will choose for you!"

Merco raised his hand. "I will go with her," he said, and Usha's jaw was not the only one there that dropped at his words. "Take us both. Now get on with it. I'm sick of all this waiting around."

"**W**here are you? Where are you?"

The voice echoed around Corin's head as he struggled through a writhing sea of strange shapes that tore and plucked at his garments with a life of their own. *Trees!* he thought wildly, though in truth he had never seen so many trees all together, like a great army tossed in the gusts of a mighty wind. Holding his hands over his face, he burst through a thicket and into a small clearing, and almost collided with a tall man who stood towering before him. For a second he thought it was his father, and started away in fear, before he recognized the face of the stranger, the dark-haired man with a pale face that he had painted from a sense other than memory.

"Who are you?" he cried, but the wind tore his words away. "Who are you?"

A hand seized him from behind and dragged him up. Corin kicked and fought, but another voice was shouting in his ears, and the shapes that held him became bedclothes entwined around his arms and legs.

"Master! Master! Wake up!"

Corin groaned as he took in the face of his servant, shaking his shoulder to wake him up. "Another nightmare, Ivar. I can't sleep! I don't know what's happening to me!"

He rubbed listlessly at his tired eyes and crawled to the window, refusing Ivar's offer of tea. Lack of sleep and constant vigilance had taken their toll on him. Already disgraced since the Enquiry, only the newly-formed, burning hatred of his father gave him strength to carry on from day to day, hiding his Emotions from all around him. Since the failed attempt to break Usha out of the clutches of the guards, the Regis had taken measures to clamp down the City and secure a military guard around the ports and the marina. Although Corin did not think that he himself was suspected in the attempted escape, he had nonetheless decided to keep to himself for the time being. In any case, hope had failed him since Usha had been taken away.

"Midsummer Night. Tell him. Midsummer Night."

Gazing at the distant sea, and wondering about the Gemini girl, doubt and loneliness seized him. Why had she not taken his chance of escape? What was the message that she had given him? And to whom should he give it?

There was a sudden fusillade of knocks at the door. Ivar opened it, and immediately Clarence, the new slave, stood gasping in the doorway, his maimed wrist raised in salute. "Please, sir . . . I've got someone to see you, sir."

Ivar moved to object, but Corin, his curiosity pricked, waved him aside. "What is it? Show him in, Ivar."

Clarence shook his head. "I can't bring him up here, sir. Would you," he asked timidly, with a glance at the hulking Gemini beside Corin, "be able to come with me? It won't take very long, but it's important, sir."

In some surprise, Corin got to his feet. Any break in his dreary day would be welcome, though for the life of him he could not think what it would be. But something in Clarence's eyes made him follow him without question.

Unwillingly, the heavily-built Gemini swung into position behind them, and the next second they were making their way down the twisting stairwell that led towards the dungeons. Corin glanced around cautiously several times, but there was no one to be seen. As they neared the dungeon door where Usha had been imprisoned, Clarence opened the gate cautiously and ushered them through.

Corin caught his breath. Ragged and stained with all sorts of nameless filth, he saw, crouched in the corner, the red-haired boy who had been so much in his thoughts of late. Next to him was another older and scruffier boy with one eye. For a moment he stared, unable to speak. At that moment it all made sense, and Usha's words came back to him with a meaning that he had never before understood. A strange and almost overriding impulse came over him, of an urge to throw his arms around the red-haired boy and embrace him, though he did not know the reason.

"You're Arlo, aren't you?" he said, his voice barely more than a whisper. "I'm Corin. I've always wanted . . . to meet you."

With smoke belching from its chimneys, the Regeneration Factory towered above Usha and Merco as the Simians dragged them across the deep plain that lay in the ninth circle and the very centre of Pharmopolis. Contingents of Simian guards bounded past them on their way to quell the tumult in the Bestiary, which after Usha's arrest had been fanned into an uproar. From the extent of the noise, it seemed as if some of the cages had already been broken beneath the weight of the rioting inhabitants. But for Usha the sound of the fledgling rebellion was fading beneath the clatter and thump of the pistons that powered the greedy Regeneration machines. A deep rumble and crash shook the ground beneath them, and the remaining Simians who manned the searchlights and the outer gates saluted Whitemane's party as they passed the first of many barriers along the path that led to the gaping mouth of the entrance. Against the blue fumes, the watchtowers and twisted wire that encircled the factory rose black and menacing before them.

Disoriented and bewildered, Usha clung to the moonstone around her neck. What should she do? What *could* she do? She tried to struggle, but the Simian held both her and Merco in a tight grasp and escape from any direction was impossible.

She gazed up at her last sight of the clouded, smoky sky. Perhaps rousing the Bestiary was all the part she was meant to play. Now it was up to Sofia and the other Citizens to try to speed the rebellion, and in her heart, Usha hoped that they would succeed. The members of the Circle were far better equipped to take over the boats and attack Genopolis than she. For her and Merco, it was too late. Yet despite the turmoil in her brain, Usha felt oddly at peace. For the first time in her life she felt that she had discovered – and fulfilled – her purpose.

The next moment the glow of the sky was abruptly cut off as they entered the darkness of the Factory. Doors clanged behind them and they were thrown roughly to the gritty floor.

Wreaths of what seemed like gaseous mist wove around them in the blackness, and Usha felt an odd sensation over her skin, as if it was being slowly constricted, bit by bit. It was a sensation that she had never felt before. Puzzled, she could see her breath hanging in the air before her, as if turned to a small white cloud. The next moment she realized what it must be, for nowhere in Genopolis nor in the Regions had this happened to her. For some reason – perhaps in the interests of preserving cells for Regeneration – the air of the Factory was freezing cold.

This must be the icy fire that Whitemane had spoken of. She felt the floor sticking to her feet, and the numbness rising up her legs, as if she might turn into a statue any moment, blue and petrified, and crusted with ice.

Looking about her, Usha could see in the dim light that they were in a small iron chamber, the walls of which were scarred with desperate scratches, as of claws or fingernails; but it was empty save for a long moving track, laden with cages, which ran along the centre of the floor, and disappeared through a small arch in the adjoining wall. Whitemane stood over them, his breath steaming through his wide-set nostrils.

"Hair, teeth and eyes!" he snarled.

"Are you sure, sir?" asked the other Simian. "Usually the eyes is last, so that they can see everything that's—"

"Eyes, I said," growled Whitemane. "For traitors, you take the eyes now."

Suddenly Merco lost his composure, and swiped at the guards wildly. "No!" he screamed. "No!"

But the orange-haired Simian stepped forward and held him with a vice-like grip, while with a pair of shears he cut roughly at Merco's lank locks until they lay in clumps around him. Usha put up no resistance, and instead closed her eyes as she felt her own head pulled forward and the freezing metal of the clippers as it cut her hair close to her scalp. So all that she had seen in the vision was coming to pass, she thought. She hoped it would be quick. Cradling the moonstone between her palms, she opened her eyes for a last glimpse into its creamy depths.

But before she could do so, the cord was wrenched from her neck by Whitemane and the stone clattered to the floor. The Simian picked it up and gazed at it, sudden greed flickering in his eyes. Usha snatched at it wildly, but Whitemane held it out of reach, turning it over and over, as if in a trance. For a moment Usha feared that Whitemane would be able to see her visions in the stone, but then Onofre's voice came back to reassure her.

"*For those who cannot see, it will be just a thing of beauty...*"

"'Ere! What's that?" growled the orange-furred Simian abruptly, releasing his grip on Merco, and turning to Whitemane. "What you got there?"

"Nothing," snapped Whitemane, thrusting the moonstone into his pocket. "Shut up, you. Get on with it."

The orange-haired Simian threw the iron tongs that he had been holding down on to the floor. "Nah! You know the rules. Any loot from prisoners is to be shared fifty-fifty. Give it 'ere!"

Whitemane turned, and at the same time, brought up his booted foot into the other's stomach, sending him staggering backwards. With a roar, the orange-haired simian recovered and charged at him, sending Whitemane crashing into the chamber wall. As they fought, rolling over and over, ripping and snarling at each other, Usha was dimly aware of Merco pulling at her and forcing her towards the moving cages on the track.

"Come on, Blondie! In here!"

Not needing to be told twice, Usha dived inside the nearest cage, and the next second Merco had clambered inside too, squashing her against the frosted metal sides. As their guards fought, the cage began to move towards the archway of the adjoining chamber. The freezing gusts of cold gas intensified, and as they passed through the arch, Usha heard Whitemane's outraged roar from behind them.

"The eyes, you fool! You didn't get the eyes!"

Arlo returned Corin's gaze with steady amazement. Now, at close quarters, he could see the boy who had smiled at him during the Ceremony, and whom he had glimpsed so fleetingly at the Circus. He was a year older now, and taller, with his fair hair already starting to darken to brown, but the same ink-black eyes looked frankly back at him. For a moment they looked at each other, unable to speak.

"I've come to ask for help," said Arlo quietly. "Clarence told me about all the trouble you had with your father, and I thought you might be able to help me."

"Usha's gone, you know," Corin replied, as soon as he had breath enough. "They took her for Regeneration. I tried to help her escape, but. . ."

Arlo bit his lip, feeling as if all the wind had been knocked out of him. Behind him, Ozzie gasped and swore.

"When?" Arlo muttered, aghast. "When was she taken?"

"A few days ago," answered Corin slowly. "But she gave me a message, Arlo. She said I would know who to give it to when the time came. I didn't understand at the time, but now I can only think that it is meant for you."

Arlo shook his head. "What message, Corin?"

"She said, *Midsummer's Night*," repeated Corin slowly. "That's all she said. Midsummer's Night."

Arlo gazed at Corin, thunderstruck. Ozzie stepped forward. "Midsummer's Night? What does that mean?"

"I'm not really sure," said Corin thoughtfully. "But one thing I am sure of. I'm sick of my father, the Brigadier, and the way things are run in the City. I don't know why you're here, Arlo, but I hope that what you're doing will bring about an end to all this. Now tell me everything. I've only got an hour before dinner, and we'd better make the most of it."

In muttered voices they shared the experiences that they had spent over the last year, of the Regions and the Hunt, of Usha's capture, and lastly, Corin's experience with Emotions and of his feelings towards his father.

"At least you *have* a father," Arlo protested, but Corin shook his head.

"Not really," he said flatly. "Not a good one, anyway. He's not really anything like me, you know."

For the first time, Arlo found himself wondering whether he had, indeed, been better off without a father, than with a bad one.

"Listen, Corin," he said eventually. "I think Usha had something in mind when she left you the message. Can you tell us what the Midsummer Ball is, and where exactly it will be held?"

Crammed though she was between the heavy bulk of the Ringmaster and the freezing metal bars of the cage, Usha could not help but feel relief that they were out of the clutches of the guards, despite what might lie before them.

A bluish glow illuminated the tunnel, and by its light she could make out that the track was moving slowly down towards another archway, from where came a flickering pale light and an acid stench. Mindful of what the Naturals had told her in the Regions, Usha knew it was essential to keep moving, as intense cold could slow down all bodily reactions and make you unable to speak or move, even if you were a Citizen.

"What do we do now?" she cried above the tumult of the machines.

Quickly, the Ringmaster knelt down, and with his remaining arm pulled aside the rough prison tunic to reveal the skin of his calf. Usha stared as she saw that the flesh was reddened and puckered, as if mutilated with a knife and stitched hurriedly together. With a long fingernail, he slashed a deep groove down his skin, and a trickle of blood seeped out. Then slowly, precise as pincers, he reached inside the wound and extracted a small metal object that he licked clean and held between his teeth as he ripped a strip from his tunic and roughly bandaged the wound.

"What are you doing?" cried Usha, but Merco ignored her, standing upright in the cage and peering ahead of them.

"This is the tricky bit now. You've got two arms, so you'll have to go first, Blondie."

With a juddering motion, the procession of iron cages passed through into the third chamber, and instantly the huge network of the Regeneration machines surrounded them. Huge hissing tubes carried steam and power up from below, while great cogs and wheels turned in giant machinery around the walls. Through the freezing fumes spurting from above and below, Usha made out that they were inside a huge metal canister, which stretched high to a vaulted ceiling and dropped many feet to the distant floor beneath. Looking down, she could see, far below them, teams of what must be specially created Gemini, impervious to the cold, turning the vast wheels that kept the machinery moving. And below them – she saw with an uncharacteristic shudder – stretched out on racks, were rows of frosted bodies, some of Gemini appearance, others of Chimaeran or Androgynous appearance, all petrified like statues into the same frozen attitudes.

Directly below them, at the end of the mechanical track, lay a great icy lake, with bluish flames licking over the surface and steaming with frost. The cages passed overhead and tipped upside down, before righting themselves and rattling around in a huge arc to return to the outer chambers. Above the lake hung a huge ventilation shaft that led up to the high ceiling of the chamber, its sides crusted with frost by the white vapour. Wraiths of mist obscured her vision, and she could not at first see or hear what Merco was asking her to do.

"Before the cage tips upside down, Blondie," he was shouting above the din, "you need to stand up and hang on to that vent above as best you can. I'll climb up on to your shoulders and pull you in. Otherwise if we fall into that lake, it will turn all the water in our cells into ice faster than you can say Regeneration!"

Pulling herself together and trying not to think of the awful fate that awaited them, Usha peered into the fog and braced herself. As the track started its passage across the huge lake, she put one foot on the side of the cage, then stepped up and reached above her head to where the smoke-vent hung down. She saw an overlapping rim at the edge of the vent, and gripped it tightly with her fingers. The next second she felt Merco's foot in the small of her back as he used her for a springboard to clamber one-armed up her body and wriggle into the top of the vent.

Usha's feet fell from under her as the cage tipped upside down over the lake, and for a moment she was kicking and wriggling and spinning over the dizzying drop down to the icy fire below. Merco's weight was full on her shoulders, and though he was not a heavy man, she felt her fingers slipping and her bones creaking under the pressure.

"I can't!" Usha gasped, as she felt the chill breath of the lake below leaping up and licking wickedly at her ankles. "I can't hold you!"

But abruptly the pressure eased, and Merco was now crouched inside the vent with each foot pressed against the lip. With his spare hand he reached down and grasped her wrist even as her grip slackened. She would have fallen in another second, but with a hefty pull, he hauled her up so that she could grip the vent with her other hand and struggle up beside him.

In the gloom, she could see that there were a series of handholds cut into the side of the vent, presumably for maintenance purposes. But where he hoped to go she did not know. She could only trust that the plan that he had obviously worked out for himself would serve both of them. It seemed clear that Merco needed her in the climb so that he could hold on to her with his remaining arm, as climbing without a limb would be impossible.

"Come on, Blondie!" cried the Ringmaster in her ear. "Or we'll be frozen to death in a few minutes!"

Gritting her teeth against the white fumes that threatened to overpower her, Usha reached up, took the first handhold, and began.

Toby lay in a puddle of water in the stern of the barge, his hands and feet bound. Next to him lay Kira, curled in a huddle, her long hair obscuring her face. Over them stood Kristo, his empty Citizen's rifle trained threateningly on them, and from time to time he stepped forward and gave Toby a savage kick. Toby moaned and writhed, giving the best impression he could of Natural suffering. He was rather proud of the effect.

"He'd better not think that he can kick *me* like that," muttered Kira. "That's *enough*, Toby, nobody screams like that unless they're dying."

"Silence!" commanded Kristo, the ghost of a smile hovering around his lips.

But as the boat rapidly covered the waves and headed for Genopolis, it became clear that there was a disagreement between the crew. At least one of the crew members seemed opposed to returning to the City, and a fierce dispute had broken out in the bows. At first, Toby imagined that someone must have become suspicious of them, but as he raised his head cautiously, he caught sight of the boat-captain remonstrating with a dark, thickset man, whose straggling hair and beard seemed strangely out of place amongst the crew-cropped sailors.

"But I have an important business meeting in the

pharms at daybreak!" protested the thickset man. "If I'd known that you were going to be picking up every squaddie that got himself stranded, I'd have taken another ship!"

"Quiet, Zadoc," snapped the captain. "You can't blame us for going back to the City tonight. You heard the soldier. Orders from the Brigadier."

"But I am expected!" cried the man. "You stupid boat-people! You do not understand!"

"That's enough," replied the captain sharply. "Any more from you, and you'll be thrown overboard and you can swim your own way to the pharms."

Kristo sighed and turned to the boat-captain, tapping his rifle warningly at the other. "What seems to be the problem, Captain?"

The thickset man threw himself into the stern of the barge, and the boat-captain turned to Kristo, ushering him away. "He is a merchant of Pharmopolis, and we offered him a return ride. His token is in order, and he said he was in a hurry. Well, he's lucky we managed to fit him in the crew at all. Never worry about him, sir. We'll get you back to Genopolis in a few hours."

But Toby was already peering in confusion at the thickset man, who, in quite an unCitizenly fashion, growled and glared at the retreating Regions behind him, throwing pellets of corn-cake ill-temperedly into the sea.

Zadoc! It was an unusual name within Genopolis, and Toby had heard it only once before. Something about Usha ... he could not quite remember the details ... but he was quite sure that the name Zadoc had been associated with trouble.

He resolved to whisper to Kira as soon as the boatman's back was turned, but the captain sat down only a few feet away, and lit a pipe packed with some evil-smelling herb. Passing on the information to Kira or Kristo was impossible under the keen eyes of the boatman and he had to bite his tongue.

Yet if Zadoc was not all he seemed, Toby shivered to himself, then it would mean that they were not the only stowaways on the ship. And when they were in Genopolis, they would need to be looking over their shoulders for him too, along with everything *else* they needed to watch out for!

Machinery clanged and whirred around them, and the din was so magnified inside the vent that Usha was half-dazed and disoriented. She knew her skin was freezing and splintering against the icy metal but she dared not stop to look. It was almost impossible to breathe, and she could only give thanks that neither she nor Merco were Naturals, otherwise they could never have survived the torment of the punishing climb. Up and up they went. The vent narrowed as it reached the top of the chamber, and despite the dragging burden of Merco's weight as he climbed behind her with one arm wrapped around her waist, Usha heaved herself up on to the last handhold. Every movement cost her an enormous effort. She half-wished that she could stay still for a moment, and her body and brain freeze into nothingness and sleep.

This is how it must feel to be dead, she thought.

Above her she could see a huge grid, through which the fumes escaped and dissipated into the night air. She pushed at it with one hand but it would not budge.

"It's locked!" she screamed above the noise of the machinery. "We're stuck!"

But Merco had lodged himself against the wall of the vent, and was already reaching up past her with the twisted strip of metal clutched in his remaining hand.

"Welcome to the wonderful world of the skeleton key, Blondie."

Usha held him braced against her shoulder as he inserted the thin strip of metal and jiggled it experimentally in the lock from side to side. But the grid did not seem to budge. Merco swore as he withdrew the key, tinkered briefly with its shape, and tried again. Usha pushed her knee against the side of the shaft, as Merco changed his position, leaning the other way. Again the lock refused to turn, and again Merco withdrew the key, all bent out of shape.

"Is it working?" cried Usha. "What do we do now?"

"Shut up, Blondie," snarled Merco as he reached forward. "There's just a little – ah, there it is."

Usha held on grimly to the side of the vent as Merco made a final effort. The grid fell back with a clatter. With the last of her strength, Usha heaved the

Ringmaster out of the vent, and tumbled after him on to the rocky lip of the volcano and the cold night air. Sprawled and gasping they lay still for some minutes, blackened with frostbite and crusted with ice, coughing and almost unrecognizable.

"We did it!" gasped Usha. "We did it!"

Merco looked at her, an evil leer twisting the corner of his mouth.

"Well done, Blondie. Now you and I are officially dead, nobody's going to look for us, are they? And nobody is going to hear you scream."

As Arlo and Ozzie, still stinking from the filth of their return scramble through the sewer-pipes, stumbled into the midst of the Rebel meeting, Tambar turned to meet them, furiously.

"Where on earth have you *been*? I gave orders for *nobody* to go off alone!"

Liana, her eyes fierce and wild, stepped forward and clouted Arlo on the side of the ear. "Do you realize how dangerous this was? What could have happened if you had been caught? How dare you endanger our plans, you stupid little boy!"

Quick as a flash, Ozzie sprang forward, and it might have gone badly between him and the Rebel girl, had it not been for the intervention of Tambar, who forced himself between them and by sheer strength held the two apart. For a moment, all was confusion, and the other Rebels surged around them in a tussle.

Despite his ears ringing from Liana's blow, Arlo shouted desperately, "Stop it, Ozzie! Tambar, please listen! I know it was dangerous, but after all we didn't get caught, and we've got a direct way into the Palace! Do you know what this means, Tambar? We've got help – help inside!"

He realized that, whatever happened, they could not afford to fall out over something like this. Didn't the Rebels understand what a valuable thing he and Ozzie had done? But finally Tambar shouted aloud and forced a silence between the boys and the simmering Rebels. Haltingly, Arlo finished relating the story of what had happened to Usha and the message she had left Corin.

"And the most important thing is that Usha has a plan!" he gasped. "She must have! She was telling us not to attack until Midsummer's Night!"

"But that is two days away!" objected Tambar. "We cannot wait until then! Every hour that passes we run the risk of discovery!"

"But Usha *sees* things," said Arlo frantically. "She knows what is going to happen. That's the truth. She wouldn't have left the message, if it wasn't meant to be. And if we attack before, Tambar – I'm scared – I'm scared that something will go terribly wrong!"

"But what could one girl have planned?" asked Liana scornfully. "I have heard of these witches before. Most things that they predict do not happen. Yet they only remember those things which do!"

"I haven't ever known Usha to be wrong," replied Arlo stubbornly.

"And how do you know that we can trust this Corin?" asked Tambar at length. "How do you know that this is not a plot in itself?"

Arlo shook his head. "I just feel that we can, Tambar. I've always felt that way, ever since I first saw him. And Clarence – well, there's no question about him. They took his father, and it seems to have changed him somehow. Citizens can *feel*, you know, when something inspires it. Look at Ozzie, for instance –" gesturing towards the Citizen-boy, who stood glowering sulkily at Liana – "he was born a Citizen, but he's changed. There's got to be hope, Tambar, hope for everyone. Because otherwise, what are we doing this all for?"

"But I wager that Corin does not know," said Tambar dangerously, "that we plan to kill his father."

"Well. . ." hesitated Arlo. In all the excited plans that they had made in that brief hour in Corin's apartments, the talk had all been about "bringing freedom" to the Citizens. And for the first time, he started to consider how exactly Tambar proposed to do that. "But Corin hates his father! All he spoke of was how much his life would be better without him!"

Tambar sighed. "When I was younger, Arlo, I too hated my father. Often I wished him dead. He was hard on us, and on all his children, in the service of the Cause. But when he died – shot by a Citizen-soldier as he carried out a raid on a gunship – I knew that in truth I did not really want him to die. And it will be the same for a Citizen. Though Corin is with us now, I am sure that if he knows the true price of freedom, he will shrink from it."

"Then come with us next time," said Arlo desperately. "We arranged to meet tomorrow, at the same place, at the same hour. Talk to Corin, and then you will know for yourself."

Tambar turned away for a murmured discussion with Liana, while Arlo flung himself in a corner to think. The prospect of what the Regis's death would mean for Corin was not something that he had considered. But after a few terse words, Tambar came forward.

"It is decided," he said finally. "I will come with you tomorrow. *Alone*." And he gestured his sister to silence. "And then we shall see what we shall see."

Usha opened her mouth to shout, but Merco was faster. Clapping his hand over her mouth, he tripped her over his foot and pulled her into the shadow of the chimneys. Usha had time only to note that the sixth level of the pharms appeared to be in flames and that the walkways were alive with swarming creatures, before Merco was dragging her into the shadow of the rocks. A Simian guard-party was charging to the Bestiary along a walkway not twenty feet beneath them, but gave no glance in their direction.

Though a small man, Merco's one arm was wiry and strong and Usha was pulled towards a jumble of rocks on the volcano wall. The Ringmaster cast around for a moment, before discovering what he sought; a passage hidden in the shadows. With his hand on her neck, Merco pushed Usha in front of him into the darkness, as their feet slipped and slithered on the rocky floor of the tunnel.

For almost an hour they trudged in grim silence.

"Thought you'd get away that easy, Blondie?" muttered Merco darkly as he forced her along. "Didn't you know that old Merco's always got something up his sleeve?"

Suddenly it all became clear to Usha in a blinding flash.

"You know exactly where to go! You've been here before, haven't you?"

"Once a smuggler, always a smuggler," returned Merco scornfully.

"Tell me," murmured Usha faintly. If she could only manage to keep him talking and distracted, she could seek her chance to escape. "Tell me how you did it!"

As she had thought, Merco was all too happy to boast.

"That Brigadier thinks she's so all-seeing, but every time there's the likes of me who manage to slip through the net. I had another name, once. I was the best smuggler there was! Without me, the entire East Quarter would've starved three summers ago. Then they caught me and sent me here for Regeneration."

"And you got out?" asked Usha, feeling vainly with her fingers for a loose rock in the darkness. If she could turn around quickly enough, if she could hit the Ringmaster with a true enough aim. . . But all the rocks were small or tightly wedged, and she dared not pull too hard at them and give Merco an inkling of her plan.

Mcrco snorted. "I was with another smuggler who showed me how to escape the icy fire. But then I was as good as dead. I was left with nothing, nobody who would shelter me. I had to change my name and everything I was. So I built myself up again from nothing, and became Mephisto Merco, the Ringmaster!"

"And you thought you could do it again?" returned Usha, seeing the first glimmer of light enter the tunnel from the other side. "How do you plan to escape from the pharms now?"

The Ringmaster smirked evilly. "I couldn't have escaped with one arm, and no eyes, and that's where you came in! But you'll not be of use for much longer, Blondie. Merco's got a friend waiting around that headland, and in half an hour, he will have both his revenge, and his freedom!"

As they crawled out of the tunnel, Usha smelt a welcome scent, of fresh air and the sea. The tunnel had brought them through the rock of the north-west wall of the volcano and out on to the rocky outer cone, where the waves pummelled far below them. Slipping and slithering, they descended gingerly, gripping at tufts of grass to steady their passage. Below them Usha could see a small culvert, similar to the docking-station that they had arrived in, but deserted and tiny, with only a thin sliver of dawn-light snaking over the water.

For the first time Merco's grip slackened, and he stood dumbstruck, gazing at the empty water. "I can't understand it," he muttered, almost to himself. "He was to be here at this hour. I trusted him! Something must have gone wrong!"

Seizing her chance, Usha pulled away and scrambled along the rocky shelf, but there was nowhere to run to. She needed all her fingers and toes to keep stable on the dizzying slope. In a sudden Outbreak of Fury, the Ringmaster lurched towards her, arm outstretched. "At least I will have my revenge, Gemini!"

Usha clung to the rocky incline and felt her foot slip on a loose pebble. A small flurry of stones fell rattling down the volcano-side to the drop beneath.

"Merco, listen! Nobody is here to meet you. You're alone!"

The Ringmaster's hand closed on her throat. "You lie! Zadoc would never have let me down!"

So he had been waiting for Zadoc! Usha struggled vainly, gasping to speak as best she could through the vice-like grip.

"If you kill me, Merco, you'll have nothing! You'll be trapped here, between two sides that are your enemies. But if you come with me, then you won't be alone. If you know your way about the pharms, then the Rebellion needs you! You can help us! But you can't do it on your own. It's your choice!"

Merco's eyes showed his doubt. Usha's brain swam with the pressure, and her fingers slowly began to loosen. But suddenly the Ringmaster's hand slackened on her neck and dropped away. She clung to the rock, gasping for breath and coughing. Impervious to her plight, Merco stood for some moments, deep in thought. With his quick, calculating brain, he had evidently seen the worst of his position and was pondering his options. The Gemini could only hope that logic would triumph over hatred in the mind of a Citizen.

And in the end, it did. "There is a path," Merco said at length. "There is a path that goes to the Bestiary, and connects to the lower quarters, where the Gemini are bred. The Simians do not use it, and I do not think they even know of its existence. It was in this way that the other smugglers and I used to take creatures to the Circus."

"Where is it?" gasped Usha, pulling herself together. She must give him no time to reconsider his decision. Speed now was the most important thing. "Which way?"

EIGHT

In the grey of the early morning, the noise of hammering and welding and a strong smell of fish filtered into Toby's sleep. Half in a dream and almost convinced that he was back taking part in a raiding party with the Kids, he sat up dizzily and saw with shock the walls of Genopolis rising out of the mist before him. They were sailing through the huge crescent-shaped harbour that guarded the docks on the south of the City. Although without his spectacles he could not clearly see through the fog, he could hear the cries of sailors repairing the pharm-barges along the waterfront, and the Gemini slaves loading cranes with boxes of supplies. For a moment he gaped in confusion, wondering if he was still asleep, before the sensation of his bound hands woke him fully, and he knew that their desperate predicament was real.

The shadow of the harbour wall fell over the boat. Behind them stood Kristo, the barrel of his empty rifle pressed into Kira's neck. Neither of the prisoners dared to talk. Toby was well aware of the consequences if their ridiculous bluff was discovered, and in his mind he was wondering how he could manage to get away if they were arrested. He was quick on his feet, but he knew that any guard seeing a fleeing boy would undoubtedly shoot first and ask questions afterwards.

"Who goes there?" called a group of guards from above, and the boat-captain replied, "We are the Palace delivery-boat, sir, with a rescued Genopolis soldier and his prisoners aboard."

"Prisoners?" said one suspiciously. "We had no advance notice of any prisoners being brought to the City."

"I am Soldier Number 24093242, of Black Patrol," answered Kristo, holding up the dead soldier's identity token. "My radio was broken in a raid, otherwise I would have told my patrol-captain of my position. We were on a special mission for the Brigadier and I have orders to put the prisoners in a cell immediately."

"Then you should report to the military marina," objected the guard. "This port is to be used for supplies only."

"The reasons for this are confidential," replied Kristo calmly. "If you will allow me ashore, I will give you a fuller explanation."

The guard hesitated, and then motioned them to follow him with a movement of his rifle. Toby struggled up the steps with Kira, followed by Kristo. "Remove your weapon," he said curtly, and Kristo obediently handed it over with a salute. Toby stared at the ground, and stumbled along the grey stone quay with his head bowed until they were ushered into one of the guard cells at the entry-station, and the door closed behind them. They were standing in a dim grey-stone building, empty apart from a desk and chair. On the other side of the cell was an external door that led through the Genopolis Customs and the docks.

"Remove your cap," said the guard warily, and as Kristo did so, a look of uncertainty crossed his face. He fingered Kristo's identity token and checked the number in the patrol-register on the desk before him. Kristo feigned impatience, and Toby and Kira fidgeted behind him.

"We received reports that the raid had run into trouble," said the guard, "and that Number 24093242 was missing, believed killed."

"I was not killed, merely separated from the patrol," said Kristo briskly. "I made my way back as soon as I could, which took long enough. How long am I to be kept waiting now?"

"The Brigadier is at the Palace on business," replied the guard shortly. "You need to wait here for your patrol-captain to come and vouch for you."

"But I cannot delay," said Kristo sharply. "The Brigadier herself authorized me to bring the prisoners to the Palace straight away."

The guard looked disbelieving, and his finger

discreetly clicked the safety catch off his rifle. "How could you have received this authorization, if your radio was not working?"

"My authorization is here," said Kristo, taking a step forward as if to show the guard something, but immediately his left fist shot into the man's stomach, and as the Citizen crumpled, Kristo's right fist connected with the soldier's jaw. Stunned, the soldier slid without a sound to the floor, and Kristo caught the rifle as it fell. Quickly, he hurried to the door, and checked outside, but all was quiet.

"I couldn't help it," he said quickly to Kira, who was standing aghast at the door. "One more second, and he would have raised the alarm. I had hoped to be escorted through, but they're too sharp. It's a shame, but it couldn't be avoided."

Quickly switching the identity token of the dead soldier that he wore with the one that hung around the unconscious guard's neck, he pushed it into the slot of the door that led through to the Customs, and the door swung open with a click. With the soldier's flick knife, Kristo cut the bonds from Toby and Kira's hands, and knotted them into a loose circle so that they could release themselves if needed. Together, they rolled the body of the guard behind the door that they had entered through, and wedged it shut with Kristo's bent rifle. It would hold, but only for a short time.

"Now move quickly, and if I say run, then run," said Kristo, taking the pistol from the slumbering form of the guard. "We'll have about a minute before someone comes and checks up on us. Toby, where's the nearest sewer from where we are?"

"There's one by the docks, but there's an iron grid over it so you won't get in there," answered Toby. "There's an open pipe a hundred metres up from there if we can make it, but it's on open ground."

"Then walk in front of me, and lead the way to the den," ordered Kristo brusquely. "We need to be far away from this part of town before the alarm is raised."

Arlo shifted uncomfortably in the darkness of the stinking latrine, until Tambar's head and shoulders appeared with some difficulty through the pipe, retching and coughing in the reek.

"A fouler place I have never been," muttered the Rebel, as soon as he was able to speak again. "I wonder that anyone – even a Citizen – could bear it for so many years."

Ozzie shot him a dirty look. "There is a first-class staircase at the front of the Palace instead if your Lordship would prefer," he said with heavy sarcasm. "It is just a matter of fighting one's way through the hundreds of soldiers that guard it."

"Stop it, Ozzie!" snapped Arlo, irritated by the sniping and the constant danger that surrounded them. "Keep your voice down. We're getting close."

Startled by his friend's uncharacteristic outburst, Ozzie fell silent and led the way up the staircase. Yet, as they crawled up the dungeon stairs Arlo was gripped by a powerful sense of unease. Something was wrong, but he could not put his finger on it. The whole Palace was unaccountably quiet, with a stillness that could not be accounted for by the unused nature of the dungeons. Everything around him seemed watchful, as if waiting for something.

Arriving at the entrance to the corridor, Arlo craned around the gate. "Corin?" he whispered softly.

But there was no reply. Arlo tried a couple more times but no answering murmur came out.

"I thought you said he would be here?" hissed Tambar darkly.

"He will come," said Arlo uncertainly. "I know he will."

But long though they waited in the darkness, there was no sound from the corridor above. After half an hour, Tambar grew restless.

"Something is not right," he muttered. "We should go."

"No!" insisted Arlo. "If we miss him now, there's no telling when we can see him again. I can't just wander up to his bedroom and knock on his door, you know!"

The Rebel pulled at him impatiently. "The first rule of any engagement: know when to retreat. I do not trust this Corin boy of yours."

"He's right, Arlo," agreed Ozzie. "Something's obviously happened, and he can't make it today. But we can't be sittin' here like lemons if any guards happen along."

Stubbornly, Arlo reached out and pushed the gate. It swung open, noiselessly, on its hinges. Immediately Tambar's strong arm was around his neck, dragging him back.

"You have been betrayed!" he hissed. "Citizen-soldiers have been here! Look at the marks in the dust!"

Arlo looked down, and indeed, alongside his own small prints and Ozzie's, there were the marks of other, larger booted feet. While he was still taking in the significance of what he had seen, there came the sound of footsteps in the corridor. Springing to their feet, the group were about to hurriedly retreat down the staircase, when Arlo heard a whistle, the sound of "Genopolis Above All Others".

The next second Corin appeared in the corridor before them. His eyes were red and puffy, and he held a dark cloak around him with a shaking hand.

"Arlo?" he stammered.

A blood-red sunrise hung over the smoke from the pharms as Usha and Merco finished their wearisome trek around the hidden path, which encircled Pharmopolis, to the rim of the plateau. For the first time, Usha thanked her extraordinary good fortune – or from Merco's point of view, necessity – that had given her an ally in an unlikely place. No other way could they have made their approach without being seen.

From the vantage point where she and Merco crouched, Usha could see that the sixth level of the pharms where the Bestiary had stood had been burned to the ground during her escape from the Regeneration machine. How her friends had managed it, Usha had no idea. But despite their difficulties, the members of the Circle had evidently managed to organize themselves well. They had a bird's-eye view of the rioting prisoners that had broken out of the inferno and now spilled across the other levels and the plain. The Simian guards, tiny as ants, hurtled to and fro, distracted by both the need to bring water and the need to control the prisoners, with the result that utter confusion reigned. Only the clanging of what must be a warning bell sounded across the plain, and the searchlights circled wildly in the smoky gloom, picking out first a struggling knot of Androgynes, the next, the heaped corpses of some of the Simians, and above them all, the circling shapes of the Furies as they wheeled and shrieked against the ghastly fumes.

"They've broken out!" cried Usha excitedly. "The Simians can't do anything! Look at them run! This is wonderful!"

Merco leaned his arm on a rock, morosely. "Better hurry up, though, Blondie. Only one of the levels has been set free so far, and at the rate your lot are going, they'll still be dancing around by the time the Citizen airships get here. And once they do. . ." He mimed slitting his own throat with grim humour.

"Then come on," cried Usha, leaping to her feet. "You've got a skeleton key, haven't you? You have to help me free the rest of them!"

A swift climb down the stony incline, and they found themselves overlooking the first of the high walkways that the Simians used as access tunnels. Keeping a sharp eye out for patrolling guards, Merco swung himself down and helped Usha after him. They stood opposite an iron gate on the first level while the Ringmaster fumbled for the key.

"In here, they've got some of the other, er ... *Chimaeras*, but I don't know what you'd think of 'em. Are you sure you want to let them *all* out?"

"Yes!" blazed back Usha impatiently. "Everyone's a prisoner here! Don't they all deserve the same freedom?"

"Fine." Merco shrugged, tinkering inside the lock. "But don't say I didn't warn you."

He threw the doors open. Usha had only a momentary impression of utter chaos within, of a writhing and rippling of limbs, before a huge wave of bodies surged up before them and knocked her flat. Over them leapt a strange and horrific multitude of creatures, roughly of human appearance but with a mass of spindly, hairy limbs, some with eight or more legs, others on two legs with a myriad number of whirling arms. So hideous was the sight that Usha rolled away and covered her face with her arms, as the monsters passed over them with a horrid, scuttling motion like enormous spiders. When the last of them had climbed the walls or vanished down the walkway, Usha dragged herself dazedly to a sitting position, and saw Merco similarly getting shakily to his feet.

"Happy now, Blondie??"

"What in Genopolis were *they*, Merco?" stammered Usha, still appalled at the memory of their gruesome appearance.

"From the look of 'em, they were the Arachnids, and the Scorpions," answered Merco shortly, glancing warily around in all directions. "Had some of 'em in the Circus once. Great at fighting, but not too particular who they attacked, if you know what I mean. At least there weren't any Gorgons. All those snakes hanging from their heads. Got to look out for their bite."

"Oh no," murmured Usha, as a renewed babble of screaming broke out from the plain, as the newcomers evidently managed to enter the fray. "I hope they don't attack any of our friends. . ."

"*Friends?*" sneered Merco. "They're just *animals*! A Chimaera that is half-man, half-animal still thinks as half an animal. You're trying to make them human, getting them on your side, trying to organize them! But they're not *Citizenly*! You won't do it! It's a shambles! They'll just be looking out for themselves!"

Usha sighed. The Rebellion was evidently going to be more complicated than she could have imagined. And though she disagreed with Merco's treatment of the creatures, Merco was still right. Some of them would not be – *could not be* – on her side. It was not the way they had been Created. They would not understand.

"Then let's go and find the Gemini. Lead me to the Gemini."

But secretly she recoiled at the idea of leaving any creature, however grotesque, to face torment and death at either the hands of the Simians or the fire that was rapidly sweeping through the pharms. For she knew that, but for lucky chance, she herself might have been made into something so monstrous as an Arachnid or a Minotaur. Yet there was nothing that she could do. The Rebellion was the most important thing, and anything that might endanger it could not be risked. For the first time she felt the burden of leadership and the choices that she must make for others – be they beast or human – weighing heavy on her shoulders.

Corin pulled the dark cloak close around him and peered through the dungeon door. "I'm sorry I'm late, Arlo," he said slowly, a strange tone to his voice. "I had . . . I had some homework to finish off first."

Arlo beckoned him inside, eagerly. "But come in, Corin," he whispered. "If you're seen in the corridor. . ."

Corin shook his head, and something in his expression made Arlo's instincts twitch. The boy's hands looked red and mottled, as if he had been scratching himself violently.

"I'd better stay out here," he replied flatly. "Ivar's

keeping guard by the staircase, and if I come inside, I won't be able to hear him."

Arlo glanced at Tambar, who pointed wordlessly at the footprints in the dust.

"Corin," whispered Arlo, "there's been someone here since yesterday. Is everything still all right?"

Corin nodded, and cast his eyes down. "Those are Ivar's footprints," he asserted, but still with the strange tone in his voice. "He came to oil the gate."

Watching him, Arlo's skin prickled. Again, his instincts seemed to be warning him very powerfully that something was wrong. Corin seemed totally different to the eager boy of yesterday. But why would this be?

"Corin, this is Tambar," said Arlo, encouragingly, pulling the Rebel forward. "He wanted to come and talk to you about Usha, and for you to tell him about our plans for Midsummer's Night."

"That's right," said Corin. "That's what . . . the Gemini said."

The Rebel eyed him slowly and carefully. "And that was all her message?"

Corin did not understand the Rebel's heavily accented speech, and Tambar had to repeat the question a couple of times before the Citizen could understand what was being said. "That was all," he replied finally. "But Arlo, listen. I need to know. Nothing's going to happen before Midsummer's Night, is it?"

Again, Arlo glanced at Tambar, who nodded. "We can wait another day," he agreed. "But at the stroke of midnight we will attack. You say that the Ball will be in full swing during this time?"

Corin nodded, and the effort seemed to cost him dear. "It will," he said slowly. "But . . . I've bad news. There's one other thing you should know."

"What's that?" whispered Arlo.

"I'm not sure how to tell you this, Arlo, but . . . Professor Ignatius is going to be executed during the celebrations, as an end to treachery in Genopolis. And . . . and with him, your friend Talia."

The shock that hit Arlo on hearing this news was so blinding that for a moment he was unable to speak. It was Ozzie who stumbled forward.

"They're going to *what*?" he bellowed, almost incoherently. "They're going to *execute* Talia?"

"Sssh!" warned Corin, shooting a sharp glance up towards the corridor. "You cannot shout like that. Listen, I have to go now. But if you attack on the stroke of midnight, you will be able to rescue your friends as well. So, will you and your group still follow the plan we arranged?"

Wordlessly, Arlo nodded, and the next moment Corin turned away and Tambar was manhandling both of the stunned boys quickly down the staircase towards their escape route.

"That's nice, Blondie," taunted Merco as they crept along the high wall that bounded the walkway over the fifth level. "All those high Citizenly ideals that you had. All creatures are equal, eh? Let 'em all out, indeed!"

Rolling her eyes at the Ringmaster's words, Usha ignored him. But as they crawled around a bend, they saw, directly below them, a party of Simians, who were clustered around a heavily-barred gate.

DANGER. ARMAMENTS AND COMBUSTION. KEEP OUT.

"Merco, look!" hissed Usha. "Armaments! They'll have weapons there! That's what Sir Herbert was speaking of!"

"I wouldn't try it, Blondie," muttered Merco. "If what they said was true, then inside there's things more powerful than anything you can imagine. If you can't control the Arachnids, then don't even think of looking in there. Better go straight to the Gemini."

But stubbornly, Usha leaned over for a closer look. This move was her undoing. Though intent on their task, the sudden shadow thrown by the fugitives fell over the Simians and made them look up. Usha and Merco froze, but it was too late. They had been seen in a minute. One of the guards shouted an order, and the next second a scowling Simian was climbing up the wall towards them.

Usha shoved at Merco, frantically. "You know the way! Quickly! To the Gemini!"

Merco nodded curtly, and disappeared. Usha started

to run in the opposite direction up the wall, as slowly as she could to cause a distraction, but the Simian was bigger and stronger and within seconds he had topped the wall behind her. She could hear him gaining on her, felt a grasp at her shoulder, hot breath on her neck. . .

But the next moment, there was a swoop from above, and the air was suddenly black with a flurry of wings and screeching. Usha ducked as a vicious claw seared through the air, but the Simian, clutching at the blood that streamed from his eyes, toppled from the wall, hit the path and scrambled away, howling. Again and again the screaming attack dived from above, this time assailing the guards on the path beneath her. A Fury alighted on the wall before Usha, silhouetted against the fumes, her beak dripping with blood.

"Alive!" she shrieked triumphantly. "The Usha is alive!"

Gratefully, despite the bird's hideous appearance, Usha flung herself towards it. "Thank you!" she cried. "Thank you!"

The Fury strutted and clicked her beak with pleasure. "What next? You want blood to drink?"

"Er . . . no thanks," replied Usha uneasily. "I have to do something first."

The bird looked nonplussed. "What you want? You want join your friends?"

"No, I can't, yet," whispered Usha. "But go and tell them – tell Sofia – that I'm alive, and we're releasing the Gemini. I will come down and join you—"

"The Sofia is gone. She say, gone to port with others."

"Then who's down there on the plain?" asked Usha incredulously.

"Only the Sphinx and the Androgynes and the old Herbert," replied the harpy, cleaning her beak fastidiously with her claws. "Other monsters come, all attack, all fight. The Simians running away. The Citizens, they go to port, get ships."

"Oh no," muttered Usha. "Listen, tell the Sphinx that if we can release the Gemini, then we'll have enough troops to overthrow everyone."

The Fury shrugged, and flapped slowly away. Usha watched her go, and worried for an instant that she would be distracted by the bloodlust and forget to pass on the message. How much could she really rely on such creatures, whose minds worked in a different way, and did not hold the same ideas as she did?

Once the bird had disappeared into the fumes, Usha slithered down the wall and made for the Armaments door that the Simians had unbarred before they fell.

"Don't go in there!"

A Simian, sprawled against the wall, cowered in the shadows, shielding his bleeding face with his paws. "Don't go in there alone, sir," he protested, evidently mistaking, in his blindness, the sound of Usha's footsteps for one of his superiors. "It's too dangerous—"

But Usha was already inside. Before her in the murkiness, stretched rows of guns and armaments, and in front of her, a small cage, unlocked, open, and empty except for two small huddled figures that sat alone on the floor. At the sudden entry they looked up in amazement, but no surprise was greater than Usha's at that moment.

"Nanda! Mindie!" cried Usha in sudden joy and recognition, and leapt forward, her arms outstretched.

Corin sighed and turned to look at the party of heavily-armed Guardians that stood each side of the corridor, rifles trained on him. For the last time he gazed longingly into the darkness of the dungeons, but Arlo and his group had long since disappeared.

"Was that what you wanted?" he asked, and in that moment, Emotions rose up inside him like a thunderstorm, and he could have wept.

A spark of tinder and flint flared, illuminating the face of the Brigadier, who leant idly against the wall of the corridor next to him, the claw of her artificial arm hooked carelessly into her belt.

"That was exactly what I wanted," she said calmly. "I know how effective half an hour in the company of Fear can be. And, Ivar, thank you for your information, and I promise that you will be spared Regeneration for the neglect of your duties as a result."

Ivar stepped forward, and Corin eyed him full in the face. "Why did you do it, Ivar?" he asked. "Why did you tell her?"

But Ivar's eyes were blank as he gazed down on his master. "I had to," he replied. "It was my purpose."

"But. . ." struggled Corin, and for a second, an

Outbreak brimmed in his eyes. "I thought . . . I thought you were my friend."

The Gemini shrugged. "I was never bred to be your friend," he said tonelessly. "I was only ever destined to protect you."

Corin stood back as Ivar was escorted away. The Brigadier smirked at him with triumph in her eyes.

"What are you going to do with Arlo?" he asked the Brigadier, miserably.

"We wait," replied the Brigadier. "We wait, until the appointed hour, and then we will have all of them, like rats in a trap."

The Guardian captain clicked his heels and saluted briskly. "But, ma'am, if we follow them now, we can surprise them in their den before they even start their plan!"

The Brigadier shook her head. "No," she said thoughtfully. "It is better to take them all together, with one fell swoop. And now that they know that Ignatius will be there to be rescued, they will not run any risk of change. Yes, it is best to destroy them all, together, at once. Indeed, this will be the best Midsummer that Genopolis has ever seen."

Mindie's eyes widened in shock, and she shrank away as Usha approached.

"Stay back! Stay away!"

"Who is it?" gasped Nanda, staring around with her petrified blind eyes. "Who is there?"

Bewildered, Usha sank to the ground before them. "It's me, it's Usha!" she cried. "Don't you remember me? I've come to get you out!"

But Nanda and Mindie both shook their heads, and in their eyes, Usha could see an expression of blank despair that she had never seen on the faces of the lowest Naturals.

"I've come to rescue you! Come with me!" begged Usha, bewildered.

What on earth had *happened* to her friends since she had left them in the sewers of Genopolis a year before? She could see no marks of torture or of Regeneration on them. Though Nanda's face was still scarred, and Mindie's legs were still missing, in all other respects they looked healthier than she even remembered.

"I remember your voice," muttered Nanda quietly. "Yes, I remember you."

"You can't rescue us, Usha," said Mindie dejectedly. "We are all prisoners here. There is nowhere for us to go."

Usha shook her head. "No! You don't understand. We have started a revolution in the pharms, and we're going to bring Genopolis down!"

"Bring Genopolis down?" asked Nanda, a sudden light coming across her face. "But how?"

Quickly, casting wary glances towards the open door of the cage, Usha related a brief summary of her plans and their alliance with the inhabitants of the Bestiary. As her friends took in the news, Mindie turned her head to Nanda.

"Nanda? Do you think. . .?"

Nanda sighed, got to her feet, and gently picked up Mindie. Usha reached forward to help, but Mindie raised her hand.

"Listen, Usha. We'll come with you, but on one condition. Neither you, nor anyone else are to touch Nanda, or . . . say anything to her. Anything at all. Unless we speak first. Do you understand?"

Usha nodded doubtfully. "But *why*? What's happened, Nanda? What have they done to you?"

Nanda hoisted Mindie firmly in her arms, and prepared to follow Usha out of the cage. "It is better you don't know, Usha. When the time comes I will have to tell you, but not yet."

Toby and Kira walked fast, head down, with the point of Kristo's rifle at their backs. It was the hour of the changing of the guard, and different patrols of soldiers were making their way down to the docks to relieve their comrades of their duties. A few glanced curiously at the group as they passed, but the black scarf of the Customs officer around Kristo's neck avoided any unpleasant questions for a few minutes. Still, the air crackled with tension. It was only a matter of time before the scene in the entry-cell was discovered. The large wall of the barracks loomed before them, but before they could clear it, distant shouts rang out from the marina.

"Alert! Spies! Stop! Arrest them!"

"What do we do?" gasped Kira, petrified.

"Keep walking," said Kristo calmly, glancing through the various windows of the barracks as they passed, as if looking for something. Suddenly he tensed. "Ah – this looks possible. Come with me."

Smartly he wheeled them through a door and into a small guard cell. A young, fair-haired guard was sitting on a chair with his legs up on the desk, smoking a cigarette. His rifle leaned carelessly against the wall, out of reach. At Kristo's entry, he jumped and stood up, grinding the cigarette out with the heel of his boot.

"I'm sorry, sir," he stammered, evidently mistaking Kristo for one of his superiors. "I was just on my way to duty. . ."

With a quick bound, Kristo was on him and forcing the muzzle of his pistol against the guard's neck. "Do exactly what I tell you, and you will escape with your life. Understand?"

Dumbly, the soldier nodded, and Kristo motioned Kira and Toby to take the rifle and conceal themselves behind the door. Dragging the stupefied guard in front of him, Kristo marched him to the window, where he positioned himself out of line of the window, with the pistol against the back of the soldier's neck. Within seconds, the sound of running feet came around the corner.

"Alert all guards!" came a cry. "Have you seen a Customs officer and two unidentified prisoners pass this way?"

Kristo pushed the barrel of the gun warningly against

the soldier's head. Without a flicker, the man replied, "I'm sorry, sir. No one has passed this way."

"They must have gone the other way, towards the docks!" shouted another, and immediately the pursuit took off in the other direction. Kristo waited a second, then pulled the stunned soldier away from the window and closed the door.

"Now take your uniform off," he snapped sharply, and as the man objected, "If you cooperate with me, I promise you your life. Now hurry up."

"Kristo, what are you doing?" gasped Kira, appalled, but the Citizen was already undressing himself, throwing his crumpled uniform at the guard's feet.

"Change of plan," he said shortly. "We won't get through into the sewers with everyone looking for us now. Trust me, Kira. There's nothing else we can do."

"Turn right. Now walk eight paces. Now turn left. . ." With Mindie held in Nanda's arms murmuring softly to the blind girl to guide her in the right direction, Usha slowly led her friends down to the ninth level of the pharms, from which she had escaped only hours before. Now that she was free to walk on her own, she could see that the vast centre plain that housed the Regeneration Factories was surrounded by a deep moat or ditch filled with fire. At intervals stone bridges spanned the great trench, and beneath some the flames had been extinguished and smouldered into the blood-red sun. Coughing and spluttering in the fumes, they crept over the bridge that led into the plain, and Usha caught her breath, unprepared for the sight that met her eyes.

In place of the rioting that had been going on not an hour before, instead rows and rows of Gemini stood listlessly in the centre of the plain, hundreds and hundreds of them, all without speaking, all without moving. Some were so huge that they seemed like giants, sitting staring dully at the blood-soaked ground and the heaped bodies of the dead.

"Who are these creatures?" whispered Mindie. "What are they doing here?"

In amazement, Usha looked at the multitude before them. Every conceivable type of Gemini was there, from those who had clearly been created to order, to those who had been bred for other limbs or for the menial work of digging, pulling levers or dragging wagons. Most had never seen the daylight before, and stared bewildered and confused at the unknown world around them. She could see Gemini of all shapes and sizes, all skin colours, old and young, male, female or androgynous, from those whose forms she knew and remembered, to ones that she had never seen before, all perfectly created for the use of the Citizens.

"They are not creatures," muttered Usha. "They are Gemini. Like me."

As they stood, staring at the throng before them, Merco forced his way to the front with Tutu and Tarissa at his heels.

"Thank Genopolis you've come, Blondie!" he cried. "The Gemini are released, but we can't do a thing with 'em! They're just standing around! They can't even talk! What's going to happen now?"

Usha forced herself to concentrate. "Where are the Simians?" she called.

"They've retreated to defend the port," shouted Yuma from the side where she, Yoshi and Sir Herbert were collecting weapons from the fallen Simians. "Sofia and the others tried to commandeer the ships, but they'll have their work cut out – there's not enough of them. Can't you do anything, Usha? Unless the Gemini can be made to follow us, it's all over!"

"They're brainwashed," replied Usha, securing Mindie and Nanda behind a small boulder, where they crouched, wide-eyed and blinking. "Every Gemini must be programmed with a duty. *The first purpose of every Gemini is to serve a Citizen*, remember?"

"But then they are useless!" cried Tarissa. "How can they possibly help us?"

Usha shook her head. "They *can* help us, but they won't be able to do anything by themselves. Unless – they believe it first."

"Then hurry up!" snarled Merco, pushing a curved horn towards her, still scarred and bloodstained from its former Simian owner. "Make them believe it!"

"But I can't!" cried Usha. "Sofia's in charge of the Rebellion, not me!"

"She's not here, and you are!" returned Sir Herbert,

helping her up on to the boulder, where she stood uncertainly, outlined against the sunrise. "Call them!"

Reluctantly, Usha blew into the horn, but only a feeble squeak came out. Shrugging her shoulders in despair, she turned to her friends.

"I don't know how!" she protested. "What should I say?"

"Remember, Usha!" cried Nanda suddenly. "You are a Gemini yourself! You know the words you need to speak to them!"

Encouraged, Usha blew again, stronger, and this time a loud blast echoed around the plain.

"Fellow Gemini!" she cried, and at the sound, all faces turned towards her. "Listen to me! Listen to your purpose!"

Arlo shivered miserably in the den as Ozzie strode to and fro, flinging pieces of debris fiercely at the walls. A wheel from Mindie's chair flew through the air towards him and he ducked just in time.

"I can't believe it!" Ozzie roared. "The cowards! They're going to execute Talia, just like that!"

"Shut up!" cried Liana. "You'll bring all the Guardians down here!"

Tambar stepped forward, and wrestled the boy against a wall. "Stop that, Ozzie!" he said sharply. "Keep your mind on what we have to do!"

Biting his knuckles, Arlo watched Liana and the rest of the group busy assembling the fire-mines from the waterproof packs that they had brought with them. An uncomfortable feeling kept gnawing at his stomach. What was this sensation of unease that kept coming upon him? Why had Corin seemed so different from yesterday? There had been something in his eyes. . . And, most importantly, why had he not looked him in the face?

But then, he tried to console himself, the Citizen *had* been bringing him terrible news. Perhaps Corin himself liked Ignatius, or perhaps he was starting to realize what the attack would mean for his father. Or . . . perhaps . . . no. *No.* The other possibility was too terrible to even contemplate.

Corin was on their side, he reassured himself sternly, and the plan was there to be followed. He should be happy that everything was working out the way that he had wanted. But still. . .

Liana got to her feet. "Tambar," she said crisply. "The mines are all ready."

Tambar nodded. "Then we have a few hours in which to lay them," he said determinedly. "Ozzie, if you have calmed down, we will need you to show us to the places in which they are to be put. Arlo, you must stay here, and keep your strength up. The plan is still to be followed, but if you wish, you may devise a way to rescue your friends in the confusion. Once the attack has been sprung, all will be chaos and the last thing they will be thinking of is the prisoners. So I advise you to make full use of your time."

Wearily, Arlo bent, and patted Rem. The dog panted trustingly up at him, and slowly Arlo tied a length of rope around Rem's neck and secured him next to a pile of crumbled ship's-biscuit.

"Wait here till I get back," he murmured in the warm, deliciously dog-smelling ears. "Understand, Rem? Until I get back."

From where she stood overlooking the port of Pharmopolis, Usha gazed down at the conflagration below. In the seas that surrounded the pharms, fierce fighting thronged the ships as Sofia and her hybrid troops fought for mastery of the harbour. The defending Simians, desperate to the last, were battling against the combined forces of the Citizens, the Chimaeras, the Sphinx and the Androgynes; but even though the Simians were outnumbered, their aggression and bodily strength meant that the Rebellion was going badly. Sofia's troops had still not managed to capture any of the ships, and the tight knot of Simians that protected them remained unbroken.

Usha turned to regard the rows of Gemini who stood at attention behind her, unsmiling and poised, carrying the guns that they had taken from the Armaments store. Suddenly she became aware of a strange sensation, of ultimate power, as at a word from her the strength of hundreds, of thousands of Gemini could be unleashed.

No longer would they be the slaves, the downtrodden,

the fuel for higher beings. At long last they would be coming into their own, and their masters would flee before them!

"Usha, quick," muttered Sir Herbert in her ear, and Usha blinked back to consciousness. "We've got to go, or the airships will soon be here."

Usha raised her arm, and at the signal, her troops stiffened into readiness.

"Charge!" she shouted.

As Kira covered the stunned guard with his own rifle, Kristo and the soldier exchanged uniforms and security tokens, and Kristo fastened the black Customs scarf around the soldier's neck. Toby squinted perilously out of the window.

"I can hear a patrol coming down from above!" he squeaked, but Kristo seemed unperturbed, smoothing his uniform and adjusting his collar. "What's the password for today?" he asked the soldier.

"Leuwenkind 431," replied the guard quickly. Kristo nodded. "Now close your eyes," he said calmly, and as the man did so, he punched him full in the face. The soldier crumpled and fell backwards, unconscious. Kira flinched at the sight, but the next second Kristo had stepped forward and wrenched the rifle from her hands.

"Get down on the floor and put your hands over your head," he said. "You too, Toby. Act scared."

Toby didn't need to be told twice, and cowered on the

floor, but Kira grabbed at the Citizen wildly. "But, Kristo! We'll be taken prisoner! You can't—"

But Kristo merely pushed her to the floor, opened the door and stepped out to meet the advancing patrol.

"We've got them, sir," he said, saluting. "They escaped as far as here but I intercepted them. Dirty Natural rats."

The captain of the patrol came forward, peered into the cell and saw the unconscious form of the soldier in Kristo's ill-fitting uniform, the stolen security token from the Customs officer still around his neck, and the bedraggled forms of Toby and Kira kneeling face down on the floor.

"Password?" he asked, shortly.

"Leuwenkind 431," replied Kristo smartly.

"Good work," said the captain crisply. "We had a bit of a shock when we heard about the break-through, but they couldn't have hoped to get far, not with our security systems in place."

Kira, unexpectedly, laughed, and vainly tried to turn it into a cough. The captain gave her a strange look.

"What's the matter with her?" he asked curiously.

"Probably got some filthy Natural disease, sir," answered Kristo coolly, shooting Kira a warning glance. "Better get them out of here as soon as possible. I'll escort them up to the cells myself shall I, sir?"

"That's my job, corporal 59438," snapped the captain, glancing at the patrol stripe on Kristo's tunic. "But your lot are supposed to be up guarding the Palace yourself, aren't you? I'd better tell them you're coming to the guard room to make your report."

"I was just on my way," replied Kristo, but the captain had already lost interest. "Pick him up," he ordered to his patrol, and two soldiers ducked into the guard cell and hoisted the unconscious soldier up. "And you two –" he motioned to Toby and Kira, who still knelt on the floor, their arms above their heads – "come with us, you dirty Natural rats."

As the sun started to set over the horizon in a blazing orange ball, the grey waters that lapped against the shores of Pharmopolis were stained a dark crimson. Smoke rose dully from the ruins of the port, as here and there broken ships and heaps of debris lined the portside. Against the streak of the reddened sky, the Furies circled overhead, screaming savagely.

Usha stared at the ranks of Gemini, who, by sheer numbers, had overwhelmed the port and the ships. The Simians had been forced back into the water and drowned, overpowered or slain. Now many of the Gemini and Chimaeras rested from the battle or tended their wounds. What little food could be found was shared between all present. In the slight lull, Usha brought morsels of bread and cheese to give to Nanda and Mindie, who nibbled timidly, as if unused to such kindness.

"Who is this?" asked Sir Herbert in surprise as he passed, taking in for the first time the blind girl with the burned face, cradling the smaller girl without her legs. "Who are these children?"

Usha swallowed. "They are my friends, Nanda and Mindie," she said. "I found them imprisoned in the Armaments and Combustion Store."

Sir Herbert's face paled and he stepped away.

"The Armaments and Combustion Store? Do you know what this means?"

"What do you mean?" cried Usha, noting in surprise how some of the Gemini fell back warily from her friends. "What's wrong?"

Nanda turned towards her, eyes large and blank in her pale face.

"They have Experimented on me, Usha," she said softly. "They have done something terrible to me, and now I am a danger to everyone who comes into contact with me."

"How?" asked Usha, mystified. "What did they do?"

Sir Herbert shook his head. "Something terrible indeed," he said softly. "Originally, it was conceived as the ultimate punishment for expressing Emotions, and an example of their destructive power. The Brigadier planned to raise an army of such people as this, but it was thought too lethal. . ."

"I don't understand!" cried Usha miserably. "What did they do to you, Nanda?"

"Don't tell her!" begged Mindie suddenly. "Please, Usha. Please don't ask so many questions!"

Exasperated, Usha turned away and made her way to

the docks, where the long barges were alive with activity of a different sort. The Circle had made good progress in the hours after taking the port. Tariq and Sasha had taken control of loading food and the little amount of weaponry available on to them, Tutu and Tarissa were organizing raiding parties of Gemini, Androgynes and Chimaeras on to each boat, and Yoshi and Yuma were working out the navigation charts. Sofia and the other Maia were in charge of organizing sufficient numbers of Gemini to guard the Regeneration Facility, the arms factory, and the food-pharms.

"We've left almost a thousand to safeguard the pharms," gasped Sofia, as she came running up, "and there's another five hundred surrounding the merchant-houses on the north side. I think Sasha and Tariq should stay here; they know the pharms well, and they'll be able to deal with any trouble if it arises. But, Usha, I think that we need to be going as soon as we can. Yoshi thinks he's spotted Citizen airships on the radar, and the sooner we can be launched, the better."

"How far away are they?" asked Usha.

Yuma replied, "A few hours still. The first thing we did was dismantle the radio systems, so they won't have any idea of the true scale of the Rebellion, so they'll probably just send a few for reconnaissance. But we don't have air-power to fight them with, and if we leave the Gemini troops on the ground, then they'll be burned to cinders."

"We'll have to put the Gemini inside the important places such as the Regeneration Facility and the food-factories," replied Tutu. "Genopolis soldiers won't risk destroying the means of production and Regeneration from the air, so they'll have to force a landing. If we leave our troops outside, they'll be sitting ducks on the plain, and if they're all on the ground, then there's at least a chance."

"Good idea," returned Sofia, issuing a swift order to the Maia next to her, who quickly departed with the message. "But the airships worry me. Once we're seaborne, we won't have any proper means of defence, and we could be blown to pieces. Our guns won't reach the range that the airships can."

"But we've hundreds of ships," argued Usha, and Sir Herbert shook his head. "One airship can destroy fifty ships with the firepower it carries aboard," he replied softly. "Teeth, claws and determination are of no use if we can be destroyed from a distance!"

"And once we surround Genopolis, we will be cut to pieces, unless we can gain a landing." supplied Tarissa. "We have the weight of numbers on our side, but we will lose many of them."

Tutu shook his head. "Then we must change our plans. Stay here and barricade ourselves in our stronghold. We can starve Genopolis into submission by cutting off their food supply. It is the only way."

The vision of Arlo in the Palace flashed into Usha's head, alone and surrounded. "But we can't!" she cried desperately. "We must attack the City directly! We must reach Genopolis by nightfall tonight!"

"We don't have enough time!" argued Tarissa. "It is a whole night's journey away! We'll never manage!"

"But I'm still going!" argued Usha stubbornly. "It was my plan! You can't change it all! Not now!"

Sofia suddenly raised her gun and fired a few rounds into the air. The other members of the Resistance turned and stared at her.

"Enough talking! I know how we can sail to Genopolis, *and* defend ourselves! Board the ships!"

The Regis stood, his back to Corin, gazing out of his study window at the evening sunset. As he spoke, his tone was solemn.

"Who are you, Corin?"

Corin stared down at the floor, unable to think of anything to say. From her position on guard by the door, the Brigadier snorted contemptuously. The Regis himself sighed and shook his head.

"You are the son of the Regis," he said finally. "But when you are faced with traitors, you help them. Do you realize what this means?"

"You are becoming a Natural," rapped out the Brigadier. "You think as a Natural, you act as a Natural. You have been contaminated by this . . . *Arlo*."

"No!" cried Corin, unable to control himself. "You made me! You made me feel Emotions!"

"This is called Anger, Corin," replied his father

quietly. "The most destructive of emotions. Anger can destroy you. Do you really want that?"

Corin looked up at his father, white-faced. "No . . . no, sir."

"Then there is only one way to bring you back to the Citizen way of life," replied the Regis as he turned from the window and came towards him, bearing a small wooden box, which he placed in front of the boy.

"Open it."

Corin pulled at the hinge of the lid. His fingers felt all thumbs, and he fumbled as he released the catch and opened it. His eyes widened as he saw what was inside.

"But, father . . . you can't possibly. . ."

The Regis leaned forward, and from the depths of the box brought out a small duelling knife that shone dully in the dying rays of the sun.

"Only blood will wash you clean now, Corin. Once you kill someone, it will take away the part of you that fears, hates and loves for ever. When these . . . *animals* are captured tonight, it will be up to you, my son, to deal the death-stroke."

Corin shook his head wildly. "Father . . . I can't. . . Don't make me do this! Please!"

But the Brigadier was already behind him, reaching over for the box, which she tucked carefully under her clawed arm.

"The gongs are already sounding," she said with satisfaction. "We will go to your chamber and I myself will make you ready. As you know, Ivar will no longer be your bodyguard. Instead, I will fill those duties, and I will make a better job of it. There will be no more chance of any more of your tricks while I am watching you."

The dark sea that surrounded the pharms was alive with ships. Hundreds upon hundreds of barges, loaded with the combined forces of the Chimaeras, Androgynes and Gemini, launched themselves rapidly through the night. Speed and caution were of the essence if they were to get clear of the pharms before the airships arrived.

In the lead boat, under the command of Sofia, Usha pulled heavily on her oar, with Nanda and Mindie sitting beside her. It had taken some persuasion from the Gemini to allow Nanda and Mindie on the vessel with them, and because of this, Usha herself was still confounded and puzzled.

What was the matter with her friends? Why was everyone so frightened of two young girls?

"Beware!" cried Sofia, pointing upwards. "The airships are here! On your marks, Furies!"

A torrent of flames roared down from above as the first of the Citizen airships made its attack. A blossom of orange fire billowed into the night as the shot struck an outlying barge on the right-hand side. Screams and confusion rang through the air as the ship blazed alight, and the Androgynes aboard leapt for safety into the shallow seas and splashed for cover.

But the Furies were ready. Soaring into the air, faster and lighter than the large airships, they dodged and swept easily out of the lines of fire like dark birds. Using their sharp eyes to navigate through the blackness and alight on the great back of the airship, they pecked with their sharp beaks at the inflated balloon that suspended the gondola beneath.

Another streak of fire shot through the night, but missed its target and crackled harmlessly into the sea. The next second, there was a great screaming noise as the punctured airship teetered on the winds, then started to deflate, zigzagging crazily into the side of the volcano with a resounding crash. A cheer went up from the barges as the airship exploded, briefly illuminating the pharms in a ghastly glow. Immediately, the other airships pulled back and soared high out of reach in the night sky, where they clustered together to form their next strategy.

"Faster!" cried Sofia from where she stood in the prow of the boat, and the Gemini who rowed bent to their oars with renewed speed. "Again, Furies! Take the next airship down!"

Another blazing missile flared over them, this time exploding into a shower of sparks on the prow of a Sphinx-laden ship. Instantly the assembled creatures beat at the flames with their paws, and the smell of scorched fur seeped through the air. To the cheers of the Chimaeras, the Furies regrouped, and swept upwards towards the airship which hastily retreated.

"You see!" cried Sofia. "We can defend ourselves!"

But Usha's hand lay slackly on the oar. Despair now consumed her. The Rebellion had succeeded, but she had failed to help Arlo. In only a few hours, her friend would be in great danger in Genopolis, and here she was, out in the middle of the dark ocean, with miles and miles of hostile sea between them!

"We'll never make it by midnight!" she wailed. "We're too late!"

Nanda caught at Usha's sleeve. "Listen, Usha. Why do you want to get to Genopolis by midnight? What is so important?"

"My friend Arlo is there," stammered Usha. "He'll be in danger. I need to help him, and I'm worried that we'll be too late."

The blind eyes gleamed back at her. "But, Usha, there's one way that we can get out of here and over to Genopolis without being attacked."

Usha gazed up at the Furies, gorged with blood from the Simian corpses and still circling overhead like black phantoms, shrieking curses at each other against the red of the evening sky.

"I think I know what you mean," she said sadly. "But, Nanda, there's not enough of them. We can't all. . ."

But Nanda's eyes seemed even larger in her face as she drew closer to Usha. "There's no need for everybody," she said slowly. "There's only need for me."

"No, Nanda!" cried Mindie plaintively. "No!"

Confused as to what her friend meant, but thinking

only of joining Arlo in Genopolis, Usha reached over and clasped Nanda's hand without a moment's doubt.

"Then I'll come with you," she said.

Night had fallen by the time Kristo finished making his report in the tiny guard room. Toby and Kira knelt on the hard stone floor, their hands bound behind them. Neither had eaten for the past twenty-four hours, and Kira suddenly slumped. The captain looked up.

"Give them some bread and water, corporal," he said curtly to Kristo. "Can't have them dying before they meet the Brigadier, can we?"

Obediently, Kristo fetched bread and water and as he knelt over Kira, he whispered, "Listen, Kira. There's no other way around it. You'll have to be put into the cells, but I'll come and release you as soon as I get off duty. And, Toby, you stay strong and look after her. Understand?"

"Now get off to the Palace," snapped the captain, as Kristo stood up. "Your patrol are covering the Midsummer Ball tonight. We need lots of security. Word is that the traitor Ignatius Bonaventura is going to be executed, and we're on red-alert."

Kristo froze, then turned to face him, slowly, and Toby could see that it took all his Citizen composure to keep his calm.

"Ignatius to be executed *tonight*?" he asked.

"That's right," the captain said, uninterested, flapping a hand at him. "Dismissed!"

*

At a signal from Sofia, two Furies circled around the boat and alighted precariously on the side of the ship, squawking wrathfully.

"What orders? What does the Sofia wish?"

"To Genopolis!" cried Usha, scrambling towards the largest bird, and helped Nanda climb astride her. "Quickly! We must be there before midnight!"

"Follow the west star!" advised Sofia. "Keep it always before you!"

Instantly, the harpy spread her enormous wings and took off. In another second, Usha was astride the other and clinging to its feathered back. Icy wind roared around her ears as the second Fury rocketed upwards. She was aware only of a thundering in her ears and the way that the bird jolted precariously on the thermal currents as they left the decks of the ships far below them.

"Am I too heavy?" cried Usha, but the harpy did not respond. Holding tightly to her mane, Usha buried her chilled face into the feathers and hoped against hope that their desperate plan would succeed.

"Fly faster!" she called desperately, and this time the bird turned her head and snapped crossly at Usha.

"Going as fast as we can! The Usha is heavy, and the Nanda too!"

NINE

Genopolis was alive with lights and music. Golden radiance twinkled from every window as the City prepared for the celebration of Midsummer. Even the curfew had been relaxed by half an hour, and here and there groups of figures ran towards home in the deepening twilight, carrying the last of their hastily-bartered food and gifts.

In the sumptuously decorated Palace, Corin wandered miserably down the flight of steps towards the Banquet, the Brigadier walking one step behind him, as Ivar had always done. The warm scent of food drifted appetizingly up the stairs, and from below a flurry of cooks ran to and fro, calling in hushed voices to each other.

A soldier saluted the Brigadier. "We've heard there's a little trouble in the pharms today, Brigadier, and the extra supplies haven't arrived yet."

The Brigadier shot him a dangerous glance. "Make sure you sort it out sharp, and report to me, understand?"

Corin walked through to the Banqueting Hall, and saw that a raised plinth had been formed in the middle of the floor. Above it, two black nooses dangled from the ceiling, in stark contrast to the luxurious furnishings. The Brigadier showed Corin to his place and sat close beside him. Her metal claw caressed the delicate silver decanter as she poured them both a golden stream of mead.

"Well, well, Corin. Looking forward to Arlo's little reception, are we? My soldiers tell me that all the fire-mines your little friends have laid have been located, and my troops are even now manoeuvring into position. Now it's only a matter of waiting until they show their faces. I do hope they aren't late. It would be such a shame if they missed all the fun."

Corin ignored her jibe, and as he stared at the steady trickle of arriving guests, he could not help but remember the New Year Ball, only a few weeks ago, when he had sat in this same place, but with Ivar next to him, and the Gorgon had been brought in for the celebrations. On that day he had made his first break for freedom. . .

A Guardian captain suddenly hurried up to the table and saluted hurriedly. "I'm sorry, ma'am, but we've had some urgent news." He bent forward and whispered in the Brigadier's ear, and Corin caught only the words "pretending to be a soldier", and "Black Patrol", before the Brigadier got abruptly to her feet.

"Here? In the cells, you say?"

"Yes, ma'am," the soldier said, retreating at great speed. The Brigadier turned to Corin, an eyebrow raised.

"It seems that a few more of your friends have come to join the party," she sneered. "Perhaps they might care to enjoy our festivities?"

Corin stared at her dully. What on earth was she talking about?

A clatter sounded from behind them and the Brigadier wheeled around, but it was only a young, fair-haired captain standing at attention behind her who had momentarily dropped his rifle. For the Brigadier, this would usually constitute a court-martialling offence, but on this occasion she scarcely seemed to contain her delight, as she signalled at the corporal.

"You there!" she called. "Sharpen up! Guard this boy with your life! I am going down to the cells for a moment, and if I come back and he is not here, I promise you that your own neck will join the traitors!"

The corporal saluted, keeping his eyes down, and moved into position next to Corin, his rifle held at the ready. As the Brigadier hastened off, Corin slumped back in his chair. Defeat washed over him. All his rebellion had come to nothing. Arlo and the Rebels would be executed and he would be forced to have a front-row seat to the tragedy. But where on earth were the Rebels? How could they hope to enter the Palace unseen?

But in that second he could see that the corporal in

front of him was sweating slightly, unusually for a Citizen-soldier, and Corin could see that his fingers were trembling on the trigger. As he raised his eyes to that of the corporal's, he saw an expression in them, one that he had only seen in those who had experienced Emotions. . .

The Rebels were here! They still had a chance!

Cautiously, Corin allowed his lips to curve into a tiny forbidden smile, and, from underneath the shadowy cover of his corporal's cap, Kristo smiled back.

His muscles cramping with the strain, Arlo crawled cautiously along the narrow ventilation shaft that ran along the walls of the Palace, following Tambar. Both their hands and faces were stained dark with mud so that only the whiteness of their eyes could be seen in the dark. Heat and smells from the Palace kitchens rose up the pipes in gusts, making his stomach turn over.

He forced himself to concentrate on the job in hand. Through the web of ventilation systems that lined the Palace, a Rebel stood at each corner, ready to relay signals in semaphore fashion from one to the other. Around the sewers of the Palace were concealed the fire-mines, a Rebel each in position to light them, and Arlo trembled as he mentally commenced the countdown. It was only a matter of minutes before the first explosions began to tear the Palace from its foundations.

Arlo's own task was to identify the prisoners in the chaos, and speed their rescue. Ozzie had been sent to act as messenger, relaying information between one and the other, and Arlo missed his surly presence and his down-to-earth chatter. And his heart longed for Rem, tied up and waiting in the underground den. But there was nothing for it. Tambar had laid down a plan, and they could only follow.

From in front, Tambar raised his hand and made the signal to the Rebel at the end of the tunnel.

Everyone into position. Quiet.

The ventilation channels ran parallel along the Palace dining wall, and here and there were set small grids that faced into the main dining area. Through the grids came a small golden glow and the noise and hum of chatter beneath.

Tambar signalled to Arlo to look through the grid. Arlo blinked in the sudden glare and screwed up his eyes before he made out the shapes of the long tables, heaped with glittering plates and knives and bowls. Around them richly dressed guests were being shown to their seats by obsequious servants. The opulence of it all dazzled him after his long year in the penniless Regions, and he stared at the lavish scene for a moment, remembering the dinners at the Inn of Court and the lively chatter of the Doctors. With Ignatius . . . and in that moment his eyes swam into focus on the nooses dangling from the rafters, and he could have choked.

Tambar moved stealthily alongside him and jabbed his finger through the grid. Swallowing down his fear,

Arlo gazed through the arriving swell of guests until he made out the High Table almost directly below them.

There's Corin, he motioned to Tambar, as he picked out the boy's slumped form. *The Regis will probably sit next to him.* Again he felt a prickle of apprehension. What was *wrong* with Corin? His friend stared listlessly down at the table, heedless of all that went on around him, and in place of his servant Ivar, a capped corporal stood next to him, his rifle cocked.

A bell rang, and instantly the polite chatter ceased. From the back the doors opened, and a small procession entered; a group of soldiers and between them, a tall man, his polished skull gleaming in the candlelight, dressed in red, with eyes as black as coal. In horrified recognition, he stared at the man, and as he did so, the man turned his eyes to the ceiling, and for a second, Arlo could have sworn that the Regis was looking straight at him.

A fierce nudge in his back roused him, and Tambar was pointing at the group, gesturing urgently. *Is that him? Is that the Regis?*

Arlo nodded, and felt the sweat begin to trickle down his cheek. *But I don't see the Brigadier*, he signalled back. *She's not there. I don't know where she is.*

Tambar shrugged. *We cannot wait any longer*, he motioned. *It is time.* He raised his arm and sent the ready signal to the Rebel at the end of the tunnel.

Light the first fire-mine.

*

Toby crouched in chains at the back of the cell, as far away as he could from the captured soldier, whose face had swollen up, rendering him almost unrecognizable. After recovering consciousness, he had kicked and fought so much that the guards had needed to tie him down and gag him. Next to him Kira buried her face in her hands.

"I can't believe Kristo did this to us, Toby," she muttered frantically. "What if he can't get back? What if he can't come to release us?"

"He will," soothed Toby, stroking her hair with clumsy, grimy fingers, as he had seen Naturals do to anyone who felt upset. "Trust him. He'll be back."

But even as he spoke, the words died on his lips. The cell door creaked open and a red-uniformed figure, nightmarish in appearance, stood in the doorway.

Toby and Kira stared up in terror, realizing in an instant who must be standing before them, for the Citizen's ghastly face and iron claw were introduction enough. Slowly, the Brigadier entered the cell, and stood over them, hands on hips.

"So you have come to join us, Kristo," said the Brigadier, speaking to the bound soldier at her feet. "And brought a couple of your Natural rats with you. Perhaps you would care to join us for tonight's entertainment?"

The soldier moaned and writhed, mumbling as best he could through the gag, but only Toby could make out the words.

"Mmm! Nnnn! Ma'am! I'm not Kristo! I'm not the traitor!"

But the Brigadier shot him only a cursory glance. "I am sure that you are longing to meet your old friends," she said smoothly. "I am so glad that you weren't too late."

She raised her claw in a signal, and from behind a guard marched in a bent figure in prison clothes, her hair matted and tangled. Talia, dirty and exhausted, tottered into the cell and fell to the floor. On her face were deep lines of pain and fatigue, and she hardly seemed to recognize her friends. Despite himself Toby started forward with a cry, and the Brigadier snickered slightly.

"A merry meeting, I think!"

"Talia!" hissed Toby frantically. "Talia!" But she lay as if dead. She did not respond to Toby's urgent pleading or move at his frantic touch.

"And finally, the last member of the conspiracy," announced the Brigadier, motioning to the guards, who marched in a final prisoner; an old man, this time unfamiliar to Toby, bent and old as if he had suffered much in many lifetimes. "I am sure you will be happy to see your former colleague."

The soldier shook his head violently, choking on the gag that bound his mouth. "*Nnnnnn!*" he screamed incoherently. "*I don't know the traitor!*"

But out of the three of them, only one person recognized the new arrival. In bewilderment, Toby saw that Kira was staring at the old man in disbelief.

"You!" she gasped.

*

hirty seconds, came the signal back from the end of the ventilation shaft. *Twenty-nine, twenty-eight. . .*

Arlo shivered. Sickness caught at his stomach and he clutched at the wall for support. Tambar grasped his shoulder warningly. *Sssh. Be quiet.*

At the far end of the chamber, the doors opened and trumpets sounded. Almost with a feeling of relief, Arlo recognized the red-clad figure of the Brigadier at the entrance. Tambar nudged him.

Once the fire mines are set off, he signalled, *the rest is up to you.*

Instantly, Arlo's hand went slowly to the knife at his belt. As quietly as he could, he unsheathed it and started to unscrew the nails that held the grid to the wall, But as he did so, his eyes caught the movement of the entering soldiers behind the Brigadier, and he froze. After the Brigadier came the two figures whom he had dreaded seeing: Talia, bruised and broken, and after her, a crumpled old man.

Time seemed to slow almost to a standstill. In horror, Arlo gazed at Ignatius, hardly recognizing the Doctor's proud features underneath the moulting grey hair and the grime and filthy rags that covered him. Where now were Ignatius's indominitable spirit, the easy laugh and the kind eyes? The self-possession and the calm belief? Instead, Ignatius swayed and tottered on his feet, as if he were more than ninety, and he trembled like an old man as he was forced up to the dais, where he stood next to Talia by the dangling nooses. In that terrible second that seemed to last an eternity, Ignatius raised his face for the first time, and Arlo saw that tears were streaming down his face, leaving pale tracks in the grime.

Oh, Ignatius, he prayed silently, gripping the sides of the grid with his fingers. *Don't despair. I'm here. I've come to rescue you.*

Silence fell. Arlo gazed around in desperate impatience. *Come on!* Where was the first explosion, the first distraction that should be echoing through the Palace any moment now? What was Ozzie *doing*?

Next to him, Tambar signalled furiously to the Rebel at the end of the tunnel.

The mines, you fools! Light the mines!

Yet still no explosion came, and, impatiently, Tambar hurtled past Arlo, leaving the boy alone at the grid.

But the greatest shock was yet to come, and the next moment contained all the grief that Arlo had ever thought he could bear. Behind Ignatius, another figure was forced into the room, a girl with long hair, dressed in Natural rags. As she raised her head, Arlo saw Kira's face, and with a gush of horror, saw her prodded at sword-point to stand in front of the High Table.

With an involuntary start, Arlo's fingers shook on the metal grid. The shock was so great that it stilled his mind completely, and he knelt motionless, gazing at the steady face of his cousin. Kira's expression was blank and closed, and she did not acknowledge the Citizens around her.

What was Kira *doing* here? Why wasn't she in the Regions?

In his terror, Arlo's hand shook, and the grid fell forward on to his knees. In the same second the knife that he had been using slipped from his sweaty fingers and fell through the gap into the Hall, turning over and over, until it plunged, point down and quivering, deep into the Regis's table and centimetres from Corin's hand.

As the knife thudded into the table before him, the sound echoed through the room like a thunderclap. Corin leapt up. All eyes travelled from the handle of the still-shuddering knife, and up the wall to the small black hole where the small ventilation grid had been unscrewed.

The Regis got slowly to his feet. "Arlo?" he called softly, and at his tone, Corin felt himself shrink inside. "Arlo? We have been waiting for you!"

Suddenly a volley of shots and screaming broke out from the opposite side of the chamber, and the lights momentarily flickered and went out. In the semi-darkness, a flash of fire burst from the other end of the hall, and Corin had a fleeting impression of black-clad figures leaping from ropes from the other ventilation grids that lined the walls. For a second, pandemonium reigned, and Corin found himself dragged to the floor by the fair-haired corporal who had been guarding him, and forced underneath the table. A great explosion shook the ground as with an ear-splitting crash, the left wall of the Hall shuddered and broke into pieces.

But at the same second, a set of doors at the other end of the hall flew open and troops poured in. A stream of sparks leapt from the rifle of the fair-haired corporal at the entering soldiers. The vanguard fell to the floor and, stepping in front of the prisoners, the corporal blazed fire at the surrounding guards.

Ignatius turned, his face incredulous. "Kristo!" he called.

"Go!" Kristo shouted back at the dumbstruck prisoners. "Run!"

In a second, Talia leapt into life, pulling the other two with her, and the next moment they had disappeared through the dust blown up from the shattered wall.

Immediately all around was chaos. Corin scuttled into a corner, his hands over his head to protect himself. Through the dust and mayhem, his father plunged towards him, his eyes blazing with an expression Corin had never seen before. His shoulder was stained with blood from where a bullet had caught it. He grabbed his son by the scruff of his neck and hauled him upright.

"You're coming with me!" he hissed. "We are going to capture this Arlo, and capture him alive!"

Usha strained her eyes to peer through the blackness, almost blinded by the freezing winds around her. "Can't you fly any faster?" she cried again for the umpteenth time, and yet again the exhausted Furies made no answer. She felt the trembling of fatigue rippling along the back of the bird that was carrying her, and fell silent. Nothing could force the Furies to do any more than they were doing.

Needing all their failing strength to make the final stage of the flight, they coasted on the air currents to gather their bearings, scanning the murk for any signs of life. It was then that Usha saw it.

"There!" she cried, stabbing her finger to the right. "There!"

Out of the dark sea, Genopolis swam up on the horizon like a jewel of light, a marooned island of civilization in the wilderness. The Furies altered their course to meet it head on. Seen from the air, Usha was surprised at how small Genopolis seemed, how alone and vulnerable it was at the mercy of the flooded sea that lapped greedily around its roots.

As they raced towards the City, Usha marvelled at the glimmer of the citadel, the outlines of its hundred tiny towers and windows, before the Fury banked and wheeled, and started the slow glide of descent.

"The Palace!" cried Usha, leaning excitedly over the back of the harpy. "Make for the Palace!"

Arlo blundered through the web of ventilation systems. His instinct for survival had overridden everything except the need for escape. Hardly conscious of where he was going, he took turnings at random, first right, then left, seeking only a place of safety in his panic. Shouts and the sound of firing echoed up the tunnel behind him, and he knew that pursuit could not be very far behind. But without Ozzie to guide him, he was lost and could only veer here and there, blindly, by instinct.

Thoughts raced through his mind even faster than he could move. They had been betrayed, that was certain, and the Rebels had walked straight into a trap. *It must have been Corin!* And somehow they had captured Kira! Anger spurred him on, but made him heedless, so that as he hurriedly crawled left into another tunnel, he did not realize that it sloped steeply downwards.

In another second he knew his mistake. The tunnel turned abruptly into a slippery shaft, and suddenly he was rocketing down, scratching vainly at the sides, until the world around him burst into a sudden blaze of heat, light and sound. He had only a second to realize that he must be falling down one of the Palace chimneys, before he plunged out of the dirty, smoke-filled shaft and straight into an enormous cauldron of simmering soup that two sweating Gemini chefs had just hauled on to the stove.

His knowledge of climbing had made Arlo instinctively turn over during his fall, like a cat, but still he hit the liquid with a huge splash, drenching the two chefs that stood stupidly in front of him, and sending the tray of spices that they had been about to add flying across the floor. As he surfaced, coughing and gasping and covered in vegetables, they leapt back in alarm, plainly more surprised at his sudden arrival than he was.

In terror, seizing the brief advantage of surprise, Arlo clambered stickily out of the cauldron and ran through the Palace kitchens, a strange and hideous figure, blackened from the smoke and the camouflage, ragged and dripping wet. Such was the shock of his entry, that the cooks ranged along the huge tables stood stupidly aside and watched him race out of the doors.

Through the babble of voices that followed him, Arlo skidded around a corner and was faced by one of two options; the first an ascending staircase, the other a long tunnel that sloped downhill. In a second he chose the tunnel, knowing intuitively that he would be more likely to be trapped at the top of a tower, than down on ground level, where he would have the chance of escaping through the sewers.

As he ran, he felt a bone-shaking crunch beneath his feet, and screams from the upper areas. Ozzie, at least, must have escaped the trap, and managed to detonate some of the fire-mines, but it was clear that Tambar's carefully orchestrated plan had been thrown awry. Sounds of gunshots and firing echoed from above, and he could tell that the Rebels had resorted to guerrilla tactics, breaking up into smaller factions to organize their attack. But what hope was there for them, so small a group, outnumbered by the soldiers by hundreds to one?

Another crunch echoed in another part of the Palace, and the ground shook. Smoke trickling down the ventilation grids caught at his lungs and made him cough. Some of the Palace at least must be ablaze! The thought gave him confidence, and he dodged through the tunnel, taking first one turning, then the other.

Shouts and screams echoed from above, and the next second he emerged into a huge chamber and tripped over the body of a Citizen-soldier who lay face down over the threshold.

"Surrender!" cried a voice, and Arlo looked up to see a black-clad figure towering above him, a rifle pointed at his face.

"Don't shoot!" he cried in relief. "It's me, Liana! It's me!"

Liana bent down and pulled him quickly to his feet as another ear-splitting crash echoed through the Palace. Behind her Arlo could dimly see a couple of Rebels crouching at the door, firing at the soldiers beyond, while around the chamber, huddled forms staggered through the smoke. "What's going on, Liana?" shouted Arlo. "Where's Tambar?"

"He's gone to detonate what's left of the mines!" shouted Liana. "Something went wrong! We rescued the prisoners but now we're holed up here. There's a platoon outside and I don't know how much longer we can hold out!"

"Arlo!" screamed a voice, and Arlo gasped as Kira struggled towards him through the smoke. A great gladness filled his heart, wiping out all else.

"Kira!" he cried desperately. "What are you doing here!"

"I couldn't leave you," muttered Kira breathlessly, and at those words, Arlo's breath nearly stopped. "But you called me a coward."

"No you're not," moaned Arlo, throwing himself into her arms. "You never were. I was stupid. I'm sorry."

Over her shoulder he could see Talia and Ignatius stumbling towards him, and instantly all thoughts of retreat were forgotten. "Ignatius!" he cried, and ran towards the Doctor to embrace him.

Ignatius staggered slightly, and Arlo could feel the thin bones of his body protruding through the rags. "Ignatius!" he cried. "I'm so sorry! I'm so sorry!"

As if a mist had cleared from his fevered brain, the anger suddenly disappeared, leaving him cold and frightened. Ignatius pressed his cheek against the boy's. "It's all right, Arlo," he murmured, softly. "I'm here."

"Ignatius—" sobbed Arlo, suddenly overcome with the long weeks of fatigue and worry. He buried his face in the Doctor's neck, clinging to him as to the only reassurance left in his life. "Ignatius – I tried, I tried to save you. . ."

"That's all that matters, Arlo," muttered Ignatius indistinctly. "I'm so glad to see you again. Haven't you grown!"

But another voice rang over his, tight with fury. "Don't you touch him! Get away, you traitor!"

In shock, Arlo turned to see Kira, her eyes suddenly blazing, a knife in her hand. "You betrayed us!" she screamed at Ignatius. "All this is because of you!"

In shock, Arlo stared at his cousin. "What are you talking about, Kira? What do you mean?"

"Arlo," said Kira, and her voice shook. "Please get

away from him. The last time I saw this man, I was eleven years old, and he came to the cave to take you away."

Arlo wheeled frantically around to face the Doctor. "Ignatius – what – what is she saying?"

Ignatius stared back at him without speaking for a moment, and Arlo suddenly saw a flash of the old Doctor in his faded eyes, and remembered the long-ago night in the study when Ignatius had told him of his real heritage. The shock was so blinding that at first he could not even consider it. Not Ignatius!

The last time I saw this man I was eleven...

But this would mean that – he had been stolen, betrayed, by the father who had brought him up! Surely it was impossible!

"It's not true, Ignatius? Tell me! It's not true?"

Ignatius's face fell, and in his place there appeared an old and broken man, with every line of his body now weakened and crushed. The words seemed to stick in his lips as he choked them out.

"It is true, Arlo, and I am truly sorry. But I have to say to you, I am not the person that I was then. Every man will change in his lifetime, and I only did what I thought was right. But as you grew up, I changed, Arlo. I learned Emotions from you. Only later did I realize that what I did was wrong, and I tried my best to help you."

"But what happened to my father?" cried Arlo. "And my mother? What did you do to them?"

Ignatius bowed his head, but Kira was already

advancing towards them, knife drawn. "He sent the soldiers to take us!" she cried. "They came and destroyed everything! I was the only one who escaped! And you grew up with your parents' murderer, never knowing, even loving him! He deserves to die for it!"

Suddenly, like a cat, Kira sprang forward, the blade of the knife above her head. Ignatius did not move but stood, head bowed. Without thinking what he was doing, Arlo threw himself in front of Ignatius and seized his cousin's wrist. Together they fell into the dust and rolled over and over, both fighting for possession of the knife, which rattled over the floor out of the reach of both of them. Furiously, Kira pulled herself away from Arlo and aimed a punch at Ignatius. It was Liana who forced her way between them, and wrenched them apart.

"Stop it! There's worse enemies to fight, in case you've forgotten!"

But it was too late. Under a sudden fusillade of shots, one of the Rebels guarding the opposite door fell. The other – Arlo could see that it was Uther – shouted over his shoulder. "They're coming!"

"We've got to get out!" screamed Liana, ducking as another explosion sounded and rubble fell from the ceiling. "Run!"

"One of us needs to hold them off!" cried Uther. "Otherwise they'll overtake us in a second!"

But it was Ignatius who struggled to his feet from where Kira's punch had floored him, and took the rifle from Uther's hands.

"I will hold them off as long as I can," he said quietly. "This will be the final thing that I can do to try to make amends. Go now, Arlo, and I wish you good fortune."

With a rushing of wind that nearly tore Usha's fingers from thc Fury's ncck, the great birds dived towards the City. Usha had never seen Genopolis from the sky before, and as they reached the level of the buildings, the sheer immensity of it amazed her. Spread out in a horseshoe shape, the wide harbour of the Port lay in a glittering crescent beneath, with the bulk of the hill and the City that sprawled up it in a steep mass in front.

Below them passed Central Square: the ruined walls of the Inn of Court, the squat bulk of the Guardian headquarters, the high Bell Tower of the Guildhall, and the icy-white Pillars of the Consulate. At last the Furies banked and swerved as the hill of Genopolis steepened, and in a second they were plunged into the North Quarter of the City, winging their way high through the empty streets so fast that they could not be seen.

Towers swam past them like great blazing beacons of light, and turning her head, Usha could see through their highest windows. As they shot past, she had brief glimpses of the celebrations going on inside, of family units clustered round a table to eat, or hanging Midsummer decorations. A baby was cradled on its mother's knee; there were children unwrapping carefully-bartered-for presents. For a moment, uneasiness unexpectedly touched her. All around them, Citizens were carrying on their daily business, following their normal routine. Yet here they were, planning, with one fell swoop, to change their lives for ever.

No, she thought, burying her head in the rough feathers of the Fury's back. They were going to change it for the better. Their quarrel was not with the Citizens of Genopolis. What did a Citizen know of the suffering beyond their walls, or indeed, how could they know of suffering, when they had been conditioned not to feel? Was a Citizen any more than a puppet, whose strings were pulled from unseen heights to make them dance at their masters' bidding? No, their quarrel was with the puppet masters, who knew what they had turned their people into, who knew of what went on in the wilderness, and encouraged it.

Finally, with a dizzying swerve, the Palace appeared before them, a broad and high building in six levels, each bounded by a bridge, with guard-turrets at the north, south, east and west. Searchlights combed the sky, and as they soared above its outer walls, they were caught in a brilliant beam for a second. The Fury squawked and twisted, momentarily blinded.

"It's all right," shouted Usha encouragingly. "Fly through! We're here!"

In another second they had been plunged into darkness, seeming the more blinding after the brightness of the searchlights. With the last of its strength, the Fury fluttered, and almost fell as it landed on the flat roof of the Palace.

Usha dropped to the tiled floor, so drained she could not move, and was faintly conscious of Nanda on the other bird as it alighted beside her. As the girls crawled to their feet, the Furies crouched next to them, panting and exhausted.

Below them came a clamouring and the distant sounds of gunfire.

"What's that?" clucked one. "What's going on?"

"That must be Arlo," said Usha, and for a moment she stood, undecided. How to find Arlo? How to tell him that help was on its way?

The next second the searchlight swept around and pinned them to the spot with its bright beam. From outside the circle of light came an outbreak of shouting and the sound of metalled feet clattering on stone.

"Attack! Attack on the roof! All troops above!"

From the guard-turrets the doors swung open and a file of soldiers poured out, rifles cocked, training them on the fugitives.

"Hands up! Kneel down! Or we will shoot!"

"You must go," Nanda said, and in her voice there was a direct command. "You can do nothing more. Leave me here. Save yourself, Usha."

Arlo ran sobbing through the tunnels, barely aware of the others behind him. He could not think, could not look up, and he blundered painfully into a wall as he ran. Kira grabbed for his hand and he pushed her away. So great had the shock of Ignatius's true identity been that he felt that his skin had been stripped from him. He could think of nothing else but Ignatius's quirky smile at their parting, and that – despite what the Doctor had done – he had left the old man to fight alone, to his death.

"The Brigadier!" cried Talia's voice impatiently. "I'm going to find the Brigadier!"

"No, Talia!" shouted Liana. "We need you! We must keep together!"

Talia scowled, and on her face were the signs of an internal struggle that the Naturals knew well.

"I need to find her! This isn't over yet!" she muttered rebelliously.

"Please, Talia," cried Arlo. "Leave your revenge. It isn't worth it."

As they neared a set of doors, firing broke out from behind them and bullets zinged against the walls of the tunnel.

"Not that way!" cried Liana. "Make for the sewers! Quickly!"

But as they ran, smoke issued from the higher levels, confusing and dispersing them. Arlo could no longer see the way ahead. More firing broke out every time they tried to turn off down a passageway. Arlo felt that they were slowly being surrounded, and forced down the tunnel in one direction. But before he could shout out to Liana to warn her, the tunnel abruptly opened out into the corridor in which he had first met Clarence, and he saw the entrance to the prison-cells.

"Down here!" he called over his shoulder. "Into the sewers! Here!"

"Talia's gone the wrong way!" shouted Liana. "And Uther!"

"Where's Kira?" called Arlo desperately, and heard with relief his cousin's faint cry behind him.

"I'm here, Arlo! I'm coming!"

There was no possibility of searching for the others with their enemies so close around them. Through the smoke, Arlo fumbled for the stairwell that led through the prison chambers. But as he tumbled down the last of the stairs, he suddenly stood aghast. In front of him stood Corin.

With one bound, Arlo was upon him, knocking the smaller boy over and forcing him to the floor. "You!" he cried fiercely, and at his voice, Corin blanched. "You betrayed us!"

Pinned to the ground, Corin stared back up at him, his black eyes brimming with tears. "I couldn't help it," he sobbed. "I'm sorry, Arlo."

In a blaze of fury, Arlo's hand coiled into a fist and he drew it back with a savagery he had never known. Yet something prevented him from smashing it into the other's face. Wavering, sobbing from the exertion of his flight, he gazed down at the Citizen.

"Why did you do it?" he gasped. "Why, Corin?"

But before the boy could speak, the chamber echoed with the clicks of a hundred safety-locks, and staring up, Arlo could see that a hundred rifles were levelled at them. From the shadows issued a file of soldiers holding the small group at gunpoint, and behind them all, like a malevolent spectre, the Regis, his face shaded with a crimson hood.

Arlo leapt to his feet, dragging the unresisting Corin in front of him as a shield. "Go back!" he cried over his shoulder at Liana who was descending the staircase after him. "It's a trap! The Regis is here!"

Liana raised her gun and tried to fire, but her rifle jammed. Instantly a bullet sang through the air and her gun clattered uselessly to the floor. Her howl of pain echoed through the tunnel and she slumped to the floor.

From above, Kira's voice echoed down the winding stairwell.

"Arlo!" she cried. "What's happening! Where are you!"

Where are you? Where are you?

Corin flinched at her voice. "Who is that?" he screamed. The voice seemed so terribly, impossibly familiar, he feared he might go mad. "Who is she?"

The Regis strode forward a couple of paces. "Who is that, Corin?" he mocked. "Do you know? Do you remember?"

"Go away!" cried Corin, and covered his head with his arms. "I don't know! I don't know anything!"

Boots sounded on the steps and the next moment another seven troops descended down the stairway, guns drawn, pushing a helpless Kira in front of them.

Arlo grabbed Corin as he sank to the floor. "Get

away!" he cried at the advancing troops. "Or I'll break his neck! Get away!"

"Really?" mocked the Regis. "But who is he?"

"He's a traitor!" cried Arlo. "He betrayed me!"

The Regis smiled malevolently. "*Who are you, Corin?* Don't you know who Corin really is, Arlo? Can't you guess?"

Nanda pushed gently at Usha. "Go, Usha. Leave us."

Usha clung to Nanda, suddenly overwhelmed. "What are you going to do, Nanda? Where should I go?"

"You must," said Nanda calmly, unwinding Usha's arms and clasping her friend's hands between hers. "You have brought me here, so far, Usha. That was all that you could do. The rest is not within your control."

A hot tear trickled down Usha's cheek as, for the first time, the Emotions of Grief and Loss overcame her. "You can't, Nanda. Don't do this! Please!"

"Hands up!" cried the voice again, and Usha could see in the darkness that they were completely surrounded. "At the count of five, put your hands up, or we will shoot!"

Slowly, Usha and Nanda put their hands up, and out of the shadows emerged a row of rifles. Usha glanced at the Fury, who was tottering behind them anxiously.

"The Usha has to go!" it squawked. "Go now, fly!"

*

rlo jumped, as if he had been stung. "What! What do you mean?"

"Corin is your father," said the Brigadier, gazing at him with his dark, hypnotic eyes. "You have searched long for your family, Arlo. I trust that now you will be pleased at the meeting."

The foundations of Arlo's world were rocked as surely as if a fire-mine had been detonated beneath his feet. Slowly he released the Citizen, but Corin did not move. With his eyes wide and his face pale, he seemed as shocked as Arlo.

"What do you mean?" Arlo cried, and his voice sounded high-pitched and childish. "What game are you playing now, Regis?"

The Regis's face broke into a forbidden smile of pleasure. "I mean, Arlo, that Corin is your father – as he once was."

His *father*? Desperately he looked at Corin, and saw also the same dazed surprise on his face. But Corin could not be his father! It made no sense!

"I don't understand," shouted Arlo, looking wildly around. "What are you saying? Are you mad?"

"I am not mad," said the Regis smoothly. "The Brigadier captured your father, Angus, over twelve years ago, shortly after the defeat of Region Three. Yet despite our best endeavours—" and the Regis smiled thinly – "he did not give us the name of the Doctor who had taken his child, not even at the end. Knowing that we would plan to kill his son, he would not betray even the man who had betrayed him."

"I don't believe you!" screamed Arlo. "You're making this up!"

The Regis sneered. "So we decided upon a little Experiment of our own, to see how nurture could triumph over Nature. We have ways of creating life from the bodies of others. We set to work to create a perfect Citizen out of the raw material, using our Regeneration procedure. A Citizen who would be able to renounce his Natural past, and form part of the system of Genopolis. Living proof that one could rise above one's genetic heritage, and disprove the Natural saying, that blood is thicker than water."

"So this is who I am!" cried Corin, turning suddenly to face him. "This is why I have nightmares! This is what they mean!"

"So it seems," responded the Regis menacingly. "You were unable to help yourself. Being Natural is in your blood and bones."

In deathly silence, the Regis stepped forward and held out a muddied, dirty object. Gazing at it, Arlo could see that it was the old book that the Abbess had given him, inside which he and Toby had laboriously written their story during the long year in the wilderness; the story of his past, and the story of his parents. Instinctively, he reached out, but the Regis held it over his head, mockingly.

"You have heard and written much about your father, Arlo. Would you like to see him now, as he was?"

From beneath his robe he took out the painting that

he had confiscated from Corin and held it up so that the light fell across it. The face of a young man in his early twenties stared back at them, with brown hair, a pale face and sad dark eyes that seemed to be gazing at something very far away.

Kira gasped and started forward.

"Uncle Angus!"

"This is the man who you were," said the Regis maliciously to Corin, "and this is the face of your father, Arlo, years ago."

Barely conscious of Corin beside him, Arlo gazed enchanted at Angus's picture, remembering everything that Kira had told him, taking in every feature of the face, and fleshing out in his imagination every detail of his father's character.

I wish he were smiling, he thought wistfully. *I bet he would have been fun if he were happy.*

The next moment he was jerked back to consciousness by the Regis's sibilant laugh. "Look your last on him, because his time is now over. For many years he has caused us much trouble, even after his death. But in destroying the past, he will cease to exist. Now I will destroy you all, and every part of your Natural History."

Through the darkness, Usha could see that more and more troops were clustering around them. Almost the whole army of Genopolis had come up to the roof suspecting an impending attack from the air, and were filing around the walls of the Palace with their guns drawn.

"Usha," said Nanda slowly. "You must go, or you will die with me. I beg you. Do not delay!"

"No!" cried Usha, and another hot tear splashed into the dust at Nanda's feet. "Please! Don't do this!"

But another voice came commandingly out of the darkness even as she spoke. "So! The witch-girl has returned from the dead! I must congratulate you, my dear! I thought that I had bought you a one-way ticket!"

Usha trembled as the Brigadier moved forward into the light, her face livid from the smoke and dust of battle, and looked condescendingly down at them.

"You must introduce me to your little Natural friend, my dear," she said to Usha with heavy sarcasm.

Nanda moved forward to meet her, calmly. "I am no Natural," she said clearly, her voice ringing in the night air. "I was born and bred a Citizen of Genopolis. I was forced into the underworld because of my disfigurement. But when I was discovered by your troops, I was sent to the pharms."

The Brigadier peered closely at her. "Why!" she said mockingly. "It is the little girl from the sewers! I am intrigued as to why you wanted to come back to the place that you were unsuitable for!"

"I came back to show you what you have done," replied Nanda. "I came back to tell you that what you are doing is inhuman and wrong. And I came back to tell you that I am angry."

The Brigadier raised her eyebrows. "You are *angry*, my dear? Well, I am sorry to have to remind you that Emotions are forbidden in Genopolis, and it will go badly with you to express them."

"No," corrected Nanda. "It will go badly with you, Brigadier. For I was not sent for Regeneration. Instead, I was sent for Experimentation in the Armoury and Human Combustion Centre, where they gave me your supreme punishment for feeling Emotions, Brigadier, the punishment that was intended to destroy anyone who felt Anger, or Love or Hatred. You intended it as a control so that all Citizens would suppress their emotions – Fury, Love or Hatred – through the threat of self-destruction."

Understanding began to dawn in the Brigadier's eyes. "You – you mean—"

"Yes," replied Nanda softly. "You made me subject to human combustion. One human body contains enough energy as a powerful explosion if it is all released at once. Your scientists reprogrammed my genetic code in order to ensure the release of the energy spontaneously. They made Emotion the trigger, so if I feel Anger, I will die, instantaneously.

"But in doing this to me, you also gave me the power of destruction, stronger than any that you possess. You intended to control me alone, but you have underestimated how angry I am, and what I can now do with this anger. Yet I do not count this as a sacrifice. I will die, and die gladly, because I will take you with me."

*

"Then who are you?" cried Arlo, swinging around to face the Regis. "If you are not his father, then who are you?"

"That is none of your concern," the Regis replied. "I was parent and guardian to Corin for eleven years. But the Experiment has failed. This is his last chance to remain a Citizen. Now the only way in which he can be redeemed is to atone for the sins of his father. Will you atone for them now, Corin?"

Arlo glanced at Corin and saw in the other's hand the sharp point of a silver knife. For a second fear seized him. He had no weapon, and although he was stronger than Corin, he was weakened by the year of living in the Regions and the ordeal of their entry back into Genopolis. But then he could see that in the boy's eyes there was no Fury, no Anger, but only tears, and they brimmed on his lashes like drops of silver. Corin's words rang through his head once more.

Perhaps it is better to have no father, than a bad one.

"Will you do it, Corin?" asked the Regis softly. "Will you renounce your Natural character once and for all?"

Corin stretched out his hand, wordlessly, and the knife clattered harmlessly to the floor.

The Regis sighed. "Then you leave me no choice. If you cannot renounce your heritage, then you too must be destroyed."

With those words, he fell back and motioned to the guards behind him. Immediately, the soldiers cocked their rifles and took aim.

What happened at that moment, Arlo could not properly tell. The air became dark, and then blindingly white, and he covered his eyes. The ghastly face of the Regis seemed to be imprinted on his closed eyelids like a bright light shone into the eyes and suddenly extinguished. A tearing sound that was not a sound blocked his ears and suddenly it seemed as if all the air in the tunnels coalesced into a great fist and then burst, forcing its way down the tunnels, knocking everyone to the floor. The ground shook around them but he could hear nothing. Then the entire world seemed to explode around him and everything went black.

As Nanda spoke her last words, the Fury seized Usha with her sharp beak, pulled the Gemini across her back, and soared upwards at breakneck speed. A searchlight circled wildly to try to follow them, but the bird dodged and twisted in and out of the beam. Shots followed them but went wide. But even as the Fury's strong wings bore them away from the outer wall of the Palace, the sky around them suddenly blazed with an unnatural brilliance. Usha buried her face in the bird's back, as a screaming roar erupted from behind them.

From the top of the Palace, a great mushroom of fire billowed out like a flowering rose, engulfing the roof where the Brigadier and her troops had been standing. Night seemed to have changed momentarily into day. A strong wave of hot air seemed to lift them up and throw them across Genopolis with no more effort than a child throwing pebbles, and Usha felt the bird beneath her shriek and begin to tumble as its wings seared in the heat.

The next moment all the air around them seemed to be sucked in with a huge gasp, and they were suddenly falling through a great vacuum of space, turning over and over, down and down, into nothingness.

From the shadow of Sir Herbert's cloak, Mindie turned her head to see a crimson light break against the horizon in a shower of flame, illuminating the hundreds of barges bearing their loads of creatures, humans and Chimaeras that sculled rapidly beside them. Shouts and screams arose from the boats as the watchers saw the flames of the towering destruction blistering over the dark seas.

"What is that?" gasped Sofia from her place in the prow. "What is going on?"

A shadow crossed Mindie's face. "It is the Anger," she said. "The blind rage that consumes, and destroys. The same could have happened to me too, but Usha saved me, just in time."

Toby clutched at the bars of his prison cell as the ground shook beneath his feet. Aghast, he stared through the window of the Guardian headquarters and saw to his horror, the enormous bulk of the Palace on the North Hill quake, blaze and erupt with the force of a hideous roar. He hung on for dear life as the turrets and watchpoints collapsed, raining rubble down upon the City. In the ghastly red glare that illuminated the skies, he saw the Pillars of the Consulate fracture and crumble, sinking to the ground like child's skittles. The huge wave of energy rocketed across the ground, levelling the great tower of the Guildhall and the Bell Tower as it came.

In the same second, an enormous chasm tore its way through the great stone floor of Central Square as Genopolis was rocked to its foundations. The next moment the great gates that barred the prison burst apart and shattered into fragments. And outside the Guardian Headquarters, the attack-siren sent up its lonely, inhuman wail, as of a great monster howling in its death throes.

Arlo coughed his way awake, and his first thought was that they were buried alive. His lungs seemed to be filled with fire. No chink of light penetrated through the darkness, and the air tasted thick with dust and ash. He tried to move but his body would not function. He lay as if in a leaden tomb, feeling only the motion of his panting chest as he struggled to breathe. But no bodily pain possessed him, and only a strange haunting feeling of peace pervaded his dazed brain.

Perhaps I am dead after all, he thought, and surprisingly the thought did not worry him. All around him was perfect silence, and at first he lay, pleasantly dreaming, as warm and safe as if he had been in the skin-lined bed in the Natural catacombs.

But suddenly, a sound broke the deathly silence, of a patter of approaching paws, and a strange, snuffling growl. As he strained to see through the darkness, he felt a warm wet tongue begin to lick his face.

"Rem!" he muttered indistinctly. "Rem! You're here!"

With a supreme effort, he willed himself to move, and managed to raise a shaking arm to touch the dog's shaggy coat. The contact gave him new strength, and slowly, centimetre by centimetre, he rolled himself over and sat upright. A ringing in his ears and a trickle of blood from his eardrums had affected his balance, and he wavered, clinging to Rem for support until the nausea and sickness had subsided.

"Hello?" he faltered into the darkness. "Is anyone here?"

But no answer came. Once he had recovered his balance, Arlo reached cautiously into the Rebel pouch underneath his tunic and fumbled for the tinder and flint. But the small amount of kindling that he had kept in his pouch was no longer there. He cast around on the floor but could find nothing. Then suddenly his fingers connected to something cold lying on the floor next to him. As he touched it, he realized in panic that it was Kira's face.

"Kira!" he choked, trying to waken her. "Kira!"

But she gave no answer. Swaying to and fro, Arlo pulled himself forward until he was crouched over her, and placed his ear on her chest. Faintly, very faintly, he could hear the noise of her heart beating. A great surge of relief swept through him, invigorating his shattered body. She was unconscious then, but still alive. But how many others might be lying in the dark rubble around him, friend or foe?

I've got to get help, he thought dizzily. I have to get out of here. But his dazed brain could reach no further than that. Where he was going and who would help him were beyond him for the moment. He was in no condition to try to find more of his friends – or his enemies. Instead, he reached out and held on to the dog's shaggy pelt, and with many faltering starts, managed to crawl down through the sewer flue after his pet.

Sensing his master's distress, Rem padded slowly in front of him, pausing every now and then to blow encouragingly in his ear, or lick him back into wakefulness when Arlo showed signs of collapsing.

As Arlo dragged himself along like a dazed beast, he thought he could see Ozzie and the Rebels crawling in front of him as they entered Genopolis. Yes, that was it. They had been here for almost a year, they had just left the Circus, they were hurrying down the maze of passageways with the two girl-gladiators and the Regis in hot pursuit. But why was Ozzie going the wrong way? Why was he leading them back into the City? Didn't he know that the Minotaur was waiting in the darkness ahead of them?

Then he knew that he was swimming through the seas that surrounded Genopolis. And the electric fence –

he had a feeling that he needed to warn them about it, but the words would not come out of his mouth. There was an electric fence around the Inn of Court too, and if you touched it. . . For a moment the brightness and beauty of the Inn's courtyard was suddenly about him, and he was clasped in the boughs of the swaying oak tree, with the soft murmur of the February sunshine against his cheek. The memory was so pleasant that it brought an idiotic smile to his face. But then the soft swaying of the green leaves became the surge of the sea, and all around him the walls of the Inn flickered as if he were underwater. He was drowning. . .

He had fallen out of the tree; he was lying on his back on the green grass. Winded from his fall, he was too shocked even to groan.

"Arlo! Arlo! Are you all right?"

A voice was calling his name. Dizzily, he pulled himself on to his elbows and looked up. Through the schoolroom window leaned Ignatius, eyes wide, gripping the sill with both hands.

"Arlo! Are you all right?"

"Ignatius—" Arlo tried to reply, but the vision dissolved and the next moment he was back in the grimy tunnel alone. Feeling he could go no further, he lay down, heedless of the stink and Rem's urgent tugging at his shoulder. Perhaps Citizens had the right idea after all. No worse punishment existed than to feel Pain. *If I were a Citizen.* . . he thought, before Rem raised his head and howled. Something about the desperation of the sound gave Arlo new strength. What would Rem do without him, if he gave up now? What would any of them do?

One more try, he thought, pulling himself to his elbows. At that moment he saw that a pale light was filtering through the darkness, and the smell of the sea air filled his nostrils. In a second he realized where Rem had led him to. It was the entrance to the guardroom where the Rebels had entered, underneath the ruined steps where his grandmother had led Region Three exactly thirteen years before.

It's my birthday today, he thought.

The thought gave him new strength. Kicking with his legs and using his arms only to hold himself up, he struggled towards the pale light. Rem was already nosing in front of him, but as Arlo reached the final turning, he paused, suddenly confused. Something had changed.

Instead of the submerged guardroom, the ancient steps had been torn away by rubble raining down from the force of the explosion. The bricked-up archway had been broken open, and the light and sound of the outside world poured in to meet him. With an incredulity bordering on insanity, Arlo tottered forward until he stood on the very edge of the City wall, holding tightly to the ruined stonework next to him for support. At first the light was too great for him to bear, and he held his hand over his eyes to shield him from the dazzle.

Behind him Rem pranced and barked, and the joyous sound echoed over the water. Peering through his outstretched fingers, Arlo saw the great spread of the bright ocean lying before him in the morning sunrise. As his eyes sharpened into focus, he could see that all around and on every side, the City was ringed with ships and barges, carrying an assortment of creatures that to Arlo's dazed mind seemed both human, yet not human.

"Who are they, Rem?" he asked, confusedly. "What are they?"

As he blinked, bewildered, he faintly heard the sound of victorious shouts rising from the boats and drifting over the waves.

"They're cheering, Rem!" he gasped excitedly. "They're cheering!"

Forgetting his body's pain, he tore off the green rope of the Rebels and waved it to and fro with new hope, as Rem capered beside him. Renewed celebrations broke out from the boats as they spied the small figure signalling from the doorway, while above him, smoke and steam rose from the shattered ruins.

The great doors of Genopolis were open at last.

Dazed and confused, Toby crawled through the devastated remains of the Guardian Headquarters, and out into the fearful rubble of Central Square. His heart hammered in his chest and he tasted blood in his mouth. Great buildings had been burst apart and the huge stones crumpled as if by a giant fist and they were no more than paper. Upon one side of Central Square the buildings had been flattened and a thick cloud of dust rose from the ruins, giving the appearance of thick mist or fog. And through the white haze he saw an army approaching, an army so great and terrible that, Citizen as he was, he could only crouch and stare.

First came a vanguard of many loping, four-footed beasts, covered in fur and with tails, but with eyes and faces that seemed human beneath the sweeping manes. Leaping nimbly from broken stone to broken stone, they swept past the astonished Toby, taking no more notice of him than if he were a pebble himself.

After them poured a wave of human-like creatures, yet they were not like any form that Toby had seen before. Some were of male or female appearance, but with more legs or arms than usual; others were grotesquely distorted with great outsized arms or limbs with which they propelled themselves up the slope. Hundreds upon hundreds of smooth-faced, hairless humanoids ran behind them, bearing rifles and spears, but they ran with a silence, a grim intention, that struck terror into Toby's heart more than any fearsome beastlike cry.

Stumbling into the shadow of a ruined wall, he watched as they poured past him and towards the Palace, and over the roads that led towards the fragments of the Consulate. Silent and purposeful they were, and even as the few remaining guards challenged them and steel met steel, it was the eerie quiet of everything that puzzled Toby more than anything. Then he realized that the lips of the creatures were indeed moving as they cried to each other, but that he could hear nothing, deafened as he was by the power of the explosion.

In confusion, he turned away but almost immediately tripped over a reclining marble figure and recoiled. The statue of the Brigadier from the doors of the Guardian Headquarters had been flung down and lay shattered in front of him, and only one baleful, unseeing eye, so similar in stone as it had been in life, glared back at him.

Unsettled by the sight, he crawled away and into the ruins behind the Headquarters, in his dizzy state wishing only to be away from the slaughter and lie down to sleep. Yet even as he pulled himself along, he was suddenly knocked to the side by a small group of fleeing figures, wrapped in grey robes, escorted by black-uniformed Citizen-soldiers carrying rifles, though their purpose appeared to be escape rather than shooting. As they passed, one of them turned and looked down at him, and Toby had a sudden impression of a pale, skull-like face and ink-black eyes, before the group disappeared into the dust.

Blindly, Toby peered after them, but immediately a great flying shape rose from the ruins next to him, the wind from its expulsion whipping gritty dust into his eyes. Rolling on to his back, Toby watched the airship take off with a grinding roar even as the first of the Furies came rocketing through the mist, falling back with frustrated screams of anguish when they saw their enemies disappear into the clouds.

Arlo slept and slept as he had never slept before. In his more lucid moments, he could tell that he was lying in a bed, but which bed it was, whether in the Inn of Court or in the Natural catacombs, he did not know. At other times, he was convinced that he was lying still buried in the ruins of Genopolis, and started from his fevered sleep, shouting for Rem. Then cool hands would come and lay cloths on his burning forehead, and a glass containing a bitter-tasting liquid would be forced between his teeth before he was lowered back down to his pillows and into black unconsciousness.

Many people wandered in and out of his fevered imagination. Sometimes it was Kristo, bending concernedly over him, and other times it was a girl with a burned face whom he did not know, crying at the foot of his bed. He tried to tell her not to weep, not to worry, but to hurry and find Kira, but his lips would not frame the words, nor could he find the energy to make a sound. Once he woke to find Tambar leaning in the doorway, surveying him sadly, his face blackened and bloodied, and on the evening of the final terrible night, in the middle of a bad dream, he started from sleep to find Ignatius sitting quietly on the end of the bed watching him.

"Ignatius!" cried Arlo, and to his surprise, he found

he could move and speak quite naturally. "Ignatius! I thought – I thought—"

But Ignatius just smiled at him. For a moment, Arlo could see again the spirit of the younger Ignatius, of the Doctor that he had known and played with in the gardens of the Inn of Court. The older Ignatius – the one that had crumpled before him and admitted his sin – was no more. Instead, he seemed years younger as he gazed at the boy tenderly.

"Well done, Arlo," said Ignatius at last, and in his eyes there came again the merry sparkle, the caustic raised eyebrow. "You've done well. Better than anyone could really have expected."

"I thought I'd made a mess of things," replied Arlo soberly. "But this seems to be the end of it, doesn't it?"

Ignatius grinned. "No, this isn't the end, you know. Not for you young ones, at any rate. You've got a lot of work in front of you especially, my boy. You'd better rest and sleep while you still can."

Arlo gazed at him, levelly. "Ignatius – I know. I know who my father is."

The Doctor looked back at him but said nothing.

"It's Corin – well, I mean he was Regenerated out of my father. Anyway, it's all too confusing. I just don't understand – how something so good could turn into something so bad, and how—"

"And how something that started badly could ever end up good?" supplied Ignatius softly. "That is the mystery of life, Arlo. We are all part of the same thing.

Every light casts a shadow, and every darkness is followed by the morning. Good men die in the service of bad causes, and for every evil-doer, there is always the possibility of forgiveness. What I did I can never undo, and all that I could then do was try to change things. And it was you who changed me, Arlo."

"Ignatius. . ." choked Arlo, and for a moment he could feel an Outbreak welling up inside him. What did he know of the person that Ignatius used to be? All he could remember was the Ignatius that had played with him and tutored him in the gardens of the Inn of Court. "You were my real father, you know, more than anyone ever was, or could be."

Ignatius smiled. "Thank you for your forgiveness, Arlo. It is freely given, and because of that, at last I can leave you."

"But—" began Arlo, and suddenly he could see Tambar and Kristo behind Ignatius, smiling at him.

"Good work, Arlo," said Kristo. "Take care of yourself. We'll be thinking of you."

In a second Arlo realized, or thought he realized, what they meant, but somehow the thought did not disturb him. "But why do you need to go?" he asked quietly. "Who's going to look after us?"

"Kira's still here, you know," said Ignatius lightly. "She'll look after you. She's got a good right hook. Almost as good as the thump you gave me." And he patted his right eye with a wink.

"You still have Liana and Talia too," said Tambar

softly, as Ignatius rose from the bed. Arlo noticed that he left no imprint on the covers. "And do not grieve us now we are gone. We did not come to say farewell, for endings and beginnings are all the same, really."

"And Usha?" cried Arlo, as they passed silently out of his sight. "What about Usha?"

TEN

"Once upon a time," said Annis, leaning over to tickle her baby underneath the chin, "there was a girl who could fly like an eagle. Nobody knows where she came from, for she had no father or mother. Some say that she came from the sun, and others that she was born from the tears of the Goddess. Her skin was so pale that the sun did not darken it, and she felt no pain when she fell on stony rocks. She could see things that had not yet happened, and warned others about the dead branch, the treacherous snake behind the rocks, and the floodwaters that came down from the mountains.

"But one day there came soldiers who wanted to take the girl and imprison her, because they were jealous of her powers. So the girl flew up into the sky and summoned the brightness of a million suns to throw the soldiers into the ocean, where they all drowned. Then the people that she had saved were able to come out of hiding and return to their homeland, where they had a huge feast to celebrate."

"She won't understand," said Talia, scornfully, reaching for a roast hog's leg that was being carried past by a young Citizen boy on a tray. "She's too young. *This* is what you need to be teaching her!"

And she threw the hog's leg into the air, and with a quick flick of her knife, impaled it. But her hand quivered as she laid down the blade, and for the first time she rubbed her shoulder where the bruising had not yet subsided from the explosion in the Palace. After the change wrought on her by the Brigadier, for all her physical strength, she was not yet accustomed to Natural weakness nor to their love of stories. Watching her, Arlo knew that she had a lot still to learn.

"Of course she understands!" said Annis defensively. "She understands every word. Don't you?" And she tickled the baby again, whose laugh and gurgle knew nothing of the world into which she had been born.

Arlo smiled as he turned away from them and gazed over the evening sunset. Around them the picnic was in full swing. On the shattered upper ruins of the Palace the crumbling remains of the walls had been knocked down and cleared by the work of many hands, until the high hill where the Palace used to stand lay bare underneath the golden rays of the last sun. In Central Square, hundreds of different humans and creatures – Naturals, Citizens, Chimaeras and Androgynes – lay around on the rubble, feasting and chatting together.

There were so many of them that even the barges had been commandeered as temporary picnic spots, and the sparkling sea had drawn many to jump and dive in the warm water by the docks. Against the brightness of the clouds, the Furies held flying competitions, and every so often a bird would soar overhead in a dizzying display of flight, to the appreciation of the younger children.

"Arlo!" cried a voice, and looking up, Arlo could see Yuma waving at him from the overturned Pillar of the Consulate on which she sat next to Yoshi. "We're so glad to see you up and about!"

"Careful with that leg!" called Tutu from his perch opposite on the shattered staircase of the old Guardian Headquarters.

Tarissa chimed in, "We need you fit and in one piece, remember!"

Arlo whistled Rem to his side, and set off down the hill to where he could see Sir Herbert sitting sharing pieces of bread and honey with Clarence and Cecilia, who swung their legs over the edge of the chasm that had rent the stone of Central Square in two pieces.

"Come and sit with us, Arlo!" they cried, but Arlo shook his head regretfully.

"I'd love to, really, but there's something I have to do first!"

Picking his way through the groups of assorted creatures, he let Rem gambol ahead of him, leading the way.

While he had been unconscious, the greater part of the fighting and the capture of Genopolis had taken place under the leadership of Sofia and the Circle. The explosion of the higher levels of the Palace had wiped out the Brigadier and her army, and with the arrival of the Pharmopolis barges, any resistance had been quickly overcome. Most of the ordinary Citizens had been reprieved, and only the remains of the soldiery had been taken into custody. Even those that had been working in the lower levels of the Palace or the institutions had been freed once they had sworn allegiance to the new order. Only the Regis, Lawlord Kane, the di Angelos and a few other Higher Citizens remained unaccounted for amongst both the living and the dead, and it was believed they had escaped in the confusion.

Arlo had pieced together scraps of the rebellion at the pharms from the survivors, who were now under the control of Tariq and Sasha. In fact, Tariq and Sasha had been responsible for sending over the food on which they were now picnicking. This was now to be the last night of celebration on the ruins of the Old City, before the hardship of reconstructing the New City began on the morrow.

Down on the water's edge, he could see the group of his friends, sitting on the harbour wall and gazing over the lapping waves of the marina. In the midst of the group was a large heaped pile of flowers that they had gathered from the Palace gardens. He waved at them and quickened his pace, while Rem pranced happily up to them, questing for stray scraps.

"Get off, you mangy mutt," objected Ozzie, holding

his sandwich out of reach of Rem's snapping jaws. "There's enough around without you stealing my grub!"

"He can have one of mine," said Liana, grinning, and tossed a sausage towards the dog. Rem caught it easily with a flick of his jaws and gulped it down hungrily.

Kira turned her head, and though she smiled at Arlo's approach, there was also sadness in her eyes that was echoed in the faces of many of the group. Impulsively he hugged them all, noticing as he did so that Liana had her arm comfortingly around his cousin.

"Everyone's still with us, you know," said Arlo, not quite knowing why he said it. "We won't forget them. And remember, they're together."

Mindie managed a grin. "This one's for Nanda," she said, selecting a large yellow flower from the pile, and throwing it into the water, where it bobbed in the sparkling waves as it was carried out to sea.

Kira reached over and picked up a flowering purple briar, dropping it into the waves with a muttered prayer. "This one is for Kristo."

Liana deliberated briefly before picking up a green trailing ivy leaf with white berries, and flinging it into the water. "This one is for Tambar."

Arlo searched the heap of blooms before finding what he sought. With some difficulty, he extracted a silver twig, with fluffy seeds and grey, beard-like wisps curling around the stem, and threw it after the others.

"This one is for Ignatius," he said, dry-eyed, watching it bob away until it was lost to sight.

In the pause that followed, Corin leaned forward and picked up a small crimson bud with sharp prickles that ran along the stem. Hesitantly, he glanced at Arlo.

"This is for my. . ." he stammered. "For my. . ."

"Go on," encouraged Arlo. At that moment he did not begrudge Corin his grief, any more than he begrudged himself his grief for Ignatius. Hadn't the Regis been the same figure in Corin's life that Ignatius had been in his? Love was Love, and Grief was Grief, and nobody could ever really explain that.

Corin turned, held the flower out over the harbour, and took a deep breath.

Suddenly a voice broke in. "Arlo! Corin!"

"Usha!" cried Toby. "You missed all the flowers!"

"I'm sorry," smiled Usha as she drew near. Her head was wrapped in a white cloth over her short-cut hair, and though her pale skin had been scorched and blackened by frostbite, her grey eyes were now clear and sparkling.

"I think you're famous," whispered Arlo teasingly to Usha, as they walked over to where Corin stood on the harbour wall. "They're making up stories about you and all sorts."

"I'm not famous," said Usha, smiling. "I didn't do anything, really." And she reached out and touched Corin lightly on his shoulder.

Corin turned and smiled at Usha with a warmth that made Arlo feel a sudden pang of jealousy. Then the next second he pushed the feeling away decisively. After all, both Corin and Usha had a special bond that he did not know. They were both created in the image of another person, while he, Arlo, was forever and unalterably himself.

"Listen," said Arlo, slipping his arm through Corin's and squeezing it, while on the other side, Usha did the same. "Tomorrow we'll make plans and decide what we're going to do. In the meantime, you're not alone. You've got us, haven't you?"

Corin managed a smile, and together they set off back towards the picnic from where the scent of sausages was drifting. As they neared the pier, they could see that Annis had made her way down and stood waiting, holding her baby.

"I thought you might like to see her," she said, holding the child out to Usha. "I thought you might like to hold her for a little while?"

Usha smiled with happiness, and a light broke out over her face.

"Thank you," she said. "Yes, I think I would."

ACKNOWLEDGEMENTS

Many many thanks to everyone whose ideas, advice and suggestions were welcomed in the writing and revision of this book, especially Zöe Duncan, David Mercatali, Jennifer Fieldsend, Cristina Teixeira, Tiffany Jean-Baptiste, Jean Fieldsend and Giles Alderson.